ANTOINETTE DE MIRECOURT

The Centre for Editing Early Canadian Texts (CEECT) is engaged in the preparation of scholarly editions of selected works of early English-Canadian prose. *Antoinette De Mirecourt* is the sixth text in the Centre for Editing Early Canadian Texts Series.

Antoinette De Mirecourt

Or Secret Marrying and Secret Sorrowing
A Canadian Tale

Rosanna Leprohon

Edited by
John C. Stockdale

Carleton University Press
Ottawa, Canada
1989

ISBN 0-88629-092-9 (casebound)
      0-88629-091-0 (paperback)

Printed and bound in Canada by The Alger Press Limited, Oshawa, Ontario. The paper in this edition is 50 lb. Finch Opaque Vellum (pH 7.8-8).

Canadian Cataloguing in Publication Data

Leprohon, Rosanna Eleanor, 1829-1879.
    Antoinette De Mirecourt, or, Secret marrying and
    secret sorrowing

(Centre for Editing Early Canadian Texts Series ; 6)
First published: Montreal : Lovell, 1864.
ISBN 0-88629-092-9 (casebound)
ISBN 0-88629-091-0 (paperback)

I. Stockdale, John C., 1929- . II. Title. III. Title:
Secret marrying and secret sorrowing. IV. Series.

PS8423.E6A75 1989   C813'.3   C89-090163-5
PR9199.2.L42A68 1989

Distributed by: Oxford University Press Canada
                70 Wynford Drive
                Don Mills, Ontario
                M3C 1J9
                (416) 441-2941

ACKNOWLEDGEMENT

Carleton University Press and the Centre for Editing Early Canadian Texts gratefully acknowledge the support of Carleton University, the Social Sciences and Humanities Research Council of Canada, The Henry White Kinnear Foundation, and the Birks Family Foundation in the preparation and publication of this edition of *Antoinette De Mirecourt*.

The illustration on the cover of the paperback edition is Place d'Armes, Montreal, a lithograph after C. Krieghoff, courtesy of the Royal Ontario Museum, Toronto, Canada.

Contents

Abbreviations

ALS	Autograph letter signed
CEECT	Centre for Editing Early Canadian Texts
DCB	*Dictionary of Canadian Biography*
NA	National Archives of Canada, Ottawa, Ontario
OKQ	Queen's University Library, Kingston, Ontario
OLU	University of Western Ontario Library, London, Ontario
OOCC	Carleton University Library, Ottawa, Ontario
OONL	National Library of Canada, Ottawa, Ontario
OTU	University of Toronto Library, Toronto, Ontario
QMBN	Bibliothèque Nationale, Montréal, Québec
QQLA	Université Laval, Québec, Québec

Foreword

The Centre for Editing Early Canadian Texts (CEECT) at Carleton University was established to prepare for publication scholarly editions of major works of early English-Canadian prose that are now either out of print or available only in corrupt reprints. Five of these editions, Frances Brooke's *The History of Emily Montague*, Catharine Parr Traill's *Canadian Crusoes*, James De Mille's *A Strange Manuscript Found in a Copper Cylinder*, John Richardson's *Wacousta*, and Susanna Moodie's *Roughing It in the Bush* have already been published, and another half-dozen, thanks to continuing funding from Carleton and from the Social Sciences and Humanities Research Council of Canada, are being prepared. *Antoinette De Mirecourt*, Rosanna Eleanor Mullins Leprohon's "essentially Canadian" story originally published by John Lovell in 1864, is the sixth volume in the CEECT series.

In the preparation of these editions, advice and guidance have been sought from a broad range of international scholarship, and contemporary principles and procedures for the scholarly editing of literary texts have been followed. These principles and procedures have been adapted to suit the special circumstances of Canadian literary scholarship and the particular needs of each of the works in the CEECT series.

The text of each scholarly edition in this series has been critically established after the history of the composition and first publication has been researched and its editions analysed and compared. The critical text is clear, with only authorial notes, if any, appearing in the body of the book. Each of these editions also has an editor's introduction with a separate section on the text, and, as concluding apparatus, explanatory notes, a bibliographical description of the copy-text and, when relevant, of other authoritative editions, a list of other versions of the text, a record of emendations made to the copy-text, a list of line-end

hyphenated compounds in the copy-text as they are resolved in
the CEECT edition, and a list of line-end hyphenated com-
pounds in the CEECT edition as they should be resolved in
quotations from this text. An historical collation is included when
more than one edition has authority, and, as necessary, appen-
dices containing material directly relevant to the text.

In the preparation of all these CEECT editions for publication,
identical procedures, in so far as the particular history of each
work allowed, have been followed. An attempt has been made to
find and analyse every pre-publication version of the work
known to exist. In the absence of a manuscript or proof, at least
five copies of each edition that was a candidate for copy-text have
been examined, and at least three copies of each of the other
editions that the author might have revised. Every edition of the
work has been subjected to as thorough a bibliographical study as
possible. All the known information about the printing and
publication of each work has been gathered, and the printed
versions of each have been subjected to several collations of
various kinds. Specialists from the University's Computing Ser-
vices have developed several programs to help in the proofread-
ing and comparison of texts, to perform word-searches, and to
compile and store much of the information for the concluding
apparatus. The edited text, printed from a magnetic tape pre-
pared at Carleton, has been proofread against its copy-text at all
appropriate stages.

Editor's Preface

My first flirtation with Rosanna Eleanor Mullins Leprohon and her literary offspring *Antoinette De Mirecourt* (1864) took place in 1970, when I was asked to prepare the entry on the author and her works for the *Dictionary of Canadian Biography*. Since I was still a novice in early Canadian literature, I agreed to undertake the task as an educational experience. On looking back, I have to admit that my opinion of Mrs. Leprohon and, particularly, of *Antoinette De Mirecourt* has risen a good deal since then. I regret now that in the *DCB* entry on Mrs. Leprohon, which was published in 1972, I called this novel the worst of the group of longer works of prose fiction she published from the late 1850s on. The remark was made because *Antoinette De Mirecourt* seemed much more "romantic," to use the word as the author herself did when she applied it to Antoinette, than *Armand Durand* (1868) and "The Manor House Of De Villerai" (1859-60), both of which contain generous helpings of realism. Like most other critics, I did not see, at that time, the close relationship that the plot of *Antoinette De Mirecourt* bore to the military and social history of Montreal.

Primarily because of this first encounter with Rosanna and Antoinette, I was given a second opportunity to meet these two ladies in the mid-1970s. Maurice Lemire, the general editor of the *Dictionnaire des oeuvres littéraires du Québec*, asked me to write an article on each of Mrs. Leprohon's novels, five in all, that had been translated into French and published during her lifetime. These entries were published in late 1978.

A year after these appeared, in late 1979, while I was peacefully composing poetry during a sabbatical in Rothesay, New Brunswick, I received a telephone call from Mary Jane Edwards, who was then organizing the Centre for Editing Early Canadian Texts project at Carleton University. She asked me if I would consider preparing the Centre's proposed scholarly edition of *Antoinette De Mirecourt*. Flattered to have been selected, seduced by the idea that the project was sufficiently far in the future for any number of events to intervene, and persuaded by the enthusiasm of my caller, I agreed. And my two initial flirtations grew slowly into a full-fledged affair, a durable, long-term commitment of a nature to drive most wives into a frenzy of jealousy, although in this case mine was actually most forbearing.

My preparation of the scholarly edition began in 1986, when the CEECT project received a Major Research Grant from the Social Sciences and Humanities Research Council of Canada. One of my first tasks was to identify the passages in *Antoinette De Mirecourt* that needed annotating and to prepare the explanatory notes.

The research these required provided many clues and sources for material that Mrs. Leprohon used in the construction of her plot. The writing of the "Introduction" itself, while often a frustrating procedure, proved to be a most enjoyable adventure into the past of Montreal in the wild, exciting period from the Conquest to 1864 and beyond. After long hours poring over microfilms of old periodicals in French and English, searching records from the times of the seigneuries, snooping in parish registers and in military histories, and reading old letters and memoirs of visitors to our new land, I became more and more convinced that Mrs. Leprohon, using her knowledge of life in Montreal, the "imperial garrison" town, was writing, in the guise of an historical romance, a contemporary moral tale that addressed the challenges inherent in the cultural mélange of nineteenth-century Canada. Although a number of reviewers saw a relationship between the novel's past and the author's present—one anonymous reviewer even going so far as to say that as he wrote there were numerous British officers of Sternfield's type walking the streets of Montreal—Mrs. Leprohon apparently got away with her potentially dangerous ploy. I think, however, that the fact that the French translation of *Antoinette De Mirecourt* was more popular than the original

English version may well have arisen from a realization on the part of the upper levels of "English" society in Montreal that the Irish Mrs. Leprohon had caught them "to the life" in a somewhat unflattering pose.

Uncovering material that might have contributed to the making of *Antoinette De Mirecourt* was relatively simple in comparison to trying to unearth new information about the character of the novelist. There are literally hundreds of references to Mrs. Leprohon's works, but only a few accounts of the woman herself. None of her private papers—letters, diaries, notebooks, etc.—appears to have survived. It is difficult, moreover, to draw from her prose and poetry a truly satisfying picture of the writer as human being.

Although I was largely frustrated in this regard, in general my research was made comparatively simple by the fact that the library of Université Laval possesses an extensive collection of early periodicals in French and English, and that the National Archives of Québec are only a step away across the Laval campus. The library of the National Assembly of Québec and that of the Quebec Literary and Historical Society have also supplied me with a good deal of information; the staff of each institution has been unfailingly helpful. I wish to thank the researchers at the offices of the *Dictionnaire des oeuvres littéraires du Québec* project for their assistance, as well as the dozens of my colleagues at Laval who have listened to my problems and offered advice and solutions.

Other institutions and people have contributed to the preparation of this scholarly edition. My thanks go to the librarians at the National Library of Canada, Queen's University, the University of Toronto, and the University of Western Ontario for lending CEECT copies of the first edition of *Antoinette De Mirecourt* and for allowing them to be microfilmed. I would also like to thank the Bibliothèque de l'Université de Montréal and les Frères de l'Instruction chrétienne for their kindness in allowing CEECT to use as frontispiece the portrait of Rosanna from "The Life and Works of Mrs. Leprohon, née R. E. Mullins," the thesis of Brother Adrian (Henri Deneau). Carolyn Donnelly, a former graduate student at Carleton and research assistant at CEECT, has been most generous in sharing the data she has collected on Mrs. Leprohon's life and works. Through the generous funding of CEECT by Carleton University and the Social Sciences and Humanities Research Council of Canada, I have been able to consult sources in Montreal and Ottawa. Also, through that funding, CEECT employed research assistants who collated texts, gathered and verified archival and other material, and helped prepare various bibliographical tools; a computer assistant who maintained, and improved, the project's complicated software; a secretary who entered the text of the novel on the computer and the many drafts of the apparatus, especially the "Introduction"; and a word processor who entered a second version of the novel onto the project's computing system. These tireless men and women, some of whom have now left the CEECT project for other endeavours, include Joseph Black, Robert Chamberlain, Mary Comfort, Michelle Kelly, Andrew Kerr-Wilson, Nadia Shewchenko, Deborah Wills, and Daniel Wilson.

Finally, I wish to thank Mary Jane Edwards, the general editor of the CEECT series, for having given me the opportunity to turn detective for a time, and for her cheerful, encouraging voice, which always came over the telephone when I needed prodding on my way, and never failed to help me focus on what had to be done next.

John Christie Stockdale
Université Laval
March 1989

Editor's Introduction

The narrow streets of Montreal teemed with British troops. Drawing admiring glances from the women of the city, officers in scarlet strutted, or rode in carriages and sleighs. Talk of conquests filled the air and feelings ran high. The time was "the year 176—, some short time after the royal standard of England had replaced the fleur-de-lys of France,"[1] the historical setting of *Antoinette De Mirecourt; Or, Secret Marrying and Secret Sorrowing. A Canadian Tale*, the novel written by Rosanna Eleanor Mullins Leprohon (1829-79) and published by John Lovell in Montreal in 1864. The time could also have been the 1860s, however, when the American Civil War (1861-65) was in progress and when Montreal, "'the principal strategic point'"[2] in the province of Canada, had an unusually large garrison. In choosing as the setting for her apparently "simple Tale" (CEECT, p. 1) a past that corresponded to her present, Mrs. Leprohon achieved the aesthetic distance she needed to deliver her important national statement about the cultural mélange that was and is "essentially Canadian" (CEECT, p. 1).

Mrs. Leprohon knew well Montreal's recent and more distant past. The daughter of a Montreal businessman, Francis Mullins, and his wife Rosanna Connelly (or Connolly), Rosanna was born in Montreal and lived there most of her life. Educated at the Convent of the Congregation of Notre Dame, she received an excellent grounding in geography, history, language, literature, morals, and religion. Mrs. Leprohon later commemorated both this "beloved Institution in which the happy days of [her] girlhood were passed,"[3] and the nuns who taught her there and who evidently encouraged her to write. Shortly after she left the Convent in 1846, her first published poetry appeared in the *Literary Garland*, the seminal Canadian literary periodical begun by John Lovell; her earliest prose fiction came out in the same periodical in 1847. Throughout her life she continued to publish both poetry and prose in periodicals in Canada and the United States, and a number of her works, including *Antoinette De Mirecourt* and her two other novels about French Canada, "The Manor House Of De Villerai" (1859-60) and *Armand Durand* (1868), were translated into French.

In 1851 Rosanna married a medical doctor, Jean-Baptiste-Lucain (or Lucien or Lukin) Leprohon whose great-grandfather had come to New France with the French army in the late 1750s and remained after the Conquest.[4] Dr. Leprohon had studied in France and had established his practice at St. Charles-sur-Richelieu, where he and his new wife went to live. He founded the *Lancette Canadienne*, one of the first French-Canadian medical journals, in January 1847; printed in Montreal by John Lovell and published twice monthly, it was suspended in June 1847 for lack of support. Later, after the Leprohons had returned to Montreal in 1855, he was active in the teaching of medicine, in the improvement of public health, and in city politics; at one time he was also Spanish Consul. Rosanna bore him thirteen children, several of whom died in infancy.

It is not difficult to discover facts about Mrs. Leprohon from newspaper announcements, church records, and other archival documents, but it is nearly impossible to find material that will hang flesh on the bare bones of these data. One source of information, albeit biased, does give glimpses of the author's private character. This is a series of letters that Dr. Leprohon wrote to his friend Pierre Margry, a French historian, between 1848 and 1885. In a letter dated 23 June 1865, Dr. Leprohon speaks of the ill health of his daughter Gertrude Ida (called Clémence), Margry's godchild, born on 29 June 1863:

> Je vous assure que les premiers qui[n]ze mois de son exis-
> tence ont été une lutte continuelle entre la vie et la mort,
> bien souvent sa chère mère et moi, nous avions presque faits
> le sacrifice de cette frêle existence. Mais je vous avoue que la
> bonne et tendre petite maman qui lui prodiguait des soins
> qu'une mère seule peut donner n'a pas hesité un instant de

passer des nuits au chevet de son Baby pour le rechapper de la mort qui paroissait imminente.

Dieu Merci, elle va mieux, et sa chère mère a pu quitter la ville pour aller passer quelques semaines à la campagne près d'un lac *Memphamagog* qui offre au regard des points de vue fort remarquables. C'est, la, avec le cadet de mes fils (Claude) qu'elle passe quelque tems pour recruter sa santé et se donner le repos qu'une assez nombreuse famille comme la mienne a un peu altéré. Aussi à chaque lettre que je recois de cette tendre épouse j'ai la satisfaction d'apprendre que sa santé va de mieux en mieux et que bientôt elle reviendra me trouver sous le vieux toit de mon père, parfaitement retablie.

J'avais quelque chose à vous envoyer mais le fait est que ma femme a pris le volume en question et je ne puis mettre, dans le moment, la main sur un autre exemplaire. C'est un livre publié en Anglais par un litterateur sur les personnes qui ont contribué à la poesie du Canada—et comme ma chere Épouse a sa place avec une notice critique sur les ecrits qui ont paru d'elle en differens tems j'aurais voulu vous l'envoyer.[5]

Two years later, on 31 May 1867, Dr. Leprohon again writes to Margry that Clémence has been "bien malade" and that his wife "depuis quelque tems, n'a pas été, non plus très bien. Mais, j'ai lieu de [croire] que tout va aller mieux depuis que le beau tems commence à se faire sentir."[6] Three years later, on 11 Mar. 1870, he writes about himself and his family:

Mes cheveux portent des flocons de neige c'est l'outrage des années, mais je n'ai pas (*de glace dans mes culottes, Dieu merci*). Je personnifie la force et la vigeur presque 6 pieds de taille poids *200* livres. Ce n'est pas mauvais à quarante huit ans, Je suis père de sept enfans, dont trois garcons et quatre filles; je suis franchement fier de cette posterité. Car tous mes enfants sont bien constitués et tous vigoureux; la langue Francaise et anglaise se parle indifferemment par eux à table, et si j'osais l'avouer il y a une plus grande affinité pour l'anglais que pour le Francais, à cause des parents de mon épouse qui ne parlent pas ma langue.[7]

In the last paragraph of this letter, Dr. Leprohon says that Rosanna, who joins him in wishing that they might meet Margry and see the sights of France together, is still publishing, and "Sa plume est mise a contribution par les prêtres, les sœurs, et pour toutes affaires religieuses."[8]

In another letter dated 27 July 1877, the Doctor reports that "Madame a passé un bien triste hyver, la perte douloureuse de sa mère et de sa sœur, mortes trois jours, l'une après l'autre, a beaucoup miné sa santé, j'ai cru même qu'elle serait forcé de quitter le pays pour aller passer quelques mois au Midi de la France, mais, heureusement qu'elle s'est rétabli peu à peu, et elle est aujourdui parfaitement bien."[9] Finally, on 18 June 1884, almost five years after his wife's death, Dr. Leprohon writes: "Je suis toujours le même, regrettant la perte de cette chère «Rosanna» qui a charmé mon existence pendant 30 années. J'irai la rejoindre bientôt, car ma santé laisse à désirer."[10] In a postscript to this letter, he sends his respects to his friend's wife and hopes that they will be united for many years to come, for "La vie est triste et monotone quand il n'y a plus de compagne pour égayer le passage d'ici bas."[11] One cannot help but be impressed by the adoration Mrs. Leprohon obviously inspired in her husband and the pride he took in her literary accomplishments.

Mrs. Leprohon died on 20 Sept. 1879. In a long article entitled "DEATH OF MRS. LEPROHON. The Canadian Poet and Novelist" published on 22 Sept. 1879, the Montreal *Gazette* reported that she had "died after a prolonged illness at her late residence, St. Antoine Street, on Saturday last."[12] Another long article appeared in the *Opinion Publique* (Montreal) on 2 Oct. 1879. The author of this article, signed "J. D.," was probably Joseph Doutre, a prominent Montreal lawyer who had himself written a novel and several short stories and who knew Mrs. Leprohon and her family.[13] "J. D." states that "Madame Leprohon était dans la force de l'âge. A la voir, il y a quelques semaines, pleine de vie, gaie et souriante, nous étions loin de prévoir que nous aurions aujourd'hui à déplorer sa perte. Elle a succombé à une maladie du cœur, le 20 septembre dernier." He continues that if it was a pleasure to read Mrs. Leprohon's works, it was an even greater pleasure to listen to her talk: "Elle possédait au plus haut degré l'art de la conversation, et elle savait l'amener sur des sujets sérieux et d'un ordre élevé, sur des questions de morale, d'art et de littérature, sans qu'on pût y trouver la moindre teinte d'affectation ou de pédantisme." "J. D." ends his article with a touching account of Rosanna's last moments. She gave, he says, her last advice and "adieux" to her family and joined them as they prayed for her; then, with faith and piety, "elle a rendu son âme à Dieu."[14]

Every writer is the product of his or her environment, and Rosanna was no exception. The most important influences in her childhood, and in her adult life, came from her religious and moral training, from her marriage into a French-Canadian family, and from her willingness to assimilate early French-Canadian history and culture and to sympathize with at least some of the more moderate views and aspirations of the French-Canadian people. Rosanna also read novels, poetry, and drama in both English and French. These influences all helped form *Antoinette De Mirecourt*, but it was, clearly, Mrs. Leprohon's knowledge of life in the city of Montreal, past and present, that gave shape and substance to the novel.

After the capitulation of Montreal in 1760, the British established a garrison there that was maintained at varying strengths for over a century, and the conquering troops became the nucleus of a growing British presence that inevitably had to meet and mingle with the *Canadiens* who remained. At first there was antipathy between the two groups, but by the time the fate of New France was officially sealed by the signing of the Treaty of Paris in 1763, the French Canadians had adjusted at least partially to the continued British presence and to the growing stream of British government officials and immigrants. Romances and marriages between the two nationalities were not uncommon, although there were periods of particular tension that coincided with the influx of extra troops to meet the threats of the American Revolution, the War of 1812, the Rebellions of 1837 and 1838, and the American Civil War.

The political situation in Canada between the 1830s and 1860s was in a constant state of uproar and change. Appointed British officials held the real power until 1841, but their right to rule was contested vigorously by both French and English groups. The desire for self-government led to the uprisings of 1837 and 1838 in Upper and Lower Canada. One consequence of these was the union of the Canadas that came about in 1841 as a result of Lord Durham's recommendations in his *Report On The Affairs of British North America* (1839). This union gave the united provinces an elected assembly with a capital city first at Kingston and later at Montreal, and began a tradition of French and English political co-operation. The arrangement, however, was fraught with difficulties. When the Rebellion Losses Bill was passed in 1849, for instance, tempers flared. The period of the 1850s was relatively calm, but with the beginning of the American Civil War, Montrealers became apprehensive of an attack from their militant neighbours, and Britain, because of her preference for the cause of the South, shared this fear.

On 8 Nov. 1861, the Northern forces had removed two Confederate representatives from the British steamer *Trent* and the British reacted with angry words. If war were to break out between the Union forces and the British, Canada would almost certainly be the battleground, and Montreal a target of attack as Canada's largest and most vulnerable city. The British government immediately dispatched 10,500 troops to Canada. "So many were posted to Montreal that the barracks proved insufficient; several colleges and stores were leased by the government, and fitted out as living quarters."[15] Still more troops arrived in the spring of 1862, and, although the Trent Affair soon blew over, they remained.

It is not difficult to envisage the impact of this sudden influx of thousands of soldiers and officers on the frontier city of Montreal, with its population of approximately ninety thousand.[16] There were bound to be frictions and incidents of many kinds, since the soldiers were, for the most part, young and thousands of miles away from the restraints of home and their well-ordered society. Many would be contemptuous of the colonial men and their militia, prejudiced against French Canadians, and searching for women willing to offer them companionship as an antidote for homesickness and the ennui of barrack-room life. In *The Story Of A Soldier's Life* (1903), Field-Marshall Viscount Garnet Wolseley, recording some of his experiences in Canada in the 1860s, writes:

> Life in Montreal was very pleasant. Of course I bought horses and a sledge, in which I daily drove very charming women, both Canadian and American. . . . We had very successful garrison theatricals in the winter, and many were the sledge expeditions we made into the neighbouring country. Altogether, it was an elysium of bliss for young officers, the only trouble being to keep single. Several impressionable young captains and subalterns had to be sent home hurriedly to save them from imprudent marriages. Although these Canadian ladies were very charming they were not richly endowed with worldly goods.[17]

The girls who sought to take part in the many sleigh-rides were known among the officers as "muffins," and "the tendency of muffinage to merge into marriage was very real."[18]

The problem of the officers and the "muffins" reached such a state that Frances Monck, the daughter-in-law of the governor general of British North America, recorded the following in a letter home written in 1865: "Captain Eliot amused us at lunch yesterday, by telling us that the priest at Montreal preached since Lent began against *officers*, and discouraged young ladies from associating with them. Last Sunday our Bishop Fulford of Montreal preached a great sermon *at* the ladies: spoke against their seeking and loving admiration, and particularly warned married women against setting the bad example."[19] This quotation proves the seriousness with which these liaisons were being taken. Mrs. Leprohon, living in this atmosphere of red-coated officers, sleighing parties, "muffins," and intrigues, and herself the mother of young daughters,[20] had many reasons to compose her story about "Secret Marrying and Secret Sorrowing."

Mrs. Leprohon's first "essentially Canadian tale"[21] was "The Manor House Of De Villerai." Subtitled "A Tale Of Canada Under The French Dominion," it was set in New France between "December, 1756"[22] and "a calm and pleasant Autumn day" in 1760, when "the chivalrous De Lévis, Colonel De Bourlamarque and others of equal fame and dauntless courage" were sailing from "the harbour of Quebec"[23] on their way to France. Initially published as a serial in the Montreal *Family Herald* between 16 Nov. 1859 and 8 Feb. 1860, it was one of the stories translated by Joseph-Edouard Lefebvre de Bellefeuille, the Leprohons' nephew. His translation was serialized in the Montreal *Ordre* from 14 Nov. 1860 to 3 Apr. 1861; in 1861 it also appeared in volume form.

The success of "The Manor House Of De Villerai" undoubtedly encouraged Mrs. Leprohon to contemplate a second "essentially Canadian" story. The echo of phrases like "the proud standard of England" and "the old *Fleur De Lys*" from the "Conclusion"[24] to "The Manor House Of De Villerai" in the opening paragraph of *Antoinette De Mirecourt* and the repetition from the former novel's "Conclusion" of the autumn setting in the opening of the latter work suggest, in fact, that Mrs. Leprohon saw *Antoinette De Mirecourt* both as a kind of continuation of her first "Canadian Tale" and as an alternative, and undoubtedly more realistic, moral and social exemplum. For, in contrast to Antoinette De Mirecourt, who sins and suffers, Blanche De Villerai, the heroine of the earlier story, never marries and leads a "pure blameless life" in post-Conquest Canada, a life that "was one of those rare careers of exemption from care, which fall, alas! so rarely to the lot of earth's children."[25] The similarities between the two works may also indicate that Mrs. Leprohon began the composition of her second "Canadian Tale" in the early 1860s, shortly after the completion of "The Manor House Of De Villerai," and developed and shaped it, thus, precisely at the period when the British troops in Montreal were causing so many concerns.

The story told by Mrs. Leprohon in *Antoinette De Mirecourt* is that of the misadventures of Antoinette De Mirecourt, the beautiful, innocent young daughter of a rural Quebec seigneur, who in 1763, while a guest in the Montreal home of her relations, comes into social contact with officers from the British garrison. Madame D'Aulnay, her frivolous cousin, decides to open her house, against her husband's wishes, to the British officers, who, she claims, are all cultivated gentlemen. She organizes first a soirée, and later a sleighing party, at which she arranges that Antoinette, who has already been smitten by Major Audley Sternfield, will ride with a professed woman-hater, the taciturn, older Colonel Cecil Evelyn.

As the reluctant companions are driving along close to a high river bank, the horses, frightened by a gun-shot, bolt. The reins break as Evelyn tries to control the team. He seizes Antoinette, who has sat silent and motionless, throws her from the sleigh onto the snow, and leaps after her while the horses and sleigh plunge onto the rocks in the river below. As Evelyn conducts Antoinette to a nearby house, he reflects on how calm she has remained in the face of possible death, and contrasts her response to what one might have expected from any other girl of her age. This incident helps establish the necessary conditions for the final resolution of the plot.

The central incident in the novel is Antoinette's sudden, clandestine marriage to Major Sternfield, an English Protestant, a gambler, a womanizer, and a fortune hunter. When he is introduced into the upper class of Montreal's French society, he meets Antoinette and is attracted by her beauty but takes care, nevertheless, to investigate her expectations. He finds her an only child, who will, at eighteen, inherit her dead mother's modest fortune and eventually her father's considerable assets. Abetted by Madame D'Aulnay, Antoinette and Audley marry secretly before the Protestant chaplain of the British garrison, Dr. Ormsby.

The ramifications of this precipitous marriage lead directly to the next major incident of the plot, the fatal duel between Sternfield and Louis Beauchesne, the young neighbour whom Monsieur De Mirecourt has chosen to be Antoinette's husband. Antoinette tells Louis that she cannot marry him, but begs him to continue to be her friend. He agrees and often calls on her in her father's house and in Montreal. These visits drive Sternfield into a jealous rage. Finally Beauchesne and Sternfield have words, and the former mortally wounds the latter in a duel. Beauchesne, to escape the law, flees to France. Colonel Evelyn, after swallowing his pride and digesting his shock, asks for Antoinette's hand in marriage. Monsieur De Mirecourt, who has formed a good opinion of Evelyn, is glad to find any man who will take such a disobedient and scandalous daughter off his hands and sensibly agrees to the union. Evelyn's virtue is further enhanced by the fact that he has been brought up a Roman Catholic. Thus Mrs. Leprohon concedes that under certain circumstances, a sterling English character of the right religion could be an acceptable partner for a French-Canadian heiress. Despite her reservations, then, Mrs. Leprohon confronts the fact that marriages between members of the British armed forces and *Canadiennes* had taken place over the years since the Conquest and had sometimes led to "unclouded domestic felicity" (CEECT, p. 238).

The source of the first major incident in the plot of *Antoinette De Mirecourt*, the sleighing accident caused by Colonel Evelyn's runaway horses, is easy to trace. In the days before railroads and automobiles, the horse-drawn sleigh was the only method of winter travel, and although there were accidents, sleighing was a favourite winter pastime. Montrealers, furthermore, "who lived by standards of sophistication had to have elegant sleighs and elegant horses. Sleighing as an expression of opulence increased as the 19th century advanced and Montreal moved into greater and greater prosperity."[26] Mrs. Leprohon would certainly have been thoroughly familiar with travelling by horse and sleigh, courting in sleighs, and the pleasures and perils of both. In fact, the author shows her precise knowledge of winter driving in her description of the accident, even to the sad necessity of shooting the injured horses.

There seems to be no single source for all the circumstances of the second important incident in the novel, the sudden secret marriage between the young Roman Catholic Antoinette and the Protestant Audley, but it is not difficult to piece together such a plot from incidents that had taken place in and around Montreal from the time of the Conquest. As an English-speaking Montrealer of Irish descent whose spouse was a French-speaking *Canadien*, Mrs. Leprohon herself had married across "racial" and linguistic lines. In her own lifetime, furthermore, when people seldom bothered to temper their words or actions towards those of other races, religions, or political beliefs, Mrs. Leprohon as an Irish Roman Catholic in Montreal must also have experienced prejudice among the English, Irish, Scottish, and American Protestants.

The secret aspect of Antoinette's marriage was most likely suggested to Mrs. Leprohon by her nephew de Bellefeuille. In November 1859, he had defended a thesis at the Law School of Collège Ste-Marie in Montreal on the subject of "secret marriages." Serialized by the *Ordre* in 1859-60, "Thèse sur les Mariages Clandestins" was based on a controversial court case that involved a French-Canadian couple who had crossed the border into the state of New York in 1849 and secretly married before a justice of the peace. Shortly after their return to Canada East, they signed a marriage contract giving the wife control of her property, and married again, this time in the Roman Catholic church. A legal problem arose over who had control of the wife's fortune. One side claimed that, since the first marriage had been legally contracted according to the laws of New York, the couple's property was held in common. The other side contended that the New York marriage was illegal, a matter of convenience only, since the two were domiciled in Canada East and should have married there, and that, according to the marriage contract, the wife had control of her own property. The long-drawn-out case, which finally ended in March 1858, was decided in favour of the first side. In his thesis de Bellefeuille was not concerned with the matter of control of property but with the question of the legality of the New York marriage. He maintained that a civil marriage set at nought the authority of the Church and that it defied the written word of God, views that Mrs. Leprohon obviously shared.

Divorce, which Mrs. Leprohon mentions briefly in *Antoinette De Mirecourt*, was also a subject being discussed in the early 1860s. The topic, for example, was taken up in a front-page article entitled "Divorce" published in the *Ordre* on 10 June 1864. Although this particular article appeared too late to have a direct influence on *Antoinette De Mirecourt*, the writer shares Mrs. Leprohon's horror of divorce, expressed by Antoinette in the novel, as a sin against the Roman Catholic church.

A further source of certain circumstances of the marriage between Audley and Antoinette may be found in the history of the Barony of Longueuil, to which Mrs. Leprohon refers in *Antoinette De Mirecourt*, and from which she may have derived Antoinette's surname, aspects of the history of her family, and the location of the family's seigneury. A particularly fascinating story of Quebec under the rule of the British immediately after the Conquest that may have supplied the broad outlines of part of the plot of *Antoinette De Mirecourt* involves the widow of Charles Le Moyne, third Baron of Longueuil, Marie-Anne-Catherine Fleury Deschambault, who, fifteen years after the death of her first husband in 1755, married William Grant, "merchant, seigneur, office holder, and politician."[27] In the fall of 1759, Grant, the brilliant bilingual son of the Laird of Blairfindy, Scotland, had been sent, at the age of fifteen, to Quebec by a relative to be his business agent. Grant set up offices in Quebec and Montreal and began to speculate in furs, salmon and seal fisheries, and in French paper currency. During the 1760s he acquired real estate in Quebec and Montreal and bought up rural seigneuries. By 1766 he was one of the principal businessmen in Quebec, although he was notorious for not paying his debts. In 1770, having declared that he was a Roman Catholic, Grant was married secretly in Montreal to the Baroness of Longueuil by a Jesuit priest, and publicly, on 11 Sept. 1770, by an Anglican minister. This marriage put at Grant's disposition the seigneurial lands of Longueuil, including the farm on "St. Helen's" Island mentioned in *Antoinette De Mirecourt* (CEECT, p. 217).

The Baroness had a young daughter, Marie-Charles-Joseph Le Moyne de Longueuil, who was to inherit the Barony, and Grant, who evidently wished to have both the land and the title for his family, saw to it that she married his nephew, Captain David Alexander Grant, of the 84th Regiment. "Le contrat de mariage, signé devant l'avocat . . . à Québec, stipule que les futurs époux seront 'unis et communs en tous biens meubles, acquets et conquets immeubles.'"[28] Two days after the contract was signed, the marriage was celebrated, by special license, at the Anglican church in Quebec on 7 May 1781. "Ce qui fera," says, somewhat sourly, Robert Rumilly, the author of *Histoire De Longueuil* (1974) "passer la baronnie entre des mains anglaises."[29] The same year David Alexander "replaced" Joseph Fleury Deschambault, the Baroness' father and Marie-Charles' grandfather, as "trustee" of his wife's inheritance and thus manager of the Barony of Longueuil.[30] A son, Charles William Grant, born to David Alexander and Marie-Charles in 1782 and baptised an Anglican, eventually inherited both the estate and the title of Baron of Longueuil.

Rumilly adds an interesting though somewhat sad touch to this story of greed. After David Alexander died in 1806, his widow passed her winters in Montreal and her summers on St. Helen's Island, where she owned a manor and very fine gardens. She carried, people said, the spirit of economy to the point of avarice. To her ancient carriage, she hitched a nag, grown old in the service of a baker. The local street urchins amused themselves "à faire arrêter le cheval, fidèle à ses anciennes habitudes, en criant: 'Bread!'."[31] Marie-Charles died in 1841 at the age of eighty-six.

In 1841 the twelve-year-old Rosanna was not of an age when she might have been expected to take much interest in the doings of the Barony, but there was one more event, a most unhappy one for future historians, that took place because of the influx of

British soldiers in the 1860s and that would have brought the story of the Le Moynes and the Grants to her attention. This was the destruction "des papiers de la famille de Longueuil, si intimement liée à l'histoire de Montréal":

> C'était pendant l'affaire d[u] *Trent*; on avait besoin d'installation pour les troupes envoyées à Montréal. Des magasins appartenant à la famille Grant, de Longueuil, furent retenus. Or, dans le grenier d'un de ces magasins, il y avait une grande quantité de paperasses. Il s'agissait de s'en débarrasser. Le moyen en était simple. On les fit transporter, sans même se demander ce qu'elles pouvaient être, sur la ferme Logan, et là, elles furent réduites en cendres. En passant, quelqu'un arracha de cet amas de paperasses quelques pièces. Une était la lettre d'anoblissement de l'illustre Charles Le Moyne, le bras droit de Maisonneuve dans la fondation de Montréal; une autre était les lettres patentes érigeant en baronnie la seigneurie de Longueuil. *Trente tombereaux* remplis de ces papiers, s'acheminèrent vers la ferme Logan. C'était là la haute appréciation que la famille Grant montrait des gloires de la famille de Longueuil qui a donné à notre pays, d'Iberville, et que le baron Grant était tenu de respecter en assumant son titre.[32]

This disaster, coupled with the already unpleasant reputation of the Grants as fortune hunters, must certainly have created a good deal of resentment among the French Canadians. For Mrs. Leprohon the story of the Barony of Longueuil may well have provided both specific historical instances of the "adventurers, who sought to build themselves positions on the ruined fortunes of the vanquished people" she described in *Antoinette De Mirecourt* (CEECT, p. 29), and an outline for a plot that included the marriage of a French-Canadian heiress to a British adventurer, a secret marriage, and the same couple being married twice, once in a Protestant ceremony, once in a Roman Catholic.

Mrs. Leprohon's most likely sources for the third incident in *Antoinette De Mirecourt*, the Sternfield-Beauchesne duel, are two duels, both described by Aegidius Fauteux in *Le Duel au Canada* (1934), that took place in the late 1830s. These are the Ormsby-Rodier duel in October 1837, and the Warde-Sweeney duel in May 1838. The first is of interest because of the name of one of the men who took part, Lieutenant Ormsby, the name Mrs. Leprohon gives to the English clergyman in her novel. This duel also provides an example of a British officer being challenged by a French Canadian. According to the Montreal *Vindicator* of 31 Oct. 1837, "An affair of honor took place this morning, at the Race Course, between E. E. RODIER, Esq. M.P.P., attended by T. S. BROWN, Esq., and Lieut. ORMSBY, of the Royals, attended by Captain Mayne, of the same Corps. After the first fire Captain M. removed his principal from the ground."[33] The timing of the duel, just a few days before the outbreak of the Rebellion of 1837, and the fact that both Edouard-Etienne Rodier and Thomas Storrow Brown were well-known *patriotes* guaranteed that the story of the duel would be remembered and retold in connection with the Warde-Sweeney affair, especially since Captain Mayne was also Major Warde's second.

The Warde-Sweeney duel was one of the most notorious ever fought in Montreal and would have been of particular interest to Mrs. Leprohon because she herself lived in the Sweeneys' old house in the 1860s; in fact, she probably wrote at least part of *Antoinette De Mirecourt* there.[34] There are numerous accounts of the duel, the events leading to it, and the aftermath, including the coroner's inquest. Henry John Warde, a major in the Royal Regiment, had been receiving flowers and messages from an unknown woman, and Warde, a great lover of women, set about discovering the identity of his secret admirer. According to some accounts, Warde had the young messenger who delivered the flowers to him followed; and the boy turned into the house occupied by Robert Sweeney, a lawyer, an officer in the militia, and a published poet, who had a very attractive wife. Warde, thinking that he had indeed found someone worthy of his attention, immediately wrote a steamy letter to Mrs. Sweeney and had it delivered to her house.

In *Old Montreal* (1906), Adèle Clarke repeats a story her mother told her of the Warde-Sweeney duel that, even at the distance of about seventy years, has a ring of truth:

> In the old Leprohon corner house on Beaver Hall Hill . . . lived Captain and Mrs. Sweeney (née Miss Temple, an American). He was one of the Voltigeurs, and she afterwards became Lady Rose, her second husband being Sir John Rose, Bart. One night when they were at dinner, the servant came in and handed Capt. Sweeney a note. On reading it, he immediately jumped up from the table and left the room. The contents of the note had enraged him against Major Ward, in some connection with the name of Mrs. Sweeney. Capt. Sweeney sent a note to Major Ward, who was a very popular officer, challenging him to a duel to be fought on Lachine Road on the old race course. In the duel Major Ward was killed. Major Ward was so great a favorite, that his death caused general sorrow, and Mrs. Sweeney left for New York.[35]

Sweeney apparently also fled briefly to the United States.

A coroner's inquest was convened, at which a doctor did a post-mortem as he explained how the bullet had killed Warde, and the jury decided that Warde had died from the effects of a bullet fired by "quelque personne inconnue."[36] Four days later, the *Montreal Gazette*, under the heading "*THE ARMY*," announced:

> Yesterday, at three o'clock, the remains of the late Major WARDE, of the Royals, were interred with military honours. The body was followed by Major General CLITHEROW, Colonel WETHERALL, the Hon. Lieut. Colonel GREY, Lieut. Colonel MAUNSELL, and the whole of the officers in garrison. The pall was borne by five Majors and a civilian. The whole of the Royal Regiment attended the funeral, as a firing party; the hearse being preceded by the bands of the Royals, 34th, and 85th Regiments.[37]

The story does not end with the inquest and the burial. The people of Montreal and especially the clergy were disturbed by this needless loss of life. In *Montreal: The Days That Are No More* (1976), Edgar Andrew Collard describes the reaction of the Roman Catholic clergy:

> It happened in 1838 that the Fête Dieu, with the Corpus Christi Procession, came on the first Sunday after Warde's funeral. On that Sunday afternoon the bishop was to carry the Host through the streets around the cathedral. . . . Arrangements had been made to have the Montreal Volunteer Rifles line the streets as a guard of honor. The bishop, horrified at Warde's death in a duel, made a request to Captain De Bleury, commanding officer of the Volunteer Rifles. He asked that Lieutenant Leclere should not be present at the sacred ceremony. His reason: the lieutenant had recently been concerned in a duel. Captain De Bleury made a spirited reply. He informed the bishop that the reason given for excluding Lieutenant Leclere was unfortunate, for he, the captain, had also once been concerned in a duel. He refused to make an invidious distinction between the lieutenant and himself. The bishop, however, held his ground. The result was that the Montreal Volunteer Rifles did not appear to line the route of the Corpus Christi Procession. To Bishop Lartigue their absence was not undesirable. It served to make public that any Roman Catholic who fought a duel, or who had any part in its arrangements, would risk the condemnation of the Church.[38]

Later, in August 1838, the Reverend William Taylor, of the United Secession Church, preached a sermon against the custom of duelling as a sin against society and against God, and prayed his fellow citizens to put an end to this deplorable *"relic of barbarism."*[39] One can well imagine the nuns at Rosanna's Convent and her parents at home lecturing the young girl on the perils of such scandalous behaviour. This affair surely became part of Mrs. Leprohon's bank of youthful memories, memories undoubtedly reinforced by her residence in the Sweeneys' old house.

Two years later, on 28 May 1840, the *Montreal Gazette* reprinted the following:

> It is our painful duty to report the fatal issue of an affair of honour which took place at Montreal; the antagonists were Lt. Colonel White, of the 7th Hussars, and Mr. Grant, late of the 79th Regiment. We are not in possession of the particulars, but it is understood that the Colonel fell from the fire of his opponent, and that the cause of the quarrel had reference to the conduct of Colonel White towards a young lady related to Mr. Grant. In every point of view, the incidents are of a most distressing character.—*Toronto Transcript, May 21.*[40]

Whatever the real circumstances that gave rise to this account, which the *Montreal Gazette* dubbed a "most absurd story,"[41] White (or Whyte) obviously endured in some kind of "conduct . . . towards a young lady related to Mr. Grant." The *Montreal Gazette* of 8 Oct. 1842 announced, "MARRIED. By the Rev. Messire Manseau, Vicar General, and afterwards by the Rev. Mr. Ramsay, Lieut. Colonel Whyte, 7th Queen's Own Hussars, to Mary Anne Jessy, third daughter of the late Mons. de Montenach, Patrician of Fribourg, Switzerland, and of Mary Elizabeth Grant, daughter of the late Baroness de Longueuil."[42] These reports tie the Grants of Longueuil to the practice of duelling and, for the second time, to marrying twice, once in the Roman Catholic church and once in the Anglican.

The past and present of Montreal were not the only sources upon which Mrs. Leprohon drew in her writing of *Antoinette De Mirecourt*. She made use of the books that she had read as well. One of her most important printed sources was the third edition of François-Xavier Garneau's *Histoire Du Canada Depuis Sa Découverte Jusqu'à Nos Jours*, which appeared in 1859, and from which she apparently translated extensively. From evidence in the novel it is also clear that Mrs. Leprohon was familiar with contemporary French authors. How much more she owes to Balzac's *La Femme de trente ans* (1842) than the reference to his preference for mature women is less obvious, but there are similarities between *Antoinette De Mirecourt* and Balzac's novel. The background of *La Femme de trente ans* is one of warfare. It opens with a scene of a father and his only daughter, young, beautiful, and motherless, watching a military parade in Paris. The daughter, Julie, marries a handsome young officer who proves to be a very limited husband. Because of the war, Julie is rushed away from Paris to the safety of the estate of her husband's aunt. While she rusticates with the aunt, a worldly one-time frequenter of the French court, she begins to be aware of the attentions of a young British officer on parole. The aunt, in the same way as Madame D'Aulnay, undertakes to direct her niece in the art of love and succeeds so well that the two young people begin a long affair. Julie's problems become so desperate at one point that her mental condition causes physical illness in the same way as Antoinette's agony of conscience over her secret marriage literally makes her sick, and both heroines consider death as a possible alternative to their unhappiness.

In *Antoinette De Mirecourt* Mrs. Leprohon's reference to the heroines of the Fronde as well as her chief character's name may indicate another source of the novel. Charles-Jean-Baptiste Jacquot, *dit* Eugène De Mirecourt, was the author of several novels, including *Les Confessions de Marion Delorme* (1848) and *Mémoires De Ninon De Lenclos* (1852). These works are of interest, first, because of the name of the author, and, second, because the chief character of each is based on an actual woman who frequented the French court at the time of the seventeenth-century uprising sometimes called the "Fronde of the women."[43] *Ninon De Lenclos* is the more relevant of the two because of its plot and some of its characters. Ninon, the heroine of this picaresque novel, has incredible adventures, numerous lovers, and illegitimate children. She also suffers a grave physical illness brought on by psychological problems.

Ninon De Lenclos, anticlerical and immoral, would certainly have qualified as one of the "novels, love-tales of the most reprehensible folly" condemned by Mrs. Leprohon in *Antoinette De Mirecourt* (CEECT, p. 139). Yet at the end of an edition of

Ninon De Lenclos published in 1857, the chief character introduces "Anne-Antoinette Ligier de la Garde,"[44] Madame Deshoulières, another woman of the Fronde who, like Mrs. Leprohon's Antoinette, does not seem at first glance to have "all the necessary qualifications for a genuine heroine" of a love story (CEECT, p. 154). According to Ninon, "Antoinette, à l'âge de seize ans, devint une aimable et délicieuse personne."[45] Educated by her father, who permitted her to read only "des ouvrages philosophiques ou religieux," she flirted briefly with the novels of "d'Urfé . . . de la Calprenède et de mademoiselle de Scudéri."[46] She soon became disgusted with "ces livres frivoles," however, and "revint d'elle-même à des lectures plus saines."[47] In later life, a virtuous married woman, she was known for her "poésie tendre."[48] Before she died, "elle paraphrasa les *Psaumes* et composa les *Réflexions morales*."[49] Such a figure, especially among the courtesans connected with the Fronde, demonstrates Mrs. Leprohon's theme in *Antoinette De Mirecourt* that a virtuous life is both possible and desirable even in a licentious world.

What seems to be the first published indication that Mrs. Leprohon was preparing *Antoinette De Mirecourt* appeared in the Quebec *Morning Chronicle* on 29 Mar. 1864. An item called "A NEW CANADIAN BOOK IN PRESS" announced that "ANTOINETTE DE MIRECOURT; or Secret Marrying and Secret Sorrowing, by Mrs. Laprohon" was "To be published by John Lovell, in April 1864." A letter from an unidentified "literary correspondent" that followed the publication notice described in more detail both the work and its author:

> "The English reading public of Canada will soon have to thank the talented authoress of which Montreal is proud for a thrilling tale of Canadian life, and we have been favored with the introductory chapter of this new novel. The scene is laid in Lower Canada, the time, that portion of our history following the cession of Canada to England, when the British officers who had come over to the newly conquered colony, amongst other achievements occasionally wooed and won, as they still do at the present day, one of

our Canadian belles. "Antoinette," the heroine, secretly marries an English officer, and then . . . but, dear reader do you really imagine I shall disclose to you all the thrilling events which followed. Mrs. Leprohon, despite her name, is, as every one knows, an English lady, whose graceful pen has contributed in no inconsiderable degree to Canadian literature. We are much mistaken if her present work should not prove even more attractive than those she has already written."

The letter concluded with the information that the new novel would be published by subscription and that "the subscription list exhibits several of our best known citizens."[50] On 6 April the *Montreal Gazette* reprinted the publication announcement "from the Quebec *Chronicle*."[51]

In the meantime, on 1 April, a similar notice had been inserted in the *Ordre*: "Nous apprenons avec un vif plaisir que Mad. Leprohon, la charmante auteur de *Ida Beresford* et du *Manoir de Villerai* que les lecteurs de notre feuilleton ont eu occasion d'apprécier, est sur le point de publier en anglais une autre Nouvelle intitulée *Antoinette de Mirecourt*." The *Ordre* predicted a "brillant succes" for the novel and indicated, "si nous sommes bien informé,"[52] that the work would be translated.

It was not until late June 1864, however, that the newspapers and periodicals began receiving copies of *Antoinette De Mirecourt*, and it is possible that the book, priced at a dollar a copy,[53] was not readily available for sale until well into July. One possible reason for the apparent delay in publication was the sickness of the Leprohons' infant daughter Clémence described by Dr. Leprohon in the 1865 letter to his friend Pierre Margry. The first fifteen months of Clémence's life were, according to her father, "une lutte continuelle entre la vie et la mort,"[54] which exhausted, and threatened the health of, her mother. At any time during these months (roughly July 1863 to September 1864), then, Mrs. Leprohon may well have been totally distracted from her literary career and unable to compose a preface, read proofs, or approve revised pages.

On 23 June 1864, the *Ordre* announced that Mrs. Leprohon had just published "le nouvel ouvrage" that it had indicated was forthcoming "il y a quelque temps." It predicted "une grande vogue" for this Canadian story and urged "les amis de la bonne littérature à en prendre connaissance." It also wished that the work would be translated into French. Finally it thanked Mrs. Leprohon for having sent the newspaper "un magnifique exemplaire cartonné."[55]

In the following months other notices of the novel's publication appeared in the Canadian press. On 8 July 1864, for example, the Montreal *True Witness* gave it several lines. Calling *Antoinette De Mirecourt* "an interesting well-told story," the anonymous author of the notice remarked, "the object of the amiable and accomplished writer of this pleasing story is to do her part towards fostering and encouraging a Canadian literature, racy of the soil—and she has done her part well."[56] A notice in the July issue of the *Journal Of Education For Lower Canada* is particularly interesting because it points out the close connection of the plot of the novel to life in nineteenth-century Montreal: "The narrative ascends to the epoch immediately following the Conquest of Canada; but the moral of the tale is quite as applicable to our own days."[57]

For the next year reviews of *Antoinette De Mirecourt* appeared in both the English and French press of Canada. One of the longest, and most serious, was written by Joseph-Edouard Lefebvre de Bellefeuille, the nephew whose thesis had helped inspire the plot of *Antoinette De Mirecourt* and who had translated "The Manor House Of De Villerai." De Bellefeuille begins his review by pointing out the relationship between the two novels. "On pourrait presque dire," he comments, that *Antoinette De Mirecourt* is "la continuation naturelle du *Manoir de Villerai*." He then congratulates Mrs. Leprohon on her happy choice of setting the second novel at the moment when "deux peuples naguère ennemis, naguère rangés en bataille" are "appelés à se donner le baiser de paix, à fraterniser, à vivre ensemble et à ne plus former qu'une seule nation." Despite the work's historical setting, it is a "roman de mœurs" rather than a "roman historique," and Mrs. Leprohon's particular talents lie in her ability to delineate the details of "la vie domestique," to describe characters, and to express emotions "d'un tact et d'une noblesse qu'on ne rencontre pas partout." The one fault he finds with the novel, a "reproche, plus ou moins sérieux," has to do with Antoinette's marrying in succession "deux officiers anglais":

> Je pense bien que l'auteur n'a pas voulu la proposer en cela comme un modèle à nos jeunes Canadiennes; mais la peinture d'un bonheur fictif peut quelquefois vivement séduire un jeune cœur nourri d'idéal loin de la trompeuse réalité.
>
> Une morale qui m'aurait beaucoup plu dans le livre de Mme Leprohon, c'est celle qui aurait résulté d'une peinture expressive de l'infortune, du malheur et des disgrâces accompagnant toujours les deux unions d'*Antoinette de Mirecourt*. La première, il est vrai, nous est dépeinte comme excessivement triste; c'est la punition juste d'un mariage secret fait malgré le vœu des parents et les lois de l'église. Mais il nous est dit que le second fut marqué de toutes sortes de bonheurs et de félicités. Il est vrai que le Col. *Evelyn*, le second mari d'*Antoinette*, était catholique; c'est quelque chose, mais ce n'est pas tout ce que je désire voir dans l'époux d'une de mes jeunes compatriotes: il n'était pas Canadien.[58]

Thus, de Bellefeuille, good mid-Victorian French-Canadian Roman Catholic that he obviously was, stressed the relevance of the "moral" of the story to his times.

Other reviewers echoed de Bellefeuille's comments. The *Montreal Gazette*, for example, on 13 Sept. 1864, welcomed the work, "issued some weeks ago from the press of Mr. Lovell," as "not only pleasantly readable, but highly interesting." Recommending the book to "Youth especially," it noted that "the lessons it teaches and moral it enforces, are well worthy of being remembered and observed, especially by the generation of girls now budding into womanhood, or about venturing on this world's busy life."[59] The reviewer in the *Ordre* of 12 Dec. 1864 likewise pointed out the relevance of the story to nineteenth-century Montreal. One could, for instance, find "une foule" of English soldiers and officers like Major Sternfield "sous nos yeux," and the "anglomanie" that led Madame D'Aulnay to welcome "avec tant d'empressement les militaires étrangers" was still too much in evidence among "quelques-unes de nos familles Canadiennes."[60] Like de Bellefeuille, both these reviewers also emphasized the importance of the work for the stimulation of "Canadian authorship."[61]

The French translation of *Antoinette De Mirecourt* mentioned in the *Ordre* in its notices of the novel in April and June 1864 and affirmed in its December review as a "demi-promesse"—"un de nos collaborateurs nous ayant laissé espérer qu'il en fera bientôt une traduction pour notre Feuilleton"[62]—appeared in 1865. The fact that a translation was being prepared was officially announced by the *Ordre* on 16 Jan. 1865. Joseph-Auguste Genand, one of the editors of the *Ordre* itself, had been "gracieusement autorisé" by Mrs. Leprohon to prepare the translation. It would be published as the "Feuilleton" in the *Ordre* soon. In describing the novel for this announcement, the anonymous writer emphasized its importance by making a direct connection between the setting of *Antoinette De Mirecourt* and the 1860s: "La scène de ce roman qui est une esquisse de mœurs parfaitement touchee, se passe à Montréal même à l'époque de la conquête, ce qui donne un nouveau cachet d'intérêt à ce livre déjà très intéressant, dans lequel on trouvera une peinture exacte de notre état de société actuel."[63]

Two more announcements appeared in the *Ordre* before the serial actually began. On 29 Mar. 1865, the newspaper informed its readers that its "Feuilleton," suspended during the Parliamentary session "pour faire place aux importants documents que nous avons publiés," would recommence:

> Pour la rentrée nous avons choisi l'œuvre de Madame Leprohon, ANTOINETTE DE MIRECOURT qui est destinée, nous le pensons, à un grand succès de vogue

auprès des lecteurs de L'*Ordre*. Cet ouvrage . . . est essentiellement national, Canadien par le fond autant que par la forme, et digne à tous les points de vue de la plume si élégante et si estimée de Madame Leprohon.[64]

On 31 Mar. 1865, the day "*Antoinette de Mirecourt*" first appeared as the serial in the *Ordre*, the newspaper introduced its "Feuilleton" as a sketch of manners that traced "la peinture exacte . . . de notre état de société actuel tout en rappelant celui de nos ancêtres lors de la cession du Canada à l'Angleterre."[65] Thus *Antoinette De Mirecourt* was emphasized again as a tale for the present times.

Genand's translation ran as the serial in the *Ordre* from 31 Mar. to 4 Aug. 1865. When important news pre-empted the novel's usual place on the bottom of the front page, the paper would print a brief announcement to explain its absence. For example, in the issue of 24 Apr. 1865, articles on Abraham Lincoln and John Wilkes Booth pushed the installment aside, as did news of an important meeting organized by the St. Jean Baptiste Society on 14 July 1865. On 10 May 1865, the paper reprinted in its column "Notre Feuilleton" notices concerning the *Ordre*'s serialization of Genand's translation of *Antoinette De Mirecourt* from four other Quebec newspapers: the *Union Nationale* (Montreal), the Montreal *Pays*, the *Courrier De St.-Hyacinthe*, and the *Gazette de Sorel*.[66] These "éloges" were enthusiastic about both the novel and its translation. The *Pays*, for example, congratulated Genand on the "service éminent" he was rendering to "notre littérature nationale" by translating this "belle œuvre littéraire écrite avec toute la richesse dont la langue anglaise est susceptible."[67] The *Courrier De St.-Hyacinthe* asked that the translation of "ce délicieux roman canadien" be published "en brochure."[68]

By late July 1865, when the serialization of *Antoinette De Mirecourt* was drawing to a close in the *Ordre*, the newspaper announced that the "accueil favorable ainsi que la sollicitation d'un grand nombre d'amis de la littérature canadienne" had made Genand decide to publish the work as a volume. It was, thus, "sous presse et formera une jolie brochure in-12, genre

français, de 340 pages." Copies of the work were expected to be
in the bookstores in about two weeks; the price of each copy
would be twenty-five cents. Its cheapness—each copy would
normally retail for seventy-five cents—was due to "Les facilités
d'impression offertes à l'Editeur."[69] In fact, except for the parts
of the serial that had been printed on page two of the *Ordre* and
that had to be reset, the volume was impressed from the type
used for the newspaper. In the *Ordre* on 14 Aug. 1865,
"ANTOINETTE DE MIRECOURT, OU MARIAGE SECRET
ET CHAGRINS CACHÉS. ROMAN CANADIEN" was adver-
tised for sale for "25 centins" a copy at its publishers, the book-
sellers "C. O. BEAUCHEMIN & VALOIS" at "237 et 239, Rue
St. Paul" in Montreal.[70]

This first edition of the French translation of *Antoinette De
Mirecourt* begins with an untitled *avant-propos* signed by Genand
and dated "Montréal, 4 Août 1865."[71] In his note Genand
explains that he had hesitated to publish in volume form "une
traduction originairement destinée à occuper le rez-de-chaussée
d'un journal politique" (1865, p. [i]) and worked on only in his
rare moments of leisure. He was finally convinced, however, to
let the work be published. First, he wished to prove to his readers
that "si la lecture des romans est une nécessité, il est du moins
possible de lire honnêtement des romans honnêtes" (1865, p. ii).
For, in contrast to most novels "importés en ce pays" that almost
without exception "s'étudient à embellir le Vice et à enlaidir la
Vertu," *Antoinette De Mirecourt* is "une grande leçon de morale.
Ecrit dans le but de démontrer les funestes résultats d'un mariage
clandestin, ce roman est rempli d'enseignements utiles qui ne
peuvent manquer de produire d'heureux fruits dans la position
sociale où nous nous trouvons en Canada" (1865, p. iii). Secondly,
both the novel and its author were "essentiellement Canadien."
The novel "se rapporte à l'Histoire de notre pays. . . . L'auteur
. . . appartient à une famille Canadienne" (1865, p. iii). Genand
states that haste is to blame for the numerous faults in his work,
but that he is scrupulously faithful to the original despite small
errors in the rendering of words and phrases and in his neglect in
the matter of reproducing Mrs. Leprohon's style.

On the whole, Genand's assessment of his translation is just. It never deviates in any detail of plot or theme from Mrs. Leprohon's original. Genand's style is readable, but it does not capture Mrs. Leprohon's. Genand did apparently take the opportunity to have a few changes made to the newspaper version before the standing type was used to reprint the book. The "faible soleil de novembre"[72] in the opening line of the serial became, for example, the "tiède soleil de novembre" (1865, p. [1]), an alteration that was at once a less English and a more accurate rendering of "The feeble sun of November"[73] of the original. Errors and infelicities remain in the translation, however.

Genand made a few obvious errors. For example, "after questioning and cross-questioning me" (1864, p. 119), Antoinette's description of Madame D'Aulnay's constant queries about the young girl's love for Major Sternfield, becomes "après m'avoir questionnée et transquestionnée" (1865, p. 107). This is a word-for-word rendering of Mrs. Leprohon's English rather than idiomatic French. Genand made another error of a different sort in translating Sternfield's phrase "a mere farce, an empty mockery" (1864, p. 146), as "une comédie, une sanglante moquerie" (1865, p. 132). "Bloody" was a tabooed word in nineteenth-century English, particularly in the mouth of a polished English gentleman. "Sanglante," moreover, in French means "very offensive, very bitter," neither of which suggests Mrs. Leprohon's "empty." The translator also made small errors in the names of birds and flowers. The "Canadian nightingale, or song-sparrow" (1864, p. 282), for example, becomes simply the "rossignol," or nightingale (1865, p. 262). The nightingale is not native to Canada, and without the mention of the "song-sparrow," the author's intended comparison is lost.

To balance these errors, Genand tried to improve or correct passages in Mrs. Leprohon's text. In the description of autumn at Valmont, the "gloomy back-ground of firs and evergreens" (1864, p. 295) is made to read the "fond sombre des sapins et des tamarets" (1865, p. 274). Neither the author nor the translator had a very exact knowledge of Canadian trees. Mrs. Leprohon's error lay in not seeming to know that firs are evergreens, and Genand's in not realizing that tamaracks are not evergreens. Immediately preceding this passage is a not unusual case of gratuitous meddling with the English text. The "crimson berries of the ash" (1864, p. 295) is replaced by "les baies cramoisies du chêne" (1865, p. 274), or "the reddish bays of the oak." This is an accurate description of autumn oak leaves, but it is not what Mrs. Leprohon wrote. Many of the apparently pointless changes made by Genand involve the omission of descriptive words. "Shortly after, Mrs. D'Aulnay floated gracefully up to them and exclaimed" (1864, p. 215) becomes "Quelques instants après, Madame d'Aulnay vint à eux et leur dit" (1865, p. 196) and "her lips rivalling her cheeks in their death-like pallor" (1864, p. 72), part of the narrator's description of Antoinette after the sleighing accident, is shortened to "pâle de terreur" (1865, p. 62).

Genand added to the original text less often than he cut from it, but there are over forty cases of this type of change. ""Never, never!" she rejoined, with a slow, hopeless shake of the head" (1864, p. 326), Antoinette's passionate denial to Dr. Manby that her life could again become "light and pleasant" (1864, p. 326), is changed to "Jamais! jamais! dit-elle en fesant une légère inclination de tête, qui indiquait parfaitement l'état de désespoir où elle se trouvait" (1865, p. 303). Some of these variations added as many as fifteen words, but in only one or two cases were they in any sense necessary.

Genand, finally, had to solve a number of difficulties that cause problems for all translators. One was Dr. Manby's observation that Sternfield's "shadow, like that of the upas-tree, seems fairly to blight that poor young creature" (1864, p. 323). Genand translated this clause as "Son ombre seule semble flétrir cette pauvre jeune fille" (1865, p. 300). Genand undoubtedly omitted the "upas-tree" either because he did not know the fable connected to it, or, if he did know the fable, because he felt that almost none of his readers would recognize the term and understand the allusion. Genand also omitted the reference to

Benedict in Evelyn's comment that his brother teased him about "turning Benedict, as he called it, so soon" (1864, p. 210) by translating the clause, "mais il me railla parce que je me mariais aussi jeune" (1865, p. 191). This is certainly the sense of the original, but the allusion to Shakespeare's character, a reference that would have been understood and appreciated by many readers of the translation, is lost. A different sort of problem can be seen in Genand's translation of the expression "fine lady's cant" (1864, p. 130) as "des subtilités d'une femme fashionnable" (1865, pp. 117-18). The anglicism "fashionable" entered the French language about the beginning of the nineteenth century and is therefore an anachronism in a novel set in 1763.

The translation of *Antoinette De Mirecourt* was warmly welcomed. The first announcements of the new work appeared in mid-August 1865. On 14 Aug. 1865, for example, the *Courrier du Canada* (Quebec) acknowledged that it had received a copy of "une petite brochure de plus de trois cents pages intitulée: "Antoinette de Mirecourt". . . . C'est une excellente traduction, faite par M. J. A. Genand, d'un intéressant roman anglais qui sort d'une plume canadienne bien connue, Madame Leprohon."[74] Other notices continued to appear over the next year. One of the longest, written by Louis-Honoré Fréchette for the *Journal de Lévis*, was reprinted in the *Ordre* on 6 Oct. 1865. Between August 1865 and February 1866, in fact, the *Ordre* continued to promote its editor's translation of *Antoinette De Mirecourt* by republishing items about it from other serials.

Both the English original and the French translation of *Antoinette De Mirecourt* have been republished several times since 1864-65. From 20 Oct. 1866 until 4 Oct. 1867, at the request of friends "que nous estimons trop pour qu'il nous soient permis d'hésiter un instant," the *Pionnier de Sherbrooke* serialized Genand's translation of the "charmant petit roman de Mde. Leprohon."[75] A second edition of the French version was published in 1881 by "J. B. Rolland et Fils, libraires-éditeurs," of Montreal. Advertised in Quebec newspapers in July 1881, it was "Un beau volume in-12, broché"; its price was "50 cts."[76]

In the "Note Des Editeurs" that began this new edition, the publishers reminded their readers that the translation of *Antoinette De Mirecourt* had first appeared "il y a près de seize ans."[77] At that time, despite the "considérable" number of copies printed, the edition "fut bientôt épuisé, et quelques mois après il n'en restait plus un seul exemplaire" (1881, p. [iii]). This success, "assez rare dans les annales de la librairie canadienne," had persuaded the publishers to issue "une seconde édition d'un roman essentiellement canadien par la forme et par le fond et qui renferme une grande leçon de morale" (1881, p. [iii]). The sympathetic welcome that the novel had formerly received was "un garant que le public saura reconnaître les sacrifices que nous nous sommes imposés en entreprenant cette nouvelle publication" (1881, p. [iii]). Presumably both to inform the public about the work's author and to garner sympathy for the work because of her untimely death, the "Note" concluded with the obituary on Mrs. Leprohon written by "J. D." and published in the *Opinion Publique* in October 1879.

Both the title-page of this edition and the "Note Des Editeurs" make clear that the work is a translation; neither, however, mentions the name of the translator. Moreover, although the Rolland version of Mrs. Leprohon's novel was based on Genand's translation, numerous alterations had been made to his text. Some of these seem to be changes for the sake of change. Others are attempts to bring Genand's translation closer to the sense of the original English version, or even to improve on the original. The phrase "the flight of birds and flowers" (1864, p. 303) in Mrs. Leprohon's description of an autumn day as "one of those glorious October days which almost reconcile one to the flight of birds and flowers," for example, is rendered by Genand as "de la fuite des oiseaux, de la chute des fleurs" (1865, p. 281) and by the Rolland version as "de la fuite des oiseaux, et de la chute des feuilles" (1881, p. 281). Neither translates literally Mrs. Leprohon's somewhat awkward phrase; Genand's is closer to her original, but that of the Rolland edition seems more felicitous in that autumn in Canada is associated with the falling of leaves.

Although it did not receive as much attention as the first edition of the translation, the Rolland version was noted by the Quebec press. On 14 July 1881, both the Montreal *Patrie* and the *Gazette Des Campagnes* (Sainte-Anne-de-la-Pocatière) carried the same review. It pointed out Mrs. Leprohon's talents for delineating "les scènes de la vie élégante, . . . les mœurs du grand monde, . . . les accidents et les aventures des gens heureux" and praised her "grande connaissance du cœur humain." The merit of Mrs. Leprohon's novel, it concluded, "réside surtout dans le travail des détails, dans les épisodes qui reposent l'attention du lecteur, dans la conception des caractères, dans la peinture des personnages, dans la délicatesse des pensées, dans la douceur des sentiments, dans la beauté du style, dans l'harmonie des rôles et dans la morale toujours religieusement respectée."[78]

In 1887 Genand's translation of *Antoinette De Mirecourt* was serialized in the *Nouvelles Soirées Canadiennes*. The name of the translator "J. A. Genand" was stated at the beginning of each part, and the text, with the exception of the inevitable changes that come from a new typesetting, followed that of the 1865 Beauchemin & Valois edition.

That *Antoinette De Mirecourt* had taken firm hold on the minds and hearts of French Canadians was further confirmed in 1901. On 16 February, the *Patrie* announced in their column "DANS NOS THEATRES" that a group of Montreal actors, the "SOIREES DE FAMILLE," would be presenting on 21 February a dramatic adaptation of *Antoinette De Mirecourt*, "un drame de salon en quatre actes, que MM. Elzéar Roy et Adélard Lacasse ont tiré du roman de Mme Leprohon." A brief resumé of the plot and main themes of the story follows, and the opinion is offered that the costumes will be "très brillants. . . . Ils représentent les costumes des officiers anglais et des gentilshommes français à l'époque de la conquête du Canada par les Anglais. Le rideau lève sur un bal chez Mme d'Aulnay et fournit les décors les plus brillants." The announcement ends with a list of the names of the players; it notes particularly that Elzéar Roy will play the principal role "dans le personnage du major Sternfield."[79] On 21 Feb.

1901, the *Patrie* reminded Montreal theatre-goers that the drama "Antoinette de Mirecourt" would be presented that evening at the National Monument.[80] The next day the *Patrie* reviewed the presentation. The drama, which played before "un public élégant" that filled "la vaste salle des spectacles," was "un succès extraordinaire." The setting was "parfaite"; the costumes, "d'une richesse étonnante, et les décors rivalisaient avec tout ce qu'il y a de plus [luxueux]." The execution of all the roles was "sûre."[81] Unfortunately the script for this stage adaptation seems not to have survived, although the presentation was recorded in an article by George H. Robert in *L'Annuaire Théâtral* (1908-09).[82]

Although there is evidence to suggest that *Antoinette De Mirecourt* was serialized in a Montreal periodical entitled *Life* in the 1890s,[83] the first reprintings of the English version in book form since 1864 did not occur until 1973. That year the University of Toronto Press issued a photographic reprint of the first edition of *Antoinette De Mirecourt* in its Toronto Reprint Library of Canadian Prose and Poetry series under the general editorship of Douglas Lochhead, and McClelland and Stewart published a new edition of the novel as No. 89 in its New Canadian Library series; for this edition Carl F. Klinck wrote an introduction and compiled a chronology of Mrs. Leprohon's life and works. The CEECT edition of *Antoinette De Mirecourt*, then, is the third in English.

Since the 1860s Mrs. Leprohon and her works, particularly *Antoinette De Mirecourt*, have been included in basic reference works on Canadian literature in both English and French. In *Bibliotheca Canadensis* (1867), for example, Henry J. Morgan concluded his entry on Mrs. Leprohon by quoting reviews of *Antoinette De Mirecourt* from the *Montreal Gazette* and the *Saturday Reader*.[84] In *Histoire De La Littérature Canadienne* published by John Lovell in 1874, Edmond Lareau discussed Mrs. Leprohon at some length. Calling "*Antoinette de Mirecourt*, de beaucoup le meilleur écrit de Mme. Leprohon,"[85] he quoted most of the review written by de Bellefeuille and originally published in 1864. Her works, particularly her poetry and short stories, have also been frequently anthologized. Five of her poems, for instance, were included in the first anthology of Canadian poetry, Edward Hartley Dewart's *Selections From Canadian Poets* (1864). *The Poetical Works Of Mrs. Leprohon (Miss R. E. Mullins)*, a collection of her poems selected and introduced by John Reade and also published by Lovell, appeared in 1881.

Mrs. Leprohon's long-standing connection with John Lovell, the most important publisher in the Canadas throughout much of the nineteenth century, undoubtedly helped her reputation as an author while she was alive. Long after her death, however, Mrs. Leprohon and her works were still frequently mentioned. In the *Canadienne* for May 1922, for example, Gaetane de Montreuil dedicated almost half her article on "Mme Rosanna-Eleanor Leprohon" to *Antoinette De Mirecourt*. In all her novels, she said, Mrs. Leprohon "a mis des caractères comme nous en avons connus, tels que nous en rencontrons chaque jour; cela établit entre l'auteur et le lecteur une sympathie de compréhension qui fait aimer ses oeuvres."[86]

One impetus for the increasing interest in Mrs. Leprohon in the latter half of the twentieth century has come from "The Life and Works of Mrs. Leprohon," a thesis by Brother Adrian (Henri Deneau) accepted by the Université de Montréal in 1948. This study gathered together a good deal of data about Mrs. Leprohon and her publications and thus provided a factual basis on which later scholars and critics could build. Carl F. Klinck, for example, is indebted to this thesis for much of the information in his "Introduction" to the New Canadian Library edition of *Antoinette De Mirecourt*. Such works as the first edition of the *Literary History Of Canada* (1965) and Norah Story's *Oxford Companion to Canadian History and Literature* (1967) had already covered Mrs. Leprohon and paid special attention to *Antoinette De Mirecourt*. John Stockdale's biography of Mrs. Leprohon appeared in the *Dictionary of Canadian Biography*, Vol. 10, in 1972; his entry on each of her novels translated into French, including *Antoinette De Mirecourt*, in the *Dictionnaire des oeuvres littéraires du Québec* in 1978.

In recent years some of the most sustained analyses of *Antoinette De Mirecourt* have been produced by women. In "Essentially Canadian" (1972), for example, Mary Jane Edwards, calling *Antoinette De Mirecourt* "probably the best novel about English-French relations in Canada published in the nineteenth century,"[87] emphasized its importance as a contribution to this subject in Canadian fiction in both English and French. In "Towards a happier history: women and domination" (1975), Elizabeth Brady chose *Antoinette De Mirecourt* as one of the three novels she used to "perceive the meaning of domination in the lives of Canadian women and trace the gradual evolution of a distinctly feminist consciousness alongside the parallel and necessary growth of political awareness."[88] Brady's two other novels were Frances Brooke's *The History of Emily Montague* (1769), a work frequently compared with *Antoinette De Mirecourt*, and Margaret Atwood's *The Edible Woman* (1969).

In "Three Writers of Victorian Canada" (1983), Carole Gerson deals at some length with Mrs. Leprohon's life, her works, and their popular and critical reception. One of the most interesting questions she raises has to do with the apparent lack of popularity of Mrs. Leprohon's three novels on French-Canadian subjects, including *Antoinette De Mirecourt*, in "English Canada," especially in comparison with their obvious popularity among French-Canadian readers. Gerson suggests that one reason is that Mrs. Leprohon's works were "written at least a decade too early to benefit from the wave of English-Canadian interest in Quebec which was inspired by Parkman's histories and James Le Moine's series of *Maple Leaves* and which peaked after 1875."[89] Another reason, especially relevant to *Antoinette De Mirecourt*, may have to do with the shock many English-Canadian readers undoubtedly felt as they perused this "essentially Canadian" story about an English officer's marriage to a young girl from a good French-Canadian family. For, in depicting life in Montreal in the 1760s, Mrs. Leprohon revealed not only a fascinating, vivid world that was romantic and exciting, but also a physically destructive, morally dangerous wilderness that bore a striking resemblance to the Montreal these readers were experiencing in the mid-nine-teenth century.

THE TEXT

The aim of this edition of *Antoinette De Mirecourt* is to provide the reader with a reliable text of this important nineteenth-century Canadian novel. No manuscript or proofs of the novel have been located. The earliest extant version of *Antoinette De Mirecourt*, therefore, and the one that best reflects Mrs. Leprohon's intentions about it, is the edition published by John Lovell in Montreal in 1864 and probably corrected by the author. This, then, is the copy-text of the CEECT edition.

This edition, furthermore, is the only version of *Antoinette De Mirecourt* that carries authority. No other edition of the novel in English was published during Mrs. Leprohon's lifetime. The 1865 translation was, according to the *Ordre*, authorized by the author, but there is no evidence that she had a hand in Genand's actual rendering of her text into French. Neither the altered translation of 1881 nor the second edition of the English original published by McClelland and Stewart in 1973 contains revisions that can be attributed to Mrs. Leprohon. As a result, the editor does not have a published version of *Antoinette De Mirecourt* that can be considered as a source of authorial emendations.

The emendation of the copy-text of *Antoinette De Mirecourt*, with a view to creating a text that is as close to Mrs. Leprohon's intentions as possible, then, has involved two processes only. Obvious errors in Lovell's edition have been corrected. In so far as this edition indicates the author's intention in regard to such matters as the spelling of certain proper nouns and titles and the use of quotation marks, these have been rendered consistent. In the absence of other authorial versions of the novel, and docu-ments like publishers' archives—and despite the crucial role John Lovell played in nineteenth-century Canadian publishing, his papers have not survived—the editor has no authority to do more.

On the whole, the text of Lovell's *Antoinette De Mirecourt* contains relatively few obvious errors. There are some, however. For example, the "the" in the clause "in which the were uttered" (1864, p. 88) has been changed to the obviously intended "they" (CEECT, p. 53). In another subordinate clause, "in which it so" (1864, p. 118) the necessary "is" has been inserted (CEECT, p. 74). Later in the novel the "Mademoisolle" in the phrase "Poor Mademoisolle Antoinette" (1864, p. 237) has been corrected (CEECT, p. 150); "illusion" in the phrase "any illusion to his own ill-starred passion" (1864, p. 311) has been emended to "allusion" (CEECT, p. 201), the word that the context clearly demands; and "gentlemen" (1864, p. 322) has been changed to "gentleman" in the speech in which Audley warns Antoinette to bring her "flirtation" with Louis "to a speedy close" (CEECT, p. 208). In two instances a line-end hyphen missing from the copy-text (1864, pp. 308 and 337) has been supplied in the CEECT text (CEECT, pp. 199 and 217), and the missing "t" in "agita-/ion" (1864, p. 363), dropped after a line-end hyphen, has been restored (CEECT, p. 234).

Most inconsistencies in the Lovell edition with regard to such matters as spelling and punctuation have been left in the CEECT edition. It does seem clear, however, from the overwhelming majority of cases in which "D'Aulnay" and "De Mirecourt" are spelled with a capital "D" and "Major" with a capital "M," and in which "Mrs." is closed by a period that these were probably Mrs. Leprohon's intended usages.[90] The few cases in which these words do not appear in this way in the Lovell edition, then, have been emended to make them consistent with the majority. Because of the amount of dialogue and reported conversation in *Antoinette De Mirecourt*, many quotation marks are used. The intention seems to have been to put double quotation marks around all direct and indirect quotations. The editor, thus, has supplied opening or closing quotation marks when one or the other was missing in the Lovell edition. Single quotation marks have also been changed to double when these were more appropriate. All these corrections and emendations are listed in "Emendations in Copy-text" in the concluding apparatus.

A few silent emendations have been made to the 1864 Lovell copy-text. The period after the title "PREFACE" has been removed, as has the period following each chapter number. The Roman numerals of each chapter have been replaced by Arabic. All the letters in the first word of each of Chapters 10, 18, 20, 21, and 23 have been capitalized in order to make these chapters consistent with the others in the Lovell edition.

In the preparation of this edition five copies of the first edition of *Antoinette De Mirecourt* were microfilmed for CEECT. In order to verify that these copies all belonged to the first edition and to establish an ideal copy, two light-table collations and one oral collation were performed by members of the CEECT staff. Photocopies from the microfilms made especially for CEECT were used in each collation, and in each case a copy of the 1864 edition of *Antoinette De Mirecourt* owned by the University of Western Ontario (OLU PR9298 L6A75) was the standard of collation. A copy of the edition from the National Library (OONL PS8423 E6A65) was the comparison copy in one light-table collation; a copy from Queen's (OKQ LP PS8423 E67A7 copy 2) in the other. Another copy from Queen's (OKQ LP PS8423 E67A7) was the comparison copy in the oral collation. A copy of the edition from the University of Toronto (OTU B-11 1847) was used to verify further the results of each collation. Oral and ocular collations of all or part of each of the two later published versions of the text in English were used to help establish their relationship to the 1864 Lovell edition. Genand's translation of *Antoinette De Mirecourt* in the *Ordre* in 1865 was read orally against the translation as it was published by Beauchemin & Valois the same year and in the *Nouvelles Soirées Canadiennes* in 1886-87. The results of this collation were compared with the relevant passages in the revised Genand translation published in 1881. Selected passages of the text of the translation in the *Pionnier de Sherbrooke* and in its 1881 version were also compared with the Genand translation published in volume form in 1865. The results of these collations are available at the Centre for Editing Early Canadian Texts.

To prepare the text of the CEECT edition, the photocopy made from CEECT's microfilm of the 1864 edition held by Western was entered by a typist on the computer. By means of a computer program especially prepared for CEECT, the Western copy was then proofed and corrected against the copy of the edition held by the National Library that had been microfilmed and photocopied for CEECT and entered by a second typist on the computer. The "corrected" Western copy was further proofread against a privately owned copy of the 1864 edition. Before the CEECT edition was sent to the printer, it was proofread orally, and the text of the CEECT edition of *Antoinette De Mirecourt* compared to its copy-text so that all emendations made to Lovell's edition could be verified. The CEECT text was also proofread at each stage of the printing process.

ENDNOTES TO INTRODUCTION

1 *Antoinette De Mirecourt Or Secret Marrying and Secret Sorrowing. A Canadian Tale*, ed. John Stockdale (Ottawa: Carleton University Press, 1989), p. 3. All subsequent references to this edition are included in the text as (CEECT, p. 000).

2 Kathleen Jenkins, *Montreal Island City of the St. Lawrence* (Garden City, New York: Doubleday, 1966), p. 372. Jenkins quotes the phrase from a "British report of 1862." In this, and in all other quotations included in the introduction, the grammar, punctuation, and spelling of the original have been retained except in a few cases where the style of the passage makes its meaning unclear. In these instances the editorial changes are indicated by square brackets. When the first letter of a word in the title of a work cited is capitalized, this initial capitalization has been retained.

3 *The Poetical Works Of Mrs. Leprohon. (Miss R. E. Mullins.)* (Montreal: John Lovell & Son, 1881), p. 91.

4 See "La Famille Leprohon," *Bulletin Des Recherches Historiques*, 39 (1933), 513-14. Dr. Leprohon was baptised "Lucain," but "Lucien" is the name he used at the time of his marriage to Rosanna; in later life he seems to have favoured his mother's family name "Lukin."

5 *Lettres À Pierre Margry de 1844 à 1886 (Papineau, Lafontaine, Faillon, Leprohon Et Autres)*, ed. Ls-P. Cormier (Québec: Les Presses De L'Université Laval, 1968), pp. 137-38. The quotations from these letters used in the introduction do not include Cormier's footnote numbers. The "volume" on poetry in Canada was undoubtedly *Selections From Canadian Poets*, edited by Edward Hartley Dewart and published by John Lovell in 1864; five poems by Mrs. Leprohon were included in this anthology.

6 Ibid., p. 141.

7 Ibid., p. 143.

8 Ibid., p. 144.

9 Ibid., p. 145.

10 Ibid., p. 149.

11 Ibid.

12 *Gazette*, 22 Sept. 1879, p. [4].

13 In 1848 Doutre, known for his radical liberalism and anticlerical-ism, had also fought a duel with George-Etienne Cartier, who was then beginning his career as a conservative. Although the motive for the duel was political rather than sentimental, Rosanna Mullins undoubtedly knew about this event and the energetic young author of *Les Fiancés De 1812* (1844) who fought in it; as the more mature Mrs. Leprohon she may well have recalled it as she plotted the Sternfield-Beauchesne duel.

14 "Madame Leprohon," *Opinion Publique*, 2 Oct. 1879, pp. [469]-470.

15 Jenkins, p. 371.

16 Figures vary on the actual number of people living in Montreal in the 1860s. Jenkins says that in 1861 the population was 91,006; Jean-Claude Robert puts the number at 90,323 in the same year and com-ments that Montreal was "la ville la plus populeuse des colonies britanni-ques de l'Amérique du nord." See Jenkins, p. 358, and Robert, "Urbanisation Et Population: Le Cas De Montréal En 1861," *revue d'histoire de l'amérique française*, 35 (1970), 523-24.

17 *The Story Of A Soldier's Life* (1903; rpt. New York: Kraus Reprint Co., 1971), Vol. 2, pp. 115-16.

18 Edgar Andrew Collard, *Montreal: The Days That Are No More* (Toronto: Doubleday, 1976), pp. 204 and 207.

19 Frances E. O. Monck, *My Canadian Leaves An Account Of A Visit To Canada In 1864-1865* (London: Richard Bentley and Son, 1891), p. 324.

20 By the time *Antoinette De Mirecourt* was published, Rosanna had had three daughters: Gabrielle Louise (b. 23 Nov. 1853), Marie Geraldine Rose (b. 25 Dec. 1857), and Gertrude Ida (b. 29 June 1863). CEECT is indebted to Carolyn Donnelly for this information.

21 "The Manor House Of De Villerai. A Tale Of Canada Under The French Dominion," ed. John R. Sorfleet, *Journal of Canadian Fiction*, No. 34 ([1985]), p. 13.

22 Ibid.

23 Ibid., p. 149.

24 Ibid., pp. 149-50.

25 Ibid., p. 151.

26 Collard, p. 203.

27 *DCB*, Vol. 5, p. 367.

28 Robert Rumilly, *Histoire De Longueuil* (Longueuil: Société d'Histoire de Longueuil, 1974), p. 74.

29 Ibid.

30 *DCB*, Vol. 4, p. 269.
31 Rumilly, p. 90.
32 A. C. De Léry Macdonald, "Le soin qu'on prend de nos archives," *Recherches Historiques*, 4 (1898), 311-12.
33 *Vindicator*, 31 Oct. 1837, p. [3].
34 Dr. Leprohon's father lived in the Sweeneys' old house in the 1840s and 1850s; some time after he died in 1859, possibly after the death of his widow in March 1861, Jean Lucien and Rosanna occupied it. In *Mackay's Montreal Directory* for 1861-1862, Dr. J. L. Leprohon is listed as living at "31 Radegonde, Beaver hall hill." See *Mackay's Montreal Directory, New Edition, Corrected In May & June, 1861-62*, p. 133.
35 Adèle Clarke, *Old Montreal John Clarke: His Adventures, Friends And Family* (Montreal: The Herald Publishing Company, 1906), p. 33. Robert Sweeney died in 1840.
36 "Duel Fatal!!," *Canadien* (Quebec), 28 May 1838, p. 2.
37 *Montreal Gazette*, 26 May 1838, p. [2].
38 Collard, p. 169.
39 Rev. W. Taylor, *A Testimony Against Duelling: A Sermon* (Montreal: Campbell & Becket, 1838), p. 8.
40 *Montreal Gazette*, 28 May 1840, p. [2].
41 Ibid.
42 *Montreal Gazette*, 8 Oct. 1842, p. [2].
43 See, for an example of the usage of this term, G.R.R. Treasure, *Seventeenth Century France* (London: Rivingtons, 1966), p. 195.
44 Eugène De Mirecourt, *Mémoires De Ninon De Lenclos* (Paris: Gustave Havard, 1857), Vol. 2, p. [395].
45 Ibid., p. 396.
46 Ibid., pp. 396-97.
47 Ibid., p. 397.
48 Ibid., p. 404.
49 Ibid.
50 *Morning Chronicle*, 29 Mar. 1864, p. [2].
51 "A New Canadian Book In Press," *Montreal Gazette*, 6 Apr. 1864, p. [2].
52 "Faits Divers," *Ordre*, 1 Apr. 1864, p. [2].
53 "New Books," *Montreal Gazette*, 13 Sept. 1864, p. [2].
54 *Lettres À Pierre Margry*, p. 137.
55 "Faits Divers," *Ordre*, 23 June 1864, p. [2].
56 *True Witness*, 8 July 1864, p. [5].
57 "Notices of Books and Publications," *Journal Of Education For Lower Canada*, 8 (July 1864), 99.
58 "Bibliographie," *Revue Canadienne*, 1 (1864), 442-44.
59 *Montreal Gazette*, 13 Sept. 1864, p. [2].
60 "Bibliographie," *Ordre*, 12 Dec. 1864, p. [2].
61 *Montreal Gazette*, 13 Sept. 1864, p. [2].
62 "Bibliographie," *Ordre*, 12 Dec. 1864, p. [2].
63 "Notre Feuilleton," *Ordre*, 16 Jan. 1865, p. [2].

64 "Notre Feuilleton," *Ordre*, 29 Mar. 1865, p. [2].
65 "Notre Feuilleton," *Ordre*, 31 Mar. 1865, p. [2].
66 "Notre Feuilleton," *Ordre*, 10 May 1865, p. [2].
67 *Pays*, 6 May 1865, p. [3].
68 *Courrier De St.-Hyacinthe*, 9 May 1865, p. [3].
69 "Notre Feuilleton," *Ordre*, 28 July 1865, p. [1].
70 *Ordre*, 14 Aug. 1865, p. [2].
71 *Antoinette De Mirecourt Ou Mariage Secret Et Chagrins Cachés. Roman Canadien* (Montréal: Beauchemin & Valois, 1865), p. iv. All subsequent references to this edition are included in the text as (1865, p. 000).
72 *Ordre*, 31 Mar. 1865, p. [1].
73 *Antoinette De Mirecourt; Or, Secret Marrying and Secret Sorrowing. A Canadian Tale* (Montreal: Lovell, 1864), p. [9]. All subsequent references to this edition are included in the text as (1864, p. 000).
74 "Publications," *Courrier du Canada*, 14 Aug. 1865, p. [3].
75 *Pionnier de Sherbrooke*, 20 Oct. 1866, p. [2].
76 See, for example, *Gazette Des Campagnes* (Sainte-Anne-de-la-Pocatière), 14 July 1881, p. 399.
77 *Antoinette De Mirecourt Ou Mariage Secret Et Chagrins Cachés* (Montréal: J. B. Rolland & Fils, 1881), p. [iii]. All subsequent references to this edition are included in the text as (1881, p. 000).
78 *Patrie*, 14 July 1881, p. [1], and *Gazette Des Campagnes*, 14 July 1881, p. 399.
79 *Patrie*, 16 Feb. 1901, p. 16.
80 Ibid., 21 Feb. 1901, p. 6.
81 Ibid., 22 Feb. 1901, p. 5.
82 George H. Robert, "Le Théâtre Canadien: Monographie," in *L'Annuaire Théâtral* (Montréal, 1908-09), p. 199.
83 An undated clipping apparently from the Montreal *Life* held in the C. C. James Collection at Victoria University Library, Toronto, indicates that Mrs. Leprohon's "story of Montreal after the Conquest" had "just been commenced in *Life*." Unfortunately, few copies of this periodical that began in 1891 are available, and those that are do not contain *Antoinette De Mirecourt*. If the story did appear in *Life*, however, it was probably serialized in the 1890s, for Mrs. Leprohon's son, writing in 1911, encloses in his letter a "short Biography of my dear Mother, which I have found in the Montreal Life printed many years ago." See C. C. James Collection, Box 4, and NA, Mrs. C. M. Whyte-Edgar Collection, MG 30, D261, File 10, ALS, R. E. Leprohon to Mrs. Whyte-Edgar, 15 Mar. 1911.
84 *Bibliotheca Canadensis: Or A Manual Of Canadian Literature* (Ottawa: Desbarats, 1867), p. 224. Morgan quotes from the *Montreal Gazette* review of 13 Sept. 1864, and from the review in the Montreal *Saturday Reader* of 9 Sept. 1865.
85 Edmond Lareau, *Histoire De La Littérature Canadienne* (Montréal: Lovell, 1874), p. 307.
86 *Canadienne*, 5 (May 1922), 3.

87   "Essentially Canadian," *Canadian Literature*, No. 52 (1972), p. 9.

88   "Towards a happier history: women and domination," in *Domination*, ed. Alkis Kontos (Toronto and Buffalo: University of Toronto Press, 1975), p. 18.

89   "Three Writers of Victorian Canada," in *Canadian Writers And Their Works*. Fiction Series. Vol. 1, ed. Robert Lecker, Jack David, Ellen Quigley (Downsview, Ontario: ECW Press, 1983), p. 197.

90   CEECT's word-search computer program revealed that "D'Aulnay" appeared 295 times, "d'Aulnay" 2; "De Mirecourt" 126, "de Mirecourt" 4; "Major" in phrases like "Major Sternfield" 100, "major" 1; and "Mrs." 275, "Mrs" 1.

ANTOINETTE DE MIRECOURT;

OR,

Secret Marrying and Secret Sorrowing.

A CANADIAN TALE.

BY MRS. LEPROHON.

Montreal:
PRINTED BY JOHN LOVELL, ST. NICHOLAS STREET
1864.

PREFACE

THE simple Tale unfolded in the following pages, was not originally intended to be issued with any prefatory remarks. Advised, however, that it is usual to do so, the author, having no wish to deviate from the established custom, will merely say:

Although the literary treasures of "the old world" are ever open to us, and our American neighbors should continue to inundate the country with reading-matter, intended to meet all wants and suit all tastes and sympathies, at prices which enable every one to partake of this never-failing and ever-varying feast; yet Canadians should not be discouraged from endeavoring to form and foster a literature of their own.

More than one successful effort towards the attainment of this object has been made within the last few years, and more than one valuable work, Canadian in origin, subject, and sympathies, has been produced and published among us. To every true Canadian this simple fact must afford no little gratification, and any fresh contribution will not prove unwelcome. Therefore, remembering that the smallest stone employed always helps a little in the construction of even the loftiest building, the author, not altogether without some hope of a favorable reception, ventures on introducing to the public this work; satisfied that if ANTOINETTE DE MIRECOURT possesses no other merit, it will, at least, be found to have that of being essentially Canadian.

1

CHAPTER 1

THE feeble sun of November, that most unpleasant month in our Canadian year, was streaming down on the narrow streets and irregular buildings of Montreal, such as it existed in the year 176—, some short time after the royal standard of England had replaced the fleur-de-lys of France.

Reflecting back the red sunlight in the countless small panes of its narrow casements, stood a large and substantial-looking stone house, situated towards the east extremity of Notre Dame street, then the aristocratic quarter of the city. Without going through the ceremony of raising the ponderous knocker, we will pass through the hall-door, with its arched fan-light overhead, and, entering the mansion, take a short survey of its interior and inmates. Despite the lowness of the ceilings, so justly incompatible with our modern ideas of elegance, or even comfort,— despite the rough wood-carving and tarnished gilding encircling the doors and windows, and the quaint, useless wooden architraves running round the walls of the different apartments, there is a stamp of unmistakable wealth and refinement pervading the abode.

Glimpses of fine old paintings, costly inlaid cabinets, antique vases, and other objects of art, revealed through the half-open doors, confirm this impression, even before we are told that the mansion is inhabited by Monsieur D'Aulnay, one of the most distinguished among the few families of the old French *noblesse*, who continued to dwell in any of the principal cities after their country had passed under a foreign rule.

The master of the house, a plain-featured but gentlemanly-looking man, was seated, at the moment in

3

which we introduce him to the reader, in his large and well-lighted library. The three sides of this, his favorite apartment, were covered, from ceiling to floor, with compactly-filled shelves, whilst a few well-executed busts or good portraits of literary men were the only ornaments of any sort which the room contained. The serviceable, dark bindings of the volumes, innocent of gilding or gaudy lettering, betrayed they were valued by their owner more for their contents than their appearance; and in his earnest, unostentatious love of literature, might have been found the key to the tranquil placidity of character which distinguished him under circumstances which would have often severely tried the patience of less philosophic men. When hosts of his personal friends and relatives urged him, after the capitulation of Montreal, to do as they were doing, and return to *la vielle France*, or at least seek the solitude of his wealthy seigneurie in the country, and bury himself there for the remainder of his days, he looked round his library, sighed, and shook his head. In vain some fiery spirits indignantly asked him how he could brook the arrogance of the proud conquerors who had landed on their shores? how he could endure to meet, wherever eye or footstep turned, the scarlet uniforms of the epauletted heroes who now governed his native land in King George's name. To their indignant remonstrances he sadly but calmly rejoined he should not see much of them, for he intended establishing himself henceforth permanently in his beloved library, and going abroad as little as possible. When farther pressed on the subject, he referred his friendly persecutors to Madame D'Aulnay; and as it was well known that that fair lady had on several occasions expressed her fixed determination to never bury herself during life in the country, though she had no objections to their burying her there after death, he was generally, at this stage of the argument, left in peace.

As we have said, Mr. D'Aulnay was seated in his library, absorbed in the perusal of some abstruse and learned work, no political regrets or projects disturbing for the moment his intellectual enjoyment, when the door of the apartment opened, and an elegant looking woman, on the shady side of Balzac's admired feminine age of thirty, and dressed with the most exquisite taste and care, entered.

"Mr. D'Aulnay," she exclaimed, laying a dainty, heavily-ringed hand on his shoulder.

"Well, what is it, Lucille?" and he half closed his book with a regretful though not impatient look.

"I have come to tell you that Antoinette has just arrived."

"Antoinette," he absently repeated.

"Yes, you moon-struck man," and the little hand inflicted a playful tap on his cheek. "My cousin Antoinette, whom I have been vainly begging of that cross uncle of mine, for the last six months; and who has been at last granted a chance of seeing a little of life under my auspices."

"Do you mean that rosy, good-humored little girl I saw two summers ago, in the country, at Mr. De Mirecourt's?"

"The same, but instead of a little girl, she is now a young lady, and a wealthy heiress besides. Uncle De Mirecourt has consented to her passing the winter with me, and I am determined that she shall see a little society during that time."

"Ah! I understand too well what that means," groaned Mr. D'Aulnay. "So our present domestic rules are to be subverted, the house completely upset, and the whole place overrun with idle young fops, or unknown men with swords clashing against their heels, as you have been studiously hinting to me for some time past. Alas! I thought when the Chevalier de Lévis and his gallant epaulettes left the country, there was to be an end to all this military fervor or fever; and I must to my shame acknowledge, that if anything could have tended to console me during that darkest episode of the history of my country, it was the supposition I have just mentioned."

"What would you, *cher ami?*" plaintively questioned Mrs. D'Aulnay. "Have we not mourned in sackcloth and ashes, as it were, for many a long and dreary month since; but people must live, and to live they must see society. I really would as soon assume the garb of a female Carmelite, and see you don a Trappist's cowl and robe at once, as live any longer in the cloister-like seclusion in which we have been vegetating for an interminable time past."

"Nonsense, Lucille! As to the Trappist's cowl and robe, I think they would be more suitable to my age and tastes, and certainly far more comfortable, than the silk stockings and ball-room costume which your new projects will compel me so often to assume. But to discuss the matter seriously, surely you who used to talk so pathetically over the woes of Canada with the brave French soldiers who have left our shores—who used to enthral your listeners by your eloquent and patriotic denunciations of our enemies and oppressors, and were compared by Col. De Bourlamarque to one of the heroines of the *Fronde*,—surely you are not going to entertain and feast those same oppressors now?"

"My dear, dear D'Aulnay, I again repeat, what alternative have I? I cannot invite clerks or apprentices to my house, and our own people are nearly all dispersed in one direction or another. Those English officers may be tyrants, ruthless oppressors, what you will; but they are men of education and refinement; and—conclusive argument—they are my only resource."

"Pray, tell me, then, when this reign of anarchy is to be inaugurated?" questioned Mr. D'Aulnay, silenced though not convinced.

"Oh, on that point, my dear André, I am certain of meeting with your approbation. The good old Canadian *fête* of *la Sainte Catherine*, a day which our ancestors from time immemorial have joyously observed, will be the evening I will choose for again opening our doors to something like life and gaiety."

"And I fear closing them against peace and comfort; but, do you know any of the men who are destined henceforth to fill our *salons* and to eat our suppers?"

"Yes; Major Sternfield called here yesterday with that young Foucher, who, in times past, would scarcely have obtained admittance into my house; but, alas! society is so reduced in point of numbers, we cannot afford to be too exclusive now."

"Was that long-legged flamingo I caught a glimpse of in the hall, Major Sternfield?" questioned Mr. D'Aulnay.

"Long-legged flamingo!" reiterated the lady, petulantly, "what an extraordinary choice of unsuitable epithets. Major Sternfield is certainly one of the handsomest and most elegant men I have ever met; and, what is more to the point, he is a perfect gentleman in manner and address. He expressed, in the most deferential terms, the earnest, anxious desire of himself, and many of his brother officers, to obtain an entrance into our Canadian *salons*—"

"Yes, to pick up any heiresses among us, and after turning the heads of all the rest of the girls, jilt them," grumbled Mr. D'Aulnay.

"Ah, you are mistaken," rejoined his wife with animation. "Myself and country-women will take good care that in all cases they shall be the sufferers, not ourselves. Antoinette and I shall break dozens of their callous hearts, and thus avenge our country's wrongs."

"Heaven preserve me from a woman's logic!" muttered the sorely-tried husband, hurriedly re-opening his book, and settling himself back in his chair. "There, there, invite them all, from General to Ensign, if you will, but leave me in peace."

CHAPTER 2

ELATED by her success, Mdme. D'Aulnay traversed, with a light step, the long, narrow corridor, leading from the library, and turned off at the right into a pretty, airy bedroom, furnished with every possible attention to comfort. The apartment, however, at the moment in question, was in considerable confusion. Shawls and scarfs lay scattered on the chairs; whilst a half-opened trunk, with innumerable band-boxes, lay heaped upon the floor.

Standing before the tall *Psyche*, adding a last smoothing touch to her rich waves of hair, stood a young girl, with a slight, exquisitely-formed figure, and very lovely, expressive face.

"Dressed already, my charming cousin!" smilingly exclaimed Madame D'Aulnay. "You have done much with very little;" and she glanced significantly, if not contemptuously, at the dark gray dress, as simple in its fashion as it was in material, which the young girl wore. "But, come, let me look at you well. I had only a glimpse of you, just now;" and, suiting the action to the word, she drew her guest towards the window, first pushing entirely back the heavy damask curtains that hung before it.

"Why, Antoinette, child, do you know that you have grown positively beautiful? Such a complexion—"

"Mercy, mercy, Lucille!" laughed the object of this eulogium, deprecatingly raising her pretty little hands before her face; "just what Madame Gérard prophesied before I left home."

"And, pray, what did that tiresome, punctilious, scrupulous old governess prophesy? Come, tell me;" and, placing her young companion in a cushioned *fauteuil*, she drew another towards her, and sank into its soft depths.

8

"Well, first of all, she did all in her power, talked more in one week than I have heard her do in months, to induce papa to prevent my coming. She spoke of my youth and utter inexperience—the dangers and snares that might beset my steps, and then, dear Lucille, she spoke of you."

"And what did she say of me?"

"Nothing very terrible. Simply that you were graceful, accomplished, and fascinating ('tis your turn to hide your blushes now), but that you were eminently unfit for the responsible office of mentor to a girl of seventeen. Whilst you were imaginative, thoughtless and impulsive, I was giddy, childish and romantic; so she argued that nothing good could come of committing me six long months to your guidance."

"And what said Uncle De Mirecourt to all this?"

"Not much at first, but I am tempted to think poor Madame Gérard said too much. You know papa always says he possesses a good share of the firmness—to use a mild term—constituting from time immemorial one of our family attributes; and when Mrs. Gérard became so urgent and earnest, he began to say just as decidedly that, as I was seventeen, it was time I should see something of society; or, at least of town life,—that Madame D'Aulnay was his niece, and an amiable, kind-hearted woman,—with many other flattering speeches, of which I will spare you the recital. Still, the day was beginning to go against us, for he thinks a great deal of Mrs. Gérard's judgment; and he concluded by remarking that I might postpone my town visit to another winter,—when I, overwhelmed by this sudden disappointment of all my hopes and prospects, burst into tears. That decided the matter. Papa declared he had already half engaged his word to me, and that unless I chose myself to free him from his promise, he must keep it. Then Mrs. Gérard turned to me, and for two days her kindly-meant entreaties, and gentle counsels, made me the most miserable little girl in the world. Indeed, I had finally made up my mind to yield to her wishes, when your last urgent, kind letter arrived. After its perusal, I embraced her tenderly,—for she has been, from my early childhood, a true and loving friend,—and implored her to forgive me this once for disobeying her. She said—but, no matter, here I am!"

"And most welcome you are, you dear little creature! I declare, I would have had neither heart nor courage to enter on this season's campaign, without some such auxiliary as yourself. You are a wealthy heiress, high-born and handsome, and you will meet here the very *élite* of those elegant English strangers."

"English!" repeated Antoinette, with a slight start. "Oh, Lucille, papa hates the very name."

"What of that, child! If we do not have them, who are we to have? Our darling French officers have left us for ever, together with the flower of our young *noblesse*. Any that remain of the latter are dispersed throughout the country parishes, burrowing in dismal seigniories or lonely old family mansions, and would prove at best but uncertain and occasional visitors. Surely, then, I am not to fill the drawing-rooms that have been crowded, night after night, with men like De Bourlamarque and his chivalric companions, with such creatures as the occupants of the inferior government or other offices, which our English masters have judged too paltry to be worth destituting. But, tell me, are the two Léonard girls coming to town soon?"

"Yes; I received a few lines yesterday from Louise, mentioning they were both coming to spend a couple of months in Montreal with their aunt."

"*Tant mieux!* They are handsome, elegant-looking girls, and will be quite an addition to our circle. But, I must warn you in time that you must have a charming evening dress ready for next Thursday, the purchase and making of which, by the way, I must superintend myself. I intend that we shall celebrate *la Sainte Catherine* with all possible splendor. In the meantime, if you should feel lonesome, or find yourself at a loss for amusement, you have only to look from the window at any hour in the afternoon, and you can see the fine imposing figures of our intended guests, lounging up and down our rough pavements."

"Do you know any of them yet, Lucille?"

"I have made the acquaintance of only one; but if he is anything like a fair specimen of the rest, I assure you we shall waste no more sighs on any of De Lévis' gallant followers. Major Sternfield,—that is the name of my new military acquaintance,—and (*par parenthèse*) he has placed the whole regiment at my disposal, guaranteeing that they shall make themselves equally useful and agreeable;— Major Sternfield, then, is superbly handsome, polished and courteous in manner, in short a most accomplished man of the world. He got young Foucher to introduce him here; and though I received him somewhat coldly at first, my reserve soon yielded to the deferential homage of his address, and the delicate flattery of his manner. By way of climax to his many perfections, the dear creature speaks French charmingly. He told me he had spent two years in Paris. In taking leave, he asked permission to return soon with a couple of brother officers, who specially desired an introduction."

"And what says cousin D'Aulnay to all this?"

"Why, like a true philosopher, and a good, sensible husband as he is, he grumbles, but—submits. And 'tis better for us both he does so, for though scarcely a shadow of real sympathy exists between us (he is matter-of-fact, practical, and intensely literary, whilst I am romantic, enthusiastic in temperament, and cannot endure the sight of a book, unless it be a novel, or volume of sentimental poetry), we are still, in spite of such startling dissimilarity of tastes and character, happy, and mutually attached to each other."

"Were you very much in love, then, with cousin D'Aulnay, when you married him?" questioned Antoinette, hesitatingly, for she felt she was treading on what had hitherto been almost forbidden ground to her young imagination.

"Oh dear, no! My parents, though kind and indulgent in other respects, showed me no consideration in this. They simply told me Mr. D'Aulnay was the husband they had chosen for me, and that I was to be married to him in five weeks. I cried for the first week almost without intermission. Then, mamma having promised me I should select my own *trousseau*, and that it should be as rich and costly as I could desire, a different turn was given to my feelings, and I became so very busy with milliners and shopping, that I had not time for another thought of regret, till my wedding day arrived. Well, I was happy in my lot, for Mr. D'Aulnay has ever been both indulgent and generous; but, my darling child, the experiment was fearfully hazardous,—one which might have resulted in life-long misery to both parties. Remember, Antoinette," continued the speaker, with a pretty little air of sentiment, "that the only sure basis for a happy marriage, is mutual love, and community of soul and feeling."

Apparently, mutual esteem, moral worth, and prudence in point of suitable choice, counted for nothing with Madame D'Aulnay.

Well might the trustworthy governess have raised her voice against entrusting to such a mentor, Antoinette De Mirecourt, with her childish inexperience, rich, poetic imagination, and warm, impulsive heart.

CHAPTER 3

HAVING introduced our heroine to the reader, we will devote a few pages to her parentage and precedents.

Twenty years previous to the opening of our tale, on a golden October day, general rejoicing and gaiety reigned throughout the *seigneurie* and Manor-House of Valmont, in which Antoinette first saw the light, and which had belonged to her family from the early date at which the fief had been conceded to the gallant Rodolphe De Mirecourt. This *beau gentilhomme*, who had landed in Canada possessing little else than a keen bright sword and a pair of shining spurs, soon found himself installed, in return for some services rendered the French crown, lord and owner of the rich and fertile demesne of Valmont, which had descended since in direct line to its present owner, Arthur De Mirecourt. Arrived at the age of manhood, the latter yielded to a natural desire to see that gay sunny land of France, that polished brilliant Paris of which he had heard such marvels recounted. But though the splendor of the latter at first dazzled, and its countless attractions fascinated him, the young man soon began to weary of its glittering dissipation, and to long for the simple pleasures, the quiet life of his own land. Despite then the entreaties, the indignant representations of his gay young Parisian friends; despite the reproachful glances of the dark eyed graceful dames who used to shed such pitying glances on him when allusion was made to the land of "snow and savages,"—he returned to his native country, fonder and more devoted to it than when he had left its shores. His sojourn in the brilliant French capital, had in no degree changed the simple healthful tastes of his boyhood, and never had he entered into the varied amusements of a

13

Parisian *fête* with more buoyancy of spirit, and freshness of enjoyment than he did into the simple rejoicings succeeding his return to his own quiet home in Valmont.

Warm and loving hearts were waiting there to welcome him back,—the widowed mother, who had found so powerful a solace in his thoughtful affection, for the loss of the husband and children who lay sleeping beneath the seigneurial pew from which Sunday or holiday so rarely found her absent; friendly neighbors and censitaires too, not omitting the orphaned Corinne Delorme, a young girl distantly related to Mrs. De Mirecourt, whom the latter had brought up with a mother's care, and whom he had always looked on as a dear sister.

This same Corinne, though possessing a graceful figure and regular small features, had never obtained the title of a beauty,—a circumstance which may have arisen in part from her total want of that gaiety and animation in which Canadian girls are so rarely deficient, or from a certain look of languor and pallor, the result of a very delicate fragile constitution.

A more exacting woman than Mrs. De Mirecourt might have occasionally taxed her young *protégée* with ingratitude, so undemonstrative, so quiet was she in word and manner; but then it must be remembered that the young girl never forgot those silent unobtrusive attentions, that respectful deference which daughter owes to parent. Never perhaps had Corinne's constitutional coldness showed itself more plainly, or in a more annoying form to her benefactress, than on the occasion of Arthur De Mirecourt's return to his native land. Whilst household, friends and neighbors, were planning festivities and rejoicings to duly honor the expected arrival, she alone displayed a provoking calmness amounting to indifference; and on the morning of his return, when he turned towards her, after tenderly folding his mother in his arms, and drew her towards him in a brother's frank friendly embrace, she evinced no more emotion or joy than if they had only parted the day previous. Happening to touch upon the circumstance, in one of the pleasant confidential conversations which his mother declared amply repaid her for the loneliness she had experienced during his absence, Madame De Mirecourt found a dozen excuses for the delinquent. Poor Corinne was so sickly— subject to such frequent headaches—such great depression of spirits,—which benevolent pleas meanwhile did not prevent the young man from setting down the object of them as a cold unamiable egotist.

It might have been expected that Mrs. De Mirecourt, having but recently recovered her son as it were, would have been in no hurry to share the large place she held in his heart with any rival, and yet such was really the case. No sooner was he fairly installed at home than a restless desire to see him settled in life,—married, took possession of her. Acting on this maternal wish, a hint was given here and there to lady friends, and Arthur was soon besieged by invitations in every quarter, certain of meeting, wherever he went, fair young faces which would have looked to singular advantage in the low dark rooms of the old Manor-House. Arrived at the age of twenty-eight, rejoicing in a heart and fancy entirely free, young De Mirecourt by no means sought to keep aloof from these social meetings; and before long, he began to acknowledge secretly to himself, that he returned in some slight degree, the evident partiality that a certain graceful young heiress, possessed of radiant health and spirits, bestowed upon him. Matters not advancing however with that rapidity which Mrs. De Mirecourt desired, that wily lady determined on inviting the young girl she had privately selected as a future daughter-in-law, together with a few other young people, on a fortnight's visit. The visit was now drawing to a close, and nothing tangible had come of it. Arthur had indeed talked, danced and laughed a great deal with Mademoiselle

De Niverville, who, in reality, was as good as she was charming, but that was all. No honeyed word, no tender love-vow had fallen from his lips; and she was now about returning home, and both parties were as free as if they had never met. Still the young man sincerely admired her, indeed he could scarcely do otherwise; and more than once, as the sweet gaiety, the winning kindness of her disposition, showed itself in such striking contrast to the apathetic indifference of Corinne, who seemed to grow colder and more reserved every day, he could not help wishing for his mother's sake, whose life-long companion the young girl, if she continued single, was destined to be, that she more nearly resembled the fair young heiress of De Niverville.

Meanwhile, Mrs. De Mirecourt, anxious and uneasy about the success of her matrimonial plans, bethought herself of seeking the co-operation of Corinne, and asking her to urge the dilatory Arthur to come to an understanding with Miss De Niverville before she left Valmont. Mrs. De Mirecourt would willingly have done this herself; but the two or three attempts she had made in that direction had been so firmly though laughingly parried by her son, that she deemed it unavailing. Corinne accepted, though perhaps somewhat reluctantly, the delicate mission confided to her, and sought one morning the breakfast room, in which Arthur, always an early riser, was reading alone. Very patiently he heard her, for her manner possessed more sisterly kindness than it usually betrayed; and she earnestly enlarged on Louise's merits and many good qualities—the hopes and expectations which she and her friends had probably founded on the attentions he had lately paid her, and on the happiness he would confer on his devoted mother by fulfilling the wish nearest her heart.

The quiet yet persuasive eloquence with which Corinne spoke, surprised whilst it half convinced her auditor. He made no answer, however, beyond smilingly replying that he had ample time yet, that the party were all going out sleighing that very afternoon; and as he intended driving the fair Miss De Niverville himself, he had a splendid opportunity for satisfying public expectation generally. Seeing that Corinne still looked very earnest, he took her hand, and added more gravely:

"Laughing or jesting will not prevent me, my kind little sister, from seriously reflecting, and perhaps acting on your recent kindly-intended counsels. The drive this afternoon will certainly afford a most favorable chance, if I can only make up my mind to avail myself of it. Of course you will join us?"

"I fear I cannot. I have a letter to write, and it is better for me to get rid of the task during the day, so that I may be free to join you all in the drawing-room on this, the last night that our guests will be with us. For this morning I have more work laid out than I can possibly accomplish."

What charming weather it was for a drive! How smooth were the dazzling white roads, how glorious the sunshine! Even Madame De Mirecourt had been induced to join the party, and buried under bear-skin robes, in her own comfortable roomy *cariole*, looked as cheerful as the light-hearted Louise herself.

Corinne, true to her previous determination, remained behind; and as she stood at the window waving them a friendly farewell, looking so pretty with that quiet smile on her delicate colorless features, and the sun-light gilding her rich silky hair, De Mirecourt again thought what a pity it was that so little feeling or warmth of character lurked beneath that fair exterior. But these thoughts were soon forgotten in the excitement of starting, and in the pleasurable duty of attending to his fair companion, and gathering the sleigh robes carefully around her. But, behold, after they had driven a short distance, the pretty Louise took it into her graceful head to imagine that she felt cold, and commenced bemoaning the want of a certain dark grey shawl, whose thick warm texture was a certain protection against the coldest of wintry blasts. Of course, a gallant cavalier like De Mirecourt instantly proposed returning to the house for it, and the sleigh was soon drawn up again at the starting point.

"I will hold the reins, Mr. De Mirecourt, whilst you run in for it. I left it in the little sitting-room. Pray do not be angry with me for being so forgetful and troublesome?"

The young man replied to the charming speaker with a dangerously tender smile, and then entered the house. Lightly and rapidly he ran up the staircase, into the apartment indicated. There, on the end of the sofa, he perceived the object of which he had come in quest; but as he hastily caught it up, the sound of a low though passionate sob fell on his ear. Surprised and startled, he glanced around. The sound again repeated, came from an inner chamber opening off the sitting room, and which a couple of book-cases had invested with the dignified title of library.

Who could it be? What did it mean? Suddenly, through the half open door, his eye fell on a mirror suspended opposite him, on the wall of the library; and clearly reflected in that mirror, was the figure of Corinne Delorme seated on a low stool, apparently in the utter abandonment of grief, her face bowed over some object which she held tightly clasped in her slender fingers, and on which she was showering impassioned kisses. That object was his own miniature, a gift which he had brought his mother from France.

All was made clear to him now. The coolness, the indifference, was all feigned—an icy veil assumed to hide the devoted love that had grown with the young girl's growth, and become an engrossing sentiment of her life, a sentiment, however, which maiden pride and modesty had taught her so effectually to conceal. Yes, loving him as she did, she had found courage enough to plead the cause of another—to dismiss him with smiles when she supposed him on the point of offering the prize of his love to a rival.

Very quietly, very softly, De Mirecourt retreated, and when he rejoined Miss De Niverville, his face was much paler and graver than was its wont. During the drive, notwithstanding his utmost efforts, he was unusually pre-occupied, and had to bear, in consequence, a considerable amount of raillery from his fair companion; but whatever course the conversation took, no profession or vow of love escaped his lips. Arrived at home, he soon made his escape from the lively group that gathered around the large double stove, and it was not till a couple of hours after that he rejoined them.

The first person he met on entering the drawing room was Corinne; and with a quiet smile on her pale still face, she "hoped he had enjoyed his drive."

"Tolerably; but shall I tell you, sister mine, whether I followed out your counsels or not?"

Brave young heart! Not the quivering of a feature, not the twitching of an eyelash, betrayed the terrible anguish that reigned within!

Softly, distinctly, the answer came:

"Yes; tell me that you have fulfilled the wishes of the best of mothers—of all your friends."

He looked earnestly, searchingly, in her face. "Will *you* congratulate me, Corinne, if I have done so, and if my suit has prospered?"

A crimson flush, fading as rapidly as it rose, overspread her face, and turning away, she rejoined in a quiet, almost cold tone:

"Why should I not? Your choice is one against which no objection could possibly be raised."

Without openly avoiding him, Corinne contrived that, during the course of the evening, she and De Mirecourt should not find themselves again in proximity. He could read aright now, however, that apparent indifference and egotism which he had till lately so greatly misjudged and so strongly condemned.

The following day, Louise De Niverville left Valmont, and her tardy suitor had not spoken. With De Mirecourt's delicate sense of honor, his chivalrous generosity of character, it seemed to him that he was no longer free, that he belonged of right to her who had lavished on him unsought the hidden wealth of her secret love. After a week's quiet reflection, during which he found his fancy for Miss De Niverville had taken no root whatever in his heart,—a week during which Corinne had endeavored unceasingly to avoid him, struggling all the while as only a woman can struggle against that affection which was daily gaining in intensity and depth,—he sought her side one snowy winter evening, as she stood at the sitting room window, silently watching the white flakes falling outside, and, without many vows or protestations, asked her to be his wife.

She turned fearfully pale, and after a moment's silence whispered, "was she, a poor dependant, the bride his mother would choose, his friends approve of?"

"That is not what I ask you, dear Corinne. I do not marry to please either friends or mother; and besides, the latter loves me too well to find fault with choice of mine. Tell me, simply, do you love me well enough to become my wife?"

Slowly, hesitatingly, as if the secret, so long and so jealously kept, could scarcely be yielded up, came the little monosyllable—yes; and a few weeks later, they were married, quietly and without pomp, in the little village church,—Mrs. De Mirecourt, the first disagreeable sensation of the surprise over, easily sacrificing her own private wishes to those of her idolized son.

Once married, the indifference and coldness of Corinne's character vanished like snow before April sunshine, and never was wife more loving and more devoted. De Mirecourt never told her that he had surprised her secret, never told her that she owed as much to pity as to love; and soon his generosity met its reward, for an affection as ardent as that which his young wife had so long secretly cherished for him, sprang up in his heart towards herself. Alas! that union, blessed and trusting as theirs, was doomed to be so soon severed! Two years of domestic happiness, unclouded by look or word of estrangement, during which period Antoinette was born, was accorded them, and then the young wife, always delicate and fragile, began to droop.

No affection, no care could save her; and before many months had elapsed, she was taken from De Mirecourt's loving arms, and laid in her last earthly home. Ere the first anniversary of her death had arrived, Madame De Mirecourt had joined her, leaving the Manor-House as gloomy and silent as a tomb. The appointed time of mourning over, friends began to hint to the young widower that his home required a mistress, that he was too young to devote himself to a life-long sorrow.

Mr. De Mirecourt, however, remained deaf to all such friendly suggestions; and after procuring in the person of the estimable Madame Gérard, a suitable governess for his infant daughter, he subsided into the quiet country life he had led ever since.

Fortunate beyond measure was the little Antoinette in having found so kind and prudent a guide to replace the mother she had so early lost; and notwithstanding the excessive indulgence of her father, and the impulsive thoughtlessness of her own disposition, she had grown up an amiable and winning, though not wholly faultless character.

CHAPTER 4

IT was St. Catherine's Eve, that day always marked in French Canadian homes, whether in the *habitant's* cottage or the *seigneur's* mansion, by innocent mirth and festivity, and which answers so nearly to our Hallow-E'en.

On the night in question, Madame D'Aulnay's abode was blazing with waxen tapers and resounding to the strains of lively cotillion and contre-danse; whilst her handsome rooms, filled with glittering uniforms, and gauzy, perfumed dresses, presented a brilliant and enlivening scene.

Leaning gracefully beside the mantle-piece of the grate, the bright reflection of whose clear fire cast a most becoming glow on her really fine features, stood the elegant hostess herself, engaged in conversation with a tall, fine-looking man, whose clear bright color and dark blue eye betrayed his Anglo-Saxon descent. The lady had brought the whole artillery of her charms to bear on her companion, speaking glances, bewitching smiles, and sweetly modulated tones; but though he was courteous and attentive, she felt she had made little or no impression; and to the courted and fascinating Madame D'Aulnay this was indeed a mortifying novelty.

Meantime, whilst she was thus vainly lavishing her powers of attraction on her unimpressionable guest, her cousin, Miss De Mirecourt, was succeeding much better with her partner of the hour. The latter was Major Sternfield, "the irresistible," as he had already been styled by some of the fairer portion of the company; and certainly as far as outward qualifications went, he almost seemed to deserve the exaggerated title. A tall and splendidly-proportioned figure—eyes, hair and features of faultless

22

beauty, joined to rare powers of conversation, and a voice whose tones he could modulate to the richest music, were rare gifts to be all united in one happy mortal. So thought many an envious man and admiring woman; and so thought Audley Sternfield himself.

A fitting partner for this Apollo was the bright-eyed, graceful Antoinette De Mirecourt, whose rare personal charms were doubly enhanced by the witching *naiveté*, and shy vivacity of manner which many found more fascinating than even her beauty itself. Major Sternfield was bending over her, apparently heedless of every thing but herself, and certainly leaving her no cause to complain of the devotion of *her* partner; when, skilfully enough for such a novice, changing the tone of the conversation from the shade of sentiment to which Sternfield, even in that early stage of their intercourse sought to bring it, she exclaimed:

"Pray tell me the names of some of your brother officers? They are all strangers to me."

"Willingly," he smilingly rejoined, "and their characters too. It will be but a proper preliminary step to their introduction to yourself; for they have all vowed, with but one exception, that they will not leave this evening till they have obtained, or attempted to obtain, an introduction to you.

"To begin then. That dark, quiet-looking man on your right is Captain Assheton, a very amiable and very harmless sort of person. The good-humored, ruddy personage beside him is Doctor Manby, surgeon of ours, who would amputate a limb as smilingly and cheerfully as he would light a cigar. That very pretty, very exquisitely-dressed young gentleman, dancing opposite us, is the Hon. Percy Delaval; but, as I have promised to introduce him to yourself, provided you will permit it, when this dance is over, and he will probably claim your hand for the next, you will have an immediate opportunity of knowing and judging for yourself."

"But who is that stately-looking, gentleman talking with Mrs. D'Aulnay?" and Antoinette glanced towards the mantle-piece where the hostess still stood, conversing with her impassible companion. "That is Colonel Evelyn:" and as Sternfield pronounced the name, an expression of mingled dislike and impatience flashed across his face. It was instantly repressed however; and in a lower tone he rejoined:

"In the first place, he is the *one* exception I hinted at just now, who did not pledge himself to become acquainted with you this evening, if possible. Is not that enough; or, do you still wish to know more of him?"

"Decidedly. He interests me now more than ever."

"A true woman's perverse answer," inwardly thought Sternfield: but with a low bow, he replied:

"Well, your wishes must be obeyed. In a few words then, confidential of course, I will tell you what Colonel Evelyn is. He is one who believes neither in God, nor man, nor yet in woman."

"You almost frighten me! Is he an infidel?"

"Not perhaps in open theory, but in practice he certainly is. Born and brought up a Catholic, he has never, in the memory of the oldest member of the regiment, entered church or chapel. Cold and distant in manner, he is on terms of friendly intimacy with no man; but worst and greatest crime of all," and here the chivalrous speaker deprecatingly smiled, "he is a professed, incorrigible woman-hater. Some disappointment in a love affair, early in life, the particulars of which none of us have ever heard, has embittered his character to such a degree that he openly declares his contemptuous hatred for all of Eve's daughters, vowing they are all equally false and deceitful. Pray, forgive me, Miss De Mirecourt, for uttering such shocking sentiments in your presence, even whilst condemning them heart and soul; but you commanded me to speak, and I had no alternative but to obey. But here comes Mr. Delaval to solicit an introduction."

The usual formula was gone through, Antoinette's hand asked by the new-comer for the ensuing dance, and then Sternfield turned away, first whispering in the young girl's ear:

"I yield my place with such regret, that I shall soon venture on claiming it again."

If Major Sternfield had chosen his successor with the intention that he should act as a foil to himself, he could not have succeeded better in his choice.

The Honorable Percy Delaval was a golden-haired, pink-cheeked, delicate-featured youth of twenty-one summers. Lately come into a considerable fortune—belonging to an old and wealthy family in England, and possessing, as before hinted, considerable personal attractions, Lieutenant Delaval was as thoroughly infatuated with himself as ever lover was with mistress. To his natural gifts he had added some acquired ones, such as a lisping, drawling form of speech, a lounging mode of standing or reclining (he rarely sat, in the proper acceptation of the term), and a peculiar mode of languidly half closing his large blue eyes, or occasionally calling up into them an abstracted vacancy of gaze and expression,—all of which numerous and varied attractions, rendered him, at least in his own estimation, more irresistible than the handsome Sternfield himself. Such was the young gentleman, who, after a protracted silence, during which his eyes had listlessly wandered round the room, apparently unconscious of the existence of his partner, at length turned towards her, and half patronizingly, half languidly, enquired "if she were fond of dancing?"

"That depends entirely on the species of partner I chance to have," replied Antoinette, with as much truth as spirit.

The infatuated Percy, however, saw only in this plain speech, an implied compliment to himself; and after another five minutes' imposing silence and abstraction, he resumed—"They say it is intolerably cold here in the winter!"

To this proposition there was no reply beyond a slight inclination of his companion's head.

"What do the men wear to protect themselves from the Siberian rigor of the climate?"

"Bear skin coats," was the laconic reply.

"And the women—haw—I beg pardon, the ladies—the fair sex, I should have said?"

"Blankets and moccasins," rejoined Antoinette, slightly tossing her pretty little head, for she felt her patience rapidly giving way. The Honorable Percy stared.

Was it really the case; or could this "obscure little colonial girl," as he inwardly characterized her, be quizzing him?

Oh, the latter supposition was improbable—totally out of the question. It must be that in some of the country parts, the women still wore the singular costume just mentioned, a reminiscence probably of the peculiar customs of their Indian predecessors.[1]

Returning to the charge, he resumed with more impertinent *nonchalance* of tone and manner than before:

"They say that for eight months the ground is covered to the depth of four feet with snow and ice, and that everything freezes. How do the unfortunate inhabitants contrive to support nature during that time?"

Antoinette's first feeling of irritation was fast giving place to one of amusement, and she smilingly rejoined:

"Oh, if provisions are very scarce, they eat each other."

Heavens and earth! It was then possible, nay, actually true. She *was* quizzing him! His very breathing seemed suspended by the discovery, and for a considerable time, indignant amazement kept him silent. But, he must condignly punish, annihilate his audacious partner; and calling up as contemptuous a sneer as his pretty, effeminate features would permit him to assume, he rejoined:

---

[1] The reader will please remember that this was nearly a century ago, when such a thing was possible, though not probable.

"Well yes, Canada is as yet so utterly out of the pale of civilization, that I am not surprised at your tolerating any custom, however barbarous."

"True," serenely replied Antoinette; "we can tolerate everything here but fops and fools."

This last sally was too much for Lieutenant Delaval, and he had not recovered from the effects of the shock it had given him, when Major Sternfield hurried up to again claim Miss De Mirecourt's hand for another dance.

Antoinette carelessly placed her arm within that of the new-comer, and turned away, totally unconscious that Colonel Evelyn, who had been examining some prints at a table behind them, having succeeded in making his escape from his hostess, was an amused auditor of the whole of the preceding singular dialogue.

"Well, what think you, Miss De Mirecourt, of the Honorable Mr. Delaval?" smilingly enquired her present partner. "If you remember, we decided that you should form your judgment of him unbiassed by any previous opinion of mine."

"I request of you, Major Sternfield," was the petulant reply, "to introduce me in future to no more foolish boys. They make tiresome partners."

Sternfield's eyes sparkled with suppressed mirth; and that evening the mess room rang with jokes and laughter which made the Honorable Percy Delaval's ears tingle with mingled wrath and desire of revenge.

CHAPTER 5

AND now will our readers forgive us if at the risk of being thought tedious, or, of repeating facts with which they may be as well acquainted as ourselves, we cast a cursory glance over that period of Canadian history which embraces the first few years that followed the capitulation of Montreal to the combined forces of Murray, Amherst, and Haviland— a period on which neither victors nor vanquished can dwell with much pleasure.

Despite the terms of the capitulation, which had expressly guaranteed to Canadians the same rights as those accorded to British subjects, the former, who had confidently counted on the peaceful protection of a legal government, were doomed instead to see their tribunals abolished, their judges ignored, and their entire social system overthrown, to make way for that most insupportable of all tyrannies, martial law.

It is true the new government may have thought these severe measures necessary, for it is well known that the Canadians, for three long years after King George's standard floated above their heads, still persisted in believing and hoping that France had not abandoned them, and that she would yet make a final and successful effort to regain the province when the cessation of hostilities should have been proclaimed. This last hope, however, like many others that the colonists had fixed on the mother country, was doomed to disappointment; and by the treaty of 1763 the destinies of Canada were irrevocably united to those of Great Britain. This circumstance determined a second and more extensive emigration of the better classes of the towns and cities to France, in which country they were received with marks of

28

special favor, and honorable places found for many of them in the government offices, in the navy and the army.

Never perhaps was government more isolated from a people than was the new administration. The Canadians, as ignorant of the language of their conquerors as these latter were of their own cherished Gallic tongue, indignantly turned from the spurred and armed judges appointed to preside among them, and referred the arrangement of their differences to their parish clergy or some of their local notables.

The installation of the English troops in Canada had been followed by the arrival of a host of strangers, among whom unfortunately were many needy adventurers, who sought to build themselves positions on the ruined fortunes of the vanquished people. Of these, General Murray, a stern but strictly honorable man, who had replaced Lord Amherst as Governor General, remarks: "When it had been decided to reconstitute civil government here, we were obliged to choose magistrates and select jury-men out of a community composed of some four or five hundred merchants, mechanics, and farmers, unsuitable and contemptible on account of their ignorance. It is not to be expected that such persons can resist the intoxication of power thus unexpectedly placed in their hands, or refrain from showing how skilful they are (in their peculiar way) in exercising it. They hate the Canadian *noblesse* on account of their birth and their other titles to public respect; and they detest other colonists, because the latter have contrived to elude the illegal oppression to which it was intended to subject them."

The chief-justice Gregory, drawn from the depths of a prison to preside on the bench, was entirely ignorant not only of the French language but also of the simplest elements of civil law; while the attorney-general was not much better qualified for the high charge he held. The power of nominating to the situations of provincial secretary, of council recorder, of registrar, was given to favorites, who rented them to the highest bidder.

It is true the governor was soon compelled to suspend the chief-justice, and to send him back to England; but this, and one or two other conciliatory measures failed to counteract the painful impression which had been made on the minds of the conquered people, that such a thing as justice no longer existed for them. The dismemberment of their territory was a point that grieved them almost as much as the abolition of their laws. The islands of Anticosti and Magdalen, as well as the greater part of Labrador, were annexed to the government of Newfoundland; the islands of St. John and Cape Breton were joined to Nova Scotia; the lands lying around the great lakes, to the neighboring colonies; and finally New Brunswick was detached, and endowed with a separate government and the name it bears to-day.

Royal instructions were received to compel the clergy and the people to take an oath of fidelity under penalty of being obliged to leave the country, as also to deny the ecclesiastical jurisdiction of Rome, which every Catholic is bound in conscience to acknowledge and submit to. They were also summoned to yield up all their weapons and defensive arms, or swear that they had none concealed. These latter orders, which were equally severe and unjust, the government hesitated about enforcing. A spirit of restless dissatisfaction, of open murmuring and complaints began to take possession of the people, hitherto so submissive to their new rulers. These latter felt it was necessary to relax the severity of their measures; and when at a later period, the American colonies broke out into the revolt which ended in the establishment of their independence, Great Britain, either through policy or justice, finally accorded to Canadians the peaceful enjoyment of their institutions and their laws.

CHAPTER 6

MADAME D'Aulnay and her young cousin were now fairly launched into that life of fashionable gaiety in which they were so well fitted to shine, and an *entrée* to madame's pleasant *salons* was sought as a singular favor and advantage. Of course the lady's new military acquaintances were assiduous in their visits. Among the latter, Colonel Evelyn occasionally came, but farther intimacy made no change in his grave, quiet demeanor, nor did it soften, in any degree, his remarkable reserve. He never danced, and scarcely ever addressed a word to Antoinette or any of her pretty young rivals. Though refined and courteous in manner, he never paid a compliment—never uttered any of those commonplace gallantries which pass current in society as successfully as remarks on the weather. Surely Major Sternfield was right; and this man, so reserved, so inaccessible, had little faith or trust in woman.

Ample amends however did Audley Sternfield make for his Colonel's indifference, and few days passed without his presenting himself, under one pretext or another, in Mrs. D'Aulnay's drawing room. A project deferentially proposed by himself, and acceded to by both ladies after some pressing on his part, farther increased their intimacy. This was his becoming their preceptor in the English tongue. With the latter language Mrs. D'Aulnay was but slightly acquainted; but Antoinette, however deficient in point of pronunciation, possessed a very accurate knowledge of its grammatical construction, thanks to the lessons of her governess, who, though experiencing, like most foreigners, great difficulty in the pronunciation, read and wrote it with perfect accuracy.

What dangerous means of attraction were thus furnished Major Sternfield in his new capacity. To sit daily for hours with his fair pupils at the same table, reading aloud some impassioned poem,—some graceful tale of fiction, whilst they listened in silent enjoyment to the rich intonations of a remarkably musical voice; or watched the expressive play of his regular, faultless features. Then when he arrived at some passage of peculiar beauty or fervent sentiment, how eloquent the rapid glance he would steal towards Antoinette—how ardent, how devoted the expression of his dark speaking eyes.

Was it to be wondered at that the young and inexperienced girl, thus exposed to such powerful and novel temptations, learned lessons in another lore than that of languages; and that after those long and pleasant hours of instruction, she often sat wrapped in silent reverie, with flushed cheek and downcast gaze that plainly told something more interesting than English verbs and pronouns occupied her thoughts.

It was the first really good sleighing of the season, for the few slight falls of snow that had hitherto heralded winter's approach, descending on the muddy roads and side-walks, had lost at once their whiteness and purity, and becoming incorporated with the liquid mud, formed that detestable combination with which we Canadians are so familiar in the spring and fall, and which we recognize by the name of "slush." A hard frost, however, succeeded by a sufficiently abundant fall of snow, had filled with rejoicing all the amateurs of sleighing; whilst a clear blue sky overhead, and brilliant sunshine, flooding the earth with light if not warmth, left nothing to be desired.

Before Mrs. D'Aulnay's door was a tiny, exquisitely-finished sleigh, whilst a pair of glossy black ponies of the pure Canadian breed, stood tossing their gayly-tasseled heads, and ringing out musical peals from the host of little silver bells adorning their harness. 'Tis unnecessary to say that this fairy-like equipage was waiting for Mrs. D'Aulnay and her cousin, who were both in the former's dressing-room, adding the finishing touches to their elegant and becoming winter toilettes. On a chair, lay a pair of lady's riding-gauntlets, which the fair lady of the mansion took up, exclaiming:

"You may safely trust yourself to my driving, Antoinette, for I am a practised hand. My ponies too, though pretty, spirited-looking creatures, are very gentle, and admirably broken in."

From this speech it will be seen that Mrs. D'Aulnay, amongst her other accomplishments, possessed that of driving two in hand; and though few ladies of the time either sought or admired this gift, Madame D'Aulnay was a leader of fashion, and did as she pleased.

"Do you know, *petite cousine*," she remarked, glancing complacently in the mirror, "those dark furs of ours are very becoming! They harmonize well with even my sallow complexion, whilst they become your glowing carmine cheeks divinely. But what have we here, Jeanne?" and she turned towards a middle-aged woman who entered with a couple of letters in her hand.

"For Mademoiselle Antoinette, madame"; and the newcomer placed the epistles in the young girl's eagerly outstretched hand.

Jeanne was a somewhat privileged person in the household, for she had lived with Mrs. D'Aulnay in the capacity of lady's-maid before the latter's marriage, and had followed her to her new home, probably never to separate from her; for she was fondly attached to her mistress, and frequently favored her with proofs of her devotion in the shape of remonstrances and reproachful counsels, which the petted and capricious Madame D'Aulnay would have borne from no one else.

Antoinette hastily opened her letters, both of which were very long and closely written; and as Mrs. D'Aulnay's glance fell on the well-filled pages, she somewhat impatiently exclaimed, "Surely, dear child, you do not intend waiting to read those folios through now! There, there, put them away: they will keep till our return."

"Not so, dear Lucille. They are from papa, and poor Mrs. Gérard, both of whom have been but very little in my thoughts for the last couple of weeks; so, by way of penance, I intend remaining at home, and reading the letters over till I have them by heart."

"What nonsense!" exclaimed her hostess. "Do you really mean to lose this beautiful afternoon, and the first good sleighing of the season? Surely you will not be so absurd!"

"It must be, dear friend, for this once; so forgive me."

"Ah!" rejoined Mrs. D'Aulnay, half pettishly, half playfully, "I see you possess a considerable share of the family firmness, or, to give it its true name, obstinacy; but I must make up my mind to exhibit myself in Notre Dame street alone this afternoon. Well, adieu!" and with a light step she descended the stairs.

CHAPTER 7

ANTOINETTE, after Mrs. D'Aulnay's departure, hastily divested herself of her out-door clothing, and then entered on the perusal of her letters. The first, which was from her father, was kind and affectionate; spoke of the void her absence made in the household; told her to enjoy herself to her heart's utmost desire; and ended by warning her to watch well over her affections, and bestow them on none of the gay strangers who might visit at her cousin's house, for assuredly he would never under any circumstances countenance any of them as her suitors. A burning blush suffused the girl's cheek as she read this last sentence; and she hastily laid down her father's letter, and took up the other, as if to banish the peculiar thoughts thus suddenly evoked. But the second epistle was still more unfortunate in the reflections it gave rise to; and as Antoinette read on, the glow on her cheek deepened to a feverish crimson, and the large bright tears gathered in her eyes, and fell one by one on the paper.

No harsh reproaches, no severe denunciations, had found place in Mrs. Gérard's letter; but with gentle firmness she spoke of duties to be fulfilled, of errors to be avoided, and then implored her pupil to question her own heart narrowly, and find in what and how far she had been unfaithful since she had entered on the gay life she was now leading. For the first time since her arrival beneath Mrs. D'Aulnay's roof, Antoinette entered on that trying task of self-examination; and at its close, she stood before the tribunal of her own heart, self-condemned.

Was she really the same innocent, guileless little country girl, whose thoughts and pleasures a few weeks previous had been as simple as those of a child?—she, whose long conversations with Mrs. D'Aulnay ever turned on dress, fashion, or silly sentiment; who lived in a round of glittering gaiety, that gave no time for serious reflection or self-examination? What amusements had replaced her former quiet country walks and useful course of reading— her religious and charitable duties? Aye! blush on, Antoinette! for the answer is one both condemning and humiliating;—the perusal of silly novels and exaggerated love-poems; the conversation of frivolous men of the world, whose whispered flatteries and lover-like protestations had become so familiar to her ear that they had almost ceased to make her blush; and idle day-dreams, planning equally idle pleasures for the future.

Whilst the remorse evoked by these thoughts was busy at her heart, Jeanne entered to say that Major Sternfield wished to see her.

"Impossible!" sharply replied Antoinette, for the fascinating Audley had much to answer for in her present severe self-retrospect.

"But, Mademoiselle," expostulated Jeanne, endeavoring to explain that the gentleman, certain of admittance, had unceremoniously followed her into the hall, and now stood outside the threshold of the adjoining apartment, which was one of the drawing-rooms, awaiting her appearance.

"I tell you, 'tis impossible, Jeanne," was the quick impatient reply: "I have a headache, and can see no one."

The clear ringing tones of the speaker certainly indicated nothing like severe suffering, and considerably disconcerted, the visitor retraced his steps. At the hall-door he paused, and, suddenly turning to the dark-eyed *soubrette* who stepped forward to open it for him, expressed his earnest hope that "Mademoiselle De Mirecourt was not very ill."

"Well, no sir," hesitatingly replied Justine, touched alike by the dark appealing eyes and perfectly spoken French of the handsome interrogator. "Mademoiselle received some

letters from home a short time since; and they may have
contained some unpleasant news, for, on passing the half-
open door, I could see that she was crying." The gallant
Sternfield bowed his thanks, and passed into the street.

"Letters from home and crying over them!" he
murmured to himself. "I must find out from Madame
D'Aulnay, to-morrow, what it all means. My little country
beauty is too great a prize to be let carelessly slip through
my fingers."

A half-hour afterwards, Mrs. D'Aulnay in the highest
spirits returned home. Not finding Antoinette in the
dressing-room, where she had left her, she hurried up to
the latter's apartment, meeting Jeanne on the way, who
informed her that Major Sternfield had called during her
absence and had been refused admittance.

"Why, what new phase of my little cousin's mood is this?"
she inwardly asked herself. "I suppose she has received a
long epistolary lecture from home, which has given her
over a prey to vexation or remorse."

Antoinette was lying on a couch, on which she had
purposely thrown herself, intending to feign headache,
and thus escape the remarks and suppositions of her
hostess. The latter, however, without appearing to notice
the swollen eyelids of her young companion, expressed her
regret at her indisposition, and then entered on an
animated description of her afternoon's drive. "It had
proved delightful; she had met everybody worth meeting,
and had organized with Madame Favancourt, a driving-
party to Lachine for the following day. Major Sternfield,
whom she had met on the way, was to see to the whole
affair; and, in short, they would have a most delightful
excursion. But now," she continued, in a still livelier strain,
"I have come to the cream of the story. Whom should I
meet in the Place D'Armes, in a splendid sleigh, driving a
pair of superb English bays, but our misanthropic Colonel!
The temptation of adding such a faultless turn-out to our

expedition to-morrow was irresistible, and, raising my whip, I beckoned him towards me. The bays champed and curvetted as if they hated the sight of a pretty woman as much as their master does; but reining them in with an iron hand, he courteously listened to my invitation, evidently seeking all the time for some plausible excuse for refusal. Thinking frankness best with such an extraordinary character, I laughingly declared that our resources in the way of handsome equipages and horses were somewhat limited. He eagerly commenced assuring me that his were entirely at my disposal, not only to-morrow, but whenever I should require them. Seeing, however, what the gentleman was at, I quietly interrupted him, by exclaiming,

"Not without the owner, Colonel Evelyn: both or none!"

"You never saw a man so much put out. He bit his lip; reined in the bays till he almost made them stand perpendicularly on their hind legs; and at length, seeing that I awaited determinedly his answer, he rejoined in a hurried constrained tone that he would do himself the pleasure of joining us on the morrow. He is a perfect barbarian;—but I will leave you now, awhile, for quiet will do your poor head good," and, lightly pressing her lips to the fair young cheek pillowed on the couch, she left the room.

Antoinette wearily sighed as the door closed upon her, and murmured: "Oh, if I wish to be again what I was, I must return home! The temptations of this gay house, the society of my kind-hearted but pleasure-loving cousin, are too much for my weak heart and feeble resolves."

CHAPTER 8

A GAY cavalcade of prancing horses and richly-decorated sleighs were drawn up the following day, about noon, in front of Madame D'Aulnay's mansion. Conspicuous among these was the magnificent equipage of Colonel Evelyn; but the owner himself was standing near it with a moody, constrained expression, that plainly betokened he was there against his will. Most of the party were already in their respective places, laughing and chatting in the highest spirits; when the door of Mrs. D'Aulnay's residence opened, and that fair lady issued forth, dispensing sunny smiles and friendly bows on all sides. In her wake came Antoinette; but the usually sparkling gaiety of the latter was strangely clouded, yet many thought this new and pensive shade of her beauty became her even better than the olden one.

As the elder lady stepped on the pavement, Colonel Evelyn approached her, and, in a tone which he vainly endeavored to render *empressé*, requested her "to honor his sleigh by occupying it."

She smilingly bowed assent, and then turned aside to answer some polite enquiries from some cavalier near. Suddenly Major Sternfield sought her side, and begged her to give him a seat with herself as he had something very particular to say to her. The truth was, he was most impatient to know why Antoinette had refused seeing him the previous day; as well as to learn, if possible, the cause of the tearful grief of which Justine had spoken. Mrs. D'Aulnay good-naturedly answered in the affirmative, not very sorry at the same time to inflict a passing slight on the ungallant Colonel, who seemed to think it so severe a hardship to share the occupancy of his sleigh with her charming self. Having previously, however, intended that Antoinette and Major Sternfield should drive together, whilst she should head the cavalcade with Colonel Evelyn, she now felt momentarily embarrassed how to arrange matters. After a moment's thought, she tripped up to the Colonel, and smilingly told him "that as Major Sternfield had thrown himself on her charity, she had no resource but to take him in her own little equipage. Here, however, is my substitute," she archly continued, drawing suddenly forward the embarrassed and astonished Antoinette, who had been looking around her for the last few minutes with a listless pre-occupied expression, which seldom rested on that sweet face.

Completely taken by surprise, and at the same time indignant beyond measure at being thus arbitrarily forced on the society of so unwilling a companion, Antoinette drew back, vehemently declaring "that she would not consent to such an arrangement,—that the horses looked too restive!"

With an almost imperceptible curl of his lip, Colonel Evelyn hastened to assure her "that the steeds, though spirited, were thoroughly broken in," whilst Mrs. D'Aulnay impetuously whispered in her ear,

"Do you want openly to insult the man? Get in at once."

Antoinette unwillingly complied; and as Colonel Evelyn arranged the rich robes carefully around her, he contemptuously thought within himself, "What a well-got-up piece of acting! Young as they may be,—guileless as they may look,—they are all alike!"

Whilst backing his horses to let Madame D'Aulnay and Major Sternfield (who, by the way, on seeing the last arrangement, heartily regretted his precipitancy) take precedence, the lady insisted on Evelyn's keeping the lead, declaring his magnificent bays were just the thing for opening the procession.

Proudly, gaily, the party swept on, making the air musical with the sweet ringing of bells, and, after proceeding down the length of Notre Dame street, passed through Recollet's gate, which gave them egress outside the wall encircling the city, and they soon found themselves[1] in the open country, on the road to Lachine.

Colonel Evelyn's moodiness and Antoinette's vexation yielded after a time to the charms of the brilliant blue sky and sunshine,—the beautiful appearance of the widespread fields covered with their glittering snowy mantle, and sparkling as if some enchanter had strewn them with diamond-dust. There was something, too, peculiarly exhilarating in the rapid pace of the steeds, and in the keen bracing air itself, that insensibly communicated its influence to both parties; but still, strangely enough, both remained silent. The scene was entirely new to Evelyn, and talking commonplace platitudes would have marred his enjoyment; whilst Antoinette, on her part, was determined to show him, that, though forced in a measure on his society, she had no intention of profiting by the circumstance in any manner.

At length they neared the Lachine Rapids, the roar of whose restless waters had been for some time previous sounding in their ears; and as the broad wreaths of foam, the snow-covered rocks with the black waters boiling and chafing up between them, or eddying round in countless different currents and whirlpools, burst upon their view, an involuntary exclamation of admiration escaped Colonel Evelyn's lips. The scene was indeed grand, sublime in the extreme; and the lonely wooded shores of Caughnawaga opposite, the tiny islets with a solitary pine-tree or two growing from their rocky bosoms, and standing where they had stood for ages, calm, unmoved by the wild tempest of

---

[1] This wall, which was originally built to protect the inhabitants of the town from the hostile attacks of the Iroquois tribe, was fifteen feet high, with battlements. After a time, it was suffered to fall into decay; and it was ultimately removed by an Act of the Provincial legislature, to make way for some judicious and necessary improvements.

waters so fiercely raging around them, gave fresh food to the thoughts, whilst they added increased grandeur to the scene.

In the eager admiration of the moment, the Colonel unconsciously relaxed his grasp on the reins, when a shot, suddenly discharged from the gun of some country sportsman near, startled the spirited steeds, that instantly set off at a most fearful pace. The peril was imminent, for the road led close along the bank of the rapids, rising in some places several feet above the chafing waters. Still, the hand which held the reins was one of iron, and its firm and vigorous grasp was a considerable check on the headlong career of the terrified animals. After the first moment of alarm, Evelyn turned towards his companion to deprecate by some encouraging word, the piercing shrieks, the fainting fit, or other tokens of feminine alarm, which would greatly have heightened the dangers of their position; but Antoinette sat perfectly upright and quiet, her lips slightly compressed, and in no way betraying her secret terror, save in the marble-like pallor of her face.

Noting the anxious glance Evelyn had just turned on her, she quietly exclaimed, "Do not mind me: attend to the horses." "What a brave little girl!" he inwardly thought; and assured of her perfect self-possession, he devoted every straining nerve and sinew to recovering his control over the runaways. Clear eye and strong hand were alike requisite, for they were now approaching a spot where the bank became steeper and the road narrower. An overturned cart, rising up black and unsightly by the wayside, added a fresh impetus to the terror of the already half-maddened animals. With a desperate plunge they sprang forward, and the wild effort caused the reins, already stretched for a considerable time past to the utmost tension, to snap asunder. In that moment of deadly peril there was no time for etiquette or ceremony, and, quick as thought, Evelyn snatched up the light form of his companion, and murmuring "Forgive me," threw her out on the snow-covered ground. He instantly leaped out after, narrowly escaping entangling his feet in the robes, and stumbling forward with considerable violence. His first thought was of Antoinette, who had risen to her feet, and was now leaning in silence against the trunk of a tree, her lips rivalling her cheeks in their death-like pallor.

"Are you much hurt?" he hurriedly enquired.

"Oh, no, no," was the piteous toned reply; "but the horses, the poor horses!"

Colonel Evelyn looked eagerly around. Aye, where were they? Down at the foot of the steep bank, maimed and bleeding, and still desperately struggling amid the rocks and shallow water, into which they had rolled. Evelyn dearly prized his beautiful English bays, perhaps over-valued them as much as he under-valued women; but it is only rendering him justice to state, that in that moment every thought of regret for their fate was absorbed in secret gratulation that the helpless girl committed for the hour to his charge, was safe.

"Take my arm, Miss De Mirecourt," he gently exclaimed, "and we will seek for assistance at yonder little cottage."

Antoinette complied, and their knock for admittance was followed by an invitation to come in. On entering, they found themselves in a bare, scantily-furnished room; the walls and hearth of which, however, were spotless, the small narrow panes glittering like diamonds, and the whole place shining with that exquisite cleanliness and order with which the Canadian *habitants* soften, if they do not conceal, their poverty, wherever it exists. Peacefully smoking beside the huge double-stove sat the master of the household, whilst half-a-dozen round-eyed, swarthy-cheeked children, of all ages from one to seven, played and tumbled like so many dolphins upon the floor. On seeing his unexpected visitor, the man instantly rose, and, without betraying half the astonishment he secretly felt, removed

the blue *tuque* from his head, and politely answered in the
affirmative to Antoinette's request for assistance. Looking
suddenly, however, towards the group on the floor, he
explained, in a somewhat hesitating tone, that his wife had
gone from home on business, and made him promise that
he would not leave the children in her absence, lest they
should burn themselves. The absent wife's fears were fully
justified by the state of the stove, which was nearly red hot;
but Antoinette with a smile wreathing her still white lips,
assured him she should take every possible care of the little
ones during his absence. Smiling his thanks, the man left
the cottage, accompanied by Colonel Evelyn; and
Antoinette found herself alone with her young
companions. Her first act was to bend her knee in heartfelt
gratitude to Providence for her late escape, and then she
turned her attention to consoling the youngling of the
flock, who set up a lamentable out-cry a moment after its
father's departure. The task was not difficult, for
childhood's tears are easily dried; and a few moments after,
he was installed on her lap, timidly fingering the golden
trinkets suspended from her neck, the heat of the room
having forced her to lay aside her furs and mantle; whilst
the other children grouped around her, listened eagerly to
a wonderous tale of a stupendous giant and a lovely fairy,
feasting their eyes meanwhile on the beautiful face and
elegant dress of the speaker, whom they inwardly set down
as belonging to the very class of fairies she was telling them
about.

CHAPTER 9

SOME time after, Colonel Evelyn entered the cottage alone, and, as his clouded gaze fell on the group before him, he involuntarily smiled. The little one on Antoinette's lap nestled closely to her breast on seeing the tall stranger enter, and clung there as naturally as if his little curly pate had always been accustomed to lie next a silken boddice, and press jewelled ornaments. Very lovely Antoinette appeared at the moment; and the gentle play of her features, as she kindly looked from one little auditor to another, invested her with a charm which her beauty had never, perhaps, possessed in saloon or ball-room.

On seeing Evelyn, she eagerly inquired about the horses.

"Our host is attending to them," he carelessly replied, "and will join us in a few moments. But tell me, are you really none the worse in any manner for our adventure? Do you not feel any pain or ache?"

"No—yes—there is something like a dull pain here," and baring her rounded beautifully-shaped arm to the elbow, she disclosed a large discolored bruise upon its soft surface. Colonel Evelyn's countenance betrayed considerable emotion as he looked down on that frail arm, so indicative of almost childish helplessness, and remembered the undaunted courage the brave young owner had exhibited throughout the whole of that trying ordeal.

"Yes," he said, "I must indeed beg your forgiveness for my rough handling; for you must have received that bruise when I threw you from the sleigh. It would have been as easy for me to have sprang out with you in my arms, but I dreaded that in doing so, my feet should become entangled in the shawls and skins filling the sleigh, and thus entail our mutual destruction. Can I do anything for you now? Let me bathe it in cold water."

45

"Oh, no: 'tis a mere trifle, which Jeanne will attend to when I get home," she smilingly rejoined, but coloring as she hastily drew down her sleeve.

A momentary pause ensued, and then Colonel Evelyn, who had been earnestly regarding her, exclaimed—

"Do you know that you have behaved throughout like a perfect heroine? Not a start, not even a single exclamation of fear; and yet I am certain, from the expression of your countenance, that you were greatly alarmed."

Antoinette hesitated a moment, and then an irrepressible smile broke into countless dimples around her pretty mouth as she shyly rejoined:

"They say one great fear almost neutralizes another; and terrified as I was by the mad career of our steeds, I was almost equally afraid of yourself."

"How, of me?" he wonderingly exclaimed.

"Yes. In the first place I was in your sleigh merely on sufferance: I had been, as it were, forced on you, undesired and unsolicited, and consequently felt doubly bound to behave well. No, do not interrupt me," she playfully said, as Evelyn essayed a few dissenting words, remembering at the same time with something like remorse, the harsh judgment he had inwardly passed on her previous to their setting out. "Then, secondly,"—but here the speaker paused in some slight embarrassment.

"And what, secondly?" questioned her companion, considerably amused.

"Well, I had been told that you were an inveterate woman-hater, and consequently presumed that you would show but little indulgence to a woman's fears or fancies."

A look of mental pain instantly chased the smile from Evelyn's face, and almost involuntarily he rejoined: "The unenviable character you give me, has been won and borne by many, merely because they have practised a prudence taught them by past experience."

The words were uttered in a low, constrained tone, and the speaker immediately walked to the little window as if to terminate the subject.

Suddenly, two loud reports of a gun, fired in quick succession, startled Antoinette, whose nervous system, notwithstanding her apparent calmness, had been considerably shaken by the late adventure, and an exclamation of terror escaped her lips. Evelyn winced as the shots rang through the air; but instantly recovering himself, he turned to his companion, kindly exclaiming:

"Do not be alarmed: 'tis our host, who is performing an act of mercy, and putting my poor maimed horses out of their pain."

"What! both killed!" and the girl involuntarily clasped her hands.

"Yes, I examined them well, and seeing that prolonged life would only be prolonged agony to them, I sent our kind assistant to borrow a gun at some neighboring cottage, and left to him the painful task of releasing them. I was too cowardly to wait myself for the accomplishment of the sacrifice."

After a moment's pause, Antoinette exclaimed in a low agitated voice:

"I need not say how deeply sorry I am, Colonel Evelyn, for you, as well as for the indirect share I may have had in this unfortunate event; nor how grieved I am that thought or remembrance of myself should be connected in your memory with the most unpleasant circumstance that will probably mark your sojourn in Canada."

"Do not say that, Miss De Mirecourt," he hurriedly replied. "Rather felicitate me on the fortunate chance which ordained that you should have been my companion, instead of Madame D'Aulnay, or some other timid woman whose weak fears would have infallibly destroyed two lives more precious than that of a couple of carriage-horses. But one woman out of many could have displayed the self-command you did to-day, and which tended more to our mutual preservation than any skill or horsemanship of mine. But here comes our humble friend with the wreck of our late equipage."

Antoinette approached the window and saw their host, aided by a couple of men whom he had called to his assistance, bringing forward a handsomely carved dash-board, and the rich tiger-skin robes. These latter, being thoroughly saturated by their late immersion, were instantly spread to dry on the low stone wall surrounding the garden of the cottage. Through their united efforts they then succeeded in dragging up the body of the sleigh from the foot of the bank, and placing it beside the rest of the *débris*. Whilst the men were standing round the latter, and passing some sage remarks upon the accident, the loud tinkling of numerous sleigh-bells became audible, and the driving-party soon came dashing up. Suddenly, Major Sternfield, who was driving Madame D'Aulnay, caught sight of the broken sleigh lying by the road-side, and recognizing the rich sleigh-robes, he reined up his horse with a precipitate violence which elicited a loud scream from his companion, and sprang to the ground. Hurriedly beckoning to the men, he addressed some rapid enquiries to them, the answers to which seemed in some degree to reassure both himself and Mrs. D'Aulnay, who at the first hint of the accident seemed dreadfully alarmed. Sternfield helped her to alight, and they entered the cottage, soon followed by the remainder of the party, who were all equally curious and excited.

Expressions of sympathy with Miss De Mirecourt's late fright and congratulations on her escape, were of course the order of the day; but most of the gentlemen were equally sincere in their condolences with Colonel Evelyn on the loss of his fine bays, to which professions of regret the latter listened with more impatience than gratitude. A consultation regarding the return of the actors in the late adventure was then held, and it was decided that Mrs. D'Aulnay's servant should yield his place behind to Major Sternfield, who should in turn give up his seat beside Mrs. D'Aulnay to Antoinette. Colonel Evelyn, instinctively avoiding any of the sleighs containing members of the fairer portion of humanity, found part of a seat in a narrow cutter already nearly filled by the portly Dr. Manby and a brother officer, but he contrived to cling on to it till they reached Lachine.

Here the party halted for rest and refreshment at the inn of the place, which was a very indifferent one; but through Sternfield's foresight, a large hamper containing choice wines and other refreshments had been placed in one of the sleighs, and was heartily welcomed when produced.

The early sunset of December was illuminating the front of Mrs. D'Aulnay's mansion when the party stopped before it. Friendly farewells were smilingly interchanged, and then the members of the party sought their respective homes. Colonel Evelyn kindly shook hands with Antoinette, earnestly reiterating his hope that the morrow would find her completely recovered from the effects of her late alarm; but Major Sternfield, less easily satisfied, implored Mrs. D'Aulnay to grant him permission to enter with them, or at least return that evening. This the lady smilingly but positively negatived, declaring that Miss De Mirecourt's pale cheek plainly betrayed she wanted immediate and complete repose.

That evening, Mrs. D'Aulnay passed with Antoinette in the latter's apartment, and, after some questioning and cross-questioning regarding the day's mis-adventure, she enquired if there would be any indiscretion in asking to see the letters her cousin had lately received from home. Somewhat reluctantly the latter put them in her hand, but the elder lady caressingly exclaimed as she wound her arm round the young girl's neck, "You must have no secrets from me, my little Antoinette! You have neither mother nor sister to confide in; choose me then as your friend and counsellor."

Mr. De Mirecourt's letter she read slowly over, and then refolded without further comment; but after a rapid glance at the contents of Mrs. Gérard's epistle, she crushed it up in her hand, and, opening the stove door, threw it in.

The act had taken Antoinette so completely by surprise that the paper was in ashes before she had fully comprehended her companion's intention; but recovering from her indignant amazement, she exclaimed, whilst her cheek flushed crimson:

"Why did you do that, Madame D'Aulnay?"

"Simply because I will not have my darling little cousin made miserable by dwelling over and pondering on the prosy letters of any narrow-minded, strait-laced old woman. Why, that absurd epistle caused you a head-ache and crying-fit yesterday; and, think you, I will run the risk of a repetition of the same thing to-day, especially whilst you are in such a nervous, exhausted state?"

"You did very wrong, Lucille," replied the girl, reproachfully; "but I will say no more on the subject, as I doubt not you intended well."

"Many thanks, little one, for your prompt forgiveness; and in return for it, I will impart to you a secret which I have just discovered. Why do you not ask what it is? Well, I will reveal it without any pressing. It is the pleasant fact that you have made a complete conquest of the handsomest and most fascinating man in the circle of our acquaintance. Audley Sternfield is deeply in love with you."

A rosy flush instantly overspread Antoinette's face, whilst Mrs. D'Aulnay archly added:

"And to follow up my discoveries, I do not think he loves in vain."

Eagerly the young girl strove to refute the charge, but her blushes and confusion increased, till at length she desisted and listened in silence to her companion's raillery. When the latter finally paused, she gravely resumed—

"Lucille, I am sincere in saying I do not think I love him. I admire him very much, prefer his society to that of most other men"—

"Why, you delightfully innocent little creature, what is all this but love? I did not feel the half of it for Mr. D'Aulnay, when I married him. Seriously, you are very fortunate, and will be an object of envy to all the young girls of our acquaintance. Independent of his matchless personal gifts and accomplishments, he belongs to an excellent family, and, despite his comparative youth, his military rank is high. Why, before you are six years married to him, you will probably be a Colonel's wife."

"Married to him, Lucille! how can you talk so thoughtlessly?—Have you not just read my father's letter?"

"What of it, child? Who ever heard of fathers in real or fictitious life,—on the stage or off it,—doing what they ought to do, or acting in a kind and reasonable manner? They are always either striving to force their daughters into marriages which would ensure their misery, or seeking to prevent them contracting those which would procure their happiness. A girl must have spirit, and allow no authority to come between herself and the man she loves, especially if he be a passable match in a worldly point of view."

The practical suggestion contained in the latter part of Mrs. D'Aulnay's speech seemed somewhat inconsistent with the previous romantic tenor of her eloquence; but Antoinette, without noticing the discrepancy, quickly rejoined:

"You should not speak thus, Lucille. I do not know what some fathers may be, but I know that mine has always been kind and indulgent,—has always acted in a manner calculated to ensure my deepest love and respect."

"All very well, child, whilst you have submitted, as heretofore, to his will in everything; but wait till you venture to oppose or differ from him on any material point. Believe me, dearest, I know more of life than you can possibly do; and you will yet acknowledge the correctness of my opinion."

Alas, what a dangerous guide and companion had fallen to Antoinette's lot! How little chance had her simple childish reasoning against the refined sophistries of this accomplished woman of the world!

CHAPTER 10

THE following morning Colonel Evelyn called to enquire how Miss De Mirecourt was, but he did not ask to see her, merely leaving his card.

"Well, that is more than I would have expected from such a semi-barbarian, especially after the loss of his splendid horses," was Mrs. D'Aulnay's qualified encomium.

In the afternoon the ladies went down to the drawing-room, and soon after Major Sternfield entered. There was an indescribable gentleness in his manner, which made Antoinette imagine she had never yet seen him appear to such advantage; and she began to think Mrs. D'Aulnay must be right, and that she really did love him. Contrary to her usual wont, the hostess left the room on some trifling pretext, after a half-hour's conversation, and Antoinette, with a feeling of unusual nervousness, caused probably by a recollection of the secret her cousin had imparted to her the day previous, found herself alone with Audley Sternfield.

The latter was not one to lose an opportunity he had eagerly sought and desired, and, after alluding in eloquent words, rendered still more persuasive by the musical tones in which they were uttered, to the agitation and alarm her late accident had caused him, he poured forth protestations of love and devotion into the ear of his blushing listener. 'Tis not to be wondered at that such terms of impassioned devotion, whispered for the first time to a young romantic girl, should be fraught with dangerous power; and when we remember that the speaker was one endowed with the rarest personal gifts, we will cease to wonder if Antoinette sat confused and silent, feeling that

53

she did, she must reciprocate in some measure the ardent love lavished on herself. Still the answer, the little monosyllabic "yes" that Sternfield so earnestly implored, came not; and feeling that moments to him of golden worth were rapidly passing, he suddenly knelt beside her, and taking her hand in his, renewed his petition with more impassioned fervor than before.

At that moment the sound of a door closing at the end of the passage fell on Antoinette's ear, and she hurriedly exclaimed "Rise, for heaven's sake, Major Sternfield; rise! I hear some one coming."

"What of that, Antoinette? Here will I remain till I receive some hope—some word of encouragement—till you whisper me, yes."

"Yes, then yes," was the girl's quick, almost indistinct reply. "Rise at once."

"Thanks, my own," murmured he, raising the hand he still held, to his lips, and rapidly passing on one of the slight fingers a splendid opal ring, the seal of their mutual betrothal.

Here Mrs. D'Aulnay entered, and a slight but well-pleased smile flitted across her face as her glance passed from Sternfield's handsome features, glowing with happy triumph, to the embarrassed, averted countenance of her cousin. The gentleman did not greatly prolong his stay, for his quick tact told him that his absence just then would prove a great relief to his shy betrothed; but as he took leave of Mrs. D'Aulnay, where she stood a little apart, looking from a window, he whispered:

"How can I ever thank you sufficiently, my true and generous friend! My suit has been favorably received."

A kindly smile was his answer, and then, as the door closed upon him, Mrs. D'Aulnay approached and threw herself on a sofa beside her companion. The latter however seemed in no mood for conversation; and unwilling to compel her confidence, the lady touched lightly on indifferent topics, passing, apparently without design, a warm eulogium on Sternfield, which almost set at rest sundry uneasy doubts and reflections which even then were agitating Antoinette's mind. That night, however, when the young girl, according to her wont, bade an affectionate good night to her hostess, the latter took her hand, and, glancing significantly at the brilliant ring that sparkled there, imprinted a kiss on her fair young cheek, whispering at the same time words of earnest joyful gratulation, to which Antoinette replied only by blushes and a slight pressure from her tiny fingers.

A day or two after, Jeanne entered the drawing-room to announce a visitor for Mademoiselle Antoinette, and her smiling, satisfied look presented a marked contrast to the grim disapproval with which she ever heralded the approach of any of King George's gallant officers, for whom she entertained, individually and collectively, a profound antipathy.

"Who is it, Jeanne?"

"A young gentleman, Mademoiselle. One much nicer than any we have seen about here for some time past."

Mrs. D'Aulnay quietly smiled at this unceremonious speech, but uttered no remark, whilst the privileged Jeanne continued, "I am sure Mademoiselle will be pleased to see Mr. Beauchesne."

"Louis Beauchesne!" quickly repeated the lady of the house. "Oh, he brings you letters or special messages from home, Antoinette, so I will go to the library for a little while, as I wish to speak to Mr. D'Aulnay, but I will return soon. Jeanne, show this favored young gentleman up at once."

Shortly after, a young man of five-and-twenty with a clear ringing voice and open handsome countenance, entered the apartment, and accosted Antoinette with a degree of familiarity which betokened that great intimacy, if not friendship, existed between the two parties. The first few moments of friendly questioning over, it suddenly struck the young girl that there was an unusual degree of constraint about her companion's manner; and she was on the point of frankly asking the cause, when the latter drew a letter from his breast-pocket and handed it to her, exclaiming, in a somewhat embarrassed voice, "From your father, Antoinette"; after which brief piece of information, he rose and walked towards a window.

Antoinette's quick glance rapidly scanned the contents of the epistle; and astonishment, perplexity, and annoyance successively passed over her countenance as she read on.

At length she sharply exclaimed, "Are you acquainted with the contents of this letter, Louis?"

"I might hazard a guess at its purport," Beauchesne hesitatingly rejoined, "though your father did not show it to me."

"No prevarication," was the quick reply. "You know as well as myself, that my father informs me here in the most sudden and unexpected manner, that he has chosen you as my future husband, and that I am to receive you as such."

Beauchesne's dark cheek slightly flushed, but he made no reply, whilst his companion petulantly resumed; "Why do you not speak? Surely you agree with me that the whole thing is most absurd and unreasonable?"

"Pardon me, Antoinette," and the young man's tone plainly betrayed both mortification and wounded feeling. "Pardon me, but I really see nothing so very ridiculous in the proposition. Moving in the same circle—belonging to the same race and creed—intimate together from earliest childhood—"

"Yes, there it is," she hastily interrupted. "The friendly familiarity in which we have grown up together, has taught us to love each other dearly, but only as brother and sister."

"Again, pardon me," and this time an almost imperceptible smile curved the corners of his handsome mouth. "On that point, at least, I am fully competent to judge, and can assure you that my love is something more than brotherly in its fervor and warmth."

"How provoking you are, Louis! you speak in that strain merely to annoy me."

"Antoinette, be petulant—unkind if you will, but do not be unjust," he replied, approaching close to her chair, and fixing his earnest gaze upon her face. "I *do* love you, and my affection is not the less sincere that it is unaccompanied by any of those frenzied outbursts of passion which all lovers in romances or melodramas are bound to indulge in."

Poor Louis! At that moment the perverse Antoinette was mentally contrasting, and greatly to his disadvantage, this really rational, truthful declaration of affection with the late impassioned words and looks of Audley Sternfield. Perhaps something of what was passing in her mind, betrayed itself in her countenance, for Beauchesne continued with a slight touch of bitterness:

"But, I forget, you may perhaps have been listening of late to the love-vows of those who are proficients in the art in which I am only a novice. What chance of success has my simple, unstudied speech against the polished eloquence of those gallant gentlemen of the sword, who have perhaps made love in a dozen different climes to as many different women? You forget, Antoinette, I labor under the singular disadvantage of your being the first idol my heart has worshipped—your ear the first into which I would pour promises or vows of love."

The truth of some of the allusions contained in Louis's last speech, dyed the young girl's cheek with tell-tale blushes, and she was too much confused to venture on a reply. Beauchesne partly read the truth in her embarrassment; and he quickly resumed, in tones in which regret had replaced the bitterness which had marked his previous words:

"Surely it is not really so, Antoinette? Surely you have not given so quickly to a stranger the love you refuse to the tried friend of childhood?"

"It matters not how that may be, Louis dear," she replied, deeply touched by the appealing gentleness of his last words; "but do not be angry with me if I frankly and truly declare I never can return your love."

"So be it," he calmly rejoined, but his lip slightly quivered as he spoke. " 'Tis better we should understand each other at once. May the one you have chosen prove one half as true and faithful as I would have done."

A pause followed, which was broken by Antoinette exclaiming in a troubled voice, "I fear papa will be very angry with me. Did he seem exceedingly anxious for our marriage?"

"So anxious that he never even counted on the possibility of my failure."

"I suppose, then, that whenever he learns the real state of things, he will hasten here in great anger, and terrify me to death"; and her eyes filled with tears at the prospect her fancy had thus conjured up.

The kind-hearted Beauchesne, touched, notwithstanding his late grievous disappointment, by the childish fears of his companion, encouragingly replied, "that he felt assured Mr. De Mirecourt was too just and indulgent to blame his daughter for refusing her hand where she could not give her heart."

"Ah! I do not know that. Papa is kind, but he does not like opposition of any sort. Louis dear, if you would only be generous enough to help me!" and she looked up eagerly in his face.

"How?" he briefly questioned.

"When you return, tell papa, what of course you ought and do secretly feel, that as my affections are not yours, you will no longer seek my hand."

"Most assuredly, Antoinette De Mirecourt," he rejoined, irritation and amusement struggling for the mastery in his breast, "I will do no such thing: be thankful that I do not tell him I am willing to wait for you, even seven years long, as Jacob waited for his bride."

"Well, then, tell me Louis, that you forgive me for what has just passed between us. Promise me that we shall remain as fast friends as we have hitherto been!"

There was no resisting that entreating look, that pleading, coaxing tone; and the young man frankly grasping her hand, rejoined, "I promise willingly. Yes, as we cannot be lovers, we shall at least remain friends. But I must leave you now: I have imperative business to attend to."

"You must not go without seeing Madame D'Aulnay. She would be quite angry with you."

"Frankly, I would rather forego that pleasure to-day. Lucille is no great favorite of mine."

"Nonsense! she expects you to remain here, and will be vexed with me if I allow you to leave without her seeing you. Wait but one moment: I will bring her immediately," and Antoinette hastened from the room.

During her absence, another visitor, Major Sternfield, was shown into the drawing-room. On his entrance, young Beauchesne, with his usual frank courtesy, bowed, preparatory to exchanging some commonplace remarks with the new-comer; but the latter, falling back on the sublime dandyism which he had the tact to keep in abeyance when in the society of Mrs. D'Aulnay and her cousin, or of his own intimate friends, inquiringly stared at this unknown candidate for the honor of his acquaintance; and then sinking back in the deep easy-chair which Antoinette had just vacated, and on the arm of which her perfumed handkerchief still lay, industriously commenced dusting his well-fitting boot with his tiny, agate-headed cane.

Beauchesne, humorously determined to show the Exclusive that supercilious impertinence was not the special prerogative of any class or profession, lounged across the room to the mantle-mirror, and commenced pulling up his collar and running his hand through his thick raven curls with a self-concentrated solicitude, an utter forgetfulness of time and place, which successfully rivalled in impertinence even Sternfield's super-refined dandyism. On the entrance of the ladies, Louis, exercising the prerogative of intimate acquaintance, turned languidly towards them, listlessly hoping they were well, and then sank on a couch with a wearied *nonchalance* which was a tolerably faithful reproduction of the manner in which Major Sternfield had just performed the same action.

The latter seeing at once that this daring *provincial* was actually turning him into ridicule, darted a covert flashing glance upon him, and Mrs. D'Aulnay, comprehending the position of affairs, quickly exclaimed:

"Oh! come here, Louis, I want to ask you a question about Uncle De Mirecourt."

She retreated into the hall as if to ask or impart something of a confidential nature, and when the somewhat unwilling Louis had joined her, she caught his arm and playfully shaking him, enquired in a whisper: "What sort of an impression did he intend giving her guest of Canadian politeness."

"As good as that which he has given me of foreign breeding," was the cool reply. "But tell me, Lucille, in heaven's name, is yonder handsome coxcomb the chosen lover of Antoinette?"

"He is certainly a great admirer of hers, and I believe a somewhat favored one," was the hesitating reply; "but, Louis, you must not talk of, or treat Major Sternfield so contemptuously: he is a man of rare gifts, and—"

"There, there, Lucille, that will do," and he strove impatiently to shake off the little hand that still rested on his arm. "God help her, poor child! she will learn soon that what she takes for pure gold is but dross. No, I cannot stay to-day. Do not urge me further. Say farewell to Antoinette for me. *Au revoir*"; and breaking from the hand that still sought to detain him, he hurriedly left the house.

Mrs. D'Aulnay mused a moment, and then murmuring, "Certainly a disappointed suitor!" slowly turned back into the drawing-room, thinking what a terrible sacrifice it would be to give Antoinette to such a lover.

CHAPTER 11

MAJOR Sternfield, whose equanimity had been considerably ruffled by his meeting with Louis Beauchesne, did not stay long; and after he had taken his departure, the letter which Louis had brought was again read, and its contents discussed by both ladies. The somewhat arbitrary though kindly tone of the epistle was triumphantly pointed out by Mrs. D'Aulnay as an irresistible proof of the truth of her theory respecting the unreasonable tyranny of fathers, where their daughters' affections were concerned; and her conjectures with regard to the extremities Mr. De Mirecourt would proceed to in order to enforce his wishes, put Antoinette into a state of feverish restlessness which effectually banished sleep from her pillow that night. A severe headache, which confined her the ensuing morning to her room, was the consequence; so that when Sternfield called with some book or trifling message for her, he found no one but Mrs. D'Aulnay in the drawing-room. His visit, however, proved anything but wearisome; for his companion took advantage of their *tête-a-tête* to frankly communicate to him the contents of the letter of which Louis had been the bearer; informing him, at the same time, of Mr. De Mirecourt's intense prejudices against foreigners, and of his formally declared determination to never allow his daughter to marry one. Sternfield's stay was unusually protracted; and towards its close, had any curious eye glanced into the drawing-room, it would have seen him in the act of holding Mrs. D'Aulnay's hand, whilst voice and eyes were alike eloquent in preferring some request. For a long time the lady hesitated and wavered; but at length, touched by his entreaties, she bowed her head in token of assent.

62

"Thanks, thanks, my true and generous friend!" he vehemently exclaimed. "You have saved Antoinette and myself."

"I do not feel so sure of that. I can do but little for you. Everything depends on your influence with my fair cousin herself; but you can call again this afternoon, and I will give you an opportunity of pressing your suit."

Mrs. D'Aulnay kept her word; and when Major Sternfield repeated his visit at a later period of the day, some inevitable writing obliged her to leave the room shortly after his entrance, whilst, singularly enough, though several acquaintances called, none found their way into the drawing-room. After a time Sternfield took his departure, whilst Antoinette, with a flushed cheek and contracted brow, escaped to her own room. Thither she was soon followed by Mrs. D'Aulnay, who found her pacing the apartment with quick, nervous steps, and heightened color.

"What is the matter, Antoinette? Are you still ill?" she enquired in a kind tone.

"Ill, and unhappy," was the hurried, agitated reply. "Shall I, or shall I not, confide in you?" and the speaker looked earnestly, wistfully into her cousin's countenance, which wore a look of innocent unconsciousness.

Oh! could Antoinette's better angel have spoken then, how he would have urged her to turn from that dangerous mentor, and place her confidence in those who would have proved more worthy of the trust. But it was the soft musical tones of Mrs. D'Aulnay that made themselves heard, as she gently insinuated her affection for Antoinette, and her earnest desire to promote the latter's happiness in all things. Little by little she at length drew from the young girl a confession, that Sternfield, who seemed by some wonderful instinct (so poor Antoinette in her simplicity said) to have divined the contents of the letter which Louis had brought, had been using every possible entreaty and argument to induce her to a secret marriage.

"And what answer did you give him, dear?"

"Of course, I peremptorily refused," was the petulant reply. "Why, you are almost as bad as Sternfield himself, Lucille, to ask me such a question."

"Well, child, abuse me if you will, but I really do not condemn his proposal as strongly as you seem to do. Once wedded, your father would have no alternative but that of forgiving and receiving you again into favor; whilst now, he may forbid your union with Sternfield, under threats so severe, that you dare not disobey him."

"Well, if he does so, I must submit," rejoined Antoinette, moodily. "I cannot, I dare not, deceive him to such an extent."

"What, submit! Yield up the man you love for a father's whim,—sacrifice the happiness of your whole life to a mere prejudice!"

"Filial duty and affection are neither whims nor prejudices," retorted Antoinette indignantly. "Papa has always been kind and indulgent, and to deceive him so terribly would be indeed but a poor return for all his affection."

"Perhaps you are right, child," was the quiet reply; "and I begin to think it would be as well on the whole to obey him on every point. Louis will make a good, humdrum sort of husband; and even if your connubial happiness occasionally prove somewhat monotonous—even if you regret at times the never-to-be-recalled past—your filial duty and your own conscience will prove your reward."

"Lucille, you are very provoking to-day! Rejecting a secret marriage with Major Sternfield is one thing, and wedding Louis Beauchesne is another."

"Oh! you will find them synonymous, cousin mine. Uncle De Mirecourt is not a man to be trifled with, and your refusal to wed the suitor he may choose for you will prove as unavailing as would the struggles of a linnet against the strong grasp that would seek to place it in a cage. But you look flushed and feverish, dear child. Seek your pillow, and take counsel from it."

Alas! Antoinette did so, instead of seeking direction from that unfailing source of light which would have guided her footsteps so unerringly amid the snares into which they had wandered. Still, for two days she scrupulously avoided any mention of Sternfield's name, evading, with equal care, all further discussion regarding him with Mrs. D'Aulnay; and the latter began to think the handsome Englishman's chance was a hopeless one, when help came to his cause from a quarter, the very last from which it might have been expected. This was in the shape of a very severe, very imperious letter from Mr. De Mirecourt to his daughter, mentioning that he had just heard from a lady who had recently left Montreal, of the notorious flirtation she was carrying on with some English officer, and that he was coming to town in a week to put an end to the affair by hurrying on her marriage with the husband he had chosen for her.

This letter, most certainly ill-judged and arbitrary, corroborating so fully all Mrs. D'Aulnay's late predictions, had a most pernicious effect on Antoinette's already wavering mind, and she had recourse again to her cousin for advice and encouragement. 'Tis needless to say in what shape the latter administered it; and she now openly and constantly spoke of an immediate and secret marriage as the only alternative left.

CHAPTER 12

ADDITIONAL cause of mental trouble and anxiety presented itself in the absence of Major Sternfield, who, since Antoinette's indignant rejection of his proposal, had not returned to the house.

Whether this was the result of disappointment and wounded feeling, or that of simple calculation on his part, it is impossible to say. If the latter, he certainly proved himself a clever tactician, for his absence served his cause far more effectually than his presence could have done. Left almost entirely to herself—for she felt too unhappy to see any of the general run of "callers" who daily presented themselves in her cousin's *salons*—half distracted by fears of her father's forcing on her marriage with Louis, or visiting on her the full weight of his anger if she resisted, she missed with an acuteness, a feverish anxiety, she would have heretofore deemed impossible, the honeyed words, the tender protestations, which of late Audley Sternfield had so constantly breathed into her ear.

Mrs. D'Aulnay, who, partly out of kindly feeling to Antoinette, as well as to Sternfield, whose mutual happiness she thought could be alone secured by marriage—partly out of a silly sentimentalism, seeking excitement of some sort or other—was determined to bring about their union, if possible; so far from doing anything in her power to alleviate Antoinette's very apparent wretchedness, strove rather to increase it. Now, affecting to look on the latter's marriage with a suitor she did not love, as inevitable, and pitying her in consequence; then, gently blaming her timidity, her obstinacy in refusing to wed the one she did. These exhortations she always concluded by repeating that once her young cousin was

66

united to Sternfield, they would have no difficulty in obtaining her father's forgiveness, though the latter would inevitably keep his word of wedding her to Louis if no obstacle, beyond his daughter's unwillingness, presented itself. Another time she would wonder, and comment on Sternfield's protracted absence—hint, that discouraged by Antoinette's coldness and contemptuous rejection of his suit, he had abandoned it, or perhaps turned his attentions to some other quarter where they would be more flatteringly received; and then she would leave Antoinette to reflections which dyed her brow with humiliating blushes, and made her heart ache as it had never ached before. It was at the end of such a conversation, that Mrs. D'Aulnay rose to dress for a drive, in which Antoinette had petulantly declined joining her, saying,—

"Well, it is probably better for all parties that Sternfield has ceased his visits here, for what could they avail but to render you both more wretched. In two days at farthest, your father will arrive; and before another month, you will be Louis's very obedient, very loving wife."

"Never!" she vehemently exclaimed. "I shall live and die single first."

But as reflection brought up before her the inflexible determination of her father's will when once fully bent on any point, the passionate flush on her cheek faded, and she wearily leaned her head on the small table near her, faint and sick at heart. From her father, her thoughts turned to the recreant Audley, who had wearied so soon of a lover's supplicating attitude, and the quickened beating of her heart as his image mentally rose before her, even though irritation mingled with the warmer feelings she entertained for him, whispered more energetically than aught else could have done, "that now, at least, she ought not to become the bride of Louis." The opening of the hall-door, announcing the probable advent of some visitor, but increased the morbid irritation of her feelings; and as the door of the apartment in which she was sitting unclosed, she impatiently exclaimed, without raising her head from the arm on which it was bowed:

"Not at home, Jeanne, not at home to any one."

"Still less of all others to me, Antoinette," whispered a deep musical voice beside her; and her quickly raised, startled glance, encountered the dark eyes of Audley Sternfield, fixed in pleading, deprecating entreaty upon her.

"Forgive me, my beloved, this once, for thrusting Jeanne aside, and forcing myself on your presence unannounced, but I have just learned that Mr. De Mirecourt arrives to-morrow, and I have that to say to you which must be said. Tell me, first, though, that you forgive me"; and he caught Antoinette's hand, which she passively suffered him to retain, averting from him, however, her pale and troubled countenance. "I have come, mine own, to implore your forgiveness for the annoyance I caused you in our last interview—to atone for my madness and folly."

"You have taken time to do so," returned his companion, her delicate lip nervously quivering.

Oh! unwary, inexperienced Antoinette, how much was unconsciously implied, acknowledged in that childish reproach! Major Sternfield's triumphant glance told he took in its full import; but in tones of softest humility, he continued, as he seated himself beside her:

"You ordered me from your presence, my own Antoinette, and I dared not seek you again till your anger, which my presumption had perhaps justly evoked, was somewhat appeased."

But why follow that wily man of the world through his course of passionate entreaty, deprecation, and well-feigned despair? What chance against him had the yielding, child-like Antoinette, unsustained as she then was by the religious principles, to whose holy suggestions she willfully closed her heart? As might be foreseen, the tempter triumphed; and on his again repeating, for the twentieth time, his proposal of an immediate marriage, she at length bowed her pale cheek on his shoulder, and burst into a passionate flood of tears.

"This evening, my beloved," he whispered, as he pressed her cold, still half-reluctant hand to his lips, again and again.

Antoinette's tears flowed still faster, but she spoke not. Her silence, however, was answer enough for her lover, and he continued: "kind Mrs. D'Aulnay will befriend us as she has ever heretofore done; and here, in her drawing-room, Doctor Ormsby, the chaplain of our regiment, will unite us by those sacred bonds which will give me the blessed right to call you all my own."

"Dr. Ormsby," repeated Antoinette, with a bewildered look, which told the peculiar circumstances of a secret marriage now fully dawned for the first time upon her. Yes, it must indeed be so. No Catholic priest would or dared marry her thus privately and secretly. Her father, too, was daily expected—no farther time allowed for hesitation, for delay. Wofully as the young girl had retrograded from the standard of truth, and pure, strict uprightness, which had been hers when she first arrived beneath Mrs. D'Aulnay's roof,—negligent as she had latterly grown in prayer, and in the fulfilment of all her religious duties, enough remained of olden feelings and principles, to make her shrink from the idea of a clandestine marriage, unhallowed by a father's blessing, and that religious benediction, which she had been taught from childhood to regard as so solemn and necessary a part of the marriage service. Sternfield saw her increased trouble, and divined at once the cause. Eloquently he spoke of Doctor Ormsby's worth and goodness, and gently insinuated how little mattered slight differences of ceremonies.

"Ah! yes," interrupted his companion, with a slight shudder, "to you it is but a ceremony,—to me it is, or ought to be, a sacrament."

"But, my beloved, our nuptials shall be blessed and solemnized again, if you wish it, by a clergyman of your own faith, whenever your father shall have been informed of our marriage,—nay, before then—to-morrow, if you will. Antoinette, my own Antoinette, what is there that love like mine would hesitate to grant you?"

Silenced, though not convinced, she made no reply, for passion at that moment spoke louder in her heart than principle; and now every obstacle vanquished, every objection overcome, Sternfield poured forth his ardent expressions of love and gratitude, unmindful, almost careless in the proud height of his triumph, that tears were still flowing down her pale cheek, and that the little hand he held so closely was as cold as one of her own Canadian icicles. This singular lover's interview was brought to an end by Mrs. D'Aulnay's entrance, some short time after; and a glance at Sternfield's happy, triumphant countenance, so forcibly contrasted by the pale, agitated face of his companion, enabled her to form at once an accurate guess at the real state of matters. Antoinette rose on her cousin's entrance, and left the room, but not before Sternfield had imprinted a kiss on her hand, whispering in an audible tone:

"This evening, my Antoinette, at seven."

"Well, Major Sternfield, I see you have diligently improved your time. So day and hour are settled!" exclaimed Mrs. D'Aulnay, fixing a penetrating glance on her military friend. Perhaps the exultant triumph that beamed on his handsome face, slightly jarred with her sentimental ideas of what a lover's reverential devotion should be, infusing probably, at the same time, some uneasy fears into her mind, regarding the absolute certainty of Antoinette's future wedded happiness,—a thing of which, till the present moment, she had never entertained even the shadow of a doubt. The quick-sighted Sternfield detected at once the cloud on Mrs. D'Aulnay's countenance, slight as it was, and, probably divining the cause, instantly advanced towards her, exclaiming,

"My dear, kind Madame D'Aulnay, you, who have listened so indulgently, so patiently to all my doubts, hopes, and fears, will not wonder that I am nearly intoxicated with joy, when I tell you that Antoinette has consented to become mine by the holiest of all ties, this very evening. Oh, best and dearest friend, I could kneel to you, if you would permit it, to pour forth my thanks—my unbounded gratitude."

The handsome speaker seemed very much in earnest, and the lady, completely appeased, smiled kindly upon him, as she rejoined:

"Enough, Major Sternfield: I believe in your sincerity. And now, if this solemn affair is really to come off this evening, I must send you away, for I have a great deal to do."

The young man kissed the fair hand held out to him; an act of gallantry which the speaker, who was equally proud of her pretty tapering fingers, and splendid rings, seldom objected to, and hurried away. Mrs. D'Aulnay did not at once seek Antoinette, for the one glance she had obtained of her tearful, pale face, on entering the drawing-room, told it would scarcely prove a propitious time for consultation or discussion, yet. Instead, she proceeded to her own chamber, and rang for Jeanne, with whom she was closeted a half-hour, giving her some household directions. Then she sought Mr. D'Aulnay, and chatted another half-hour with him, incidentally mentioning that she and Antoinette expected a couple of gentlemen friends in the evening, a precaution which she knew would infallibly keep her husband in his library. The early winter evening was rapidly closing in; and giving a passing glance at the drawing-rooms, to assure herself that lights and fires were brightly burning, she sought her young cousin's room. The latter was standing near the bed-room window, her forehead pressed against the panes as if she were watching the snow-storm wildly raging without, the falling flakes of which, caught up by the fierce wind, were whirled against the casement, or blown about in blinding masses, obscuring for the moment everything in earth or sky.

"Good heavens, child!" exclaimed Mrs. D'Aulnay, almost angrily, "what are you dreaming about? Five o'clock, and priest and bridegroom expected in a couple of hours!"

Her annoyance was excusable, for Antoinette still wore the soft dark stuff she had put on in the early part of the day, and no ribbons, flowers, or lighter garments lying about, betokened any intention of assuming a more suitable costume. But as the young girl slowly turned her pallid, tear-stained face, towards the new-comer, the heart of the latter smote her, and she felt she must console and encourage, instead of finding fault.

"Come here, Antoinette, darling, to the fire," she kindly exclaimed: "you will take cold near the window. It is time to think, too, about what you will wear this evening, for you must look your very best."

The bride-elect made no reply, but the expression of wretchedness on that usually bright and sparkling countenance, told how indifferent all minor details were to her then. A violent struggle, fierce as that of the storm she was watching, had been passing in her breast during the previous hour; and better thoughts, and good inspirations had been combatting powerfully for the mastery. The strife was not yet over; for as Mrs. D'Aulnay, alarmed at her pallor and silence, drew her towards her, repeating her questions, she whispered,

"Lucille, I cannot, I dare not venture on this terrible step! 'Twould be a union unblessed by God or man."

Mrs. D'Aulnay sank into a chair, in speechless amazement and indignation. Antoinette De Mirecourt's destiny was trembling then in the balance. One word of good advice, one encouraging look, would have given her strength to have drawn back from the precipice on which she was standing; but, alas! that strengthening word or look came not, and instead, her companion burst forth:

"Are you mad, utterly mad, Antoinette? Your consent, your promise given—your lover, with the clergyman, whose assistance he has asked, on their way here—"

"But my father; oh Lucille, my father!" gasped forth the girl, her cheek turning to still deathlier whiteness.

"Don't speak to me about your father!" retorted Mrs. D'Aulnay, now fairly roused to anger. "The harm, if harm there is, is entirely his doing. What right has he to dispose of you to Louis Beauchesne, as if you were a farm or field he wished to get rid of? Decide, now and for ever, between the husband he has selected for you, and the one your heart has chosen. Aye! choose between Louis Beauchesne and Audley Sternfield. But I am wasting words, my poor little cousin," she added in a softened tone: "your final choice is already made, though that wayward heart shrinks from acknowledging it. I see I must be your tire-woman for the occasion; and 'tis as well, for I am determined Audley shall feel proud of you."

CHAPTER 13

TURNING to Antoinette's ward-robe, she hastily selected a rose-colored silk dress, and, bringing it forward, exclaimed:

"You are too pale for white this evening; besides, as we are comparatively alone, it might excite the remarks of the servants. This soft, warm color will give something of that glow to your complexion in which it is so sadly deficient to-night."

Under Mrs. D'Aulnay's skillful fingers, the process of dressing was a speedy one; but if hours had been lavished on the task, the result could scarcely have been more successful. Major Sternfield had indeed a lovely bride.

"Come to the drawing-room, now, you little nervous creature," the elder lady smilingly exclaimed. "You must be seated there quietly for a half hour at least, before they come in, for I can hear the beating of your heart as plainly, almost, as the ticking of yonder pendulum."

Once in the drawing-room, Mrs. D'Aulnay took good care to leave her companion little time for serious reflections; for she passed from one subject to another, with a vivacity and rapidity of utterance, which almost overpowered Antoinette's already over-tasked brain. Once, however, perhaps from weariness, she suddenly paused, and a long silence ensued. Antoinette's eyes were fixed on the floor, and, by the light of the lamp on the table near her, in whose full radiance she sat, Mrs. D'Aulnay earnestly scrutinized her features. There was something in their peculiar set expression which sent an uneasy fear through that lady's heart as to the wisdom of the step on which she was strongly encouraging, if not almost forcing the young girl committed to her charge, and suddenly, impulsively she exclaimed:

74

"Tell me, Antoinette, darling, do you not truly, deeply love Audley Sternfield?"

For the first time that day, something like a smile flitted over the girl's face, as she replied: "Why, you have told me yourself a hundred times that I did, after questioning and cross-questioning me more strictly than any lawyer could have done."

"Yes, but does not your own heart tell you that you do?" was the rapid, almost agitated inquiry.

For a moment Antoinette was silent; and then, as memory called up before her the fascinating handsome Sternfield, with all his boundless devotion to herself, a shy smile played round her lips, and she murmured, "yes."

"Thank you, sweet cousin, for the avowal!" replied Mrs. D'Aulnay, throwing her arms around her; and feeling almost as delighted with the acknowledgment, in her new-born anxiety, as Sternfield himself could have done. "Thank you a hundred times; and now I will ring for Jeanne to bring you a glass of wine. You look bent on being nervous and provoking, by and bye."

It was Jeanne who answered the summons, and when her mistress exclaimed, "Let tea be given in the drawing-room: I expect a couple of friends," she rejoined, "Oh, madame, nobody that could help it would venture out to-night: 'tis most fearful weather!"

Her mistress quietly smiled in reply, inwardly thinking how terrible would be the storm which could prevent *one* of their expected guests from coming. As the door closed upon Jeanne, a furious blast struck the casement, and caused Antoinette to give a nervous start.

" 'Tis all for the best, dearest," was her companion's smiling remark. "We need be under no apprehensions of unwelcome intruders dropping in. Ah! there are our friends," she added as voices and footsteps sounded in the hall, and sundry stampings betokened the new-comers were endeavoring to divest themselves of the snowy covering with which the storm had favored them. In another moment Major Sternfield and his companion Dr. Ormsby were in the drawing-room, and the ceremony of introduction was gone through. The clergyman, a young, intellectual-looking man with dark earnest eyes, replied briefly, almost coldly, to Mrs. D'Aulnay's flattering welcome, and, as soon as they were seated, stole an earnest scrutinizing glance towards Antoinette, beside whose chair Sternfield was already bending. Neither the pink hue of her dress, the heated atmosphere of the drawing-room, nor yet the presence of her lover, had brought color to her cheek, or animation to her eye; and the minister's earnest gaze grew yet more serious and his expression more thoughtful, as he watched her. Rapidly, imploringly Sternfield whispered in the girl's ear; and at length, when Mrs. D'Aulnay, whose patience was almost exhausted by the want of gallantry of her clerical guest, exclaimed, "Antoinette dear, we must not trespass on Dr. Ormsby's valuable time," she briefly, almost irritably replied, "I am ready."

Mrs. D'Aulnay turned quickly to the door, which she noiselessly fastened, and then moved to the table near which the remainder of the party were now standing. For a moment Dr. Ormsby's calm, earnest glance rested on Antoinette, and he then gently said:

"You are very young, Miss De Mirecourt, and 'tis a life-long engagement on which you are about to enter. Have you weighed well its duties and its purport?"

"It seems to me that your question, Dr. Ormsby, is a very singular and unnecessary one," interrupted Sternfield, with a dark frown.

"I am but doing my duty, Sir," was the grave, stern reply; "or rather, I fear I am about to overstep it, in keeping the promise I have given you. However, as I am here, if Miss De Mirecourt is still determined to wed you thus privately and hurriedly, 'tis not for me to raise opposition now."

Antoinette again repeated in an almost inaudible voice, "I am ready." In a few moments, those solemn words, "They whom God hath joined let no man put asunder," rang in their ears, and Antoinette De Mirecourt and Audley Sternfield were man and wife. After a few brief words of felicitation, Dr. Ormsby rose to take leave. In vain Mrs. D'Aulnay begged him to remain to partake of some refreshment—in vain the handsome bridegroom, who had now completely recovered his equanimity, repeated her entreaties: he was resolute. As he shook hands with Antoinette, she laid her little hand on his arm, and whispered in a tone inaudible to her companions:

"Promise me that you will keep my secret."

"That promise," he kindly rejoined, "I have already tacitly given Major Sternfield, and to you I now repeat it. Need I say it shall be sacredly kept?"

"Thank you, and bear witness, Doctor Ormsby," she rejoined in a louder though more agitated tone, "that I tell Major Sternfield in your presence, that till the marriage shall have been publicly acknowledged to the world, and celebrated again by a Roman Catholic priest, he and I shall be but friends to each other."

Dr. Ormsby gravely, kindly bowed his head, and then left the room; and as the yawning domestic showed out the tall stranger, he carelessly wondered at his early departure, little dreaming what a powerful, life-long influence his stay, short as it had been, had exercised over the future destinies of two of the occupants of the drawing-room. Meanwhile the parties in question were standing quietly around the table as if nothing unusual had happened; and Mrs. D'Aulnay and Major Sternfield were exchanging some commonplace remarks about Dr. Ormsby's gentlemanly manners and appearance; but the lady stole many a secret, uneasy glance towards the silent bride, the pallor of whose cheek had given place to a feverish vivid scarlet, such as the keenest wintry air, or the most violent exercise, had never perhaps yet called to it.

When the door closed upon the clergyman, Antoinette abruptly withdrew from Sternfield the hand he had immediately caught in his, and poured herself out a large glass of water, which she swallowed in a single draught; but the little fingers trembled so violently in raising it to her lips, that part of its contents were spilled on her bridal dress.

Mrs. D'Aulnay, naturally thinking that the lovers might wish to exchange a word alone, had, at first, quietly turned to leave the room; but a quick glance from the bride, half imploring, half authoritative, had warned her to stay. Unwilling to increase the agitation she read so plainly depicted in the latter's face, she addressed some commonplace observation to Sternfield, and then walked to the window; whilst Audley, probably actuated by a similar dread, repressed the ardent words that rose to his lips and continued to address her in the subdued strain of gentle affection which he justly divined would alone prove welcome at the moment to his trembling bride.

"What a fearful night!" exclaimed Mrs. D'Aulnay as she drew together the crimson curtains shading the window near which she was standing. " 'Tis snowing, storming, and drifting in a manner that will effectually block up the roads for days to come. Your father, Antoinette, cannot possibly arrive to-morrow."

"A welcome respite!" was the secret thought of all parties, but a thought to which no one gave expression; and then Major Sternfield took occasion to enquire, with much seeming interest, how many miles it was to Valmont. Shortly after, Mrs. D'Aulnay rang for tea, which was quickly served up, and all three continued to affect a composure and calm which none really felt. Another hour passed over, all circumstances considered very heavily; and then the hostess warned Sternfield by a glance towards the time-piece, that it was time for him to leave.

After a friendly clasp of the latter's hand and a few whispered words of gratitude, he turned to his shrinking, girlish bride, and, folding her in his arms, murmured, "My wife, my own!" For a moment that bright young head rested on his shoulder, and then with a convulsive sob, or rather gasp, she faltered:

"Audley, Audley, never give me cause to repent the irrevocable step I have taken to-night!" Another embrace was his only reply; and he left the apartment with a light step and a proud triumph in his face which was certainly not reflected from the countenances of his companions.

"Come to rest, Antoinette, darling!" exclaimed Mrs. D'Aulnay, when they were alone. "I will go with you to your room, and wait to see you in bed."

The girl passively obeyed; and when her gay evening-dress was laid aside, and her rich heavy braids of hair gathered up beneath the little snowy cap which made her fair young face look doubly youthful, she knelt before her prie-Dieu, but only to rise from it a moment afterwards, vehemently exclaiming, "Oh! Lucille, I cannot, I dare not pray to-night!"

"And, why not, you dear, fanciful little creature? It seems to me prayer is doubly incumbent on you now that you have a handsome, devoted husband to pray for. But do not mind it to-night: I see you are really ill and your hand is burning. Lie down at once."

Antoinette passively submitted, but the step brought no repose to mind or body; and for several hours her cousin sat at her bed-side, listening anxiously to the moaning and incoherent ravings which immediately ensued whenever sleep overpowered her, or soothing the nervous fancies or terrors which marked her waking moments. At length, about an hour after midnight, she sank into a deep, dreamless slumber; and Mrs. D'Aulnay retired to her own couch, more anxious and troubled than she would acknowledge even to herself.

CHAPTER 14

THE following morning, the young girl awoke with an intense, overpowering head-ache which kept her prisoner in her room the whole of the forenoon, much to the annoyance and disappointment of Sternfield, who called at an early hour; and who, when refused admittance by Jeanne, turned from the door with a lowering frown which excited that worthy woman's wrath to a high degree.

"One would think he was the master of the house," she resentfully muttered, as she closed the door upon him. "Why, he looked as if he was about to push me aside and force himself in as he did the other day when he wanted to see *Mademoiselle*."

She failed not on the first subsequent opportunity to communicate her ideas on the subject to her mistress, whose smooth brow contracted as she listened to the tale, in a manner which proved more satisfactory to Jeanne than it would have done to Major Sternfield had he witnessed it. Antoinette came down to dinner; and just as the ladies had sought the drawing-room, and Mr. D'Aulnay his library, the tinkle of sleigh-bells stopping before the door announced an arrival.

"My father," murmured Antoinette, turning pale as marble.

"Yes, it is indeed he," rejoined her companion, taking a hasty *réconnaissance* through the window. "Who would have expected him with such roads? And now, dear child, no tremors—no nervousness. If, by ill-fortune, your father happen to be in an unpropitious humor, do not run the risk of confessing your marriage now: precipitancy might spoil all."

Ere long, Mr. De Mirecourt—a carefully-dressed, stately-looking gentleman of the old French school—

80

entered; and his daughter, dreading to meet his penetrating glance, instantly threw herself into his arms. He embraced her affectionately, and then gently raising her face, he looked earnestly into it, exclaiming, after a moment:

" 'Tis as I feared, little one! This gay, fashionable life does not agree with a simple country girl like yourself. Why, you look three years older than you did when you left home; and though your cheeks are rosy enough, these burning little hands tell that your roses are more those of fever than of health."

"Antoinette did not rest well last night, dear uncle," said Mrs. D'Aulnay, who was standing beside the new-comer, her hand resting caressingly on his shoulder. "She is unusually nervous."

"There it is, my fair niece," was the smiling reply. "The usual fine lady's cant. Why, my little Antoinette, who used to give me breakfast every morning in the country at seven, and help to eat it too, with excellent appetite, scarcely knew then what the term nervous meant."

"But, *cher oncle*, Antoinette was scarcely more than a little girl a few months ago. She is a young lady now."

"A fine lady, you mean, Lucille. But it is not that alone: I find an indefinable change in her that I cannot describe. Perhaps it is that she is more graceful, more elegant in her style of dress; in short, more like my charming niece, Madame D'Aulnay," he good-humoredly added. "However, let my little girl's external appearance pass, 'tis well enough; but I cannot say I am well satisfied with her on other points. Aye, you may well blush!" he added, as Antoinette's face became painfully crimson. "I have two serious accusations to bring against you. But to begin with the first: What is the reason you reject Louis Beauchesne, the husband I have chosen for you—to whom I promised you?"

"Because, dear papa, I do not love him sufficiently well to marry him."

"Ah, Lucille, Lucille, this is your work," exclaimed Mr. De Mirecourt, reproachfully shaking his head at his niece. "Just what Mrs. Gérard foretold, when we discussed the propriety of accepting your invitation for Antoinette."

"But, dear uncle, I know you are too just, too kind, to force my cousin into a marriage with a man she does not love."

"She loves Louis quite as well as you did Mr. D'Aulnay when you wedded him; and who will presume to say that you are not a very happy couple? But *trêve* to this nonsense! I have made up my mind; and though I give her her own way about pocket-money, household matters, and other minor details, on this point I must have mine. She has known Louis long, always treated him with affectionate kindness, and is as well acquainted as I am with his irreproachable character. He is an excellent *parti* too in a worldly point of view, and I do not intend sacrificing so many combined advantages, in compliance with a girl's sentimental whim. So prepare to return home with me to-morrow, my daughter; or if I leave you another week here, it will be only to give you the chance of at once selecting your *trousseau*,—for, before this day month, Louis Beauchesne will be my son-in-law."

"But, dear dear papa," pleaded Antoinette, with tearful eyes, throwing her arms about Mr. De Mirecourt's neck as she spoke, "forgive me if I say I cannot marry Louis. I will do anything else you wish me to do—return with you to the country to-morrow, live as quietly as a hermit there"—

"Pshaw! enough of this folly!" interrupted Mr. De Mirecourt, unwinding, though not unkindly, the little arms encircling him. "I have overlooked your singular, I might say rather undutiful letter of last week, informing me that you could not, would not, listen to my wishes; but, Antoinette dear, you must not try my patience too far!"

A pause ensued, and then the young girl unclosed her lips twice as if to speak, but her resolution failed her, and she directed a pleading look towards Mrs. D'Aulnay, mutely asking her to enter on the dreaded explanation.

"Well, it is all settled then?" cheerfully enquired Mr. De Mirecourt, misinterpreting the momentary silence into a token of consent.

"Ah! I fear not, my dearest uncle," and Mrs. D'Aulnay's hand was again laid caressingly on his shoulder. "There may be an invincible obstacle to this union—one which, perhaps, cannot be overcome!"

Mrs. D'Aulnay had scarcely calculated on the effect her words would produce, or she might have hesitated before uttering them. Dashing off her hand, Mr. De Mirecourt sprang to his feet, and, looking angrily from one to the other, sternly repeated,

"Invincible obstacle! What do you, what can you mean, Lucille? But, pshaw!" he continued, less violently, " 'Tis only your romantic, exaggerated style of speech; unless, indeed,"—and here his gaze grew darker than before,— "that Antoinette has become entangled in a ridiculous love-affair with some of the gay military gallants who are probably allowed to over-run the house. I have heard a whisper of the flirtations and nonsense going on here of late."

"Uncle, dear uncle!" gently remonstrated Mrs. D'Aulnay.

The simple appeal, uttered in the softest tones, somewhat calmed Mr. De Mirecourt, but he continued, still firmly enough, " 'Tis of no use, Lucille. Soft words and pleading looks will not prevent me saying what I have to say; and again, I repeat, I hope that my daughter has not forgotten herself so far as to enter into any secret love-engagement with those who are aliens alike to our race, creed, and tongue."

"But if she should have done so, dearest uncle—if she should have met with some noble, good man, who, apart from the objection of his being a foreigner, should have proved himself worthy in all other things of inspiring affection—"

"Then, Madame D'Aulnay," he interrupted, striking the table so violently that the vases and other ornaments on it shook again, "the first thing she has to do is to forget him; for never, never will she obtain either my consent or my blessing."

"Now is the moment," inwardly groaned Antoinette; "now, we should undeceive him—tell him it is beyond earthly power to prevent the union he so utterly condemns." So thought Mrs. D'Aulnay too; but Mr. De Mirecourt had wrought himself up to a degree of anger most unusual with him, and they tremblingly recoiled from the thought of exasperating him farther.

"Listen to me, daughter Antoinette, and you, my too officious niece, bear witness," he resumed, after a short pause, which had been merely a lull in the tempest. "I must be plain, explicit, with you both. I forbid you, child, to have any intercourse, beyond that of distant courtesy, with the men I have mentioned; and if you have entangled yourself in any disgraceful flirtation or attachment, break it off at once, under penalty of being disowned and disinherited."

"Oh! my father!" faltered Antoinette, clasping her trembling hands, "For God's sake, retract those cruel words: they are too terrible!"

A vague fear stole over Mr. De Mirecourt's heart at this passionate appeal; but as is frequently the case, it only increased his irritation, and seizing his daughter's arm, he violently repeated, "I shall not retract them, disobedient, wilful girl!"

At that moment the drawing-room door opened, and Louis Beauchesne entered. A look of mingled dismay and indignation flashed across his face as his glance took in the scene before him; but Mr. De Mirecourt, still under the influence of his late fierce excitement, exclaimed,

"I have just been telling this wilful girl that this day month, willing or unwilling, she shall become your wife."

"Oh, Mr. De Mirecourt," he replied, with a look of mingled bitterness and pain. "I seek not an unwilling bride—one forced to the altar against the wishes of her own heart. But are you not exacting too speedy a submission from Antoinette? Scarcely a fortnight has elapsed since you first mentioned your wishes to her, and you must accord her a little time to make up her mind. Why, she will require a month to recover from the effects of to-day's scolding"; and he glanced compassionately towards Antoinette, who was leaning against a chair, her cheek pale as marble, and every feature quivering with agitation.

Mr. De Mirecourt's heart smote him. During the seventeen years that his daughter had passed under the protecting shadow of his parental love, he had never addressed as many unkind and harsh words to her as he had done within the last ten minutes; and unacquainted with the secret fears and anxieties torturing her heart, he attributed her overwhelming emotion entirely to his own severity.

"Sit down Antoinette," continued Louis, reading, at once, the relenting expression stealing over her father's face. "Sit down, and I know Mr. De Mirecourt will promise to grant six months instead of one, to prepare your mind and your *trousseau*."

"You are a philosophical wooer, Louis," exclaimed Mr. De Mirecourt, sarcastically; "more so than I would have been at your age; and seem to be in no hurry to seal your happiness."

"Because I seek Antoinette's happiness before my own," he rejoined, whilst the old bitter expression clouded his countenance for a moment. "But speak, Mr. De Mirecourt, is it not settled that you will give her six months longer for reflection; at the end of which time let us hope that your wishes and mine may be fulfilled."

Poor Louis! he knew well the futility of that hope; but in his generous abnegation, he only thought of procuring a respite for the pale trembling girl before him.

"Be it as you wish then," returned Mr. De Mirecourt, with an attempt at carelessness. "Since the expectant bridegroom is satisfied, so also should I be. But, Antoinette, remember that of what I have just told you concerning foreign lovers or suitors, I retract nothing. What I have said, I have said; and if you disobey me, neither blessing nor inheritance will ever be yours. And now enough on this chapter. Where is Mr. D'Aulnay?"

"I will seek him, dear uncle," rejoined Mrs. D'Aulnay, hastily rising, for her quick ear had caught the sound of the hall-door opening. On leaving the room, instead of proceeding to the library where her husband was, she rapidly descended the stairs in time to arrest Sternfield, who was divesting himself of his outer coat, preparatory to seeking the society of the ladies, Jeanne having received no orders to exclude him.

Mrs. D'Aulnay drew him hurriedly into a small ante-room off the hall, and in a few rapid words recounted the stormy interview which had just passed up stairs. The Major's flushed cheek and contracted brow betokened the intense annoyance the recital caused him; and had his companion been as quick-eyed as she generally was, she would have perceived that at her mention of Mr. De Mirecourt's threat of disinheriting his daughter, the listener's cheek gained a deeper glow, his eyes an angrier light. "Can you tell me," he irritably enquired, "how long this tyrannical old man is going to stay, for see my wife I must and shall."

"Hush, hush, do not speak so loud. I think he will leave to-morrow morning; and till he has taken his departure, you must remain exiled from her presence. Do not get impatient; for, believe me, our penance meanwhile will be severer than yours."

Dismissing Sternfield with a friendly pressure of the hand, she turned now to the library where she found, as she had expected, her husband; and immediately entered on a narrative of the late scene in the drawing-room, condemning Mr. De Mirecourt's harshness in no measured terms, and concluding by imploring Mr. D'Aulnay to use all his influence in inducing this père *sauvage* to leave poor Antoinette a little longer with them. "Believe me, dear André," the lady pathetically added, "she will be scolded and worried into her grave, if she goes back with her still irritated father. Request, then, the prolongation of her visit as a personal favor; and if you are sufficiently persevering, uncle De Mirecourt will scarcely refuse you."

"Well, I will do as you ask me, Lucille, for I am really fond of the little girl; but still I cannot help thinking she would be better at home, than flirting and fluttering about with the military cavaliers that you and she both so strongly affect."

CHAPTER 15

THE meeting between Mr. D'Aulnay and his guest was cordial in the extreme, for they had been fast friends from early boyhood, and, though dissimilar in many points of character, resembled each other in being both honorable, kind-hearted men. On Mr. De Mirecourt's mentioning that he was about to bring his daughter back to the country, his host, with a warmth and earnestness for which the guest was unprepared, insisted that Antoinette's visit should not be shortened in so sudden and unreasonable a manner.

"It must be, my dear D'Aulnay. Your house here is too gay for an inexperienced country-girl, such as she is; and I cannot trust her any longer among the fascinating English gallants whom report says find their way so frequently into Madame's *salons*."

"But surely where I trust my wife, you may safely trust your daughter?"

"Scarcely, André. My fair niece has a store of experience and worldly knowledge which my little girl has not had time yet to acquire."

"Well, even so, you will not refuse to leave her with us a couple of weeks longer?"

Mrs. D'Aulnay here joined her entreaties to those of her husband; and after considerable pressing, Mr. De Mirecourt consented, though with considerable reluctance, that Antoinette should remain another fortnight in town, at the end of which time she was to return without fail to Valmont. The evening passed pleasantly enough to most of the little party; for Mrs. D'Aulnay and the good-natured Louis, whom the hostess had almost tearfully pressed to remain, exerted themselves to amuse the others. Antoinette alone was silent and sad; but the scene of the

88

morning, fortunately, accounted sufficiently for her unusual depression. No allusion to that event was made by any one, except once, when she herself whispered to young Beauchesne: "My dear, kind Louis, how can I ever thank you sufficiently for your generous interference this morning!"

"Aye! Antoinette, you *may* thank me, for the effort caused me a sharp, bitter pang. I am not quite the cold philosophical wooer your father thinks me. But no more of this now: it would only agitate you. Enough to say, that if I cannot be your lover, I will still continue to be your friend."

His companion's beautiful eyes, so dangerously eloquent in their gratitude, drove poor Louis from her side, but only to see him soon return again; and as Mr. De Mirecourt's watchful glance followed their long-whispered conferences together, his smiles became more genial, his laughs more frequent and prolonged. In the course of the evening he consulted his host on the project so dear to his heart, informing him at the same time of Antoinette's opposition to his wishes.

"Well, my opinion," replied Mr. D'Aulnay, as he directed, by a slight movement of his head, his companion's attention to the two young people who were standing at a distant window conversing in a low tone—"my opinion is, that you have only to let them alone, and they will soon be more anxious even than yourself to fulfill your wishes. I know very little of womanly character or peculiarities, but I have read the works of those who have most deeply studied the question, and they all unite in asserting it to be a most difficult thing to force a young girl to love a suitor against her own will. They indeed go farther, and say that to warn her against, or forbid her loving any particular individual, is the most effectual way of ensuring her attaching herself to him."

Mr. De Mirecourt smiled at this doctrine, and thought it might possibly be somewhat exaggerated; but still he had sufficient respect for Mr. D'Aulnay's opinions, to accept his counsel of leaving his daughter unmolested for some time to come, on the subject of her marriage, convinced that such would be the most effectual means of bringing it about. He would have felt more anxious respecting the truth of his theory had he chanced to overhear the conversation going on at the distant window, in which Louis, in reply to his companion's whispered avowal that she loved Major Sternfield, resigned then and for ever, all hope of her hand; promising, at the same time, with the innate generosity which formed so striking a feature in his character, to always do whatever he could to aid and befriend her. Mr. De Mirecourt left early the following day, despite the condition of the roads; and Antoinette, anxious to escape from her own harassing thoughts, seated herself at her tapestry-frame, where her white fingers were soon moving with as much rapidity as if no graver care engrossed her mind than the formation of the miniature lilies and roses she was tracing on the canvass. Bending over her frame, her thoughts as busy as her fingers, she heard not the servant's announcement of a visitor, and it was only when enfolded in Sternfield's arms that she was aware of his presence.

Startled, surprised, she abruptly withdrew herself from his close clasp, and then, with crimsoned cheek, she asked, "Why did you do that, Audley?"

"Why did I embrace my bride," he repeated with a forced laugh. "A singular question that, Antoinette!"

"Listen to me," she gently though firmly rejoined, and this time there was no tremor in her voice, no nervousness in her manner. "I again repeat what I have once before told you, that till our marriage shall have been acknowledged in the eyes of the world, I shall be nothing nearer to you than I was as Antoinette De Mirecourt."

"You are unkind, unjust to treat me thus!" he vehemently rejoined.

"Not so, Major Sternfield," exclaimed Mrs. D'Aulnay, advancing towards them. "Antoinette is right; and should I find that till the time she mentions has arrived, you should in any way annoy or grieve her, rest assured that much as I esteem you, much as I have done and would do for you, I should be obliged to deny myself the pleasure of seeing you beneath my roof. Remember, Antoinette is under my protection, and I must shield her from unnecessary annoyance."

"Good heavens!" impetuously interrupted Sternfield, "is it thus you threaten, speak to me about my own wife! It passes human patience! it passes belief! Nay, I must, I *shall* speak," he continued more violently than before, shaking off at the same time the hand which Mrs. D'Aulnay, partly in warning, partly in deprecation, had laid on his shoulder. "Think you that after a clergyman has declared us one—after I have solemnly placed on her finger the wedding-ring that now glitters there, I am not to be allowed to speak to her—to even kiss the hem of her garments without permission?"

Antoinette, terrified by this hot outburst of passion, stood motionless with changing cheek and beating heart, but Mrs. D'Aulnay, wholly undismayed, quietly replied: "Be calm, Major Sternfield, and do not compel me already to regret the share I have had in bringing about your union. Yes, it must be as you say; and till your marriage is openly proclaimed, I will run no risks of having my cousin's spotless name made a bye-word by servants and scandal-mongers through too attentive civilities on your part. Rather than that such a thing should happen, I would close my doors at once upon you."

"By heaven! you will drive me out of my senses!" he fiercely retorted. "I will not, I shall not submit to such intolerable tyranny. Antoinette, were the solemn vows you uttered before God the other evening, a mere farce, an empty mockery?"

"Oh! no, no, Audley," and the soft pleading look, the low earnest tones of the girl somewhat calmed even his fierce wrath. "Surely, I have already given you a great, a mighty proof of my love; but understand, till the conditions mentioned by me and subscribed to by yourself at the time of our marriage shall have been published, I will not look on the latter as completed—as ratified."

"And when is this ratification to take place?" he questioned, though somewhat less violently than before.

"Whenever you wish. Perhaps we had better write a full confession to my father at once," but a slight shudder ran through her frame as she spoke.

"Beware of precipitation!" exclaimed Mrs. D'Aulnay. "After yesterday's terrible scene, reflect carefully before venturing on such a step. He might cast you off—disinherit you at once. Even Major Sternfield, excited as he is at the present moment, will join with me in condemning so hasty a proceeding. The way must be prepared first; your father soothed and humored till he is in a mood to receive such a communication more favorably. Am I not right, Audley?" Sternfield, who had no wish that his bride should be portionless, felt the full justice of her remarks, and moodily replied in the affirmative.

"Well, since such is the case, let us all make up our minds to be tolerant with one another. You, Audley, will promise to look on Antoinette merely as your betrothed, till a public repetition of the marriage-service in her own church shall have made her entirely and wholly yours."

Sternfield made no reply, but walked to a window, near which he stood for some moments in sullen thought. This constant harping on the incompleteness of their marriage made him both anxious and uneasy, and, after serious reflection, he returned to the spot where his pale young bride still stood, and exclaimed: " 'Tis a hard and trying ordeal, Antoinette, to which you and Mrs. D'Aulnay wish to subject me; and you would yourselves despise me, if my heart had not at first rebelled against it. If you wish it so, however, I must endeavor to submit. In return, you must both solemnly promise, nay, swear that you will not reveal our secret union, till I shall deem the time advisable."

Mrs. D'Aulnay, giddy and thoughtless, at once rejoined, "Certainly: I see nothing wrong in that. I promise you, Audley, in the most solemn, the most binding manner that it shall be as you say. But excuse me one moment: there is Jeanne at the door, waiting to consult me on some household topic."

"Now, Antoinette, it is your turn," said Major Sternfield, as his hostess left the room. "I consent to waive, for the present, a husband's authority and privileges; to look on you, treat you—hard task!—as a stranger, instead of my own dear wife, as you really are. In return, you will bind yourself never to breathe the secret of this marriage to any one, nor to allow Mrs. D'Aulnay to reveal it, till I give you leave."

"Oh, Audley!" was the imploring rejoinder, "why must we surround ourselves with more secresy—more mystery? Alas! have we not enough already around us?"

"It must be so, dearest, for your sake as well as mine. But this mystery, as you call it, will not last long, for my impatience to openly make you, call you mine, will brook no long delay. Promise, then!"

"I do, most solemnly," she earnestly repeated.

"By this sign, which I know you hold so sacred," he added, raising to her lips a small gold cross which she always wore suspended from her neck.

She kissed it, and repeated again, "I promise," adding afterwards, with a shudder, "My vow is indeed a binding one, that cross was my mother's dying gift."

"And I know you will keep it sacredly; but sit down, Antoinette, darling, and we will talk quietly, kindly together, just as if we were but simple acquaintances; as if our destinies were not united beyond the power of aught on earth to ever part them."

When Mrs. D'Aulnay returned, she was enchanted to find Antoinette quietly seated at her frame, looking like her olden self; whilst Sternfield, on a low ottoman beside her, was reading aloud from some volume of love-verses, such passages as he deemed most suitable to the circumstances. This was something like the realization of her romantic dreams for her young cousin—something like the *piquante* mystery she delighted in; and resting her hand lightly on the young man's rich dark curls, she said with a half sigh, half smile, "What would some wives not give to have their husbands make love to them thus!"

Audley Sternfield glanced towards his young bride, and though the long lashes veiled the downcast eyes, the sweet smile that stole over her lips, the soft crimson that suddenly flooded even her ivory neck, told that she, too, inwardly thought with Mrs. D'Aulnay, it was indeed very pleasant.

CHAPTER 16

THE stated fortnight, with its hours of pain and pleasure, passed rapidly over; but alas! poor Antoinette found that for her at least pain predominated. Apart from harrassing doubts regarding the possibility of her father's proving implacable; apart from the remorse she experienced for the manner in which that kind, good father had been deceived and disobeyed, there was much in her lover's conduct to grieve and wound her. Ever passing from one extreme to another, he was either all tenderness and passion, or else a prey to the most gloomy irritability; and whilst under the influence of the latter mood, he would reproach her with her coldness and cruelty, in terms which made the girl's eyes overflow, and her heart throb with mingled grief and indignation. Her approaching departure for the country was a continual source of recrimination and upbraiding; but despite all his remonstrances, her resolution remained unchanged. She knew, if Major Sternfield did not, that her father was not a man to be trifled with.

The last day of her stay in town had arrived, and Mrs. D'Aulnay had invited a number of guests, intending that Antoinette's closing evening should be as pleasant as possible. All was gaiety and glitter—promising a time of complete enjoyment; but one young heart was destined to learn, during the course of those mirthful hours, a new and keen suffering from which it had as yet been exempt.

Antoinette had of course danced the first dance with her lover, and as they promenaded slowly round the room, he abruptly exclaimed:

"Were you speaking seriously yesterday evening, when you told me that you could not possibly say how long you would remain in Valmont?"

The reply was so low toned that he guessed, rather than heard its purport; and he rejoined irritably: "I tell you that so prolonged, perhaps uncertain an absence is more than I can patiently bear. However possible for you, it would be impossible for me; so I shall soon run over to see you."

"And what would papa say to that?" she questioned, in alarm.

"He would know nothing of it. I could go under a feigned name, and stop at some village-inn near, or at some farmer's house. You would have nothing to do then but to take your walks or drives in the right direction."

"Audley, Audley, I dare not—I cannot do that. The sharp eyes, the busy tongues, of village-gossips would soon make our meetings known, not only to papa, but to all the world."

"So you refuse me even this paltry concession! Beware, Antoinette: you are trying me too far!"

"What can I do?" she urged, turning an appealing, tearful glance upon him.

"What can you do!" he retorted, untouched by that pleading look. "Prove by your actions that you are a woman, not a silly child; prove that you really feel, in some slight degree, the love you so solemnly vowed me a fortnight since. Surely, I do not ask much. Permission to meet, to see you for a short hour; and yet even that you heartlessly refuse me. If you continue thus insensible to pity, to common justice, I shall soon insist on your showing me both."

"These reproaches are intolerable!" gasped his companion, turning deadly pale. "Audley, I will confess all to my father at once, and throw myself on his mercy. Better his open though terrible anger, than this unceasing secret wretchedness."

"No, you will not confess to Mr. De Mirecourt yet. Remember your solemn promise. When the favorable time comes, and not till then, shall I release you from that vow."

"Oh, Major Sternfield, in what a net-work of deceit and mystery you have bound me!" she rejoined with involuntary bitterness.

"Perhaps you are already beginning to weary of your bonds," was the cold reply. "Well, I acknowledge I am a tiresome lover, too devoted, too fond; I must endeavor to amend, however."

Silence followed this remark, and soon after he led her to a seat, leaving her without further comment. In another moment, she saw him by the side of a graceful, dark-eyed brunette, whispering in her ear with the devotion he usually vouchsafed herself. An uneasy feeling smote her, but she resolutely combatted it, and accepted the hand of the first partner who presented himself. The dance over, her gaze involuntarily wandered in the direction of her lover. He stood just where she had last seen him, bending over his beautiful companion, toying with the flower she had given him from her *bouquet,* and adding, by his whispered flatteries, additional brilliancy to the bright flush that glowed on her cheek. Ah, now indeed, a keen, sharp pang shot through Antoinette's heart; but too proud, too maidenly to show it, she went calmly through the penance of another dance with a wearisome partner, who almost bewildered her already aching brain by his overwhelming flood of weak, small talk. It came, however, to an end, and then the slow measured strains of the minuet, so different to the rapid polka, waltz, and galop of our days, struck up, and Sternfield and his companion pressed forward to join it. Still Antoinette bore all bravely. Another partner came up, and, though she declined dancing under a plea of fatigue, he retained his post beside her. Nothing daunted by her discouraging silence, he stood his ground, determined to have her hand for at least once during the evening; and when the music of the contra dance, which succeeded to the minuet, commenced playing, she unwillingly stood up with him. By some unpleasant freak of fate, the place that fell to her lot was very near the couch on which Sternfield and his partner were now resting; and during the course of that interminable dance, she had to stand an apparently unconcerned spectator of that mutually engrossed couple, who seemed at the moment so entirely wrapped up in each other. Notwithstanding her close proximity, never once did Sternfield's glance wander towards herself; and as she silently watched them—how could she help it! she ever and anon asked her aching heart, "Is that man really my husband? Must I see all this, bear all this, and not even dare to complain—this too, the last evening that we shall be together for perhaps many weeks! Bring me to the other room, it is too warm here," she abruptly said, when her partner, noticing her excessive pallor, asked her at the close of the dance if she were ill.

With a sentiment of relief, she entered a small sitting-room, specially appropriated to Mrs. D'Aulnay's use, which at the moment chanced to be vacant; and, longing for a moment's solitude to school her looks and voice to the calmness they ought to wear, she eagerly assented to her partner's proposal that he should procure her some refreshment. He was scarcely gone, when the clanking of approaching spurs told that an intruder was at hand. It proved to be Colonel Evelyn, who had accepted (an unusual circumstance for him) Mrs. D'Aulnay's invitation for that evening; and who now, without perceiving Antoinette, threw himself on the sofa with a wearied *ennuyé* look. His glance, however, in carelessly wandering round the room, suddenly fell upon her, when he started up, exclaiming,

"What, you here, Miss De Mirecourt, and all alone?"

"Oh, I have only just entered. Mr. Chandos has gone in quest of coffee and cake."

Colonel Evelyn at once detected that her carelessness of manner was assumed, and, as he looked at her more narrowly, there was something in the pallor of her cheek, the constrained look of her beautiful but unusually pale lips, that brought vividly back to memory the eventful drive they had once taken together, and the feeling akin to interest which she had awoke in his breast at the time. Instead of quietly escaping from the room, as was his wont when by any chance he found himself *tête-à-tête* with a pretty woman, he drew nearer, and, whilst uttering some of the commonplaces of conversation, which he generally avoided, secretly wondered at the shadow which had fallen on that young face, at the involuntary look of pain it wore.

"You have wearied soon of dancing, to-night," he said, after a short pause.

"Yes, I must keep my strength for to-morrow's journey. I will start for Valmont immediately after breakfast."

"Ah, you are leaving us then. What will your friends and admirers do in your absence?"

"Forget me," she apathetically rejoined.

The listener inwardly thought that where she had once inspired love, she was not one to be easily forgotten, but he merely said, "As you will doubtless forget them."

Ah! would she? There was *one* that now she never could, never must forget; and yet how he had grieved, how he had trampled on her feelings, through the course of that painful evening!

She made no reply to her companion's chance remark; but the tide of vivid crimson that rushed to her cheek, the look of intense mental pain that suddenly contracted her features, told how deeply it had moved her. Interested, touched by the evidence of suffering thus involuntarily betrayed, Colonel Evelyn gently changed the subject; inwardly thinking what a pity it was that a few more months' experience of fashionable life would teach that guileless young nature to dissemble completely the emotions it now so clearly revealed.

Had Antoinette been in her usual state of health and spirits, smiles irradiating her beautiful face, Evelyn would soon, if not almost immediately, have left her side; but he had known deep and bitter anguish himself, and moody, misanthropic as he appeared at times, coldly, impatiently as he turned away from human mirth and friendship, suffering or sorrow always touched his heart.

At this juncture Mr. Chandos returned with a well-loaded salver, and, as he pressed some of its contents upon Antoinette, expressed a hope "that she would soon be able to accompany him to the ball-room."

"If Miss De Mirecourt would rather remain here a little longer to rest herself, I will be happy to wait upon her," exclaimed Colonel Evelyn.

Mr. Chandos engaged for the next dance to a sprightly young lady, who was probably already impatiently awaiting him, mentioned his engagement, and joyfully withdrew. Antoinette, after making a pretence of tasting some fruit, rose with a vague, unhappy feeling that she ought not now to sit thus alone with Colonel Evelyn, or indeed with any other.

"What, anxious to go already, Miss De Mirecourt? Pray take my arm, and we will walk through the rooms till you are sufficiently rested to return to the partners who are probably growing impatient at your absence."

The forced smile with which poor Antoinette endeavored to meet this remark was more painful to see than even her late expression of misery; and Evelyn, remembering her calm, unflinching look in an hour of mortal peril, sorrowfully thought that bravely as she might meet physical danger, she was one apparently whom mental suffering would soon prostrate. Walking slowly through the rooms, he exerted himself in a manner most unusual with him, to interest and amuse her, and he partly succeeded.

Colonel Evelyn possessed a rare and powerful intellect, and, though his conversation was wanting in the graceful strain of compliment, the witty and constantly recurring

epigram, which imparted such brilliancy to that of
Sternfield, to a refined and cultivated mind, it was
infinitely more interesting. Antoinette quietly listened,
unconscious that in the short, simple observations she
occasionally made, her companion found a freshness, a
transparent candor which charmed him far more than the
wittiest repartees could have done.

In passing through one of the apartments, dimly lighted
by rose-colored lamps, and abounding in niches and angles
which seemed to make it a very temple of flirtation, they
saw Major Sternfield seated on a *causeuse* beside a pretty,
child-like creature of sixteen, whose blushing, embarrassed
face, and downcast eyes betrayed she was totally unused to
the new strain of adulatory conversation in which he was
initiating her.

As they passed on, Evelyn's lips curled, and he abruptly
asked,

"Do you admire Major Sternfield?"

"How little he imagines," inwardly thought poor
Antoinette, "that Major Sternfield is now the sole arbiter of
my destiny—my future life"; but the Colonel, without
perceiving her sudden embarrassment, or, careless of
hearing her reply, rapidly went on,—"Of course you do,
and so also do three-thirds of the ladies present to-night.
He is handsome as an Apollo, dresses, dances, and flirts
irreproachably;—surely, that is enough. Still I think I
would rather labor under the imputation of being a
woman-hater, as you once told me I was regarded, than a
woman or rather lady killer. One is not more heartless than
the other. But now, I must yield you up, for I see a claimant
for your hand approaching, and I will say farewell, for I
intend soon leaving this gay scene."

"Good bye! You have been very kind to me to-night," she
simply said, tendering her hand.

He clasped it in a friendly pressure, and whispered,
"Your last words encourage me to venture on offering you

a counsel which otherwise you might have regarded as impertinent; a counsel at least disinterested, for it comes from one who has ceased to seek or care for ladies' smiles and approbation. It is this: Remain in that happy country home, in which you have grown up candid and truthful; remain with the tried, wise friends of your girlhood. You will meet none such in the gay, heartless life on which you have lately entered."

"Too late!" inwardly sighed Antoinette, but she merely replied by a sad slight shake of the head; and Colonel Evelyn turned away, acknowledging to himself that such a thing as truth or worth in woman might still possibly exist.

Antoinette, on her part, accepted without word or comment the partner who had just presented himself, and doubly wearisome did his platitudes appear after the engrossingly interesting conversation of her previous companion. Soon her thoughts wandered back to Audley Sternfield, to his studied, cruel neglect of herself, his open devotion to others; and the olden pained look came back on her face, stronger than ever. At the end of the dance, supper was announced. That over, came a cotillion, some singing; and, finally, when the greater part of the guests were taking leave, Major Sternfield sought her side.

"How have you enjoyed yourself?" he asked; "I left you to do so, untrammelled by my wearisome attentions."

"You have made me very unhappy, to-night," she rejoined, with a quivering lip.

Sternfield read as clearly as Colonel Evelyn had done, the traces of mental anguish on that pale face, and his heart somewhat smote him.

"Forgive me, Antoinette," he tenderly whispered; "but what is the slight annoyance my conduct may have caused you to-night, compared to the suffering your coldness continually inflicts on myself?"

"I act as I do from principle, Audley; but you have grieved, tortured me to-night, either through retaliation, or through an idle wish to see how much you could make me suffer—how much I could bear."

"Not so, my little wife; but I thought the harsh lesson might render you more merciful to me than you have hitherto been. You will not surely now refuse me permission to visit Valmont?"

"Visit Valmont if you will, Audley, but come openly, without disguise; and even at the risk of incurring papa's anger and reproaches, I will receive you with friendly welcome: but to meet you in inns or lonely walks, I will not, I cannot consent."

"So be it. I shall speedily commit myself, according to your wishes, to the mercies of your father's hospitality. Meanwhile, how shall I pass the time of your absence?"

"Oh, you have many resources," she bitterly replied: "witness to-night."

"What, jealous, Antoinette!" and an almost imperceptible smile flitted over his face.

"I do not know that I have felt so; but I know that I have been very wretched during the course of the last few hours; and have asked myself more than once in alarm, can the love you profess for me be really sincere—can it even really exist whilst you treat me thus? Oh, imagine Audley, with what agony—what anguish such a doubt must have filled my heart, now, that we are irrevocably united together!"

"Yes—; fortunate indeed that it is so!" he rejoined, his eyes flashing with a moody triumph.

His companion shuddered. "Fortunate, you should say, Audley, as long as confidence and affection reign between us."

"I make no exception—fortunate in any and every case. Even with distrust, coldness, irritation, clouding our mutual relationship, 'twill always be a welcome thought to know that you are entirely, irrevocably mine!"

The words were merely one of those exaggerations of passion which sound pleasantly enough, in general cases, in the ear of a young bride of a fortnight; but they blanched the cheek of Sternfield's girlish wife, and filled her heart with nameless dread.

"What, am I not right?" he continued, almost fiercely, noticing her sudden pallor.

"For mercy's sake, Audley, do not speak so wildly! God forbid that either distrust or anger should ever arise between us now! I will be true, faithful, and devoted to you,—ah, do you, on your part, be kind and forbearing with me. Sport not with my feelings, as you have so mercilessly done to-night—"

"Even as you are constantly doing with mine," he whispered. "But, here comes our hostess. Pray, dearest, try and look more cheerful; or I shall have to undergo a private court-martial at her hands."

"What are you two conspiring about in this desolate corner?" Mrs. D'Aulnay smilingly asked. "Why, Antoinette, you look wretchedly ill! You will surely be unfit for your journey to morrow."

"There, Major Sternfield, say good night at once, for I am certain it is you who have worried all Antoinette's roses away with your melancholy fretting and grumbling. Say good night and good-bye!" and she good-naturedly turned from the lovers, still interposing her stately person between them and the half-open door of the adjoining room in which some of the guests still lingered.

"Farewell, my own Antoinette," whispered Sternfield, as he tenderly pressed the young girl to his heart. "Forgive and forget the pain I have so cruelly inflicted on you to-night."

Forgive and forget, aye, the request was easily spoken, but was it as easily granted? Antoinette's sleepless, tear-stained pillow could have answered that.

CHAPTER 17

ANOTHER day saw our young heroine installed in her own home, surrounded by her father's affectionate cares, the gentle ministerings of her devoted governess, and the friendly attentions of Louis Beauchesne, who was of course a privileged visitor of the Manor-House. Still, despite the triple wall of affection thus surrounding her—despite her return to the regular hours and calm healthful pursuits of country life, she retained the fragile delicate look she had acquired during the last few weeks of her residence in Montreal. Mr. De Mirecourt felt little anxiety on the subject, persuaded as he was that a fortnight's rest would make her as strong as ever; but Mrs. Gérard was far from being as sanguine, or as easily satisfied.

What pained and alarmed her far more than the pallor of Antoinette's cheek or the slowness of her step, were the frequent fits of melancholy abstraction in which she so often indulged; as well as her indifference, if not aversion to the charitable as well as intellectual pursuits which had formed the chief pleasures of her guileless life before her recent visit to Mrs. D'Aulnay. Gently, patiently, lovingly, as a mother would have done, did she endeavor to win the confidence of her beloved pupil; but the latter shrank with terror from every overture: and Mrs. Gérard, finding the invariable result of any such effort was to drive Antoinette to the seclusion of her room for half the day, abandoned the attempt, contenting herself with daily pouring forth prayer to Heaven in private, for the support and direction of that heavily-burdened young heart, sparing, at the same time, no effort to cheer and distract her sadness.

A source of unceasing regret and annoyance to Mrs. Gérard, was the constant correspondence kept up between her charge and Mrs. D'Aulnay. This annoyance was well-founded; for the reception or writing of a letter generally left the young girl a prey to a fit of absorbing melancholy, or to a severe headache. How much would her anxiety have been increased, had she but known that half of the letters thus received from, or sent under cover to Mrs. D'Aulnay, formed part of a correspondence with Major Sternfield.

A gentle, half-playful request on her part to be permitted to see some of the epistles in question had met with a cold reply from Antoinette, accompanied by an assertion that she had promised Mrs. D'Aulnay to show her letters to no person. Really alarmed, Mrs. Gérard applied to Mr. De Mirecourt; but the latter, grown doubly indulgent towards his daughter since her return, impatiently rejoined "that Antoinette must not be worried or vexed about trifles. She was too old to be obliged to submit to inspection a harmless correspondence with her cousin, as if she were still a school-girl."

So had it always been with Mr. De Mirecourt, whenever the governess had appealed to him; and if his child had hitherto proved a gentle and submissive pupil, it was owing entirely to her own natural sweetness of disposition, not to parental constraint. It was well for the young girl's jealously-guarded secret, that her father's time and thoughts at the present period were entirely taken up by other matters, or he could not have failed noticing the great and unaccountable change which had come over her.

We have already remarked that the greater part of the French Canadians, instead of having recourse in their difficulties to judges who understood neither their laws nor their language, were accustomed to refer them to the arbitration of the *curé*, or to that of some leading person in the parish. In Valmont, Mr. De Mirecourt was universally beloved and respected; and he found himself constituted judge and umpire in all the differences which happened to arise amongst his co-parishioners. No appeal was ever sought from his decision, for all felt that he acted with the strictest justice and impartiality.

"A letter for you, little one," he smilingly said, entering one morning the cheerful though old-fashioned sitting-room in which the ladies of the household were passing the hours of the forenoon. "As heavy a despatch as the provincial secretary ever receives."

No answering smile brightened his daughter's face as she took the epistle and slipped it into the folds of her dress, with a slight word of thanks. Mr. De Mirecourt, who had an unusual number of cases *en délibéré* that morning, soon took his departure, and a moment after Antoinette rose also.

"Why not read your letter here, my child?" questioned Mrs. Gérard. "I promise to neither speak to nor look at you during its perusal."

The young girl murmured some apologetic, half-unintelligible reply, and left the room. Ah, those letters of hers were not letters to be read under the eye of any one whose scrutiny she feared. They brought crimson flushes to her cheek, tears to her eyes, too often for that. They sent too many shades of pain and pleasure (alas that the pain should have so constantly predominated) flitting over her expressive face to permit her to let any eye study her features whilst she read them.

Alone in her room, she turned the key in the door and opened the envelope which contained, as she had previously divined, two letters, one from Major Sternfield, the other from her cousin. We will give the latter—a pretty accurate illustration of the mind and character of the writer—in full.

"My darling Antoinette, for Heaven's sake, make every effort to obtain your father's permission to return to Montreal immediately! Audley is like a perfect mad-man. He has heard somewhere that young Beauchesne is almost domesticated in your house, paying you all the while the most devoted attention; and he will have it that you are flirting outrageously with Louis, and entirely forgetting himself. He was here last night in a towering passion, and declared that if you remained in Valmont much longer, he would assuredly go there to see you, let the consequences be what they might. I have hitherto, in compliance with your urgent prayers, prevented him doing so; but I fear his patience and my influence have now reached their utmost limits. Who would have thought that such a dear, handsome, fascinating creature could so soon have turned tyrant! And yet there is something in his very violence, arising as it does out of the excess of his love for you, calculated, it seems to me, to render him ten times dearer to the one he has chosen from among all of her sex. How contemptible does the tame, philosophic love of most men appear when placed side by side with his stormy devotion!—Now, with regard to your visit here; how is it to be brought about? I think Mr. D'Aulnay and myself must drop in (of course unexpectedly) this week at the Manor-House; say we find you looking ill, which of course you do, or ought to do, separated from the being nearest and dearest to you in this world; and coax and worry Mr. De Mirecourt into lending you to us for some time. I will represent, that this being the season of Lent, I am doing penance for past gaiety in perfect seclusion—that you will meet no one at our house; and finally, if all else fail, I will invite Louis also. That last stroke of policy will I know decide the matter; for Uncle De Mirecourt will naturally suppose it will farther his own darling project of a union between you both.—But adieu, I hear Sternfield's voice in the hall, so I will not seal my letter yet. Of course, he also has a few lines, or rather a folio to send you. Your devoted, but greatly-worried, Lucille."

The lines alluded to were not calculated to diminish the mental trouble produced by the letter in which they were enclosed. They consisted chiefly of accusations that she had forgotten him, passionate protestations that he could not suffer to be much longer exiled from her presence; and a concluding assurance that he would endeavor to be patient for a few days longer, at the end of which time she must absolutely meet him at Mrs. D'Aulnay's.

Antoinette read and re-read the epistles with quivering lips, and covering her face with her hands, sobbed forth,

"Oh! Audley and Lucille, what misery ye have both brought on me!"

The words, melancholy-strange as they were, coming from the lips of a young bride, married to the husband of her choice, were not, as might have been supposed, the fretful complaining of a moment of trouble or anxiety, but the real outpourings of an overburdened heart. Yes, during the past few weeks, removed entirely from the fascinations of Sternfield's society—separated from Mrs. D'Aulnay's companionship and influence, she had leisure in the solitude of her own heart to look back on and to judge the irrevocable past. What the result of that stern scrutiny was, may be gathered from the exclamation that had just escaped her.

Had Audley Sternfield proved persistently gentle and considerate, there is no doubt that the passing fancy which she had mistaken for love, would ultimately have ripened into deep affection; for Antoinette's nature was loving and gentle, but the system of persecution and intimidation the bridegroom had so soon adopted after their ill-omened marriage, insensibly frightened away the dawning attachment she had felt for him; and with anguished fear for the future, despairing regret for the past, she now acknowledged to her aching heart that she only feared and trembled where she should have loved and confided. A dreary half-hour followed, during which she sat leaning her head on her hand, tearfully watching the bare branches of the trees as they swayed to and fro, or wildly tossed about, sport of the keen February wind; and thinking with a sort of broken-hearted apathy, how improbable it was that she would ever know peace or happiness again.

A slight tap at the door aroused her, and Mrs. Gérard gently asked admittance, mentioning that Mr. De Mirecourt and Louis were in the drawing-room, and had enquired for her.

"Please, go to them, dear Mrs. Gérard! I will be down in a few minutes."

After hurriedly bathing her eyes, and smoothing back her rich hair, yet damp with tears, she sought the drawing-room, tutoring her countenance as she went into a look of repose or indifference. Placing herself under the shade of the heavy crimson curtains, that the glow they cast might help to conceal her pallor (a precaution she had learned from the fair Mrs. D'Aulnay), she contrived to reply with apparent composure to the remarks addressed her. After a time, Mr. De Mirecourt was summoned to his private room by some neighbors who wanted his counsel and arbitration; and Mrs. Gérard, being occupied with some household details, the young people found themselves alone.

"What is the matter, Antoinette?" asked Louis, who had detected her mental trouble, spite of crimson curtains and assumed composure.

"Oh, Louis! I am very miserable—very unhappy!" was the agitated reply.

"I have seen that since the first hour of your return," he gravely rejoined. "You are not the light-hearted and happy being that you were, when you left us. But, dear Antoinette, is there anything I can do for you?"

"Oh, yes," she interrupted, clasping her hands together. "Obtain permission for me to return soon, aye immediately, to Montreal."

"Yes, to the fascinating society of the irresistible Major Sternfield," rejoined her companion with a jealous bitterness he could not at the moment overcome. "Surely, if he grieves over your mutual separation one half as much as you appear to do, your names will deserve to go down to posterity as illustrative of the noble devotion of the lovers of our day."

"Oh! Louis, spare me reproaches and taunts: I am already miserable enough. Help me, if you can; if not, pity me!"

Touched by her gentleness, young Beauchesne impetuously exclaimed, "Nay, Antoinette, 'tis you who must pity me, who must forgive my injustice. Say that you do so, and I will endeavor to prove myself worthy of the trust you have placed on me."

The assurance he asked was speedily accorded, and Antoinette then communicated to him Mrs. D'Aulnay's approaching visit and the object she had in view. Louis, of course, promised at once to do all in his power to further the project; and Mrs. Gérard entering soon after, he engaged her in lively conversation, in order to withdraw her attention from his still agitated companion.

CHAPTER 18

ON a pleasant bright morning, some days after, Mr. and Mrs. D'Aulnay dashed up in their handsome winter equipage to the door, greatly to the delight of Mr. De Mirecourt, who was equally partial to his graceful fashionable niece and her worthy philosophical husband. Antoinette brought her cousin to her own room, to take off her wrappings; and, once there, the latter carefully closed the door, saying: "Now, for home gossip; but, mercy on us! child, how dreadfully ill you look. What have you been doing to yourself? Why, you have not only grown thin, but your eyes and complexion have lost all their brilliancy. This will not do. You should never allow anxiety or grief to go farther than imparting a delicate pallor or pensive look to your features."

"Give me your receipt for thus restraining it within such moderate bounds," questioned Antoinette with a faint smile.

"Why, whenever you find yourself beginning to mope, stop thinking. Take a novel, or get up a flirtation, or overlook your wardrobe. If the latter be in a needy state, the remedy will prove infallible, for the one cause of low spirits will effectually neutralize the other. But, cheer up, darling child! We will obtain uncle's permission; and you will find yourself in Montreal to morrow evening, in my pretty sitting-room, with that dear tyrannical Audley at your feet. Hush, here comes Mrs. Gérard. Not a word about our project till after dinner."

The dinner was excellent, the wines choice, and Mr. De Mirecourt, conscious that everything was as it should be, was in a most propitious mood. Coffee served in the drawing-room, Mrs. D'Aulnay ably opened the campaign

112

by a remark concerning Antoinette's pallor and delicate appearance.

"Yes, she does look ill," replied Mr. De Mirecourt, somewhat shortly, "but we may thank her town visit for that."

"Oh, dear uncle," smilingly rejoined Mrs. D'Aulnay, "she looked far better when she left Montreal than she does now. She is just moping herself to death here, for the matter of that, precisely as I am doing in town since Lent began."

"Very complimentary that, to Mr. D'Aulnay and myself," was the reply.

"But, uncle, you are very often absent, or occupied by important duties in your study, and Mrs. Gérard has her household duties to attend to, so poor Antoinette is frequently left alone."

"Let the little lady read, play, or sew, as she used to do very contentedly before her introduction to fashionable life," replied Mr. De Mirecourt in the same short tone; but the kindly look with which he regarded his daughter, contradicted the apparent abruptness of his words.

"Rather let her return to town with us, dear De Mirecourt," interrupted Mr. D'Aulnay, who had been previously tutored by his fairer half, "and I promise we will send her back after Easter, as merry and healthy as she ever was."

Mr. De Mirecourt laughingly shook his head, and Mrs. Gérard hinted that she did not think Antoinette would wish to leave home so soon again after her previous long absence.

What chance however had Mrs. Gérard of successfully coping with the able allies arrayed against her? Even Louis, whom she had counted upon as a most efficient aid, incomprehensibly and treacherously went over to the enemy. What his motive in doing so was, she could not divine, unless it were, that, as Mrs. D'Aulnay had extended an invitation to himself, he wished to profit by the opportunity thus afforded him of becoming an inmate under the same roof with Antoinette. It escaped Mrs. Gérard's notice that Beauchesne replied to the invitation in question, in vague general terms, which left him perfectly free to accept or reject it hereafter, as best suited him. Antoinette herself, silent and spiritless, spoke very little, and, in spite of her cousin's warning looks, and significant hints, remained almost passive.

One appealing glance towards her father, accompanied by the simple sentence, "I would like to go," was all the help she gave. Had the young girl carefully studied however the most effectual means of winning her father's consent, she could not have adopted any more successful. The quietness amounting almost to apathy, the look of despondency clouding that girlish face, combined with the remembrance of his own severity in the matter of her marriage with Louis, touched him deeply, and inclined him to accede to her request. Mrs. D'Aulnay's assertion too, that they were living in due penitential retirement, as well as the knowledge that Louis was also invited, and could mount guard, as it were, over his promised bride, decided him.

"Well, child," he kindly said, drawing his daughter towards him, "we must make the sacrifice, I see, so we have only to endeavor to do it cheerfully. What, in tears!" he exclaimed, as Antoinette, overcome by his kindness and by the remembrance of her own ingratitude and treachery towards him, hid her face with a quick gasping sob on his shoulder. "In tears, little one! What does this mean?"

"Do not be so childish, Antoinette!" interrupted Mrs. D'Aulnay, more sharply than the occasion seemed to call for. "How ridiculously nervous you are to-day?"

"Well, it was yourself, fair niece, who taught her what delicate nerves were and how she might contrive to render herself miserable through them; but enough of this, Antoinette,—run up stairs and commence packing, or the half of the most indispensable things will be forgotten. 'Tis no use, Mrs. Gérard," he good-humoredly continued, as the latter commenced an earnest though respectful protestation against Antoinette's return to town. " 'Tis no use. They have been too many for us this time. There, there now. Everything is settled. Give us some music, Lucille, if you can; but I am afraid the harpsichord is out of order. Our little girl has seldom touched it of late."

Shortly after Antoinette had sought her room, in obedience to her father's welcome directions, Mrs. Gérard entered. "I have come to see, dear Antoinette, if you want my assistance," she kindly said.

"Oh! I will not take much time to get everything ready. My wardrobe and drawers are in perfect order, thanks to your careful training, dear friend."

"Ah, my Antoinette," rejoined Mrs. Gérard, with a grieved anxiety of look and voice that she could scarcely disguise, "I fear my instructions on points far more important have been sadly deficient; and yet, God knows, I have ever diligently prayed for grace and enlightenment to accomplish worthily the important task assigned me."

"Dear Mrs. Gérard, why are you so anxious and unhappy?" soothingly rejoined the young girl, as she took the hands of her governess, and gently pressed them within her own. "You have been more like a mother to me than aught else. Ever kind, judicious, prudent"—

"And yet I have failed, signally failed," interrupted the elder lady in the same grieved, dejected tone. "Nay, start not thus, Antoinette, but listen, for I am speaking truth. Where is the confidence I should have inspired and that should have brought you to me as to a mother, to relate your griefs, to consult me in your troubles? Alas, you place no more trust in me than if I were an utter stranger! You have cares and anxieties, but you weep over them in silence; you may have plans and projects, but you brood over them in secret. Oh, Antoinette, Antoinette, tell me, have I deserved that you should distrust me thus?"

The warm heart of the young girl, who was really fondly attached to the kind instructress of her youth, was deeply touched by this appeal. Flinging herself with a burst of tears into the arms of the latter, she sobbed forth, "Oh, my kind, dear friend, forgive me! Would that I had accomplished my duty one half as faithfully to you as you have done yours to me. Would that I had never left your side!"

"Then, why leave me again, dear one?" softly whispered Mrs. Gérard, smoothing back the rich hair from the fair young brow, leaning on her breast. "Let Mrs. D'Aulnay return alone to that gay town-life, in whose turmoil you have already lost your smiles and gaiety, your peace of mind."

"That cannot be!" ejaculated Antoinette, starting feverishly up. "Alas, I must go!"

"So be it, then, my child, and may God guide your steps aright. One word, my little Antoinette, one word more from the tried friend who first taught your tongue to lisp the name of our heavenly Father. Why is it that you, who were always so attentive to the duties and observances of our religion, have of late almost abandoned them?"

"Because I am unworthy of seeking their consolations now," was the girl's agitated reply.

"The very reason, my child, that you should the more perseveringly cling to them. Has not our Divine Master Himself told us that he came to seek, not the just, but sinners? But, surely, that term in its severest sense does not apply to my little, quiet Antoinette. Open your heart to me, my darling child; breathe in my ear the secret care that lies so heavily on it, and you will be lighter, happier, after."

Antoinette groaned in spirit. What would she not have given to have been able at that moment to whisper her hidden faults and griefs in the ear of that wise, prudent counsellor, to have shared the burden of that secret which was already beginning to prey upon her young life. But the remembrance of the vow of secrecy which Sternfield had extorted from her, sealed her lips, and, with another tender caress, she whispered, "Have patience with me, yet awhile, oh my kind, enduring friend; and, despite my seemingly ungrateful silence, love and pray for me still!"

"May I come in, Antoinette?" suddenly asked the silvery voice of Madame D'Aulnay; and without waiting for a reply, the new-comer entered.

"What is all this, my poor little cousin?" she questioned, glancing indignantly from Antoinette's flushed tearful face, to Mrs. Gérard. "You have been receiving a lecture, I suppose."

"Hush, Lucille! Do not speak so thoughtlessly," hurriedly interrupted Antoinette. "Are you going now?" she regretfully added as her governess rose.

"Yes, my child; but before I leave, I have one word of warning for you, Mrs. D'Aulnay. At your pressing instances, that innocent, inexperienced child was committed to your special care. To God you will have to answer for the manner in which you have fulfilled your trust. Whatever have been the snares into which her feet have wandered; whatever the errors into which she may yet fall, on your head, you, her guide and monitor, will fall the heaviest part of the punishment."

"What a dreadful old creature!" exclaimed Mrs. D'Aulnay, shivering affectedly as the governess left the room. "She reminds one of a Sybil."

"Spare your names and taunts, Lucille?" retorted Antoinette in a pained, indignant tone. "She has been friend, instructress, mother, to me since infancy, and I would indeed be a shameless ingrate if I ever permitted her name to be slightingly spoken of in my presence, when I could help it."

"Oh, enough, my darling child! 'Tis a mere waste of indignation; for I am ready to speak of her, look on her in future as perfection, if you desire it. But let us not waste our time in quarrelling, when we have something more interesting to talk about. Have we not succeeded charmingly in all our plans? We are to start to-morrow morning early, to profit by the beautiful roads, which a sudden fall of snow may at any moment render heavy. Come, smile now, Antoinette. Look like your olden self, or your father will think of retracting his permission. And now that we have a moment to ourselves, why do you not overwhelm me, you icy-hearted bride, with questions about that dear, delightful, tyrannical husband of yours? Why, you start at the epithet as if it terrified you! You have really grown very nervous."

"Well, what of him?" questioned Antoinette, in a low tone.

"Well, what of him?" rejoined Mrs. D'Aulnay, playfully reiterating her words. "Is it thus an idolized bride of a few weeks should enquire about the handsomest, the most fascinating bridegroom that ever woman was blessed with?"

"I am not quite such an enthusiast as you are, Lucille; besides, you forget I received a letter from him two days ago, which informed me that he was quite well. But since you wish me to question you about him, tell me how he has been spending the time since my departure."

"Well, the truth is," rejoined Mrs. D'Aulnay, coughing, as if to conceal some sudden access of embarrassment, "it would not have done for him to have shut himself up like a hermit. People might have suspected something; so he has acted since just as he was in the habit of always doing."

"As he did the last evening of my stay in town?" rejoined Antoinette, whilst a flush of mingled pain and resentment overspread her features.

"Oh, yes: I know to what you allude. I observed myself his disgraceful flirtation with a couple of the girls present, and I roundly scolded him for it afterwards. Among other things, I told him that you had shown far too much gentleness and patience; and that your proper plan would have been to have flirted outrageously with some partner that suited your taste, thus combining pleasure and revenge. But, my dearest Antoinette, the dark, vindictive look he gave me, in return, almost froze me with terror. 'Listen to me, Mrs. D'Aulnay,' he said; 'as you value the happiness of your cousin, never give her advice to that effect. Should you do so, and she act upon it, the result would make you both rue the day she entered on so mad a career.' 'Why, Major Sternfield, you are a perfect tyrant,' I angrily retorted. 'Blue-beard was not half as bad as you are.' 'Do not talk so childishly, Lucille,' he replied, impertinently calling me by my Christian name. 'I love devotedly, as a man ought, the woman I have chosen for my life's partner; and I could not forgive her trifling with my affections, much less my honor.' Is he not, spite of his faults, an irresistible creature, Antoinette darling?"

Antoinette made no reply, beyond what was conveyed in the faintest possible smile, and in a slight, very slight shake of her head.

"And who do you think was enquiring very particularly, very kindly about you, some short time since? Guess; I will give you twenty chances. What! you will not exercise your ingenuity at all? Well, I will tell you at once. The invincible, invulnerable Colonel Evelyn. What think you he had the coolness to say, one afternoon that he came up to speak to me whilst the carriage was drawn up near the Citadel,[1] to give me a chance of listening to the new band? After enquiring about you, and receiving the information that you were well, and that I expected to have you soon again with me, he launched forth into a diatribe something in the style of the one your governess has just favored me with, saying how inexperienced and guileless you were, and how jealously I should watch over—how prudently I should

[1] Now Dalhousie Square.

direct you. I think he must have been listening to some ill-natured remarks about yourself and Sternfield at the mess-table, though what can have given rise to them I cannot imagine. But, mercy on us! Antoinette, how flushed and feverish you are looking! Come, let us leave this packing to your maid, and go down to the drawing-room."

CHAPTER 19

THEY found the gentlemen engaged in an animated political discussion, in which the grievances of Canada and the oppressive acts of the new government formed, of course, the chief topics. In deference to Mrs. D'Aulnay, who of late professed the greatest possible dislike to politics, nothing more was said on the subject, and the conversation turned to general topics.

The next morning was mild and pleasant, and the blue sky was beautifully dotted with soft fleecy clouds. In the farm-yards the patient cattle, released from the close confinement of stable and out-house, stood turning their wondering gaze on the white landscape around them, whilst flocks of tiny snow-birds hovered round, or settled down on the leafless branches of the trees. As arranged the day previous, the party started early; and Mrs. D'Aulnay, who was in the highest spirits, enlivened with many a gay remark their long though pleasant winter drive. In due time they arrived at their destination; and most comfortable did the well-furnished rooms, with their bright fires, look. The pleasant odor of an appetizing dinner, so welcome to the hungry travellers, pervaded the house; and the dining-table set for three, with snowy damask, cut crystal, and shining silver, told they were expected.

With that kindly good nature which formed so redeeming a feature in her frivolous character, Mrs. D'Aulnay hurriedly opened one of Antoinette's trunks, and taking from it a handsome, bright-colored dinner-dress, insisted on her wearing it.

"You know Audley will be here this evening, and I want you to appear to advantage," she whispered; "so now, as

121

you have only ten minutes to dress, be expeditious. Mr. D'Aulnay, philosophic and patient on every other point, is the most irascible man in the world if kept waiting any time for his dinner."

Antoinette, ready within the prescribed time, sought the dining-room, where her host, watch in hand, was promenading the room.

"Oh what a treasure of a wife you will make, fair cousin," he smilingly said: "always ready to the moment."

The exhilarating effect of the long drive, with its natural result of an improved appetite, told with good effect on Antoinette's languid frame; and the lively sallies of the fair hostess, who was in one of her happiest moods, imparted to the young girl's spirits a cheerful tone which they had not known for many weeks past. She was freed, too, at least for a time, from the wearing fear, haunting her of late, that her lover would venture on some rash step, such as presenting himself unexpectedly under her father's roof; or, what she dreaded still more, arriving in Valmont under an assumed name, and insisting on, forcing her to grant him an interview.

After a half-hour's pleasant dinner-chat, Mr. D'Aulnay solicited permission to retire to his library, and Mrs. D'Aulnay and her cousin were left alone. The former, who was an ardent admirer of fancy-work in all shapes and varieties, brought out some new designs and patterns to exhibit to her companion. Whilst expatiating on the beauties of a certain vine which she intended reproducing on canvas, a loud summons of the hall-knocker sent the warm blood bounding through Antoinette's veins.

"Yes, that is Major Sternfield. 'Tis his impatient knock; but bless me, child, how rapidly your color is changing! Tell me truly," and she scrutinized the trembling girl more closely, "is it love or fear that moves you thus?"

"A little of both, I suppose," was the reply, uttered with a very poor assumption of gaiety.

His handsome face beaming with smiles, Audley Sternfield entered the room, and, as he gently drew his young wife to his heart, he softly whispered, "Arrived at last, my own darling. How happy—how blessed I am!"

Antoinette, remembering at that moment all the unkind thoughts, the bitter regrets that she had harbored since their last parting, forgot all her grievances, and, woman-like, accused herself of injustice and unkindness. Ah, had Sternfield been always tender to her thus, he might soon have rivetted her affections to himself as irrevocably as he had done her destinies.

The evening passed quickly and pleasantly, and unwillingly Sternfield at length rose to take leave. As he clasped his bride's delicate hand in his, his glance sought her wedding-ring, but it was no longer on the finger on which he had placed it.

"Where is *it*—your ring?" he asked, with a sudden contraction of his brows.

Antoinette raised her other hand, on one of whose fingers the golden circlet glittered, murmuring, "I used to color so deeply and feel so uncomfortable when any one even glanced towards my hand, I thought it more prudent to change it."

"Quite right, dearest; and now for another question equally allowable, and I hope equally easy to answer: Who is this Mr. Louis Beauchesne, with whom report says my little Antoinette has been so busily flirting of late?"

"Oh, poor Louis!" rejoined the girl, with a frankness which effectually disarmed his suspicions, at least for the moment.

"Why do you call him poor Louis?"

"Because I like him," she rejoined, smiling and slightly coloring.

"I hope you never call me poor Sternfield," returned her companion, divining, with a quickness peculiar to him, that Louis had been a suitor, though not a favored one.

"No, no," she gravely whispered; "you are one better calculated to inspire fear than pity."

"And love than either, I trust," was his equally soft-breathed reply.

"A truce to farther whispering, friends," playfully interrupted Mrs. D'Aulnay. "I want your attention for a matter more serious than any of your own private affairs."

"Speak your wish, fair lady. It shall be law for us both," and Sternfield gracefully bowed.

"Well, I wish to organize a sleighing-party to Longue Point or to Lachine. We can count on very little sleighing after a couple of weeks, the season is so far advanced."

"But we promised papa we should be so quiet and retired whilst I remained in town," hesitated Antoinette.

"And so we are, and so we will be, my very prudish little cousin. I do not intend proposing either ball, rout, or *soirée*, but merely a drive, to profit by the present beautiful roads. St. Anthony himself could not have objected to such a thing. Take this pencil and make a memorandum, Major Sternfield, of those I wish you to gather together."

Two or three names were mentioned and jotted down without comment, and then Mrs. D'Aulnay proposed Colonel Evelyn.

"Where is the use of asking him?" objected Sternfield. "He will not come. He did not the last time."

"Never mind that, Mr. Secretary, but attend to your duties," was the peremptory reply. "Invited, Evelyn shall be. He joined us once before."

"Yes, on which memorable occasion he lost the splendid bays he had brought with him from England, a reminiscence scarcely calculated to induce him to favor us with his society a second time. And besides, of what use will he be, now that he has neither horses nor turn-out?"

"Nonsense, Major Sternfield," sharply retorted his hostess. "You know as well as I do that he has lately procured a pair of the most beautiful Canadian thorough-breds in the country. You are either jealous, or anxious to be the only irresistible beau of the party."

"Do you call him irresistible?" sneered Sternfield.

"No, but he is misanthropic—mysterious, which is a great deal better."

The gentleman shrugged his shoulders, and, after two or three minutes' farther discussion of their plans, took leave.

The morning appointed for their expedition dawned clear and bright; and whilst the two ladies were chatting over a somewhat late breakfast, in the pleasant little morning-room, Jeanne entered, and handed a card to her mistress.

"Why, I declare it is Colonel Evelyn!" exclaimed the latter, in tones of profound astonishment. "What on earth can he want so early?"

Antoinette's color slightly deepened, but she offered no solution of the problem.

"What are we to do?" continued Mrs. D'Aulnay. "The drawing-room fires are scarcely lighted yet. We had better have him up here. Yes, Jeanne, show the gentleman up. Do you know we both look charming in these graceful French morning-dresses? and then this room, with my birds and flowers, is a perfect *niche* of comfort. Decidedly, 'tis the best place to receive him."

Stately and calm, the visitor entered. Probably aware of Antoinette's arrival, for he expressed no surprise on seeing her, he accosted her with quiet friendliness; and then, after apologizing for his matinal visit, said, with a tranquil smile,

"I wish to know from yourself, Mrs. D'Aulnay, whether your invitation was extended merely to my horses, or did it also include myself?"

"Why, what mean you, Colonel Evelyn?" was the indignant rejoinder. "I told Major Sternfield to ask you on my behalf, as I did not think it necessary to send you a more formal notice of such a very simple affair."

"Well, the invitation, to say the least, was a very equivocal one. I met Major Sternfield in the street yesterday evening;

and after felicitating me on the acquisition of my new horses, and asking me if they were well broken in, he told me that Madam D'Aulnay was getting up a driving-party and could not do without them."

"How malicious of Major Sternfield!" ejaculated Mrs. D'Aulnay, with a heightened color. "I need not explain or deny anything, Colonel, for you know well I am incapable of such rudeness."

"I feel assured of that," he gravely rejoined. "The hospitality Mrs. D'Aulnay has so kindly shown to the strangers whom chance has brought to her native land, is alone sufficient refutation. But my chief purpose in coming was to know at what hour you wish my horses and servant (which are always entirely at your disposal) to be here. Major Sternfield, unfortunately, did not wait to inform me on that point."

"I will not accept either, well trained as I know they are, without their master," replied Mrs. D'Aulnay, with a pretty air of feminine *pique*. "I know you care, in general, but little for woman's society; still I am certain you are too kind to come in person to refuse a lady's invitation, especially when she tells you that doing so will both annoy and mortify her."

Colonel Evelyn looked perplexed. His chief object in calling that morning had really been, as he had said, to place his equipage at Mrs. D'Aulnay's disposal, and to ascertain at what hour he should send it. He may also have had a passing wish, unacknowledged perhaps to himself, to see Antoinette on her arrival; but joining the sleighing-party was a thing he had in no wise contemplated. Still, when the lady urged and pleaded, he at length rejoined:

"Of course, since Mrs. D'Aulnay so kindly insists, I cannot but comply with her wishes; but I much fear that, after the catastrophe which occurred during the last excursion of the sort that I joined, no lady will be found courageous enough to trust herself with me."

"Indeed you are mistaken. Without going farther, here are two ladies willing to share the glories and perils of your turn-out. What say you, Antoinette?"

The girl blushingly shook her head, but Colonel Evelyn, without noticing the slight movement, quickly rejoined:

"Oh! Miss De Mirecourt is a heroine in the true sense of the word; and if such an accident were ever to happen again, I could be almost selfish enough to wish her for my companion. It was her wonderful calmness that saved us both."

"Joined to Colonel Evelyn's own skill and presence of mind," replied Mrs. D'Aulnay with a winning smile. "But what say you, Antoinette," she continued, animated by a sudden desire to punish Sternfield for his late shortcomings,—"what say you to giving the world, and particularly Colonel Evelyn, a proof of your courage by driving out with him to-day?"

"Pray do, Miss De Mirecourt," he kindly, nay persuasively said. "I can safely promise that your nerves and resolution will not be subjected to such a severe trial as they were the last time. It will be a welcome proof that you have forgiven and forgotten the terrors of that dangerous drive."

"Of course, she will, Colonel Evelyn," interrupted Mrs. D'Aulnay. "Consider the matter as finally arranged."

Antoinette, timid and embarrassed, was ashamed to dissent farther; but when the visitor shortly after took leave, she burst forth, "Oh, Lucille, I am afraid Audley will be very angry with our arrangement."

"Just what he deserves, the impertinent creature, for misrepresenting me in such a shameful manner," retorted Mrs. D'Aulnay, on whose cheek a spot of indignant red yet lingered.

"But, Lucille, when he is angry, I feel so much afraid of him," remonstrated poor Antoinette.

"The very reason you must learn to brave him out; but if you should feel at all uncomfortable about it, I will tell him the arrangement was entirely my own—that you had nothing to do with it, which indeed you had not; so no more worrying about such a trifle!"

CHAPTER 20

It happened, fortunately for the easy fulfilment of Mrs. D'Aulnay's plans, that Major Sternfield, owing to some unforeseen impediment, was somewhat late, and on dashing up in his fantastic but graceful cutter, he found the members of the party already in their respective places.

"Time is up, Sternfield! What kept you so late to-day?" exclaimed two or three voices, but the new-comer deigned no reply. When his eye fell on Antoinette, seated beside Colonel Evelyn, an angry flush mounted to his forehead; but, controlling his vexation, he approached Mrs. D'Aulnay, who sat back among her bear-skin robes, with a very provoking smile on her face.

"Am I to thank you for this arrangement?" he asked in a low angry tone. "Is it you who have condemned me to drive alone?"

"No need for that, Major Sternfield. Look at yon unfortunate Captain Assheton, with two ladies, crowded up in that nut-shell of his. Relieve him of one of his fair charges."

"Pshaw!" retorted the gentleman with a look of intense annoyance, "Mrs. D'Aulnay is not like herself to-day. However, you have punished me; now I shall retaliate, and inflict my ill-tempered companionship on you"; and, suiting the action to the word, he threw the reins of his horse to one of the men in attendance, and sprang into Mrs. D'Aulnay's sleigh.

"You are really becoming insufferably impertinent," she exclaimed, inwardly however, anything but dissatisfied with an arrangement which she had probably contemplated from the first.

A few smiles and satirical glances passed between some members of the party at this by-play; but Sternfield was an

idol of the ladies, and do what he would, was generally sure
of indulgence. Another five minutes' delay was occasioned
by one of the gentlemen leaving his own already
sufficiently freighted sleigh and stepping into Sternfield's
empty cutter, into which he invited one of the over-
crowded fair ones, vainly pointed out to the former's
compassionate notice, a few moments previous. All were
now ready, and, with jingling bells and nodding tassels, the
cavalcade set out.

"Now, Mrs. D'Aulnay," abruptly questioned Sternfield,
after a few moments' silence, "answer me frankly. Is this
arrangement yours or Antoinette's?"

"Entirely mine."

"And why, may I ask? Why separate me from my wife
when I have so much to say to her? when we have so little
time to spend together."

"To punish you, Major Sternfield, for delivering so
untruthfully and rudely my message to Colonel Evelyn."

"Ah, he has stooped then to explain and complain, our
most potent, grave, and reverend Colonel," said Sternfield
with a sneer.

"No such thing. It was by mere chance I found out your
supercherie; but, good heavens! do you want to break our
necks that you worry and abuse my beautiful pets thus?
Give me the reins at once! 'Tis dangerous to trust you with
them whilst you are in such a dreadful temper."

Sternfield sullenly obeyed; and for a long time
afterwards, nothing beyond an occasional monosyllable
escaped his lips. Not so silent, however, were Colonel
Evelyn and his fair companion; and it was well, at least for
Antoinette, that she was removed from her bridegroom's
immediate *surveillance,* or she would assuredly have
thoroughly expiated, at a later period, her own and Mrs.
D'Aulnay's faults. Their conversation, on setting out, was
confined to generalities; but as they entered on the Lachine
road, the remembrance of their last eventful drive in that

same direction, vividly rose up before the memory of both. A shade of emotion crossed Evelyn's brow, and he involuntarily exclaimed,

"What a narrow escape! Tell me, Miss De Mirecourt, what were your thoughts, that is, if you were capable of analysing them at such a moment, when we were dashing on at such fearful speed to what might have been our ultimate destruction?"

There was a moment's shy pause, for such frank communion with a comparative stranger embarrassed her, but then, half smilingly, half seriously, she rejoined: "I was thinking of death, and endeavoring to prepare myself for it."

"Well thought, well said," was the grave reply. "Though unfortunately I profess religion myself, neither in action nor in word, still, where I meet with it in others, I respect it."

"Are you not a 'true believer,' a Catholic like myself?" she questioned, smilingly though timidly.

"Why, Miss De Mirecourt, you are quite learned on all topics relating to my unworthy self," he rejoined, turning upon her with a suddenness that dyed her face with crimson. "I suppose the same charitable talker who informed you once before that I was a woman-hater, has also told you, that, though little better than an infidel in point of practice, I was born and brought up in the same faith as yourself. Well, I have no right to be angry, for much that has been told you is unfortunately too true. Do not mistake me, however. Though careless, indeed utterly, completely neglectful of all the precepts and duties of that Church of which I still and always will call myself a member, I have never gone so far in my impiety as to doubt even for a moment the wisdom and mercy, much less the existence, of the Sovereign Being who formed me. No, I am not an atheist, as many have charitably called me," he added with considerable bitterness, "but simply a bad

Catholic. You are shocked—startled, Miss De Mirecourt,"
he said as he noticed Antoinette's color suddenly rise, and a
pained expression flit over her face.

Not of his errors thought she then, but of her own. She
the religiously-trained, the carefully-instructed girl, who
had suffered a few months of fashionable, frivolous life to
stifle in her heart all its best and holiest feelings, and to
plunge her into a false step whose terrible consequences
left nothing open to her save a long vista of future
falsehood and misery. Again, Colonel Evelyn repeated his
previous question, and his companion startled into reply,
involuntarily rejoined:

"Has not our Divine Teacher said, Judge not lest ye be
judged!"

Wondering at the gentle aptitude which alike charmed
and surprised him in all Antoinette's replies, and won into
farther confidence by her evident sympathy, he continued;

"And now, that I have proved to you I am not exactly an
infidel or an atheist, may I venture on answering the other
accusation laid to my charge, that of being, as you have
already told me with an openness I prize in proportion to
its rarity among your sex, a woman-hater?" Antoinette
smiled, and the bright blush Evelyn almost unconsciously
took such pleasure in watching, again rose to her cheek. He
mused a moment in silence, and then, turning suddenly
towards her, looked full in her face, and said:

"Shall I or shall I not give you a little insight into the story
of my life? I cannot clear myself, or excuse my general
avoidance and distrust of women, unless I do. Yes, I will tell
it, but remember, not to be related again to Mrs. D'Aulnay,
or any others of her stamp; a breach of confidence I feel
convinced you could never be guilty of. I need not tell
you—my misspent life would almost have done so of
itself—that I never knew a mother's loving cares or
counsels. Left an orphan in earliest childhood, I retain no
tenderer recollections of my youth, than those with which

college life, an indifferent guardian, and a handsome, haughty elder brother, furnish me. To be brief, I grew up to manhood uncared for, chose the profession of arms,— of course the family estate went to my brother John,—and entered on life with a heart, despite its harsh training, capable of yielding a rich return to whoever should win its love. The time and hour soon came. Chance threw me into contact with a young girl of good family and gentle bringing up. I will not vaunt her beauty, but will only say, that fair as you are, Miss De Mirecourt, she was still far lovelier. I wooed, and was soon accepted, both by herself and family; for though I was not wealthy, I had powerful family influence, which was certain to ensure my rapid advancement in the career I had chosen. The day was appointed, the bridal *trousseau* almost ready, and, having a few days' leisure, I determined on paying a visit to the old family-home to bid it and my brother farewell. He received me kindly enough, though he rallied me most unmercifully about my turning Benedict, as he called it, so soon. Somewhat nettled by his satirical remarks, I drew forth, in my boyish vanity, the portrait of my betrothed, which, like all model "true lovers," I wore about me, and triumphantly asked him, was not that face sufficient excuse for early turning Benedict? He looked long, earnestly at it, and at last returned it with the brief remark that it was indeed a lovely countenance. When I came down the following morning, equipped for my journey, he was standing dressed in the hall, and carelessly informed me that he had business in—but names are unnecessary—in the same quiet country town in which my betrothed dwelt. Delighted at this, I expressed my satisfaction at the prospect of their so soon knowing each other, and of his being able to satisfy himself at the same time how far the reality eclipsed the pictured beauty of my bride-elect. There was nothing in the careless glance, the few indifferent words they interchanged on their mutual introduction, to warn me of coming evil. The time sped on. My brother, in his *nonchalant*, fashionable way, lounged in occasionally into the little drawing-room, but there was no reason to find fault with that: it rather gratified me. One evening he quietly said he wished to make me a suitable brotherly gift, to confer on myself and heirs for evermore the lands of Welden Holme, a fine unentailed property belonging to the family estate. My gratitude was of course as boundless as my credulity. I returned to the old house with the papers he placed in my hands, to seek an interview with the family lawyer. He was tedious, minute, detained me longer than I had expected; but what of that? I returned the eve of my appointed bridal day. Of course I went straight to her home. Secret consternation was depicted on the faces of the servants when I asked for her. Then came her mother, grayhaired and respectable; and told me to be patient, to be forgiving, but that my affianced bride was now the wife of John Evelyn, Lord Winterstow. I listened patiently, stupidly almost, so great was my woful surprise and grief, whilst she added that they had been privately married three days previous, and were now on their distant wedding-tour. Then I drew forth the miniature, with the papers which really and virtually conveyed to me the estate with which he sought to bribe me for my bride, and cast them into the flames of the grate-fire before me. 'Tell them how I have disposed of both their gifts,' I said; 'tell them—'

" 'Oh, do not curse them!' interrupted the pale trembling mother. 'Do not curse my child!' 'No,' I replied, as I turned away, 'I leave them both to the curse of their own remorse.' That very day I exchanged into a regiment ordered for foreign service. Since then I have served in India, Malta, Gibraltar; have sighed out five years of my manhood's prime in a French prison, the hard school in which I learned your language, Miss De Mirecourt, but for twelve long years I have never set foot on my native land."

"And what of them?" asked Antoinette, with a moistened eye and quickened breathing that plainly told how deeply this simple manly recital of a life's sorrow had touched her.

"Aye! what of them?" he rejoined bitterly. "In my early simplicity, I questioned like yourself, what of them, expecting that their perfidy would hourly meet with condign and striking punishment. Well, it has not been so. They are one of the happiest couples in England, with lovely intelligent children around them, she beautiful, admired—he happy, fond; whilst I am a lonely wanderer on the earth, a stray waif, a gloomy misanthrope. Do you wonder now, that I have lost faith in your sex; that I have avoided them almost as carefully as saint or anchorite has ever done?"

Antoinette made no reply, for she feared the tremor in her voice would reveal how deeply she felt, how earnestly she sympathized with the speaker; but the keen reader of face and character at her side, at once interpreted her silence correctly. After a pause he resumed:

"I have been strangely communicative with you, Miss De Mirecourt. What secret spell of yours has broken down so completely the barriers of my usual reserve?"

There was something peculiar in his tones, and Antoinette feared he was already regretting the frankness he had showed her.

Hurriedly she spoke: "I feel deeply grateful for the confidence you have deigned to repose in me, Colonel Evelyn, and it shall always be held sacred."

"I know that, young girl. Think you if I had supposed for a moment that it could have been otherwise, I should have trusted you. From the first, I saw that you were a being as different to Mrs. D'Aulnay and others of her class, as I am different from that perfumed fop, that heartless Sternfield."

Antoinette colored deeply; but that changing blush of hers came and went so often, that her companion attached no great importance to the circumstance.

CHAPTER 21

THE party were now near the humble village-inn, at which they soon stopped for warmth and refreshments, the greater part of the latter being brought by themselves. Antoinette, somewhat chilled by the long drive, was sitting in a warm corner of the room, near an angle of the huge glowing stove, awaiting the return of Colonel Evelyn, who had gone to procure her a glass of warm wine. Here she was suddenly accosted by Major Sternfield, who stepped up to her, and whispered with that stern frown with which she was, alas! already so familiar:

"Much as you may have enjoyed the previous arrangement, Antoinette, I must insist on altering it. You will drive back with me and no other."

Without waiting for a reply he turned away, and, when Colonel Evelyn returned with the refreshments he had procured, he wondered much at the taciturnity and pre-occupation which had so suddenly taken possession of his young companion. Shortly after, Mrs. D'Aulnay floated gracefully up to them and exclaimed:

"I fear I come to change arrangements agreeable to all parties; but, my dear Antoinette, Major Sternfield tells me that you had promised to drive with him when this excursion was first spoken of. He feels very sore about his disappointment, so I think you had better console his wounded feelings by driving back with him."

Antoinette remembered no such agreement, but she was only too thankful to accept any subterfuge that afforded her an opportunity of deprecating the stern anger of which she stood so much in dread.

"Well, be it so," she quickly rejoined. "I know Colonel Evelyn will as kindly consent to this arrangement as he did to our former one."

135

"I have no alternative," he said with a somewhat formal smile. "And who is to be my homeward companion; or is it necessary I should have one?"

"Certainly. That young lady (and Mrs. D'Aulnay indicated, by a slight motion of her head, one of the over-crowded damsels on whose behalf she had vainly appealed to Sternfield in the morning) has been thrown again on the world by Major Sternfield's resumption of his sleigh, and she awaits the advent of some generous knight-errant to relieve her."

"I have long since given up knight-errantry," coldly rejoined Evelyn, "but the lady is welcome to a seat in my sleigh."

The latter, though a really very pretty girl, happened to be one of the most affected and insipid of her class; so the feelings of Colonel Evelyn during the return drive may be easily imagined. To her nervous little terrors, her pretty sentimentalisms, he opposed a silent grimness which made the young lady in question inwardly compare him to an ogre. "Faugh!" thought he, as the latter, on their arrival, determined to make an impression on his stony heart, thanked him with a die-away languishing glance from her really splendid, dark eyes, which had only the effect of inexpressibly disgusting him, "who could believe that this creature and that other rare young girl really belong to the same species!"

Poor Antoinette's homeward drive had proved even less pleasant than Colonel Evelyn's. Sternfield was in one of his dark, jealous moods; and he questioned, reproached, and taunted her, with a severity alike unjust and ill-judged. Mrs. D'Aulnay, also out of sorts, invited none of the party in on her arrival, and she and Antoinette entered the house alone.

"What a stupid affair!" she petulantly exclaimed, as she twitched off her rich furs, and threw herself down on a couch in her dressing-room.

" 'Tis that ill-tempered Sternfield who spoiled all! I really think if I had not yielded to his wishes, and prevented you returning home with Colonel Evelyn, he would have made some dreadful scene or other, before the whole party. You cannot imagine how he annoyed and worried me. What did he say to you on your homeward *route?* Made love, I suppose?"

"Oh, that is unnecessary *now*," rejoined Antoinette, "it would be an idle waste of time!"

"Do not speak so singularly, Antoinette dear," hastily rejoined Mrs. D'Aulnay. "It alarms, grieves me. But you shiver, child, and how pale you are; I hope you have not taken cold. Lie down on the sofa, and I will send Jeanne to you immediately with a cup of hot coffee."

It was no cold or external physical ailment that blanched Antoinette's cheek, but mental suffering. That drive, both going and coming, had been a strangely eventful one for her. The powerful fascination Evelyn had exerted over her, whilst stooping to lay bare his proud heart to her gaze, and which she had earnestly, conscientiously, struggled against, still proved, alas! that she was capable of a far deeper, truer love, than that which she had bestowed on Audley Sternfield. Then the bridegroom himself, whose patient, thoughtful affection should have interposed an invulnerable shield between her inexperienced youth and the strange, dangerous snares that surrounded her peculiar position, yielding, instead, to jealousy, irritation, or any other unworthy feeling that happened at the moment to sway him, gave free vent to it, careless of the anguish he was inflicting on that sensitive young nature, to which the language of reproof was so new; or of the fearful rapidity with which he was weakening his own mental hold upon her.

The bitter hour of complete awakening from the feverish trance of her love-fit for Sternfield had at length arrived; and after a long hour's silent reverie, during which every little event and episode which had marked their acquaintance from its first beginning, down to the painful drive of that day, rose up before her, she suddenly clasped her hands, and murmured with a look of intense anguish, "God help me! I do not love him!"

What a terrible, but alas! what an unavailing confession for a bride to make!

But there were deeper abysses of misery yet remaining, and from which she should have prayed God on bended knee, night and morning, to preserve her. It was that of loving another. Yes, though her affection, or rather predilection, for Audley had vanished like a morning mist, still she owed him entire fidelity and allegiance, and every feeling of her heart belonged, of right, to him. Did any warning voice suggest that she should avoid Colonel Evelyn even as if he were her deadliest enemy—that that proud nature, which had so strangely unbent to her influence, was one, alas, too dangerously attractive, too wondrously fascinating? It must have been so; for suddenly, covering her face with her hands, as if ashamed of the weakness her words implied, she murmured, "I must see Evelyn no more—no more."

CHAPTER 22

A WEEK passed over quietly enough. Sternfield, who had somewhat recovered his good temper, and who had received besides some very severe lectures from Mrs. D'Aulnay, behaved himself better. Colonel Evelyn had sent the ladies some interesting books, but he had not called to see them. One unpleasant, sleety afternoon, however, that they had settled themselves down to their work, certain that no visitors would disturb them, Jeanne brought up his card.

"What is coming over the man?" exclaimed Mrs. D'Aulnay. "He is surely in love with you, Antoinette. Is it not too bad that—" she suddenly stopped and bit her lip, but her cousin's rising color told her that she had easily completed the sentence, with its unexpressed regrets over her union with Sternfield. Alas! did not her own heart, not once, but daily, hourly now, waste itself in similar unavailing regrets.

Colonel Evelyn entered with a friendly kindness of manner, very different to his usual unbending reserve; and as Mrs. D'Aulnay watched the earnest gentle glance he bent on her young cousin, the genial smile with which he listened to her expression of thanks for the books he had sent, she was conscious of a secret wish, that the "irresistible Sternfield," as she had once delighted in calling him, was in the most distant penal settlement of his Sovereign's dominions. With her unfixed principles, her lax ideas of right and wrong, it did not strike Mrs. D'Aulnay that there was any harm in permitting Colonel Evelyn to increase his evident admiration for Antoinette by intercourse with her. On the contrary, to a mind stored, like hers, with novels, love-tales of the most reprehensible folly, there was

139

something inexpressibly touching in this dawning of "*un amour malheureux.*"

Fortunately, however, Antoinette's moral perceptions were of a keener character; and as Colonel Evelyn grew more attentive, addressing his conversation more exclusively to herself, her restlessness, and occasionally appealing glances towards her cousin, plainly told the latter that she wished her to come to her aid, by giving a more general tone to the conversation. Madame D'Aulnay, however, doing as she would have wished others to have done by her, and unwilling to stop so charming a little bit of romance in its very beginning, affected to be exceedingly engrossed by her tapestry-frame. Ere long, Jeanne came in with a message from Mr. D'Aulnay, whom his wife at once sought in the library. She shortly re-appeared at the drawing-room door, ready dressed for the street, and informed her astonished auditors that "she was going out with Mr. D'Aulnay for a half-hour, on business," an assertion which was really true. Antoinette's perturbation on this announcement became extreme, and Colonel Evelyn put his own interpretation, a flattering one to himself, truly, on her deepening color and nervous embarrassment. Involuntarily he drew his chair closer to hers, and his voice assumed a lower, kinder tone, which tended in no manner, however, to put his young companion at her ease. They were thus seated together, when, chancing to look up, they perceived Major Sternfield standing in the half-open doorway, steadfastly regarding them. Antoinette gave an irresistible start of terror, which did not escape Evelyn's quick glance; but endeavoring to recover herself, she rose, and, in a somewhat faltering tone, welcomed Sternfield, and asked him to come in.

"No, I fear I might be *de trop*," he slowly rejoined, in accents of bitter irony. "It would be unpardonable on my part to disturb so engrossing a *tête-à-tête*." Colonel Evelyn's brow grew dark as the speaker's, and he fixed a stern, questioning glance upon him.

"Surely, Colonel Evelyn, you are not going to order me under arrest for my unwitting interruption," queried Sternfield, in the same mocking tones.

The Colonel hastily rose to his feet, but before he could speak, Antoinette gasped forth in tones of passionate entreaty, "Audley, for mercy's sake, hush!"

An actual storm of passion seemed to shake the young man's frame, but he evidently wrestled with himself to repress it. "Antoinette!" he at length said, in a voice hoarse from concentrated anger, "you shall account to me for this"; and then, as if afraid to trust himself longer, he turned abruptly away, and, a moment after, they heard the hall-door heavily clang to. Antoinette, white as death, and trembling in every limb, sank back in her chair, whilst her companion sternly exclaimed, " 'Tis he, rather, who shall be called to a strict account."

"Just what I feared," she whispered, growing, if possible, whiter than before. "Oh, Colonel Evelyn, you will both meet in deadly conflict, I, the unhappy, unworthy cause, and one or both may fall."

"There is no fear of that, Miss De Mirecourt, if I choose to let the matter rest. Major Sternfield will scarcely challenge his commanding officer without some more tangible cause of provocation than I have given him."

"Ah, you cannot reassure me! I know that men of your profession generally hold the cruel code that the slightest insult or offence should be washed out in blood. Oh, Colonel Evelyn," and she clasped his arm with her trembling hands, whilst her soft, speaking eyes sought his in earnest entreaty, "promise me that you will take no farther notice of this unfortunate affair—that you will not seek to exact from Major Sternfield an apology he may refuse to give?"

It was a new sensation to Evelyn to have that gentle, beautiful girl thus clinging to him in prayerful entreaty, and he inwardly rejoiced his heart was not yet so utterly insensible as to be able to resist its influence.

"For whose sake do you thus pray so earnestly," he smilingly questioned, laying his own powerful, sun-browned hand on the little fingers that lay like snow-flakes on his arm. "Is it for mine or Major Sternfield's?"

"For both," she rejoined, hurriedly, confusedly.

"Listen to me, Miss De Mirecourt, I will give the promise you exact of me—bind myself thus hand and foot, if, in return, you will frankly answer me one question, and pardon, at the same time, my indiscretion in asking it?"

"Speak," was the low-toned reply.

"Tell me, then, do you love Audley Sternfield?"

How that question flooded her heart with pain. She was asked did she love *him*, her husband, her future partner through the joys and sorrows of earth, and she could not, anxiously as she sought to deceive herself, say "yes."

"Alas! I do not!" she rejoined, with a look and tone of indescribable anguish.

"Another question, Antoinette," whispered her companion, overlooking, in the delight which that earnest denial afforded him, the peculiarity of her manner, "another question," and he bent towards her till his thick brown locks almost mingled with her own shining tresses. "Do you think you could ever learn to love me?"

The tide of vivid burning scarlet that flashed over cheek, neck, and brow, the suddenly averted eyes, as if the girl feared he might read in their depths the secret feelings of her heart, rendered him careless of her startled, impetuous exclamation: "Do not ask me so idle, so wild a question, Colonel Evelyn?"

"Antoinette," he whispered, clasping her suddenly to his breast. "You do love me. It is useless to deny it. Oh to think that such a treasure of happiness is vouchsafed to bless my long-desolate heart, my barren, cheerless life!"

Ah! in that moment she felt that death would have been welcome, aye, pleasant. There was no chance of farther self-deception now. She loved with womanly love, not girlish fancy, the true-hearted man beside her, but she must leave for ever the support of those kindly arms that would have shielded her so carefully from life's trials and cares; she must reject that priceless devotion, and follow out alone her own dreary destiny, linked as it was for ever with that of the dreaded, heartless Sternfield. The regrets that crowded upon her were overwhelming in their despairing intensity, and, with a countenance, furrowed at the moment with mental anguish, she slowly raised herself from Evelyn's embrace. "Words cannot thank you," she whispered, "for so great a proof of preference from one like you, to aught so unworthy as myself."

"But, I do not ask thanks, my Antoinette," he interrupted, troubled by her strange demeanor. "One little word of affection would be far more welcome."

"And that word can never be said. The love you deign to ask for, can never be yours."

"This is girlish trifling," he earnestly though gently rejoined. "I know you love me, Antoinette. I have read it unmistakably in your look, manner, and voice."

"So much the worse for us both, then," she solemnly rejoined. "I tell you, Colonel Evelyn, I can never be yours— must never listen to word of love from you again."

Terribly perplexed as well as grieved, he stood in silent trouble, regarding her; then it suddenly flashed upon him, that she might have entered into some thoughtless engagement with Major Sternfield, such as young girls often form as easily as they break, and that she regarded the engagement in question as an insurmountable obstacle to any other union, even though the fancy which first induced her to make it, had completely passed away.

"Sit down, Antoinette," he said. "We will talk quietly over the matter," and gently pressing her into a chair, he took her hand in his. She immediately withdrew it, but remained seated where he had placed her.

"You owe me a fair and patient hearing," he continued, "and it will be better for us both that we should understand each other at once. I, who for long years past, aye ever since that first bitter trial of my life which I have already recounted to you, have avoided woman, shunned alike her love or sympathy, have suffered unconsciously to myself your image to creep into my heart and become very dear to me. Had your own sweet guilelessness of character not betrayed that my affection was in some slight degree reciprocated, notwithstanding the disparity of age, and the gloomy unattractiveness of my nature, I would have hidden it deep in my own breast, and none would ever have suspected its existence. Destiny has decreed otherwise; and it rests with you now to decide, whether this new-born love is to prove to me a blessing or a curse; it rests with you to decide whether the remaining half of my life is to prove as desolate as the first has done." She had covered her face with her hands and was sobbing bitterly, but he went on. "Antoinette, you are in the dawning of life, I at its meridian. Oh, you know how cruelly this heart of mine has been tried before—spare it now! Make of it no young girl's toy to be cast aside after it has been won, for some childish trifle, some exaggerated sentiment. Speak to me, tell me that my future life will be gladdened by your love!"

"Would to God that we had never met!" she passionately exclaimed, wringing her hands. "Was it not enough that I was wretched, without bringing misery on others? Oh, Colonel Evelyn, I could kneel at your feet to crave forgiveness for the pain I have given, may give you, but alas! I must again say I never can be yours."

Keen and terrible was the suffering her words inflicted on her hearer, and he abruptly turned from her to hide the emotion every line of his countenance betrayed, but soon he returned to her side to make a last despairing appeal.

"Antoinette, you are sacrificing us both to some over-strained principle," he vehemently exclaimed. "You are trampling on my heart as well as your own, for some insufficient cause. You shake your head in dissent. Let me know then this obstacle that lies like a gulf between us. Give me the poor satisfaction, one accorded to the greatest criminal, that of knowing why I am condemned?"

"Alas! my lips are sealed by a solemn promise, by an oath, to never reveal it."

"Poor, innocent child! Some one has been practising on your youth and ignorance of life, to wind you into toils which may yet bring misery, if not worse, on your head. Break from them, Antoinette, turn from the false friends who would thus mislead you, and my arms will be your shelter, your home."

"Colonel Evelyn, you will drive me wild," she exclaimed, in a voice sharp with anguish. "Waste not your love or regrets on a wretched, guilty creature like myself."

"Guilty, wretched," he repeated with a violent start, whilst his face flushed. "These are wild words, Antoinette."

"Yes, but they are true ones. False to the holiest principles of my youth, false to ties which even the most hardened respect, what other epithets do I deserve?"

Earnestly, searchingly Evelyn gazed into her face, as if he would have looked into the depths of her soul, and then in an accent of indescribable tenderness, he said, "Poor wayward child, your looks belie your words; but it is time that this painful interview should come to an end. You have no gleam of hope to give me?"

"None, none," she reiterated. "I have only to say that my future lot will be far more miserable and cheerless than your own."

He looked at her a moment in silence, and what volumes of meaning, of emotion, were in that glance! No disappointed suitor's pride, no irritation, lurked there; but oh, such yearning love, such unbounded compassion for that fragile young creature on whom the hoarded affection of the best part of a life time had been lavished. "Antoinette, farewell," he at length said, and his tones trembled despite every effort. "Remember, in your hour of sorrow or trial, that you have a friend whom nothing can alienate."

Her hour of trial! Yes, it had come! Bitter, scathing trial, and he had in great part brought it about—infused into the chalice of her misery a bitterness which almost overtasked her failing strength to bear, and which left its traces so legibly stamped on her brow, that tender compassion for her almost predominated over his own wearing, hopeless disappointment. Silently he withdrew from the room, and she, stunned, almost bewildered, laid down her aching head on the arm of the couch, wishing that she might as easily lay down the burden of life.

CHAPTER 23

Of the lapse of time she took no note; and when the well-known voice of Sternfield suddenly pronounced her name, she slowly raised her head and looked at him in silence. He drew a chair towards her and sat down, saying, in a low stern tone, "I have come to ask why I found my wife closeted, an hour ago, with Colonel Evelyn?"

The expression of heavy languor shadowing the girl's beautiful face remained unchanged, and in tones, strangely unlike her usual clear, sweet accents, she rejoined, "I was not closeted with Colonel Evelyn. I received him as I would have received any other gentleman in the public drawing-room with open doors."

"Where, pray, was your model *chaperone* meanwhile, the wise and prudent Mrs. D'Aulnay?"

"Gone out with her husband. I am not surely to be rendered responsible for that."

"No. I will only ask to hear the subject of the long conversation you held with this same gentleman visitor." "That I cannot reveal to you, Audley. The secrets of others are not at my disposal."

"Is this your idea of wifely duty?"

No reply, save a moody silence.

"Answer me," he continued in tones of rising anger. "Is this ring," he caught up the small hand on which it glittered, "and the union of which it is the sacred symbol, a mere mockery?"

In his deep-restrained passion, he pressed, perhaps unconsciously, the small hand he had taken, till a line half livid, half scarlet, formed around the golden circlet.

"Press on," she murmured, giving no token, beyond a bitter smile, of the physical suffering that strong clasp caused her, "Why should not the outward symbol of our ill-starred union torture and crush the body as deeply as its reality does the soul?"

"You are complimentary," he rejoined, loosing his hold of the hand he had clasped, not in love but in anger, and tossing it from him.

"It seems to me that the union whose sorrows you are so eloquent over, does not weigh so heavily on you. It has neither taught you affection or duty to him you call husband, nor has it prevented you listening to the secrets or love-vows of other men."

"But whose is the fault, Audley?" she suddenly retorted with passionate earnestness. "Why have you placed, and why do you keep me in so cruel, so exceptional a position? I tell you I cannot bear this longer. I will acknowledge everything to my father."

"And break your solemn promise, your vow?" he interrupted. "No, Antoinette, you will not, you dare not do it. That promise made upon the cross received from your dying mother, is as binding as our marriage-vow itself."

"But why this continued secrecy and mystery? Oh, Audley, it is bad for us both. Do away with it. Acknowledge me before God and man for your wife, whilst a chance of happiness yet remains to us—whilst our hearts are not yet entirely estranged from each other!"

"Impossible child, utterly impossible."

"And why so?"

"Because," and his handsome lip curved with a movement of mingled sarcasm and irritation—"because I am not rich enough to afford the luxury of a dowerless bride."

"A dowerless bride!" she slowly, wonderingly repeated.

"Yes. Do you not know that if we were so infatuated as to confess our rash act to your father, the consequence would be your immediate disinheritance, and we would have nothing to live on but love, which would prove a most inadequate means of support. You may perhaps say that in three months, in six months, your father's resentment will be just as much to be dreaded as it is now. Perhaps not. Time brings many changes in its course, and before that period, other influences may be brought to bear on his prejudices, which will soften if not remove them. At the worst, Antoinette, you know that at the age of eighteen, nothing can prevent you coming into the enjoyment of your mother's small fortune, according to her dying wishes, which happily for us were legally expressed and recorded. Till then—'tis only a comparatively short time to wait—we may probably be obliged to keep our secret."

There was a long pause. New thoughts and fears were busy at work in Antoinette's aching brain, and for the first time the bitterly humiliating conjecture presented itself, that Sternfield had married her, not from any romantic feeling of attachment, but from cold calculation, from motives of interest.

Still with wonderful calmness she questioned, "Were you as well acquainted with my position when you married me, Audley, as you are now?"

"Of course, you simple child. Do you think that I, with an income which barely suffices to keep me in the necessaries of my rank—my gloves alone cost a dollar per day"— (Major Sternfield forgot to state what his gambling propensities cost)—"would have ventured on marriage, without previously ascertaining whether my wife possessed some golden charms as well as other more irresistible ones?"

"Thank you; I feel grateful for your candor. Now, I need not visit with such severe condemnation, nor expiate with such bitter remorse, my own waning love, my growing indifference, towards yourself."

"Whether your love wanes or grows, Antoinette," he carelessly said, "it does not matter so much, for you can never forget that you are my wife."

"There is no danger that the captive will forget the galling chain he is compelled to wear," was her bitter reply.

"A chain you assumed of your own free will, lady mine; but, a truce to heroics! I have a horror of them in private life. I have only to say before terminating this interview, which I fear we have already prolonged too far for our mutual comfort, that there are some things I will bear with—others I will not. With your indifference, or waning love as you call it, I can put up philosophically enough; but beware of rousing my jealousy by flirting with other men. Farewell. What, you will not let me take a parting kiss! Well, I will be patient: your mood may be more amiable at our next meeting."

Jeanne, who chanced to be in the hall at the moment, and let the gay handsome Major out, saw no tokens of disturbance on his smiling features; but she wondered much when she went up stairs shortly after to Antoinette's room, with a message from Mrs. D'Aulnay, who had just returned, at the ghastly paleness of the young girl's face.

"Tell Mrs. D'Aulnay, Jeanne, that I feel too ill to go down stairs this evening."

"Poor Mademoiselle Antoinette, you do indeed look very bad," said the kind-hearted woman in an anxious tone. "I will bring you up a cup of tea now, and some warm *tisanne* later, which will make you sleep soundly all night."

"I fear that is more than your *tisanne* can accomplish, Jeanne."

"Indeed, Mademoiselle, you are mistaken: it is a most wonderful cure, especially in youth, for, thank God! dear young lady, at your age, you can have no thoughts able to drive sleep from your pillow."

Antoinette shivered as if a cold wind had suddenly struck her, but she forced herself to smile kindly on the woman as she dismissed her.

"My age!" she repeated. "Yes, young in years but old in sorrow," and she pressed her hands tightly on her burning, throbbing brow.

Jeanne soon brought up a daintily-prepared repast, with a message from Mrs. D'Aulnay, excusing herself for a couple of hours, as she was engaged with a friend of Mr. D'Aulnay, who had just arrived from the country.

The time passed heavily on, and Antoinette still sat motionless, her changing cheek alone giving token of the storm of agitated thoughts and feelings that worked within. Who could describe or analyse their intense bitterness? The full complete knowledge of Sternfield's unworthiness, and the certainty which brought so cruel a pang to her woman's heart, that she had been sought and won (her cheek burned as she recalled how lightly and how easily) from a paltry motive of worldly interest. Then came the thought of the deceit she had practised on a kind, indulgent father—of her own sad falling off from truth and goodness. But keener, bitterer pang, perhaps, than all else, was the agonizing remembrance of the priceless treasure she had lost in Colonel Evelyn's love. That brave, true heart, with its wealth of noble, generous affections; that clear, powerful intellect, and honorable nature, which might have belonged to her, and her alone, and which, alas! were for ever beyond her grasp. How contemptible appeared now the girlish feeling of admiration for Major Sternfield's handsome face and fascinating manners, which, combined with the flattered gratification of her own vanity, she had once dignified with the name of love.

It was a fearful consciousness to a wife, to a woman, weak, erring as she was, surrounded by temptation, and with nothing to save her from harm but the dim spark of religious faith that still burned in her breast. She thought of Mrs. D'Aulnay, the unprincipled, ill-judging friend, whose counsels had ever led her astray; of Sternfield, her husband, who acted as if he wished to drive her to destruction; and then of her own miserable weakness, her luke-warm devotion, her undisciplined heart. From the very depths of her nature suddenly went up in the stillness

of her room, an audible cry to Him whose ear is ever open
to the accents of humble penitence: "Oh, my God, none but
thou can save me!"

On her knees she repeated it, and in broken accents
prayed, not in empty form as she had done for so long a
time past, but in passionate appeal, that she and Cecil
Evelyn might meet no more; that his love for her might
pass away; and that God would give her strength and grace
to preserve unsullied till death, even by one rebellious
thought, the fidelity she had vowed to Audley Sternfield.
In the luxury of that moment's free blessed communion
with the Heavenly Father, she had, for a time, almost
forgotten, she found strength to also ask for a wifely spirit
of submission which would enable her to patiently bear all
the bitter trials Sternfield's unkindness might yet inflict
upon her. She was still engaged in prayer when the door
softly opened, and Mrs. D'Aulnay entered.

"How are you, my poor darling? I had hoped you were
asleep," she kindly exclaimed, as the girl rose from her
knees. "Why are you not in bed?"

"I must take Jeanne's infallible *tisanne* first," was the
reply, uttered with a smile that was inexpressibly sad.

Mrs. D'Aulnay, who was really very fond of her young
cousin, watched her countenance narrowly a moment, and
then whispered, as she threw her arm around her neck,
and drew her gently towards her, "Alas! it cannot cure
heart-ache. 'Tis that wretch of a Sternfield who renders
you so miserable. I am really beginning to hate him. And
the thought that you are tied to him for life sets me wild;
now especially, that I have a secret conviction that that
delightful misanthropic Evelyn loves you."

"Listen to me, Lucille," suddenly exclaimed the young
girl, confronting her with a calm dignity, which awed for a
moment the frivolous woman before her. "You have led
me, by your counsels and solicitations, into a terrible step
which will entail on me life-long wretchedness. I say not

this to reproach you, for alas! I am far more guilty than yourself; but to tell you that having wrought me such misery, you should stop now and not seek to plunge me still lower into sin and sorrow. Mention Colonel Evelyn's name to me no more; and above all, never tell me, a wife, again, that he, or any other man, loves me. When you speak of Sternfield, too, if you cannot do so in terms of friendship, at least employ those of courtesy, for he is my husband. Oh, Lucille, if you cannot lighten my heavy cross, at least do not seek to make it more galling!"

"Antoinette, you are an angel!" enthusiastically exclaimed Mrs. D'Aulnay, touched by what she chose to regard as the lofty heroism of her companion. For every-day virtues she had no respect whatever,—in fact, as she often said herself, she had scarcely patience with them; but anything out of the ordinary routine of life, heroic or uncommon, filled her with admiration. "Yes, my child, your wishes, sublime in their self-sacrificing heroism, shall be law to me. And after all," she pensively added, " 'tis perhaps better that Sternfield should try you as remorselessly as he does. You know a modern French writer has said that in wedded life, next to love, hatred is best; that anything is better than the terribly monotonous, hum-drum indifference with which so many married couples regard each other, and under the influence of which life becomes like a dull, stagnant pool, without wave or breeze ever breaking the surface. Better the wild dash of the tempest, the sweep of the hurricane—"

"What, even though it scatter ruin and desolation around?" interrupted the poor young bride, won into something like a smile, despite her misery, by this new and extraordinary view of connubial life. "No, no," she added more earnestly. "If I cannot have sunshine, let me at least have peace. I have not courage enough to cope with the storm or the tempest."

"Then, dear Antoinette, forgive my saying that you have not all the necessary qualifications for a genuine heroine. But here comes Jeanne with the *tisanne*, which has led to so singular a dialogue."

CHAPTER 24

ANTOINETTE found the two following days singularly quiet, after the terrible agitation she had recently undergone. Mr. Cazeau, the gentleman visitor already alluded to, was a quiet amiable man, with that gentle suavity of manner and cheerful, well-bred gaiety which characterized so generally the Canadian gentlemen of the time. He was a sincere patriot, too, grieving deeply over his country's dark days, and Antoinette found a salutary distraction to her own sad thoughts in listening to him; the more so that his regrets and reveries were unmixed with the fierce, merciless denunciations of their conquerors, with which her own father ever alluded to their national troubles.

"Well, Miss Antoinette," exclaimed Mr. Cazeau, as the quiet little party separated the third evening of his stay, after a long, pleasant conversation, "when I see Mr. De Mirecourt, which I soon will, I must let him know how much report has misrepresented you, as well as Mrs. D'Aulnay. I was told you were always surrounded by a bevy of red-coats, plunged into the gayest fashionable dissipation, and totally inaccessible to common mortals, like ourselves. Now, I have been three whole days here, and I have seen you both constantly occupied with your needles or books, and asking no other amusement than the talk of a tiresome, old-fashioned man like myself."

"You forget that it is passion-week," interrupted Mr. D'Aulnay, with a very expressive shake of his head; "and these fair ladies, though passably fond of this world, have not given up all hopes of ultimately attaining to a better. Pay us a visit when Lent is over, and then tell me what you think. For my part, I could find it in my heart to wish that it were Lent all the year round. I would willingly endure the fasting and penance for the sake of the peace and quiet."

"Indeed, I do not believe him, Mrs. D'Aulnay," laughed the guest, in answer to a playful, though somewhat earnest protest on the part of his graceful hostess against Mr. D'Aulnay's last words. "I can only speak of what I have seen; and I can honestly tell my old friend that I have been charmed by the quiet domestic life you lead here, and that Miss Antoinette is all that he could wish her, only a trifle too pale."

"Do not say anything about that, dear Mr. Cazeau," pleaded Mrs. D'Aulnay; "for fear Uncle De Mirecourt should recall her to the country, out of anxiety for her health or complexion, a step which would certainly improve neither."

Mr. Cazeau's visit was so far productive of good, that Antoinette received a few days after a very kind letter from her father, saying that as she was leading such a quiet domestic life in town, she might extend her visit two or three weeks longer if she wished. He added, moreover, that he was going to Quebec on business matters, and would probably call himself on his return, to bring her home.

"Do you not find it very singular that Sternfield should be so long without coming to see us?" questioned Mrs. D'Aulnay, one afternoon, of her young cousin. " 'Tis more than a week since his last visit; in fact, he has not been here since the day that *héros de roman*, Colonel Evelyn, called."

Antoinette merely sighed, whilst Mrs. D'Aulnay resumed, with a yawn, which for the moment completely disfigured her pretty mouth, "He surely will come to-day. I hope so, for I feel in a most dreary discontented humor, and would like to see him, if only to have a quarrel. Pshaw! I am tired of this stupid work," and, impatiently throwing down her embroidery, she walked to the window. Her remarks on the passers-by were anything but complimentary to the individuals in question, when suddenly she started, and, with a deepening color, abruptly exclaimed:

"As I live, there is Sternfield driving past with that pretty Eloise Aubertin, with whom he flirted so desperately at my last *soirée*. Is it not infamous?"

Antoinette's only reply was another sigh.

"How can you bear it?" questioned Mrs. D'Aulnay, indignantly. "A week without coming near you, and then to dare drive past our very windows with a young and pretty girl at his side. If you do not punish him well for it, you are utterly destitute of common spirit."

"What am I to do?" dejectedly asked her companion, thus energetically appealed to.

"What are you to do! Why, retaliate in kind. Drive, walk out to-morrow, flirt with any handsome agreeable man. That will soon bring this refractory bridegroom of yours to his senses."

"Never, Lucille, never! I have erred and sinned enough. With Heaven's help I shall go no farther."

"Then the next time that he comes to see you, fly at him in a passion. Tell him that he is a tyrant—a heartless wretch."

"Scarcely the way to ensure his speedy returning," was the sad reply.

"Well, if you do not resent it in some manner or other, I frankly tell you that you have neither proper pride nor spirit."

"Lucille, nothing remains for me now but patience and gentleness."

"Antoinette De Mirecourt," exclaimed Mrs. D'Aulnay, with startling abruptness, "you do not love this man. If you did, your very blood would boil in your veins with indignation at his conduct."

There was no answer to this sally, and Mrs. D'Aulnay rapidly went on. "Good Heavens! this state of things is terrible—unnatural. Do you call this a love-match?"

" 'Tis a match of your own making," bitterly retorted the poor bride.

"Yes, I acknowledge it," returned Mrs. D'Aulnay, slightly disconcerted by this unsparing home-thrust. "But who could have dreamed things would have turned out as they have done? Who could have dreamed that such a handsome, fascinating, chivalrous man as Audley Sternfield would have turned out such a wretch?"

"I have already told you, Lucille, that I do not wish to hear such epithets applied to him."

"Nonsense!" and Mrs. D'Aulnay tossed her graceful head indignantly: "I will give him his due once, at least, if you oblige me ever after to hold my peace. Husband indeed! He is certainly a singular illustration of the word. I tell you what, my poor little cousin, I see plainly you do not love him; and I do not think he loves you, or he acts as if he did not, which comes to the same thing. No alternative remains for you but a divorce."

"A divorce!" re-echoed Antoinette; "since when has our church granted divorces? The most she has ever done is in cases of extreme urgent necessity to give permission to the parties to separate. But if they were living at the opposite ends of the earth, they would still be husband and wife. Ah! the chain I so madly forged for myself, however galling it may prove, I must wear to the end."

"But your case is an extraordinary one, poor child. We might appeal through our Bishop to the Pope."

"Of what use, when he holds not the power? Who or what am I, that I should expect an impossibility? What excuse for me is it that the senseless ill-judged passion which led me to infringe the sacred rules of feminine delicacy, the holy dictates of filial duty, has passed away as quickly as it rose. 'Tis but just that I should expiate my folly."

"But if Sternfield, on his side, wearying of the marriage, as you have done, should seek a divorce, obtain one, and then marry again,—a thing of sufficiently frequent occurrence, and permitted by his faith,—what then?"

"My chains would remain as firmly rivetted as ever, and in the eyes of God I would still be his wife, not only unable to contract any other union, but obliged to be as faithful in thought and deed to him, as if he were the tenderest of husbands."

"Good God! 'tis terrible!" exclaimed Mrs. D'Aulnay with a shudder. "Are you certain, Antoinette that you are not in error?"

"Alas, I have studied the subject too well to be mistaken."

"But your marriage was secret,—the only witness myself,—no banns published, and you a minor."

"Alas, alas! all that helped to render it sinful, ill-judged, but it did not render it less binding."

"Oh, Antoinette, how little I anticipated so sorrowful a conclusion to a romance that opened so brightly. You are right in the stand you have taken, however, even though it may cause strife and unkindness to arise between you and Audley. A daughter of the De Mirecourts is not to be at the beck of any husband who is afraid or ashamed to publicly acknowledge her."

CHAPTER 25

"THERE is some one up stairs whom you will be very glad to see, Mademoiselle," exclaimed Jeanne, as Mrs. D'Aulnay and Antoinette entered the house on their return from an afternoon drive. "Mr. De Mirecourt has just arrived."

"Now remember, Antoinette," said Mrs. D'Aulnay in a warning voice, as her companion was hastening up stairs, "you must endeavor to obtain permission to extend your stay in town. Should you return to Valmont with your father, Sternfield will worry us both to death, and end by bringing about some grand *esclandre* in your peaceful village."

Mr. De Mirecourt, who was in excellent spirits, received his daughter most affectionately, and dismissed the question of her delicate looks by a half dry, half-laughing remark that it was fortunate she had her husband Louis ready chosen and secured, otherwise her fading beauty might render it somewhat difficult to procure an eligible one.

Mr. D'Aulnay hastened to divert the conversation from Antoinette's personal appearance, a topic he well knew was disagreeable to her, by exclaiming: "But do tell us, De Mirecourt, how does Quebec look now?"

"How does it look!" repeated Mr. De Mirecourt, his expression instantly becoming grave; "just as a city that has been besieged and bombarded twice, might be expected to look—all ruins and ashes. The environs too, in which three sanguinary battles have been fought, the whole district itself, occupied for two years by contending hosts, all bear melancholy traces of our country's struggles and fall."

"Did you see any of our old friends?" questioned Mr. D'Aulnay.

160

"No, they all left the city after the capitulation of Montreal, and are now endeavoring, like many others, to occupy their time and repair their ruined fortunes by devoting themselves to their farms and lands. It will take a long time ere Quebec can rise Phœnix-like from her ashes."

"Did you meet any one you knew, going down?"

"No. I had but one fellow-traveller, an Englishman, as I at once detected by his accent, though he addressed the driver in excellent French."

"And what did you talk about, uncle?" questioned Mrs. D'Aulnay, becoming suddenly interested.

"The conversation would have been a very brief one, as far as I was concerned, fair lady, for I have no fancy for intercourse with our new masters, had it not been for an accidental circumstance, or, to be just, an act of courtesy on his part. Shortly after we started, a heavy snow-storm set in, accompanied by a sharp, fitful wind, which, notwithstanding my thick bear-skin coat, and woollen mufflers, so warmly knitted by my little Antoinette, soon searched me through and through. My chattering teeth plainly betrayed this to my companion, who instantly, with a kindness the more remarkable that I had previously repulsed most ungraciously his one attempt at conversation, unfolded the large cloak laid across his knee, (he had another one on him,) and insisted on my wearing it. After this, conversation flowed freely, and I soon found that my fellow-traveller was not only a person of high intellect, but also a just and liberal man, totally free from the prejudices that rule so many of his caste and race. We discussed the present state of the country with an openness certainly indiscreet on my part; but though I sometimes lost my temper, he never lost his, maintaining his point when he differed from me, with a manly courtesy which did him honor. On many subjects he thought with me, and, I could see plainly, had as great a horror of anything like oppression as myself. I had a practical proof of this at an inn where we stopped to change horses and procure refreshments. The man, Thibault, who formerly kept the place in question, embarked for France, last year, with many more illustrious than himself, and his successor is a person of the name of Barnwell,—one of the newly-arrived colonists who have come to lord it over ourselves and fallen fortunes. Just as we were resuming our seats, after partaking of some slight refreshments, our attention was aroused by the voice of our host, raised in loud angry tones. We looked round and saw him forcing back by the bridle the horse of a poor *habitant*, whom necessity had compelled to stop for some little refreshment at his hospitable establishment. Poor Jean-Baptiste energetically protested, in his own tongue, that he had already paid twice the value of what he had received; whilst his adversary, with oaths and opprobrious epithets, insisted he should hand over the full price he asked, which was most extortionate. Emboldened by the countryman's evident terror, and the tacit encouragement or indifference of the lookers-on, Barnwell tightened his grasp on the bridle of the horse, and commenced at the same time lashing the poor animal about the head in the most merciless manner, threatening to do the same to the owner if he did not at once satisfy his claim. In a second, my fellow-traveller had leaped to the ground, wreathed his powerful hand in mine host's coat collar, and with the whip, he had just snatched from his grasp, administered him two or three sharp cuts. 'Your name!' gasped the fellow; 'your name, till I have you brought up before a magistrate at once!' 'Colonel Evelyn, of His Majesty's ——th regiment,' he disdainfully replied, hurling from him the man, now thoroughly cowed and humbled."

"Colonel Evelyn!" breathlessly repeated Mrs. D'Aulnay; "dear uncle, we know him well."

" 'Tis to be hoped you do; as you are acquainted with so many objectionable people of his cloth, it would be too bad

not to know one who does it so much honor. Upon my
word, my little Antoinette, I could have forgiven you if you
had succeeded in winning this gallant Englishman's
homage."

Poor Antoinette! She had but just received another
illustration of the value of the heart which she had indeed
won, but which was beyond her reach forever.

"And how did you find the roads?" questioned Mr.
D'Aulnay.

" 'Tis time for some of you to ask me that. My journey
was as severe a one as I have ever yet made, though I have
travelled many a mile on snow and ice."

"How is that? Tell us all about it!" exclaimed his listeners.

"Well, as I have just said, shortly after we started, it
commenced snowing fast and heavily; and as it had snowed
the whole night before, you may safely conclude the roads
were anything but light or pleasant. Down it came in
myriads of large soft flakes, darkening the air; and whilst
my companion and myself were discussing Canada, its
misfortunes and destiny, the snow was as effectually
changing the appearance of everything as if sorcery had
been at work. Fences, low stone walls disappeared entirely,
and fruit-trees looked like mere shrubs. Fortunately for us,
neither man nor animal was abroad, for no sight could
have been more unwelcome just then than that of an
approaching sleigh, which, by obliging us to yield half the
track, would have probably sent us all floundering down
into the depths of untrodden snow on either side of the
narrow road. Had we been wise, we would have remained
at Thibault's Inn, but I was anxious to press on, and so was
my companion: after a minute's halt accordingly we
resumed our journey. The cold soon became intensely
severe. It ceased snowing, but the brilliant sunshine that
had succeeded was perfectly powerless, imparting neither
heat nor comfort. The wind used to catch the newly fallen
particles of snow, now hard and glittering as diamonds,

and whirl them back in our faces, blinding and suffocating us. Meanwhile we advanced at a true funereal pace. Large snow-drifts often lay right across our path, and we had to alight and take turns with the couple of wooden snow-shovels with which our driver's sleigh (probably with a view to such emergencies) was provided."

"And how did Colonel Evelyn act, uncle?"

"Just as a true man and soldier should. He neither grumbled nor wondered, but worked; and when the shovels came into requisition, handled his with as much skill and dexterity as one of your rose-water heroes, fair niece, would twist his ivory-handled cane."

"But, dear papa, you must have suffered dreadfully," exclaimed Antoinette.

"Yes, my little girl, I did. Every fibre and vein in my face ached and smarted, and my respiration became short and actually painful. And the roads—oh, how those poor exhausted horses of ours labored and floundered through the snow-wreaths, now plunging wildly forward, then bringing suddenly up. When we arrived at the little inn at which we were to pass the night, I was utterly, thoroughly done up."

"And your fellow-traveller?" Mrs. D'Aulnay asked.

"All I have to say is, that he has an iron strength of constitution, and, unused as he is to our climate, he seemed to bear its rigor better than even old Dussault, who has driven the stage for so many winters through all sorts of weather. He is most unselfish too, and showed as much wish to assist and relieve me as if I had some lawful claim upon him. But enough of this long story. Neither Colonel Evelyn nor myself will forget our winter journey for a long time to come."

Comments and suppositions followed on this narrative, and at a late hour the party separated for the night, in mutual good humor.

Mr. De Mirecourt, yielding to the united solicitations poured in upon him, consented to remain a few days, instead of starting the following morning with Antoinette, as he had intended. His stay proved very agreeable; and in witnessing the quiet regular lives the ladies of the household led, and partaking of their harmless amusements, he began to think matters must have been greatly misrepresented, and that there could be no great amount of harm in yielding to Mrs. D'Aulnay's petition, and leaving Antoinette with her till the return of spring.

CHAPTER 26

LENT over, Mrs. D'Aulnay thought it but fair to repay herself for her late seclusion by giving an entertainment to her friends, though boisterous March with its rough winds and melting snows had already set in. The late temporary cessation of gaieties seemed but to add a fresh zest to present enjoyment; and perhaps the only heavy heart in Mrs. D'Aulnay's rooms that night, was that of the once light-hearted, happy Antoinette. Yes, there was one other also, the tone of whose spirits was somewhat in unison with her own; and Colonel Evelyn took himself secretly and severely to task more than once for his folly in thus seeking scenes distasteful to him, for the sake of a chance meeting with Antoinette, who, on her side, endeavored so assiduously to avoid him. There was always, however, a vague hope lurking in his heart that the obstacle which she spoke of as insurmountable, was not in reality so, and that some fortunate chance might yet set all right between them. For the first part of the evening he respected her evident wish to avoid any intercourse with him; but happening to see her seated alone in one of the pauses of the dance, he approached and accosted her on some general topic. Though he strove to interest and amuse, he had the tact to refrain from anything like an approach to subjects of deeper interest. This was fortunate; for Mrs. D'Aulnay, suddenly finding herself at a loss for something to say, called on him, with her usual thoughtlessness, to tell them "what he had just been whispering to Miss De Mirecourt."

"Most willingly. I was repeating the remark made by his Majesty George the Third to Madame De Lery, when she was lately presented with her husband at the English Court."

"Oh, the beautiful Louise De Brouages," replied Mrs. D'Aulnay, with lively interest. "Well, what did the King say? What did he think of her?"

"He must have found her very beautiful, for he at once said with considerable warmth, alluding of course to the recent acquisition of Canada, that 'If all the Canadian ladies resemble her, he had indeed good reason to feel proud of his fair conquest.' "[1]

"The more chance then for the mission of Mr. De Lery and his companions to prove successful," remarked her fair hostess.

"And what is that mission?" questioned one of the company.

"They have been sent to represent our interests, as well as to present the expression of our homage to our new monarch."

"And behold it is His Majesty who pays homage instead, and with reason," exclaimed Sternfield, who had just joined the group.

"Oh, I suppose we shall be surfeited with compliments, now that King George has set the example!" coldly rejoined Mrs. D'Aulnay, as she turned away, for the irresistible Major was in anything but high favor with her just then.

Sternfield, who had heretofore been amusing as well as behaving himself tolerably well, no sooner saw Antoinette with Colonel Evelyn than his good humor vanished, and he commenced inwardly taxing his brains for some means of separating them. Being engaged for the next dance he could not ask Antoinette to be his partner, which would have been the surest and speediest method, so he had the inexpressible vexation of seeing them conversing together during the long contra-danse which followed. Turning a deaf ear to his pretty companion's hint that she thought promenading infinitely preferable to dancing, he

[1] Garneau.

unceremoniously deposited her at the conclusion of the dance, on the first vacant seat, and hastened to Antoinette.

"May I request the honor of your hand, Miss De Mirecourt for the next?" he asked with an elaborate politeness which struck Evelyn as savoring more of mockery than respect.

What a vivid crimson dyed that young face, and what a mingled look of pained embarrassment and anxiety stole over it as she timidly replied that she was engaged. In the trouble of the moment she did not think of mentioning the name of the partner to whom her hand was promised, a very plain unattractive person as it happened; and Sternfield, at once inferring that it was Colonel Evelyn, notwithstanding that the latter rarely, indeed never danced, cast one stern vindictive look upon her, and turned away. His coming however had left its sting; and Evelyn soon saw that his companion's thoughts were now wholly occupied by things foreign to the subject of their conversation, which was the very harmless one of his late journey to Quebec with Mr. De Mirecourt. It was almost a relief when Mrs. D'Aulnay approached them, and, after some jesting remark to Colonel Evelyn, carelessly handed her cousin a small scrap of paper on which were traced a few words in pencil, saying, "A memorandum of yours, Antoinette."

The latter, the worst possible hand in the world at dissembling, took the paper, and hurriedly glanced over it. It was from Sternfield, and ran thus:

"You are trying my patience beyond all bounds! Meet me as soon as possible in the little sitting-room upstairs, for I have that to say to you which must be said without delay. At your peril refuse my request. If you do, you will regret driving a desperate man too far! Your husband,

AUDLEY STERNFIELD."

The tenor of this missive, as well as his recklessness in appending to it the signature he had done, convinced the unfortunate Antoinette that he was in no mood to be trifled with, and with trembling fingers she tore the paper into fragments. Her agitation was so evident that Evelyn could not help speculating on the cause, the more so as he had seen Sternfield give the note in question to Mrs. D'Aulnay to deliver, a mission which she had at first declined, but which his menaces had ultimately forced her into accepting.

"What can be the secret link between that handsome villain and this innocent girl?" he inwardly asked himself again and again. "It certainly is not love, for, apart from her explicit denial of the existence of such a sentiment at least on her side, her countenance expresses anything but that feeling when he draws near her. Well, I will watch, that I may render her service if possible, and protect her from his treacherous arts."

Seeing that his companion now evidently wished to be left to herself, he uttered some indifferent remark, and sauntered to the other end of the room. Another dance was beginning, and Antoinette greatly exasperated the gentleman to whom she was engaged by declaring she felt too much fatigued to join it. Taking advantage of the slight confusion consequent upon the dancers assuming their places, she contrived to steal from the room, as she hoped, unobserved. Up the narrow stair-case she sped, and entered the sitting-room in which Sternfield was already awaiting her, and which, unlike the rest of the house, was but dimly lighted.

"You have condescended to use haste in coming," he sarcastically exclaimed, as he handed her a chair.

"What do you want with me, Audley?" she asked, placing her hand upon her heart to still its rapid beatings.

"Have I not already warned you," he said, his brow growing darker and sterner as he spoke. "Have I not already warned you, that, though I may patiently put up with your coldness, your indifference, aye! if I read at times your feelings aright, your dislike, I will not stand quietly by, and see you, my wedded wife, coquetting and flirting with other men?"

"Ever the same unjust, unfounded accusation. With whom do you say I was flirting now?"

"With that deep, dangerous hypocrite, Colonel Evelyn. Do not attempt to deny it!" he impetuously continued, bringing his hand heavily down on the back of the chair beside him. "I watched you both narrowly. I saw your sweet down-cast looks, your varying color, and his undisguised bold glances of love and admiration. Curse him! Think you I will tamely suffer all this?"

"Why do you accuse and blame me thus?" She strove to look and speak calmly, though her hurried irregular breathing told how deeply she was agitated. "If a gentleman comes up to speak to me, to stand beside my chair, I cannot bid him begone; I must not tell him that I am a wife, and that my thoughts and smiles belong entirely to yourself. I will leave here to-morrow—bury myself in the country, there to remain till you judge fit to come forward and acknowledge yourself my husband. I may perhaps have peace there."

"Yes, flirting with your first love, Mr. Louis Beauchesne," was his moody retort.

Antoinette's small hands were clasped still more tightly over her wildly throbbing heart, as she whispered, "Audley, do you think you can continue to torture me thus, without life or reason yielding in the end?"

"No heroics, please," he coldly rejoined. "I am afraid Mrs. D'Aulnay finds you too apt a pupil in the science which she is so eminently qualified to impart."

The girl, too miserable, too heart-struck to reply to his taunt, covered her face with her hands in silent wretchedness.

"Listen to me, my Antoinette," he said with a rapid change of voice and manner. "You find me thus unkind and stern, because you have shown me on your side so little love or sympathy. Say that you forgive all the past; and let me, as a token of our perfect reconciliation—of my earnest intention to show you more gentleness in the future, press for once a husband's kiss on that proud brow, which has, heretofore, so scornfully refused it. Do not say me nay! I again repeat, 'tis wrong to push a desperate man too far!"

Feeling that she dared not, perhaps ought not to refuse him so trifling a concession, she made no reply, and Sternfield, interpreting her silence in his favor, threw his arm around her, and kissed again and again her brow, her silken shining hair. A sound between a startled exclamation and a half-suppressed groan, suddenly broke the silence; and Antoinette sprang from the treacherous arms that encircled her, in time to behold Colonel Evelyn standing, white as marble, at the door of the apartment. In another moment, he was gone; and as Antoinette's wild reproachful glance fell on her companion, she saw a triumphant sneer replacing already the tenderness his features had discarded as rapidly as they had assumed.

"Methinks the dainty Colonel Evelyn will be effectually cured of his love-fit by this wholesome lesson," he mockingly exclaimed. "You may flirt with him henceforth, Antoinette, as much as you like."

Slowly the girl confronted her tormentor, and in low thrilling tones exclaimed, "You have done your worst, Audley Sternfield. Profaning the sacred name of husband, you have been to me only a cruel, heartless tyrant. Prevented by sordid paltry motives of interest from acknowledging our marriage, you would yet wish to degrade me in my own eyes, in those of others. Now, listen to me. Till the day you shall come forward to claim me as your wife in the eyes of the world, I shall resolutely avoid all intercourse with you, and laugh your threats and prayers to scorn, for despair has made me reckless. I shall return to the country to-morrow; and if you follow me there to persecute me farther, the doors shall be closed upon you."

"Will you ever dare to say you love me after this?" he impetuously questioned.

"Love you!" she repeated with a short sharp laugh of bitterness. "Yes, as the criminal loves the instrument of his punishment, as the convict loves the other wretch to whom he is chained for life."

"Be silent, girl, or I cannot answer for myself," he said in tones hoarse with suppressed passion.

"Pshaw! Major Sternfield," she replied with calm disdain. " 'Tis you who are acting now. A half-hour ago that speech would have made me tremble, would have kept me an humble suppliant before you; but I tell you that all sentiments of fear, hope, or any feeling save one, are dead now within my breast."

Sternfield glared fiercely at her. Calm, proud, she stood before him—so lovely in her graceful festal robes, so delicate and feminine in her girlish beauty; but there was an iron firmness of expression stamped upon her brow, which he had never yet seen there, telling of resolutions formed, resolutions to be rigidly kept; and with a wrathful pang he inwardly acknowledged that his own unhallowed violence had lost him, perhaps, for ever, the love of that matchless young creature.

"So be it, Antoinette; you have willed that strife should exist between us; but remember, that through weal or woe, in poverty or in suffering, in sickness or in health, till death doth part us, you are mine and mine alone."

Despite her calmness, her stoicism, she shuddered as the solemn words fell on her ear, but recovering instantly her late forced composure, she rejoined: "Do not fear, I can never forget that; but I will return to the ball-room now to enjoy myself as much as my present frame of mind will permit me."

Those who had chanced to notice the long absence of Antoinette and Sternfield, and saw them at last stealing back, one after another, inwardly judged it was a very decided case of flirtation; nor was there anything in the outward demeanor of either party to indicate the singular interview through which they had just passed. Antoinette was pale and quiet, but that she had often been of late; whilst Sternfield, as was usual with him, hovered about the fairest faces in the room, whispering words which ever won him the reward of smiles and blushes.

CHAPTER 27

WHAT Antoinette suffered during those tedious lagging hours, no words could express. Obliged to speak, to smile, whilst heart and brain were alike throbbing with agony; obliged above all, to hide her feelings from curious or cavilling eyes, there were times when it seemed to her she must drop the mask at once. To Sternfield, trained in deceit, triumphing in the success of his odious plot to degrade her in the eyes of Colonel Evelyn, a plot conceived and executed in the moment his keen eye had detected the latter approaching up the corridor, no great effort of self-command was necessary. Determined to pique and punish his refractory bride, he devoted himself with such assiduity to the young lady who had, on a previous occasion, shared his sleigh, that Mrs. D'Aulnay's indignation was excited to the highest pitch. Glancing around in search of Antoinette, she beheld her seated near a small table pretending to examine some engravings upon it. Resolved to punish Sternfield in kind, she beckoned Colonel Evelyn to her, and handing him a roll of paper, exclaimed,

"Pray go and show these new plates to Miss De Mirecourt, and examine them at the same time yourself. You will tell me afterwards what you think of them."

Evelyn looked for a moment as if he would have declined the commission; but meeting Mrs. D'Aulnay's dawning look of amazement, he took the engravings, and crossed the room to Antoinette's side. Abruptly, coldly, he said:

"Rather than excite Mrs. D'Aulnay's questions or suspicions, I have brought you these pictures as she instructed me to do."

"Oh, Colonel Evelyn, what must you think of me?" faltered the unhappy Antoinette.

174

"I will tell you," he rejoined in tones of suppressed bitterness. "My first love taught me to hate your sex; you, my second love, have taught me to despise them. She, though false to myself, was true at least to the one who had supplanted me; you, a few weeks ago, called on Heaven to witness you had no love for Audley Sternfield, and yet I saw you lie passive in his arms an hour ago, whilst he pressed his kisses on your lips and brow."

"Spare me! be merciful!" she implored with white and quivering lips.

"No, Antoinette De Mirecourt, for you have not spared me. Sternfield or his like might pardon you, for their love is as easily recalled as it is given, but I cannot. You have done me a woful wrong, young girl! destroyed the dawning confidence in human truth and goodness, beginning to spring up in my seared heart; dried up the springs of human sympathy there, and doomed back to hardened misanthropy the gloomy remainder of my barren life."

"Oh, forgive me, Colonel Evelyn!" and the speaker felt at the moment that she would willingly have laid down her life, if she could have saved him thereby one solitary suffering, one single pang.

Pitilessly he went on, "As much deeper in proportion as is my love compared to that of most other men, so is my resentment against her who has mocked that love to scorn. Oh what a wealth of affection have I not lavished on a worthless idol!"

"I have sinned," she rejoined in a low solemn tone, "and my sin has found me out; but, Colonel Evelyn, guilty in the sense you suppose me to be, I am not. Ten years would I willingly give of the life that spreads out such a dreary blank before me, to have my innocence made clear to you; but if in this life that may not be, there is another and a better world where it shall yet be made plain to you."

Evelyn gazed a moment on those clear truthful eyes, that fair youthful brow, and then hastily averting his gaze, exclaimed,

"Girl, ask of Heaven to withdraw from you that fatal gift of seeming innocence and candor, or you will win others to their destruction as you have won me to mine."

"And you will not spare me one kind or forgiving word?" she asked, clasping her hands together, reckless in the despair of the moment, who witnessed her agitation, or what construction might be put upon it.

"No. You have ruined, robbed me, and I cannot forgive you. If I were on my death-bed, on the point of appearing before my Maker, my answer would still be the same. I have loved you too well to show you mercy, but, hush!" he rapidly added, interposing his tall form between her and the other occupants of the room. "Your agitation may be noticed, misunderstood. Heavens! Miss De Mirecourt, what a finished, faultless actress you are. One would think now that my approbation or censure was a matter of life and death to you. I would believe it myself, only that I witnessed so memorable a scene in the sitting-room a short time ago. Oh, only for that terrible, damning proof of your worthlessness, nothing could ever have opened my eyes to it. Farewell now, and let us both mutually hope our paths in life may never cross each other again. You will hear that Cecil Evelyn is a greater misanthrope than ever, that he is more selfish and gloomily inaccessible to every social, kindly feeling; but knowing who has helped to make him so, you at least will hold your peace."

He bowed, turned away, and a few moments after left the house.

Sick at heart, Antoinette sat where he had left her, wondering if human breast had ever known such misery as her own; when Sternfield, who had been dancing and flirting in an adjoining room, came up to her. Narrowly he scanned her face, and then said,

"You look ill and sad, Antoinette."

"You cannot expect me to look well or gay."

"Perhaps you are angry with me for having flirted so much with that bright-eyed little Eloise?"

"I never noticed it," was the weary reply.

Sternfield bit his lip! This utter indifference was neither what he had sought or wished for, and he angrily rejoined:

"Doubtless more powerful interests and anxieties engrossed you."

"Ah, I have nothing left to hope or fear now."

"Are you really serious in your intention of returning to the country immediately, or was it merely an idle threat?"

"I go to-morrow."

"Shall I bid you farewell then to-night, or call again for a parting word in the morning?"

"As you wish. I think it would be better to say the parting word to-night."

"You are a loving bride, Antoinette."

"I am what you have made me," was the calm, passionless response.

"Then, since you wish it, Good-night," he abruptly, angrily rejoined. "I will not obtrude my unwelcome presence on you again."

He left her; and Antoinette, feeling she had suffered and feigned enough for one evening, quietly passed from the apartment.

How cheerful, how pleasant her own little room looked, with the bright fire, the wax-lights, the soft easy-chair drawn up into her favorite corner, but how heavy was the young heart of her who entered it! Closing the door, she threw herself into the fauteuil, hoping that tears might come to her relief; but that great solace was denied her, and she sat there in dry, tearless misery, recalling every trifling detail, every painful circumstance that could possibly add to the burden of her sorrow. Another hour passed, the last of the guests had taken their departure, and Mrs. D'Aulnay, as was her wont, stepped in to bid her cousin good-night. The latter looked strangely ill, but then she was very calm and quiet, so Mrs. D'Aulnay felt but little alarm.

"Are you sitting up, dear?" she asked. "You should have gone to bed immediately."

"I wished first to tell you, Lucille, that I must return to Valmont to-morrow."

"Return to-morrow, and why? Have you had letters from home?"

"None; but I have decided on returning."

"This is incomprehensible, child! What cause, what reason have you?"

"I am heart-sick, weary, Lucille, and I must have rest, utter repose."

"You are ill, dear child. Aye, I feared so. You have looked wretched for some time past, and two or three remarked it to-night. Ah, I fear my poor cousin, you are very unhappy." And she anxiously scanned the pain-worn young face before her.

"Yes, I am indeed very miserable."

"And I need not ask the cause. I suppose 'tis in great part that miserable Sternfield?"

"I will tell you in a simple sentence. You were present when those solemn words were pronounced: 'Those whom God has joined, let no man put asunder.' Do you understand, cousin Lucille! The woful past is unchangeable, irrevocable!"

"Alas, do you really regret it so much, then? I suppose you must hate me at the same time; though, indeed, I did all for the best."

"Ah, no, I neither hate nor upbraid you; but it was an unfortunate hour for me when I entered beneath your pleasant, friendly roof."

"Tell me, what has Audley been saying or doing to bring you to such a hopeless state of mind?"

" 'Twould be useless and painful for me to give any farther details than those with which you are already acquainted, but I have been sorely tried."

"Oh, as to that, dear child, so are all wives. There is André, who will sometimes get into a passion for the merest trifle, perhaps, a tardy dinner, at other times, say in his quiet way, the most sarcastic, cutting things you can imagine."

Antoinette smiled—a very bitter, strange smile—as she replied, "If Audley Sternfield never gave me greater cause of sorrow than Mr. D'Aulnay has given yourself, I would not grieve so deeply that our union is irrevocable."

"But to return to your lately formed determination, what will you gain, my poor darling, by returning to the monotony of your country life sooner than you can help? Here, at least, you have some distractions, some amusements."

"Do you include under that title the persecutions Sternfield daily inflicts upon me?"

"But he will persecute you in Valmont as well as here. You remember when you were there before?"

"Yes, but I have grown more callous than I was then, more reckless of consequences, and for his own sake he will not try me too much."

"Of course, dear, if you are decided on leaving, there is no more to be said on that point; but do you not think it would be better to brave your father's anger, violent as it may be at first, and acknowledge at once your marriage?"

"That would not suit Major Sternfield," rejoined Antoinette, with a sharp, forced laugh, that made Mrs. D'Aulnay start. "He told me he could not afford the luxury of a dowerless bride, having previously bound me by a solemn promise not to reveal my marriage till he allowed me, which will probably be on my eighteenth birthday, when I shall enter on the possession of my poor mother's fortune."

"He calculates closely as well as cleverly," was Mrs. D'Aulnay's sarcastic comment; "but, tell me, my poor heart-broken little cousin, would you like me to reveal all to your father, instead of waiting the pleasure of this tardy bridegroom? I care nothing for the promise he fraudulently extracted from myself."

"Oh no," and Antoinette shuddered. "I begin to look forward to the period when he will claim me, with sickening terror. Let me enjoy my poor father's love, my own personal liberty, as long as he will allow me!"

"Oh, Antoinette, forgive me!" exclaimed Mrs. D'Aulnay, throwing her arms round her cousin, and bursting into a passionate flood of tears. "How greatly my unfortunate counsels have helped to bring utter misery on your bright young life. What would I not give to undo the mischief I have wrought! Handsome, fascinating demon, how I hate him!"

"Enough, dear Lucille. I am very weary—very ill. Leave me to rest."

With countless tearful protestations and caresses, Mrs. D'Aulnay parted from her, leaving her, not to repose, but to a night of sleepless wretchedness. The following day, notwithstanding her feelings of severe bodily illness, she persisted in her intention of leaving for the country. In passing before the parish church, not the massive, stately edifice which now bears the title, but an old-fashioned, though solid stone structure, situated almost in the centre of the French square, or Place D'Armes, she directed the driver to stop, and alighted for a moment.[1] On leaving, shortly after, the sacred edifice, strengthened and consoled by a few minutes' closer communion with her Creator, she stood, leaning against the railings, gazing at the thickly strewn graves around her; and despite the cheerless aspect of the cemetery, covered, in some parts, by winter's icy

---

[1] The church in question, which succeeded to the first simple wooden structure in which our early forefathers united in common worship, was built in 1672, and as we have already said, occupied a portion of the French square, standing awkwardly across the middle of Notre Dame street, which it divided into two nearly equal portions, requiring travellers to pass half round the church to proceed from one part of the street to another. The burying-ground was attached to the building, and occupied the space where the present parish church stands, as well as other parts of the Place D'Armes.

mantle, presenting, in others, the muddy, sodden appearance with which the melting of the snow usually heralds Spring's approach, a wish, nay, rather a prayer, as earnest as heart ever framed, rose up from the depths of her soul, that death's dreamless sleep might be vouchsafed her before the arrival of the dreaded epoch when Sternfield should claim her as his wife.

In turning away, her eyes fell on the tall form of Colonel Evelyn approaching; but he passed her with a cold, though respectful salutation. A little later, she encountered a small party of the gay triflers she had often met in Mrs. D'Aulnay's drawing-rooms, and hats were touched, and bows made, with genuine respect, for Antoinette had ever been a general favorite. After she had passed, however, they wonderingly commented on her altered looks, and gravely marvelled if Canadian beauty was always as evanescent as hers had been.

CHAPTER 28

In the joy following Antoinette's arrival in Valmont, no one thought of wondering and questioning about her abrupt, unexpected return, and it was with something like a feeling akin to pleasure that she found herself in the calm atmosphere of her home.

Mrs. Gérard saw that her charge had returned to her, heart and world-weary; but she made no direct effort to obtain her confidence, contenting herself with surrounding the young girl with the tenderest marks of affection, which the latter, so far from shunning or avoiding, as she had done during her previous sojourn at home, now seemed to crave, to almost cling to. Passively she yielded to Mrs. Gérard's arrangements for the ordering of their time, and read, walked, studied, just as her kind friend wished. No more hours of lonely reverie now—no more long afternoons devoted to unknown correspondents. Letters she still received from town, but they were neither as frequent nor as heavy as formerly, nor did their reception bring in their train the swollen eyes and oppressive headaches which they had once done. There were times when the worthy governess became almost terrified by this passive submission, this apathetic obedience: it looked so like a species of despair. This thought struck her one evening with overwhelming force as she and Antoinette were seated near the open window, watching the dying glories of the setting sun, and listening to the liquid notes of that sweetest of all our forest songsters, the Canadian nightingale, or song-sparrow.

"Mrs. Gérard, mamma must have died very young?" was the girl's sudden but softly spoken question.

"Yes, my child. She married at eighteen and died on her twentieth birth-day, leaving you an infant of a year old."

182

"She died of decline, did she not?"

"I believe so," rejoined the governess, very unwillingly, for she did not like the turn the conversation was taking.

"Twenty," softly repeated Antoinette to herself. "Too long, too long! Oh, Mrs. Gérard, pray that I may never live till my eighteenth birth-day!"

Mrs. Gérard started, and looked earnestly, sorrowfully into her young pupil's face, but she tranquilly said, "That were asking perhaps too soon, my darling, for your heavenly crown. God may will that you should bear your earthly cross, whatever it may be, much longer than that."

"But mine is so heavy!" sighed the girl, more to herself than to her companion.

"He who sent it will give you grace and strength to bear it."

"Aye but He did not send it!" she rejoined, with a sudden irresistible burst of emotion. "It was I in my own blind folly that sought it out, that took it up."

"Bear it nevertheless, my child, with Christian courage, and exceeding great shall be the reward. Ah, my Antoinette! I seek not to penetrate your secrets, they shall be to me sacred; but all I ask is, that you should place your trust in no earthly arm or shield, but in God alone."

"You speak of secrets: young as I am, I have a heavy one, one which bears me almost to the earth by its merciless weight; and yet I was mad, rash enough to give my solemn promise on this doubly sacred symbol," and she touched the small gold cross she wore, "that I should never reveal it till permitted. Otherwise, my patient, unwearied friend, I should have confided all to you ere this."

"Thanks, thanks, dear child. How grateful I am to know that your silence has arisen from necessity, and not from any want of trust or confidence. Far from me any attempt to induce you to break your word thus solemnly given, but forgive me if I tell you to beware of the person who asked that promise. However dear they may have rendered themselves to you, however full of good or noble qualities, beware of them, for it was not for your sake but for their own it was exacted."

Some evenings after this conversation, Antoinette, unusually dull and preoccupied, sought the sitting-room where she and Mrs. Gérard usually sat together, but the latter was not there. On asking for her she learned that her governess was suffering from severe headache, and had gone to her room to lie down. Antoinette immediately proceeded thither; but seeing that the invalid required perfect rest and repose, she soon bade her good-night and returned to the sitting-room. It looked somewhat lonely; but the moonlight was streaming in, in floods of liquid silver, chequering the floor and furniture in lines of strange fantastic beauty.

"Do you want lights, Miss?" asked a servant, entering to close the windows and draw the curtains.

"No: I will sit in the moonlight for awhile. Does François expect Mr. De Mirecourt home to night?"

"He is not sure, Miss. The roads are somewhat rough since the last rain, and 'tis fully a thirty miles journey."

The girl retired, and Antoinette sat down near the open casement, the fragrant breath of verbenas and mignionette stealing up to where she sat, and adding yet another charm to the tranquil beauty of the still summer night. Soon her thoughts took the saddened character they ever assumed when she was alone; and painful recollections of Colonel Evelyn, Mrs. D'Aulnay, and bitterest of all, the worldly, heartless Audley Sternfield, rose upon her memory. Suddenly her pulses gave a bound of terror, for surely she had just heard her own name softly pronounced in the well-known tones of Audley himself.

"It must be fancy," she thought, endeavoring to reassure herself, for she was trembling with agitation. "Perhaps the sighing of the night-wind."

Ah, again! This time it was not imagination. The word "Antoinette" clearly though gently pronounced, fell plainly upon her ear. Springing to the window, she bent her straining gaze from it, and between the acacia-trees growing close to the house, saw a tall, dark figure emerge. But surely this figure disguised in ungraceful cloak and slouching hat was not that mirror of elegant dandyism, Audley Sternfield! The remembrance of what he had once said to her about visiting Valmont in disguise, flashed across her mind; and without any farther doubt as to who the intruder was, she leaned forward, and rejoined in guarded but agitated tones:

"Oh, Audley, what brings you here?"

"What brings me here! Is that the only word of welcome you have for me?" was the rapid, irritated reply. "Do you intend coming out, or will you merely condescend to speak to me from the casement as if I were a lackey?"

"Heaven direct me," murmured the girl to herself, "what to do! Should I bring him in, and my father find him here in that disguise, what fatal consequences may not ensue; and yet to steal out to meet him and be perhaps discovered, misjudged, condemned!"

"Have you decided yet what farther reception you will give me?" The voice was louder now, less cautious, showing that the patience of the impetuous speaker was rapidly giving way.

"Hush!" she whispered. "I will be with you in a moment" and, unclosing the French window which opened on the low balcony, she soon stood beside him.

Coldly disengaging herself from his embrace, she again asked, "Tell me, Audley, what has brought you here?"

"Are you really flesh and blood, Antoinette, like others, or are you not rather made of marble?" he passionately retorted. "You ask me, your bridegroom and husband, after a wearisome separation of long weeks, what has brought me here."

"Have you come to claim me openly as your wife?" she shortly questioned.

"Not yet; not yet awhile," and his accents betrayed something like embarrassment. "You know the reason."

"Oh, I do, Major Sternfield, and doubtless you think it all-sufficient, all-powerful. It may be so, but in mercy do not talk of your love afterwards—'tis empty mockery. If from prudential, pecuniary motives you can defer for months, perhaps years, claiming me as your wife, your love is not so uncomfortably ardent that you cannot also refrain from paying me visits which can entail nothing else on me save annoyance and disgrace."

"You have a merciless, stinging tongue, Antoinette," rejoined the young man, baffled by the plain, straightforward manner in which his companion, once so childish and timid, spoke to him now.

"Listen to me, Audley. You have robbed me of nearly all I value in life,—my liberty, my happiness, the approbation of my own conscience. Nothing remains to me now save my reputation, and *that* no threats or menaces of yours shall induce me to risk in stolen interviews or secret meetings with you. If your love is so great," here the speaker's tones involuntarily grew sarcastic, "that you cannot exist without occasionally meeting me, come openly to the house in your own character of a gentleman, not disguised as you are to-night."

"Yes, that your father may seek perhaps to eject me, and bring matters to such a crisis that a full explanation and acknowledgment of our marriage would become inevitable. No, that would not suit me as well as it would suit you. But let me congratulate you on your tact: you are becoming a perfect diplomatist, my little Antoinette."

Without noting the taunt conveyed in this last speech, she rejoined, "Have you anything else to say to me, for I must return to the house? I expect my father this evening, perhaps this moment."

"There is no danger of that. They told me in the shabby apology of an inn where I put up last night, that he was absent, and would not probably return till to-morrow, on account of the bad roads."

"Believe me, you are mistaken; he may be here to-night: but in any case we have said all to each other that we have to say. I have no honeyed phrases to whisper; and if you have them for my ear, they will prove at best but unwelcome."

"Do you not fear that you are laying up a terrible reckoning for a future day, lady mine?" he asked in a low menacing tone. "Think you that Antoinette De Mirecourt's bitter revilings, her scornful disdain, may not yet be remembered to Mrs. Audley Sternfield?"

"Very probably. I have seen enough, Audley, to know that you will not spare your wife more than you have done your bride; but I do not think that in any case you could make me more wretched, more hopeless than I am now."

He smiled—a cruel, meaning smile—and it was well for the frail young girl at his side, that the shadow of the acacia-boughs hid his face, or that smile would have haunted her long afterwards.

"Well, 'tis to be hoped I never will; but you have only a very slight idea of the troubles of life, young lady. Your bark has always glided over a sunshiny sea; but it may meet with storms yet, such as you have never dreamed of. Do you intend returning to Montreal soon?"

"No. Not whilst I can help it. I suffered too much during my last visit there; but I am living as secluded and quiet a life here as you could wish. I rarely go out alone, have few visitors, and am nearly always with my governess. Believe me, for both our sakes, 'tis better to leave me in peace. Let this visit, Audley, be your last."

"It certainly ought, for my reception has not been such as to encourage a renewal of it; but I will make no rash promises, lest I should be tempted to break them hereafter."

"Hush!" suddenly exclaimed Antoinette, grasping his arm tightly. "My father has arrived. Do you not hear the voices—the noise?"

A moment after, lights were glancing from the sitting-room window, and Mr. De Mirecourt's clear, pleasant voice was heard, loudly summoning his daughter.

"Oh, we shall be discovered! He is coming this way," said the girl in an agony of terror.

"Go forward, and meet him as usual, foolish child," whispered Sternfield. "He will suspect nothing."

Slowly, hesitatingly, Antoinette went forward into the bright moonlight; and had Mr. De Mirecourt's trust in his daughter been one degree less unbounded—had his suspicions in any way been previously aroused—he could not but have noticed the singularity of her manner. Fortunately, however, he was in high spirits, jested her about her sentimental love of moonlight musings, and then enquired for Mrs. Gérard, which afforded Antoinette an opening on a subject about which she could trust her voice.

Sternfield waited till father and daughter had re-entered the house, and then advancing a little closer to the open window, but keeping still in shadow of the trees, he listened.

"I thought her a much better actress," he said to himself, after a moment. "How is it her father does not see there is something the matter? Pshaw! she is a mere child yet, and still how thoroughly, how completely she keeps me in check," and a stern, dark look crossed his features. "Do I love her, or do I not? At times when her rare beauty, her wondrous grace, rises mentally before me, I feel she is a creature to be madly worshipped; then again, when she stands forth opposed to me, with that relentless firmness, that iron will, so strangely at variance with her usual character, her feminine loveliness, I feel as if I almost hated her. Still, there is a wayward charm, too, in that very coldness, which makes me rejoice in the thought that she shall one day be mine; but I cannot afford to hasten that time, even if my love were ten times as fervent as it is. My gambling losses fetter me as completely as her secret

marriage fetters her. I certainly love her more now than
when I wooed and won her. I wonder will she venture out
here again to-night! I shall wait and see. Ah! I have wofully
bungled matters to have allowed her love for me to die out
so completely. I must try another course, and coax it back
again."

The lights soon passed into a front room. Mr. De
Mirecourt was about to partake of what, according to the
customs of the time, was a singularly late tea; and the
opening and closing of a door, followed by the light
rustling of a woman's dress, fell on Sternfield's quick ear.
Yes, it was as he had expected—Antoinette had
returned,—and, stooping from the window, she hurriedly
whispered,

"Audley, are you still here?"

"Do you think I could have gone without a farewell
word?" he gently, though reproachfully rejoined.

"I have come to say good-night. Of course you leave to-
morrow," and her tones plainly betrayed the intense
anxiety she felt.

"Yes, since you appear so strongly to desire it."

"Oh, thank you, thank you. I cannot tell you how much I
dread anything like a scene between you and my father."

"Is your health not better since your return to the
country?" he enquired, with real anxiety.

"No; still I have no decided ailment—merely weakness."

A sudden fear flashed across Sternfield's mind as he
remembered how sadly changed Antoinette was from the
bright blooming creature he had first met in Mrs.
D'Aulnay's drawing-rooms. What if Death snatched his
bride from him before the time he intended claiming her
had arrived! He had heard it said that Antoinette's mother
had died in early youth of decline, and that her daughter
strongly resembled her in her delicate beauty, but he had
paid little attention to the rumor at the time. Now it
occurred to him with painful force, and he inwardly

determined to spare his bride the agitating scenes, the wearying persecutions, which he felt had strangely helped to undermine her physical health as well as happiness. Pursuant to this resolve, he gently said:

"As I know my presence in Valmont alarms and annoys you, I shall leave it to-morrow at daybreak. I will not seek to see you again for fear of discovery, so I will say farewell now."

She leaned still lower from the low casement, and extended her hand. It was of a dry burning heat, and his conscience smote him as he pressed it to his lips.

"If you should wish to see me, Antoinette, write me word. Till then I will not trouble you."

"God bless you, Audley!" she falteringly whispered, for his unusual gentleness touched her. "I will write to you often, and live as quietly as you yourself could wish."

In a moment he had vaulted on to the low balcony, through the open window, and was beside her. Not for long, however. One ardent, passionate embrace, and he was gone as rapidly, as silently, as he had entered.

Shortly after, Antoinette returned to superintend the tea-table; and Mr. De Mirecourt, noticing the scarlet flush on her cheeks, laughingly enquired "where she had stolen her *rouge*."

CHAPTER 29

SUMMER had mellowed into autumn. Not the autumn of other lands, with its leaden gloomy skies, and dark, withered foliage, but our glorious, glowing Canadian autumn, with golden, hazy atmosphere, and gorgeous woods and forests.

Has it not often struck you, reader, how wondrous is the change wrought by the first severe autumn frost? You have retired to rest, giving a pleasant parting look to green hills and emerald woods,—you awake and find earth and wilderness flooded with new lights and colours. Here the rich scarlet of the glowing maple contrasts with the pale gold of the delicate birch; there the quivering, silvery leaves of the poplar with the dotted saffron of the broad sycamore. Farther on, the crimson berries of the ash and the gorgeously dyed vines, looking yet more bright against a gloomy back-ground of firs and evergreens. If ever beauty smiled brightly forth in the midst of decay, it is certainly in the foliage of our autumnal woods.

Looking languidly out from the window of her room on the scene before her, sat Antoinette; and the pillows heaped upon her chair, the tiny vial and glass beside her, as well as the painful delicacy of her whole appearance, betrayed she was an invalid. By her side sat Mrs. Gérard, who, with a cheerful smile, exclaimed:

"Do you not wish to hear what Doctor Le Bourdais says, dear child?"

A faint smile and an inclination of the head was her only reply.

"Well, he declares that your lungs are perfectly sound, and that all you require is cheerfulness and variety. He finds the life you lead here too dull and quiet for the

191

present state of your health, and recommends an immediate visit to town."

"To town!" repeated Antoinette, in consternation. "The worst thing he could advise. No, I will not leave home. Here, at least, I have peace and quiet—all I can wish or hope for on earth."

"My darling Antoinette, you will go since it has been judged necessary for you to do so. You need only remain a few weeks, just sufficiently long to satisfy Dr. Le Bourdais' wishes, and the engrossing anxiety of your poor father."

The young girl, either too docile or too spiritless to offer farther resistance, soon yielded, and that day week she was seated in the easiest, softest *fauteuil* in Mrs. D'Aulnay's drawing-room, submitting, like a passive child, to the congratulations and caresses of that highly delighted lady.

"What a treat to have you again with us, dearest Antoinette! I am determined you shall enjoy yourself well."

"Our ideas of enjoyment are now very different, Lucille, and you must not forget, that being an invalid, I must have quiet, and early hours."

"No such thing, child; you have been moped to death in that dreary old Manor-House, and you require a little gaiety to bring you round again. Did not the doctor tell you as much himself?"

"Not exactly: he said my illness almost baffled his skill, that he could not arrive at its origin, so, *en desespoir de cause*, he ordered a change, to see what effect that would have. Remember the conditions, dear Lucille, on which I came here."

"Oh yes, I remember rashly promising that you should remain as isolated and unsocial as you liked, so I suppose I must respect my promise for awhile. Of course, you will make an exception in Sternfield's favor?"

A delicate flush rose to the girl's cheek, as she said, "Yes, I must not refuse to see him."

"Indeed, you had better not," was the somewhat significant reply. "It may serve as a sort of check upon him."

A look of painful enquiry rose into Antoinette's eyes. "Perhaps I should not tell you, my dear, but you would hear it more abruptly from other quarters: report says he has been leading a very wild life lately."

The anxious look in Antoinette's eyes deepened.

"Yes, not to speak of other failings, perhaps still more unpardonable, and which I will not even hint at, it appears he is becoming a confirmed gambler. They say his losses are enormous. 'Tis probably his complete separation, amounting almost to estrangement from yourself, that has driven him desperate."

Antoinette sighed—a long, weary sigh. Oh, how every shade deepened the gloom of the future! This reckless gambler, this libertine spendthrift, whose faults were in every one's mouth, was her life's partner, her husband; and she awaited but his will, his word, to leave the loving, tender friends of youth, her happy home, perhaps, her native land, to follow his ruined fortunes. One gleam of hope presented itself, her own failing health; and it was with a strange quickening of her pulses she remembered that death might yet free her from a union, to whose consummation she now looked forward with inexpressible aversion.

"I have no doubt," continued Mrs. D'Aulnay, "that Audley will entirely reform when your marriage is publicly acknowledged, and will probably make an excellent husband."

"Peace! peace!" implored Antoinette, tortured almost beyond her strength by the ill-chosen remarks of her companion.

"Certainly, darling child. I will not touch on the topic again since it annoys you. To speak of another, and very different character, Colonel Evelyn: you must know that he has become the most gloomy misanthrope, the most confirmed savage, you can imagine. To the several invitations I sent him after you left town, he returned the shortest, most peremptory refusals possible, never paying me the civility of a call afterwards. Like St. Paul's relapsing sinners, the last state of the man is worse than the first. Ah, I hear carriage-wheels at the door. 'Tis Sternfield. I thought he would not prove tardy in paying his devoirs. But I must go up stairs for a moment: I shall be back immediately."

Whatever had been Sternfield's late mode of life, his sins, or his anxieties, no traces of either rested on his gay, careless features when he entered; and as he stood there, so marked a contrast, in the pride of his strong, handsome manhood, to the fragile delicate, girl beside him, the latter could not help bitterly thinking, that she, and she alone bore the heavy burden of their mutual fault. With the bright smile of old, he threw himself on the low ottoman at her feet, exclaiming:

"So they have sent you to Montreal to recruit, my little Antoinette? The best thing they could do, for the dreariness of Valmont is enough to destroy the strongest constitution in less than six months."

"I have never found it dreary, Audley. I was born and brought up there, and the place is inexpressibly dear to me."

"For the matter of that, so is, to the Esquimaux, the barren waste he inhabits; but you will acknowledge I have not troubled or worried you much lately. I formed the good resolve during my first and last moonlight visit, that no act of mine should disturb your mental peace, and thus retard your recovery."

"Thank you. You have indeed been considerate, and I feel grateful to you for it."

The young man coughed as if slightly embarrassed, and rejoined, "I must tell you, though, whilst Mrs. D'Aulnay is out of the room, that, naturally feeling very lonely whilst thus separated from yourself, I sought distractions and amusements which a rigid moralist might censure; but I will take courage and hope from one of your own charming French proverbs,—*a tout péché misericorde.*"

Antoinette was silent, and he went on, "Mrs. D'Aulnay, who is as indiscreet and ill-judging as she is graceful and fascinating, took it into her fair head to bring me to a strict reckoning about my conduct, threatening at the same time to make a formal complaint to yourself about me. I told her it was quite enough for me to render an account of my actions to my wife, without having also to do so to my wife's friend. Was I not justified in telling her so?"

"I have never assumed the right to find fault with your actions, Audley."

"Adhere always to that determination, and you will make one of the most perfect little wives in the world. But to change the subject to one more agreeable: I suppose you have returned to town for a little gaiety, not to immure yourself here as you have done in the country. In furtherance of so laudable a purpose, I shall call for you to-morrow afternoon, and we will take a long drive in whatever direction you may prefer; but Mrs. D'Aulnay must not be of the party."

"In that case, I dare not go."

"Pray give me your reasons then?" he irritably questioned.

"In the first place I do not wish to offend Lucille, who is always so kind and considerate to myself; then it would not do for me to be seen out driving alone with any gentleman, the very day after my arrival. It might come to papa's ears, and—"

"In short, Antoinette you are the most prudent and circumspect of young ladies. No danger of your heart or feelings ever running away with your judgment; but, since you will not accept my offer, do not be offended if you should see me out with some less particular and cautious young lady than yourself."

The entrance of Mrs. D'Aulnay put a stop to the conversation as it was taking this most unpropitious turn;

and after a half-hour's general conversation, Sternfield took leave.

The following day was one of those glorious October days which almost reconcile one to the flight of birds and flowers, and which possess a peculiar charm in their mellow beauty, beyond that of the blooming luxuriant Summer herself. Mrs. D'Aulnay's carriage was at the door early in the afternoon, and vainly Antoinette begged to be excused from accompanying her, repeating Sternfield's request of the preceding day, and her own refusal.

"The very reason you should go with me, child. You must show him that you intend going abroad, keeping a strict watch over his actions. Come, I will take no refusal."

Mrs. D'Aulnay carried her point; and with a sad heart, which neither golden sunshine nor bracing pleasant air could enliven, Antoinette took her place beside her cousin in the latter's small though handsome carriage. Arrived in Notre Dame street, Mrs. D'Aulnay, as usual, had some shopping to do, and, promising not to delay more than five minutes, she alighted before one of the dingy, narrow-paned shops, so different to our present large-windowed, handsome establishments. She had scarcely entered the store in question, when Sternfield's light, graceful equipage passed. By his side was seated a smiling blushing beauty, one of the many who shared his attentions and his flatteries, and in passing Antoinette, she bestowed an unmistakable glance of triumph on the latter. Scarcely recovered from the unpleasant sensations which this last meeting had excited, Antoinette beheld advancing towards her a tall figure, the first glimpse of whom caused her heart to beat with unwonted rapidity. It was Colonel Evelyn, and, supposing he would probably pass her without any sign of recognition, she turned away her eyes from him. Yielding however, to an influence which he rarely allowed to sway him, that of impulse, he suddenly stopped, and with scant words of introductory courtesy, asked her when she had arrived.

Recovering from her agitated astonishment, she briefly told him.

"I have heard that you have been very ill since I last saw you."

"Such things are always exaggerated," she rejoined, with a wretched attempt at carelessness.

"You do not, however, look like one in health. Is it mind or body that is ailing, Miss De Mirecourt?" and his eyes earnestly scrutinized her face. Then bending towards her, he said in a low tone, "You told me once before, that you were very unhappy, and I scarcely believed you; now I read in your face that you spoke truth. In expiation of my incredulity, and on account of the deep powerful love I so lately bore you, I wish to whisper a word of counsel in your ear. Will it be of any use to warn you to put no trust in Audley Sternfield? He is unworthy of any woman's love."

"Too late, too late," she faltered: "the past is irrevocable!"

"Aye, after what I had seen, I ought to have known it must be so. Well, you have chosen a frail support; but regrets are unavailing. Farewell." Touching his cap, he strode off just as Mrs. D'Aulnay, having completed her purchases, left the shop where she had been tantalizing master and clerks about a certain indefinable shade of lilac, in search of which nearly all the goods in the store had been overturned.

Antoinette, agitated by her late interview with Colonel Evelyn, was in no mood for conversation, and, after taking a turn up to Dalhousie Square, in which the hill or citadel then stood, surmounted by its flag, and the few rusty cannon which had been almost the only defence that Montreal had to offer against the three besieging armies that had invested it, they returned homeward. Again, Sternfield and his blushing triumphant partner passed them. To the bows of both, Mrs. D'Aulnay only returned a cold, disdainful nod, which mortified Sternfield almost as much as Antoinette's quiet, self-possessed bow. Mrs. D'Aulnay was in a fever of indignation, and she abused Sternfield and his companion with a fervor and energy which could not have been exceeded if she, instead of Antoinette, had been the aggrieved party.

"May I tell Jeanne that you are not at home, when he calls the next time? Do not shake your head—I will. This insolent bridegroom must be brought to his senses in one way or another."

The next day, Dr. Manby, one of the army surgeons, and a frequent visitor at the house, called, and he enquired so earnestly about Antoinette's health, and expressed so great a desire to see her, that Mrs. D'Aulnay, despite her cousin's avowed intention of receiving no visitors for two or three days, went to her room, and half coaxed, half forced her down. Dr. Manby was a quiet, middle-aged man, neither handsome nor accomplished, simply respectable, so Antoinette felt no anger at his many questions, nor scrutinizing looks. As he rose to go, he kindly said, retaining in his grasp a moment, the small thin hand he had taken:

"If I were your physician, Miss De Mirecourt, I would prescribe neither quinine nor tonics, but a daily dose of heart's ease."

"But is that remedy found in every apothecary's store?" she rejoined, endeavoring to laugh off his remark. "Or have you any doses ready done up for use?"

"I am afraid not; but at your age, my dear young lady, it is easily procured. The best means is to take plenty of exercise—see agreeable, cheerful people, and religiously avoid all dull or melancholy thoughts. I will call again next week to see if my prescription has been followed, and to ascertain the results."

"What a good-natured, officious creature," said Mrs. D'Aulnay, as she watched the Doctor's short, thick-set figure traversing the street.

"Kind-hearted, and amiable, though," returned Antoinette.

Neither dreamed for one moment, that Colonel Evelyn, unable to subdue the anxiety which the sight of Antoinette's altered appearance had awoke in his breast the day previous, despite his outraged love, despite that never-to-be-forgotten scene which he had witnessed between her and Sternfield, had asked Doctor Manby, one of the chosen few with whom he was on anything like terms of intimacy, to pay a visit of apparent civility to Mrs. D'Aulnay, and ascertain as much as he possibly could about her young guest. It must not be inferred from this, that Colonel Evelyn had at all relented in his feelings of estrangement towards Antoinette, or in his severe condemnation of her conduct. No, her offence was one which that sensitive, honorable nature never could forgive; but, at the same time, there remained a feeling of powerful interest in her, one which, perhaps, he could never wholly overcome; and a deep intense sentiment of regret that the man for whom she had sacrificed so much was so utterly unworthy of her. No one was better acquainted than Colonel Evelyn with the lawless recklessness of Sternfield's career; and as he thought over the future misery of the young girl, when united for life to a man who set all moral laws at defiance, it was more with the anxious grief of a father than with the irritation of a rejected suitor.

CHAPTER 30

Mrs. D'Aulnay did not obtain as speedy a chance of saying "not at home" to Major Sternfield as she had expected, for several days elapsed without his renewing his visit; and whilst she wondered and scolded, Antoinette grew thinner and paler every day. Doctor Manby, who, without having been formally adopted as the latter's physician, took the liberty of questioning and prescribing during most of his frequent visits, began to get anxious and irritable. One day that he found himself alone with the lady of the house, he took her roundly to task, for the rapidity with which her young friend's health was declining.

"But what can I do, Doctor?" was the indignant rejoinder. " 'Tis you, a physician, who should be able to suggest or prescribe something that would be of service to her."

"So I could and would, madam, if this were an ordinary case, but it is not. 'Tis the mind that is ill with her, and you should endeavor to soothe, cheer and solace her."

"But I repeat, what can I do?" questioned the lady despairingly. "If I propose a *soirée*, dancing, or other amusement of the sort, she says she is too ill, and menaces to shut herself up in her room till the entertainment is over; if I seek to engage her in visiting, shopping, or novel-reading, or indeed in any other feminine pastime," the Doctor smiled grimly at this choice of amusements, "she begs off with such a coaxing way, that I cannot find the heart to insist. The only point on which I invariably remain firm is to bring her out driving every day, and a difficult task it sometimes is."

Doctor Manby, convinced that the case was a serious as well as difficult one, departed without another word; and

Mrs. D'Aulnay set herself earnestly to work to think what more effectual means she could adopt to amuse and divert her young guest. She was highly delighted, therefore, when, that very afternoon, a clear pleasant voice resounded in the hall, and Louis Beauchesne entered, all smiles and gaiety. Antoinette, too, was pleased to see him, for she had always looked on him as a brother, and there was something almost contagious in his exuberant spirits and kindly genial humor.

He informed them "he had come to spend some weeks in Montreal, having business of importance to transact, and that he had promised Mr. De Mirecourt at the same time to keep a strict watch over their movements."

Mrs. D'Aulnay laughingly declared that "as she wished to afford him every opportunity of prosecuting his researches, she gave him *carte blanche* for visiting at the house. Morning, noon, or night—to dinner, breakfast, or tea, he would be always welcome without farther invitation."

This pleasant species of challenge was smilingly accepted, and that evening, as well as many succeeding ones, saw Louis a welcome guest at Mrs. D'Aulnay's. Something of Antoinette's olden look and color used to steal over her face whilst listening to Louis and his mirthful sallies. His conversation awoke no disagreeable thoughts or reminiscences; it brought back only the happy golden past: and his careful, delicate avoidance of any allusion to his own ill-starred passion for herself, which he seemed apparently to have completely mastered, removed the only unpleasant feature that by any chance could have attached itself to their intercourse.

One evening the three were seated together in Mrs. D'Aulnay's drawing-room, and never had Louis been more entertaining or his companions more highly amused. Antoinette had asked him to hold a skein of floss whilst she wound it off; and to assume a convenient position, he had thrown himself carelessly at her feet on one of the low stools with which Mrs. D'Aulnay's rooms were filled, and which, that lady's enemies maintained, were intended for such purposes. The heat of the fire had flushed the young girl's face; and as Louis, perhaps wearied of his task, fidgetted about, rendering the winding of the silk a very difficult thing, she laughingly chided him for his impatient awkwardness. At that moment the door opened, and, without warning or announcement, Sternfield walked in. He stood a moment on the threshold, glancing darkly on the group before him. He had come there that evening, magnanimously thinking that he had sufficiently punished Antoinette for her obstinacy in the matter of the drive, and expecting to find her ill, pale, and spiritless. He saw her instead, with a glow on her face, and smiles on her lip, such as neither had worn for many weeks past; whilst by way of climax, Louis was seated at her feet, his gay, handsome face upturned to hers.

Mrs. D'Aulnay, who easily divined the jealous angry feelings of the new-comer, fairly revelled in the triumph of the moment, and, with a look of smiling *badinage* which he found inexpressively provoking, inquired where he had been lately, and what he had been doing with himself?

Scarcely replying, he walked over to a chair beside Antoinette, and, throwing himself into it, sarcastically expressed his delight at the improved state of her health. Of Louis he took no notice whatever; but the latter revenged himself by adjusting his low seat more comfortably, and inquiring how many more skeins Antoinette had to wind, announcing his willingness at the same time to hold any amount of them. With all his arrogance, his self-esteem, Sternfield felt somewhat disconcerted. Mrs. D'Aulnay's mocking smile, Louis's easy not to say impertinent indifference, and Antoinette's constrained embarrassed welcome, formed a reception such as he had not calculated upon. But Major Sternfield was not a man to be easily vanquished; and whilst Mrs. D'Aulnay was yet triumphing in his mortification, he had determined how to bring the latter to an end.

Giving ample time to Antoinette to finish the winding of her floss, he waited till Louis rose from his seat in obedience to a look from the young girl, and drawing his chair nearer to hers, hemmed her in in such a manner as to isolate her entirely from her companions. Then addressing her in a low familiar tone on matters which he knew could not but chain her attention, contrived to engross her completely. Louis watched this palpable and singular flirtation with mingled surprise and indignation. That Antoinette should permit such a thing astonished him beyond measure; and yet, the more he watched them, which he did very narrowly, the more leniently he judged her, and the more intense became his feelings of dislike for her companion. There was a constrained unhappy look about her, a restless glancing around, as if she were weary of her position, and longed for release, which seemed to speak of fear more than of love; and though Sternfield bent so closely over her that his dark curls almost mingled with the braids of her hair, and his eyes beamed glances that might have awoke emotion in the heart of any woman who entertained the slightest feeling of affection for himself, the coldness of her manner never wavered, nor the glow which had faded from her cheek shortly after his entrance, never mounted to it again.

Sternfield however had accomplished all his intentions: he had changed the pleasant cordiality which reigned on his entrance into embarrassed dullness, and, whilst inflicting ample mortification on his supposed rival, had punished at the same time Antoinette for having dared to be gay or amused during his absence. Mrs. D'Aulnay, however, was eagerly watching an opportunity of retaliation, and when Major Sternfield said,

"I will call to-morrow for you, Miss De Mirecourt, if you will do me the honor of driving with me," she hastily interrupted, "Impossible! Antoinette and I are engaged to drive out with Mr. Beauchesne in the country, to see a mutual friend."

Sternfield glanced at his bride, but her eyes, determinedly bent on the carpet, warned him he would get no assistance from her; and too wise to enter on a contest in which he ran the risk of defeat, he bowed and withdrew. In doing so, however, he managed to tell Mrs. D'Aulnay, in a low whisper, "to beware of making Antoinette as independent and careless a wife as she was herself, for that he assuredly would not prove as tame and blind a husband as Mr. D'Aulnay."

"Audacious!" muttered the lady with crimsoning brow; but before she had time to collect her thoughts, the offender was beyond reach of her voice.

The fierce unreasoning jealousy of Sternfield's character had been strangely roused by finding Louis on such intimate terms in Mrs. D'Aulnay's house; and the fact of subsequently meeting him a few days later, driving the two ladies out, still farther increased his anger. Shortly after the visit during which he had contrived to render himself so disagreeable, Mrs. D'Aulnay half coaxed, half worried Antoinette into promising that she would enter into the details and preparations for a small *soirée* with which she wished to enliven the present monotony of their lives. The appointed night came, and the young girl in her gauzy white robes looked so delicately lovely, but so fragile, that Jeanne, remembering how full of health and bloom that young face and form had been one short year previous, sadly and forebodingly shook her head.

Aware that many unpleasant remarks regarding her altered looks had been whispered about, Antoinette spared no effort to appear gay and cheerful; and Doctor Manby, who was among the guests, quietly rubbed his hands, and murmured to himself, "That what his young friend really wanted after all, was distraction and amusement."

One of the liveliest of the gay assemblage was Louis Beauchesne; and there were few whose reserve of manner did not yield more or less to the influence of his frank, joyous gaiety. Sternfield, on the contrary, was in one of his worst moods. Heavy gambling losses experienced the night previous had greatly ruffled his temper, and rarely man sought a festive entertainment with feelings more ill-suited to the occasion. Pre-determined to find fault with his unfortunate young bride, he felt angry with her for looking so unusually cheerful, angry with her for the calm even friendliness of her manner towards him. Availing himself of the opportunity afforded by the dance for which he had secured her hand, he contrived to effectually damp her assumed cheerfulness by favoring her with a chapter of reproaches and upbraidings such as she was now, alas! too familiar with. The dance concluded, he abruptly left her and sought out one of the budding young beauties with whom he was so fond of flirting. Whilst bending over the latter, looking and whispering tender things, he inwardly congratulated himself on the means and power he thus possessed of punishing that rebellious girlish will that ever dared to place itself in opposition to his own.

Antoinette, however, was not left to a wall-flower's fate, and eager partners thronged constantly around her. Among these, Louis was naturally one of the most attentive. Her greater degree of intimacy with him, the freedom from restraint, from the necessity of keeping up that appearance of cheerfulness or interest which she was obliged to assume, whilst dancing with others, induced her more than once to grant his demand for her hand. Still there was nothing which an unprejudiced eye would have regarded as even approaching to flirtation between them; and when Antoinette two or three times chanced to meet Sternfield's glance angrily fixed upon her, she thought the looks were merely the supplement of the lecture he had previously given her. Strangely dispirited, however, by those threatening glances, she refused Louis's request to join a cotillion then forming, declaring that she felt too much fatigued to do so.

"Then I shall sit beside you and wait for the next, for you have promised me a dance," he rejoined, carefully adjusting the cushions of the silken ottoman on which she was seated.

Kindly solicitous to make her forget the sadness which he saw stealing over her, the young man strained every faculty, though unavailingly, to interest and amuse her. Antoinette's glance was either wandering wearily round the room or stealing towards Sternfield, who stood some distance from them, apparently engrossed by his pretty partner, for he never danced with any but very young and handsome women. His companion's look strangely puzzled Louis. There was sadness, anxiety, pain in it, but no jealous anger, none of the *pique* which a girl might naturally be expected to feel or show, in witnessing her lover devoted to another. Suddenly, after studying her countenance a moment in silence, he impulsively exclaimed:

"Pardon the remark, but I think Major Sternfield is a recreant wooer. Oh! Antoinette, can it be possible that you really love that man?"

She blushed deeply, painfully at the question, but made no reply beyond a reproachful glance.

"Forgive me, dear Antoinette," he earnestly continued, "but it seems to me there is something in his manner and character that should prevent him winning, much less retaining, the love of such a heart as yours."

"And yet is he not handsome and fascinating, envied by men and admired by women?" she replied with a touch of bitterness which but confirmed Beauchesne's supposition that whatever tie still linked her to Sternfield, it was not that of love.

"I acknowledge he is all that, but methinks there is much in which he is still wanting. However patiently women may put up with slights and frowns after marriage, they rarely tolerate them before."

"Because, probably, they have then a remedy in their own hands, and can turn the despotic lover adrift; but here is the object of your doubts approaching."

"Yes, and with a stormy looking brow too," thought Louis.

Sternly, Audley drew near them, and, unceremoniously leaning across young Beauchesne, whispered in Antoinette's ear, "How much longer do you intend rendering yourself ridiculous by flirting with the brainless puppy beside you?"

"What do you mean, Audley?" she inquired in turn, her face flushing.

"I will tell you if you will favor me with your hand for the next dance," he rejoined, in a somewhat louder key.

"Miss De Mirecourt is engaged to me," said Louis, stiffly.

Sternfield cast a supercilious, negligent look at the speaker, and repeated, "Do you hear, Antoinette, you will dance the next dance with me?"

"Pray, Miss De Mirecourt, do not forget that we are engaged," interrupted Louis, still more firmly than before.

Antoinette, infinitely distressed and perplexed, glanced entreatingly from one to the other. Louis's countenance was proud and determined, but Sternfield's brow was like marble, as cold and unrelenting.

Again stooping towards the young girl, the latter menacingly whispered, "I swear if you set me aside to dance with that fool, I shall teach him with a horsewhip to come between me and my wishes."

The unmanly threat was worthy of him who uttered it, but it had its effect; for Antoinette, dreading not only the menaced insult, but the deadly satisfaction which was sure to follow, turned with a blanched cheek to young Beauchesne.

"Are you ready, Miss De Mirecourt?" inquired the latter, "I do not like to hurry you, but the dancers are taking their places."

Sternfield deigned no farther remark, but, with an intolerable sneer on his lip, waited for Antoinette's decision. The latter suddenly placed her hand on Louis's arm, and, as he bent towards her, whispered:

"Oh, Louis, dear Louis, I implore you let me dance with him. I am very wretched. Do not help to make me still more so."

The pale cheek, the tearful eyes, the voice of the speaker, touched the generous heart of Beauchesne, and he mutely bowed in assent. As Sternfield abruptly, almost roughly, drew his partner's arm within his own, he cast a disdainful arrogant glance upon his momentary rival, which the latter's kindling eye returned with interest, speaking of something more than mere anger,—of menace, of future revenge.

"What sweet words have you been whispering in that idiot's ear to make him yield his insolent claims so easily?" harshly questioned Sternfield.

Antoinette dared not reply, for her lashes were heavy with unshed tears, and there was a suffocating feeling in her throat that was almost growing beyond her control: a scene she did not wish to make, and she felt that she was on the verge of one.

"Take a word of friendly warning, sweetheart mine," resumed her companion, "and bring your present flirtation with that young gentleman to a speedy close, or I shall do it for you in a more summary and unpleasant manner than either of you could desire."

Antoinette shuddered, for well she understood the threat conveyed in his words; but the music commenced, and with what composure she could gather, she had to go through the lively dance and endeavor to look careless and indifferent, in default of looking gay or amused.

"Hang that fellow Sternfield!" inwardly soliloquized Doctor Manby, who had noticed how entirely Antoinette's tranquillity had given way since the former had accosted her: "his shadow, like that of the upas-tree, seems fairly to blight that poor young creature."

The dance at length came to a close, and Antoinette was meditating flight to her own room, but Sternfield had no intention of allowing her to escape so easily. Bringing her to a small alcove, he drew forward a chair for her, and then placed himself in front of her. "I want a word of explanation with you, for I do not think we understand each other yet. You have braved me pretty well in this last flirtation of yours with Mr. Louis Beauchesne."

"Audley, cruel and unjust as you always are, will you not believe my solemn, sacred asseveration, that Louis is nothing more to me than an old and esteemed friend?"

"Tush! the man loves you heart and soul; and as you do not care one iota for your wedded husband, it is hard to say on whom your wandering affections may be placed."

What could she say to this heartless, merciless tormentor, who scoffed at her denials, sneered at her protestations? Words were unavailing, and with hands tightly clasped, and colorless lips, she sat, determined to listen and suffer in patience. Had she not in her own blind folly filled up this cup of misery, and was she to murmur now at the bitterness of the draught?

Either encouraged or exasperated by her silence he went on: "You have hitherto been firm and unyielding as bronze on your favorite whim. Tender word, caress, or kindness, such as the most scrupulous young ladies often accord their lovers, you have perseveringly refused me. Well, so be it. You have been true to your hobby, so I will be to mine. You shall walk, drive, flirt, with no living man of whom I could possibly be jealous. If, neglecting this, my explicit command, you disobey me, I shall walk up to your cavalier of the moment, Master Louis, or whoever else it may be, and publicly insult, strike him. On your own head be the result! If you will not love, I shall at least teach you to fear me." He uttered this last sentence with the menacing sternness peculiar at times to his voice, and which was in such striking contrast to his usual rich musical tones.

"Well, God will perhaps show me that mercy that you refuse me," she said, whilst an expression of anguish momentarily convulsed her features.

At that moment her eyes encountered the fixed, sorrowful gaze of Louis, who stood at some distance, apparently watching the dancers, but in reality concentrating his attention entirely upon herself. Instantly however he turned away; but another scrutinizing pair of eyes was also fixed upon them—the light blue orbs of the worthy Doctor Manby, who with a face purple with suppressed indignation, suddenly stalked up to Major Sternfield.

"What disagreeable nonsense are you whispering in Miss De Mirecourt's ear, I should like to know?" he said, in a low tone. "You have chased smiles and color from her face."

The young man drew himself stiffly up, and "wondered what Doctor Manby meant."

"Doctor Manby means what he says," was the testy rejoinder. "And he does not like to see a young lady, whom he looks on as one of his patients, frightened and worried out of her health and wits, without interfering. Come, Sternfield," he added, more good-humoredly, "you have scolded Miss De Mirecourt sufficiently for one evening, whatever her offence may be; so let me replace you, whilst you go and relieve that pretty little girl in white over there, looking out so disconsolately for a partner."

Knowing that all farther chance of private conversation with Antoinette was now at an end, (for Doctor Manby was equally tenacious and outspoken,) Sternfield rose, and, after telling her, with marked significance, that he gave her free permission to flirt with Doctor Manby, but with no one else, he turned away.

"How is this, my fair patient?" kindly enquired the good-natured physician, secretly noting and grieving over the suffering, pain-worn look of his companion. "Have you been dancing too much? you look sadly exhausted."

"Because I am unhappy, wretched!" she rejoined, with that reckless candor which great misery often induces. "Talk to me no more of drugs or palliatives, Doctor, unless you can give me one that will set this weary heart at rest for ever."

Inexpressibly shocked at this sudden confidence, as well as at the depth of mental misery which it revealed, he hurriedly, but soothingly, said: "Courage, courage, dear child. We cannot throw down life's burden because in a moment of depression we may find it heavy. To-morrow all may be light and pleasant again."

"Never, never!" she rejoined, with a slow, hopeless shake of the head.

"Listen, dear Miss De Mirecourt, to the advice of a man old enough to be your father, and do not let a lover's quarrel prey on your spirits thus. Major Sternfield is hot-tempered, but he soon forgets and forgives."

As he uttered the name which had proved such a woful sound to her, a shudder ran through her frame, and, more perplexed and troubled than ever, he inwardly thought, "She does not love the handsome villain. What does it all mean?"

In a quiet, indifferent tone he soon resumed: "You seem so weak and nervous to-night, my dear young lady, the best thing you can do is to retire to rest at once. Take my arm, and I will pilot you to the hall, after which I will tell our friend, Sternfield, that I insisted on sending you off."

Arrived at the foot of the stair-case, Antoinette gratefully, falteringly bade him good-night, and hurried to her room. Shall we follow her there, reader? Shall we watch her during the course of that long, weary night, during which no slumber closed her burning eye-lids; no temporary unconsciousness brought its blessed balm, even for one half-hour, to that tortured heart and spirit? The lesson would be a painful, though, perhaps, a useful one. She had erred, but how speedy had been her retribution; she had violated the dictates of conscience and religion— trampled on a daughter's most sacred duties, and what had it brought her? That which guilt and wrong-doing will ever bring to those who are not utterly hardened in evil,— remorse and wretchedness.

CHAPTER 31

MRS. D'AULNAY, who had just risen from her couch, was seated in her easy-chair, the morning after her *soirée*, her feet thrust into her quilted satin slippers, whilst Jeanne was preparing to disentangle and smooth the thick masses of her hair, when a loud, prolonged knock, whose echoes reverberated through the whole house, startled mistress and maid.

"Heavens! what can that be? Run, Jeanne, and see," ejaculated Mrs. D'Aulnay.

The messenger soon returned with a small note, which she said "Mr. Beauchesne's man had just left. He must be in a great hurry, Madame, for he never waited to ask how you and Miss Antoinette were, as he generally does, but thrust the letter in my hand, and hurried away."

The note was crumpled and ill-folded, the address carelessly and illegibly written; and with a presentiment of evil, which caused her heart to throb more rapidly, she opened the missive. It ran thus:—

"He who writes this, dear Mrs. D'Aulnay, is now flying from justice, and, if not overtaken, will soon have left his native land for ever. Major Sternfield insulted me last night, goaded me to ungovernable passion by his insolent cruelty to our poor unhappy Antoinette, who seems—Heaven help her—to be strangely in his power. I controlled my anger at the moment, and waited my time. It soon came; for shortly after he left the house, which I took good care to do at the same time with himself, I went up to him and asked for an apology, which of course he was as little disposed to give as I was anxious to obtain. This morning we met, and he fell, mortally wounded. They tell

213

me he is dying. Say to Antoinette, that if, contrary to my secret suppositions and thoughts, he is really dear to her, I implore her, by the memory of the deep, true love I have ever borne her, to forgive me. Deeply I regret the mad act of which I have been guilty, not so much for the consequences it has entailed on myself, as for the terrible responsibility thus incurred of hurrying a fellow-creature, in the strength of manhood, into eternity. Ah! before the deed was done, I could never have dreamed that the remorse would have been so bitter—so weighty: but time presses. With earnest thanks for all your past kindness to myself—I dare send no farther message to Antoinette,

"Yours,

"LOUIS."

Deeply agitated, Mrs. D'Aulnay perused and reperused this painful letter, and then, suddenly starting up, hastened to her cousin's room. The latter, who had thrown herself on the bed about an hour previous, was lying motionless, her eyes listlessly fixed on the pale rays of light streaming in between the parting of the curtains, her face looking as wan as that chill, pale light itself.

"Antoinette darling, I have something terrible to tell you. Are you strong enough to bear it?" tremblingly questioned Mrs. D'Aulnay.

Neither the warning of coming evil, contained in this mysterious announcement, nor the evident agitation of the speaker, aroused anything like anxiety or emotion in Antoinette. She was too ill in body and mind at the moment for that.

"Well, child," sharply continued Mrs. D'Aulnay, with an irritability springing from her own intense agitation, "have you no question to ask, no wish to enquire farther? It concerns chiefly yourself, or rather one nearly related to you. 'Tis of Audley Sternfield I would speak."

"What of him?" languidly questioned the girl.

"There, read for yourself," and she placed Louis's letter in her cousin's hands. "But Antoinette, darling, for Heaven's sake be calm: do not faint or go into hysterics."

The latter did neither, but her cheek turned to an ashy hue, and her very lips became white as she read. The letter perused, she sprang from her couch, and, without a moment's thought or hesitation, proceeded to dress.

"Why this hurry? Where are you going?" asked Mrs. D'Aulnay.

"To poor Audley," was the whispered reply.

"Have you taken leave of your senses, child? How do you know where he is, or even whether he is still living?"

"I must ask, find out. They have probably brought him to his quarters."

"And do you mean to say that you, a young girl, will seek him in his own rooms?"

"But you will come with me, Lucille?" was the imploring rejoinder.

"You are certainly out of your mind, poor child," and Mrs. D'Aulnay's accents betrayed both irritation and compassion. "Why all Montreal would ring with it to-morrow if we were to do such a thing. Our names would be in every one's mouth."

"So be it, Lucille: I shall go alone."

"You shall do no such thing. After quarrelling and disagreeing with that unfortunate Sternfield ever since he wedded you, about the preservation of your fair name, are you going to uselessly, recklessly forfeit it now?"

" 'Tis my duty; and whatever be the consequences, I must go."

"But you do not love, you do not even like him, thoughtless child."

"Oh, the more reason that I should seek his dying bed without delay. Alas! remorse is busy enough at my heart already, without my adding farther to its weight."

"But what good can you do him?" persisted Mrs. D'Aulnay.

"My presence may smooth, may solace him. Would you have him die," and a convulsive shudder ran through her frame, "with anger towards me in his heart, perhaps curses on his lips, as might happen if I kept away from him, forgetful of his claims and my duties?"

"Well, at least wait awhile. Mr. D'Aulnay is out, but I expect him in every moment, and I will then boldly ask him to accompany us."

But Antoinette had no intention of wasting priceless moments, any one of which might be Sternfield's last on earth, in waiting for a chance that might in the end fail her, and, hastily completing her toilette after her cousin's departure, she stole softly down the back staircase, and thence through the narrow passage which led to the out-houses and court-yard. As she had partly hoped, she saw one of the servants lounging about the stable-door, and in a low tone she told him to harness one of the horses to the plain light vehicle usually employed by Mr. D'Aulnay. In a short while it was ready; she got in, and they quietly passed through the gate without attracting the notice of any of the household, save one of the maids, who saw nothing very unusual in the fact of Miss De Mirecourt's going out at so early an hour in the morning; her destination, as the girl at once decided, being of course to church.

"Now," thought Antoinette, pressing her hand to her aching head, "my first step must be to call at Doctor Manby's, and, though he will probably be with poor Audley, I may learn from some of his people where the latter is."

Arrived at the quiet boarding-house which Doctor Manby made his home, she was told he had gone to Major Sternfield's quarters, to attend the latter, who had been dangerously wounded that morning in a duel.

Major Sternfield, and three or four of his brother officers, occupied a plain, though comfortable, stone house, situated towards the east end of the city, now included in that portion which we call the Quebec Suburbs. A small garden, environed by a wall, whose rough masonry was concealed in great part by the spreading maples that kindly drooped over it, sloped from the back of the building towards the bank of the broad, blue St. Lawrence, from which it was divided by a very narrow road. Directly in front lay the graceful, picturesque island of St. Helen's, then belonging to the Barons De Longueuil, affording a pleasant resting-place to the eye, when weary of dwelling on the sparkling, dancing surface of the river.

Before the door of this residence, Mrs. D'Aulnay's coachman drew up the reeking, panting horse, which he had driven at a merciless pace, moved by Antoinette's unceasing and urgent appeals. A terrible fear had taken possession of the young girl's heart, that she would arrive too late—arrive, but to learn that the man to whom she had sworn life-long love and fidelity had passed from earth, hating and cursing her. Without waiting for assistance, she sprang to the ground, and, heedless of the amazed looks of a couple of soldiers, officers' servants, who were loitering about the door-steps, plied the knocker with what strength her trembling fingers permitted.

A soldier opened it, and she hastily exclaimed, "I wish to see Major Sternfield. Show me to his room immediately."

Lounging in the hall, with a cigar in his mouth, stood the Honorable Percy Delaval, and had Medusa herself suddenly appeared on the threshold, enquiring for the sick man, he could not have looked more utterly astounded. In an adjoining room, the door of which was open, two other officers were seated, and the expression of intense astonishment that suddenly overspread their features rivalled the wonder depicted on Lieutenant Delaval's countenance.

"Do you hear me? I wish to see Major Sternfield," repeated the new comer, with feverish agitation.

The man hesitated, fearing to introduce so unusual a visitant, without, at least, previously announcing her to the patient.

Antoinette, chafing at this additional delay, instantly turned to Mr. Delaval, and entreatingly exclaimed:

"You know me. Tell him to bring me at once to Major Sternfield."

"Certainly, Miss De Mirecourt," rejoined the young man, with an embarrassment which contrasted strangely with the young girl's fearless earnestness. "Certainly. Here, sirrah, show this lady immediately to Major Sternfield's room. I take all responsibility upon myself."

Of course the man obeyed, and Antoinette followed him with trembling limbs up the steep, narrow staircase.

"Well, I call this a case!" whispered the young honorable to his two brother officers, who had joined him in the hall as soon as Antoinette had disappeared. "A young lady who would do that in England would certainly be tabooed."

"And that poor girl will just as certainly be tabooed here," rejoined one of his companions. "They are not more indulgent to woman's weaknesses in Canada than they are at home."

"I can scarcely believe the evidence of my own senses," said a third, a clever, gentlemanly man, whom Antoinette had often met at Mrs. D'Aulnay's. "I repeat, I can scarcely believe it, for Miss De Mirecourt was such a gentle, modest little girl, the very last one I would have thought capable of venturing on such a step."

"Oh, love works miracles, Thornley,—changes people's very natures sometimes."

"Sternfield is a lucky dog," groaned young Delaval. "Living or dying, he always contrives to make a sensation. No danger of any of us, if we were at the last gasp to-morrow, having such an angel visitant."

"Well, poor fellow, it will not do him much good," resumed Captain Thornley. "He is almost beyond earthly consolation now. And I must say, that I for one do not think the less of the true-hearted girl who has had courage enough to brave smiles and sneers, in order that she might bid a last farewell to the man she loved."

"But I really do not think she loved him. She showed him no very decided marks of preference; and I have seen her sit near him for a half-hour at a time, with a look as cold, a glance as distant, as if she were made of marble."

"Oh, that was perhaps put on. At any rate, she has just given proof of a love surpassing that of most modern young ladies."

But we will leave the group to their discussion, and follow the object of it on her way.

CHAPTER 32

ARRIVED at the landing-place, the soldier who acted as guide silently indicated a door, and then, as if fearing to venture farther, disappeared. Antoinette, faint, sick with agitation, knocked hurriedly, though lightly. It was opened by Doctor Ormsby, the clergyman who had performed the marriage-service for herself and Sternfield.

"Does he still live?" she gasped, looking wildly up into the kind, though sad face that met hers.

"Yes, but his hours are numbered," he whispered, glancing sorrowfully towards the bed, on which, ghastly and deathlike, Sternfield lay.

"Oh, Audley, my husband!" sobbed Antoinette, suddenly springing to his side, and sinking on her knees beside the couch, careless in that supreme moment who might be there to learn the long jealously-guarded secret of her breast; unconscious that another, and that other, Cecil Evelyn, stood at a distant window, listening awe-struck, spell-bound, to that strange confession. Every thought or fear of hers then was absorbed in the overwhelming consciousness that the man who had been the bane, the curse of her life, but to whom nevertheless she belonged by the holiest of earthly ties, lay there before her, dying.

With an effort of strength, wonderful in his exhausted state, the wounded man raised himself on his elbow, and gazed at her a moment with a look of intense astonishment, which speedily changed to an expression of passionate anger; then he hoarsely said:

"Away, hypocrite, away, mocking dissembler! How dare you utter the word husband? Have you ever been wife to me in aught but name? Have you ever shown me wifely duty, love, or submission?"

220

"Audley, Audley," she wailed, "be merciful, be just. Embitter not this solemn moment by cruel upbraidings."

"Why have you come?" he interrupted, in a still harsher voice. "Is it to gloat over my dying agonies, and to assure yourself by witnessing them, that you are really free at last? It is not love that has brought you; for if one spark of that feeling for me had glowed in your breast, you would not have mocked at my prayers and tenderness, trampled on my rights and claims, as you have so insolently done, since the hour I placed the wedding-ring on your finger."

"But whose was the fault?" she asked, with clasped hands and streaming eyes. "Did I not tell you that the instant you would acknowledge me for your wife before the world, and have our marriage solemnized again, without which my creed and belief told me it was not lawfully completed, I was ready to follow you to the ends of the earth."

"Mere hair-splitting," he sneered. "No girl, it was not that, but it was because the short-lived fancy that had led you to consent to our secret union, had died out as suddenly as it had arisen."

"Forgive me if I interfere," said Doctor Ormsby, advancing, moved alike by compassion for the agonized suffering depicted in the girl's colorless face, and with anxiety for the unchristian state of feeling into which the dying man had lapsed. "Forgive me if I interfere; but as the clergyman who solemnized that marriage, which has been, alas! so fruitful in misery to both, perhaps I may have some slight claim on your mutual attention and confidence."

Here Colonel Evelyn, suddenly recovering from the stupor of astonishment into which this singular dialogue had plunged him, and becoming at the same time awake to the grave impropriety of his remaining there, a witness to an interview of so strange and delicate a nature, stole from the room, closing the door noiselessly behind him; and as he passed through the hall, the loungers there wondered much what had occurred in the sick chamber to move

Evelyn's iron nature so greatly, and to leave such traces of deep agitation on a countenance usually impassible as marble.

"May I speak, Sternfield?" gently questioned Doctor Ormsby, seeking to soothe the fiercely roused passions of the wounded man.

"Say on," was the sullen rejoinder. "What I could listen to from no other earthly being, I can bear from you."

"Well, my dear friend, it seems to me that you are severe, nay, unjust towards this young girl," and he kindly laid his hand on the shoulder of the still kneeling Antoinette. "I remember well her telling you what she has just said, and calling on me to witness it."

"The old story, ever the old story," peevishly ejaculated Sternfield, turning aside his head. "Go home, girl; go home: and you, Doctor, leave me in peace. I am growing weary of you both."

As he spoke, a deadly pallor stole over his face, and Antoinette, terribly startled, sprang to her feet.

"Do not be alarmed," Doctor Ormsby reassuringly exclaimed. " 'Tis a temporary faintness. He had a similar attack shortly before you entered, when Dr. Manby was here. Here are restoratives."

Their united efforts soon brought back something like life to Sternfield's pallid features; and the clergyman, fearing the sight of Antoinette might renew his agitation, motioned her to place herself behind a high screen which stood in one end of the room.

After a moment, the dying man glanced restlessly around him, and then muttered, "Where is she gone, my wife, Mrs. Sternfield? Ha! ha! Doctor," and he laughed in a ghastly manner. "Let me at least give her her title once before he who conferred it will be turned to lifeless clay."

"You told her to go home, just now."

"But why did she listen to me?" he retorted. "Why did she go? Of course she was tired of so dull an affair as a death-bed, and having made *son apparition*, as Mrs. D'Aulnay would say, prudently retired."

"Shall I send for her again?"

"No, by ——: I am not fallen so low as that. Had she remained, it would, though I hate almost to acknowledge it, have been a solace, a comfort to me."

"I have not left you, Audley. I am still here," said Antoinette, timidly, as she emerged from her retreat, and approached the bed.

Something like an expression of satisfaction stole over his features, imposing still in their death-struck beauty; but when she faltered out "Dear Audley, may I remain beside you?" he answered, with the olden sneer, which habit had rendered almost natural to his handsome lip, "Since it pleases you to act the part of a sister of charity, I will not say you nay. It amuses me, though, to see you shower on my dying hours, attentions and tender cares which you never vouchsafed my living ones."

She bowed her head submissively,—no taunts of his could move her now,—and, after a few moments' silence, gently said:

"Had you not better try to sleep? I will watch beside you. Are there any medicines to be given?"

"Pshaw! I will take none. I told Manby so. My case is beyond human skill, and why should I torture my palate with any vile drugs or mixtures?"

Knowing that insisting farther would only irritate him uselessly, she drew a chair close to his couch, and silently seated herself. After quietly watching her for some time, he suddenly exclaimed:

"So you have fairly installed yourself here as my nurse— determinedly taken up your post! Are you aware of what the world will say, of what men will think?"

"Oh, dear Audley, what is the world to us?" she sadly said. "Do not think of it. Do not torment yourself about its opinions."

"Aye! it is nothing to me now; but to you, girl, it is everything. Why, before two hours, this mad step of yours will be repeated, with exaggerations and commentaries in every corner of the city; and the fair name, of which you have been so jealously careful, will be at every one's mercy."

"If so," and the mournful eyes and voice became yet more sad, " 'twill be but the just punishment of my past folly: I have sinned, and I must expiate my fault."

"You have done so severely enough already," he rejoined, the first approach to anything like feeling which he had yet shown, softening his voice. "I have not spared you; and few young brides have ever passed through as bitter an ordeal as yourself. Well, the close of my rule and the dawn of your liberty are both at hand, sooner by thirty or forty years than you might have dared to hope for."

"Audley, talk not thus. Do not agitate yourself unnecessarily—"

"Stop lecturing, child: here comes a higher authority than yourself."

As he spoke, Doctor Manby entered the room. The newcomer's amazement on seeing Antoinette seated at his patient's bed-side, was almost ludicrous.

"God bless my soul, Miss De Mirecourt!" he ejaculated, involuntarily starting back.

"Not so, Doctor, but Mrs. Audley Sternfield," said the patient, with a forced laugh, that grated most painfully on all ears. "Nay, do not stare, man, as if you were moonstruck. Our good friend, Ormsby, here, who performed the interesting ceremony, can corroborate my words. Speak out, fair bride. Do you deny my ownership?"

Antoinette's cheek had turned from white to deep scarlet, and then to white again, at this address; but though her eyes were welling over with tears, she contrived to rejoin, with tolerable calmness, "I do not seek to deny it, Audley. Why should I? It is you, not I, who have always insisted on keeping it secret."

"Well, I acknowledge it now; so you see, Doctor, I shall, at least, leave something about a young and interesting widow to round off gracefully the paragraph announcing my decease. Do not look so reproachfully at me, Manby," he continued, as Antoinette, cruelly wounded by the mocking strain in which he persisted in addressing her, hurriedly rose, and turned away in tears. "You know the proverb, "ruling habit, strong in death"; and I have been so much accustomed to torment and worry my bride from the first, that I can not resist the temptation even now. But sit down, if you have sufficiently recovered from your amazement to do so, and tell me how many more hours this thread-like pulse of mine promises me."

Scarcely recovered yet from his first overwhelming astonishment, the physician took the chair which Antoinette had just vacated; but in the midst of all his bewilderment, he was conscious of a deep feeling of indignation excited by the mocking manner of Sternfield towards the unhappy young creature whom he called by the sacred title of wife.

"Well, speak out, man! What does my pulse say? Ah, you need not mince the matter. I am no school-boy to be frightened by a few hours' advance or delay. You will not answer? Never mind: that shake of your head tells enough. I suppose that I am booked to start on my last journey before to-night."

The physician made no reply. He could not conscientiously contradict him; for, despite the strength of the wounded man's voice, and his fluency of utterance, the faint, irregular pulse told that sudden reaction, followed by the *end*, was at hand.

"I can do no more for you, Sternfield," he said, hurriedly rising to his feet, his late feeling of irritation completely merged in compassion. "A few drops from this vial when you feel faint is all I can prescribe; at least, all that would be useful to you. Good bye. God bless you!" and after a long, friendly grasp of the hand, the kind-hearted Doctor hurried away, more agitated and grieved than he cared to show.

For some time after his departure, the patient maintained a moody silence which he at length broke by sullenly asking, "Do you know, girl, whose vile hand laid me here? Of course you do. It was that smooth-faced country lover of yours. If I have not spoken of him before, 'tis because at the very thought of him curses rush to my lips, throng through my brain. But I have a word to say to you about him. It is this: He may hereafter return, hereafter renew his suit, and I would have your solemn promise ere I enter eternity that you will never lend him a favoring ear."

"Dear Audley, could you think that the hand stained by a husband's blood—"

"Pshaw! no girlish sentiment. I want not protestations nor speeches, but a promise, aye! an oath," he added more fiercely, "that you will never be aught nearer to him in any circumstances, than what you have hitherto been?"

"Willingly," she eagerly rejoined. "With heart and soul."

"Then, kiss that," and he indicated by a look the chain to which was attached her small gold cross. "The promise you made me once before on that, has been so religiously kept, that I can put faith in any other, framed in a similar manner."

She drew forth the cross, and with an earnest solemn look kissed it.

" 'Tis well, Antoinette: I can die now without cursing him and hating you."

"Oh, Audley, my husband," she entreatingly exclaimed, presenting the cross to his lips, "kiss it also; not as I have done, merely to add solemnity to an earthly promise, but as the blessed token of salvation, of future pardon and peace."

"No, no, Antoinette," and he faintly smiled. " 'Tis too late to try proselytizing now. I have settled my spiritual affairs already with Doctor Ormsby, who has read prayers to me, and prevailed on me, though with great difficulty, I must acknowledge, to refrain from heaping curses on the wretch who has cut short my life."

"But it will do you no harm to allow me to say a prayer at your bed-side."

"I am here, my dear young lady, to accomplish that grave duty which is peculiarly my own," exclaimed Doctor Ormsby, in a firm though gentle voice, as he advanced towards them. "I have hitherto refrained from intruding on you, knowing that you must have much to say to each other; but if you wish for prayer or reading now, Major Sternfield, I am ready."

"Of course you are, Doctor," rejoined Sternfield, with a somewhat equivocal smile. "It would be a terribly mortifying affair if I should slip from your pastoral care at the last moment, into the pale of Rome."

"Oh, dearest Audley, do not talk so lightly, so mockingly of all that is most solemn and sacred on earth. If your heart leans to the faith of my fathers, do not allow—"

"Tush! child, enough of such folly! I will die in the creed in which I was born and brought up."

"Then Doctor Ormsby will read you some prayers at once: your time, my dear, dear husband, is very short."

"Do not commence croaking, Antoinette: it will do me no good. Doctor, I am ready, but excuse my saying I hope you will not be too diffuse."

"Your present state of weakness will prevent that. Believe me, I will not overtask your strength."

At that moment a knock was heard at the door of the apartment, which Doctor Ormsby instantly opened. "A messenger for you, Miss De Mirecourt," he said.

Antoinette glanced through the half-open door-way, and instantly recognized Jeanne; so whispering to Sternfield that she would return in a few moments, she went out to the new-comer.

The latter told her in a low tone that Mrs. D'Aulnay had
sent her with strict injunctions not to go back till Antoinette
should return with her. "But, *mon Dieu*, Miss De Mirecourt,
what does all this mean?" enquired the old servant,
drawing her farther into the passage so that the sound of
their whispering might not disturb the clergyman who had
commenced reading aloud. "Mr. D'Aulnay, always so quiet,
is like a madman. He says you have disgraced us all, and
that your father will die of grief and shame; and has been
scolding my mistress all morning, saying that she is to
blame as much as yourself,—he, that to my knowledge
never said a downright cross word to her since they became
man and wife. *Madame* at last told him that if you had gone
alone to see Major Sternfield, you had a right to do so, for
that you were his wife. It was that stupid Paul, who, on
being asked by Mr. D'Aulnay as he met him driving into the
yard, where he had been, told at once. But is it true, dear
young lady, what Madame said?"

"Yes, Jeanne," said the girl, sadly. "Major Sternfield, who
is now dying in yon room, is my wedded husband. I was
married to him secretly."

"Oh, Miss Antoinette! Miss Antoinette!" ejaculated the
old woman, clasping her hands in overwhelming distress.
"I could not have believed that a pious young lady, so
carefully brought up as yourself, could ever have
consented to such a thing. What will poor Mr. De
Mirecourt and Madame Gérard feel? What will the wicked
slanderous world say?"

Antoinette shuddered. "Alas, I have mourned over my
folly bitterly enough, but that has not repaired it. I have still
a long expiation before me."

"And how long will you stay here, poor dear child?"

"Till all is over if he will let me," was the faltering reply.

"Ah me, Miss Antoinette, of what service can your
presence be to him now? Come home, come home. How
unseemly it is for a young lady of your age to be alone in

this house with none but soldiers and gay young officers around you."

"Jeanne, if my dear and much-wronged father were to come himself to bring me away, I could not, would not go."

"Well, I suppose 'tis no use arguing with those whose minds are made up not to see the right; but it was an evil day for us all that we caught the first sight of a scarlet coat in our quiet home. Go in now, Miss Antoinette, dear; I will just sit down here: for that handsome Major, who always looked so scornfully at me, would'nt like perhaps to see me in his dying room."

"But, Jeanne, you will feel ill at ease here,—so many strange faces passing and repassing."

"And what harm can they do beyond staring at me, and what does an old withered woman like me care for their curious looks? It is'nt like if it was your own pretty face they were peering at. Go in, go in, and call me whenever I can be of any use. I will sit here till then."

Doctor Ormsby was still reading when Antoinette re-entered, and the young girl knelt down in a corner of the apartment and poured forth in silence her own earnest prayers to Heaven in behalf of that soul trembling on the verge of eternity. Meantime, a sort of drowsy torpor was stealing over Sternfield; and when Doctor Ormsby, having finished his ministrations, addressed a few words to him, his answer was confused and almost unintelligible.

"I must leave you for a time," said the clergyman, closing his book; "and I think, my dear young lady, you had better bring that respectable woman in, provided she is willing to assist you. If poor Sternfield should recover his consciousness, which is improbable, she can leave the room if her presence annoys him. I will return in a few hours."

Acting on this advice, Antoinette brought in Jeanne; but unwilling to run any risk of annoying the patient in case he should suddenly recover consciousness, she pointed to the latter to seat herself behind the screen which had already afforded temporary concealment to herself. Slowly the time wore on, no sound breaking that deep, hushed silence save the laborious breathing of the dying man. Prompted by a delicacy and kindliness of feeling that did them honor, the other occupants of the house permitted no loud voice, or hurried, careless footstep, to intrude on that heavy stillness.

Shortly after noon, a single knock was heard, and Jeanne hastened to answer it. It was a soldier bearing a tray containing some simple refreshments which he said, "Doctor Manby ordered him in the morning to bring to the sick room."

"I begin to think in a kindlier way of these red-coats than I have ever yet done," inwardly soliloquized Jeanne, as she arranged the things on a small table, and carried the latter close to Antoinette. "Ah, I fear me, yon handsome-faced one was the worst of the lot," and she glanced towards the calm statue-like countenance of the sleeper.

Earnestly, anxiously she pressed the young girl to taste some of the refreshments she placed before her; but the heart of the latter was too heavy for that; and she was obliged at length to remove the untouched tray, consoling herself by the reflection that if her young lady did not eat, it was not at least owing to that most deplorable of all earthly reasons, the having nothing on which to exercise her powers of appetite.

The sun had set behind thick banks of clouds, leaving here and there a sullen crimson streak, and the twilight was stealing rapidly on, its gray shadows rendering still more wan and ghastly that white upturned face lying so still and motionless on its pillow. Suddenly it stirred, the heavy eyelids parted, and Sternfield's voice, so hoarse and changed as to be scarcely recognizable, exclaimed, "Are you there, Antoinette?"

A gentle pressure of his hand, a softly whispered word of kindness, answered him.

"Determined to see me through the last stage of my journey? It must be near its close, for my sight is growing strangely dim."

"The twilight is coming on, dear Audley. It may be that."

"No, 'tis that twilight which will never know another sunrise. Well, 'tis not the death a soldier would have chosen, but it might have been worse. I am at least free from pain."

"And you have had time, dear husband, to reconcile yourself with God?"

"Yes, yes, and to dictate a short letter of farewell to the two fair-haired sisters living in that quiet town in Warwickshire in which I was born. Ah! I had not dreamed a year ago, of finding a grave amid the snows of Canada; above all, a grave at so early a period of my pleasant life. Perhaps it would have been better for me had I never exacted that promise of secrecy from you; but you had told me so often our marriage was not lawfully completed, that I dreaded such was really the case, and feared if our secret became known, that your friends would prevail on you to seek a divorce. Meantime, whilst waiting thus securely for the day which would put you in undisturbed possession of your mother's fortune, many things favorable to me might have happened: your father's death—in this solemn hour, I speak openly, Antoinette—or other circumstances which would have placed yourself and reputation completely in my power. But my dreams, like my life, are at an end."

A long silence, broken only by Antoinette's sobs, followed.

"Listen to me, child; bend nearer, for I have that to say to you which I once thought my proud lips would never say to mortal. Your patient gentleness has touched me at last, and before I go hence, I would ask you to pardon me for all that I have made you suffer, for all my past cruelty and injustice?"

"From my heart," she whispered, stooping over, and pressing her lips to that death-damp brow. "May God forgive me all my own errors as freely as I forgive you."

He faintly smiled, and his fingers tightened on the small hand that rested in his own. The twilight gloom deepened. Colder and colder became his clasp, darker and darker grew the shadows round his eyes and mouth; and when his pale young watcher, at length startled by his fixed gaze, loudly uttered his name, no look or word gave response.

"Jeanne, here, come here," she shrieked.

The woman hurriedly drew near, and, after a glance at that marble face, she gently disengaged the girl's fingers from the icy clasp in which they were still twined, and whispered, "How peacefully he passed away!"

A wild, hysterical fit of sobbing gave some relief to Antoinette's overtasked feelings; and a moment after Doctor Ormsby entered the room.

"Take her home, poor child," he compassionately said, raising her from the bed on which she had thrown herself. "Take her home: she has been sorely tried. I will see to everything."

Passively, almost unconsciously, Antoinette yielded to Jeanne's guidance, and suffered herself to be dressed, and placed in the vehicle which one of the officer's servants had procured. Arrived at home, the kind-hearted woman undressed her now almost helpless charge, and put her to bed; previously warning Mrs. D'Aulnay that she must on no account even enter her cousin's room that night. Neither all these tender cares nor the calming potion which she passively took, sufficed to chase away that grim shadow of impending sickness which was brooding over her pillow. From a heavy lethargic sleep, she awoke up delirious. A physician was sent for, and the startled household learned that she was dangerously ill of brain-fever.

CHAPTER 33

WHILST the young girl lay on that sick bed, unconscious of every thing passing around her, battling with the strength of youth against death and disease, the mortal remains of the handsome and fascinating Major Sternfield were committed to their last home. Very busy were gossipping tongues with his name and that of the hapless Antoinette; and had the latter but known half of the false rumors which malice or thoughtlessness invented and repeated, it would in all likelihood have prevented convalescence from ever revisiting her sick couch. Everything of such a nature however was carefully kept from her, whilst watchful care, medical skill, and judicious nursing were all enlisted in her cause; and after eight or ten days of anxious suspense, she was pronounced out of immediate danger. Wofully weak and altered was she though, and friends and attendants ominously shook their heads and whispered each other that she would never get wholly well.

Mr. De Mirecourt had hastened to Montreal immediately on hearing of his daughter's illness; and whatever may have been his first feelings of anger and humiliation on learning the sad tale of her secret marriage, her severe and dangerous attack of sickness, calling forth his deep parental tenderness, shielded her not only then, but even after recovery had set in, from rebuke or reproach. About two months after Major Sternfield's death, one afternoon that the invalid had yielded to Mrs. D'Aulnay's entreaties, and ventured into the latter's cheerful morning apartment, her hostess was summoned to the drawing-room to see a visitor. She soon returned, and coaxingly exclaimed:

233

"My little Antoinette, an old friend prays for permission to see you. 'Tis Colonel Evelyn. Will you not admit him?"

How rapidly Antoinette's color came and went, how wildly her heart throbbed at that name; and Mrs. D'Aulnay, taking advantage of her involuntary silence as implying consent, hastened away. A moment after, a firm, manly tread resounded through the hall,—a mist arising from weakness or agitation swam before Antoinette's eyes, and, when self-possession returned, she was alone with Colonel Evelyn, both her hands in his, and his kind, friendly glance bent earnestly on her countenance.

"You have been very, very ill," he exclaimed, in accents as gentle as his looks.

"Yes, but I am rapidly recovering," she rejoined, with a desperate effort at composure, and withdrawing her hands as she spoke.

A silence followed, silence almost insufferable to the nervous, agitated girl, for her companion's earnest searching gaze was still fixed upon her, and beneath it she felt her color come and go, and her eyes droop in painful confusion. At length he resumed in tones whose involuntary tremor betrayed that he too was moved in no small degree:

"Will you pardon me, if, at the risk of agitating you, I allude to the painful past and to that strange secret which brought so much misery to more than one? Was it—was your marriage with Audley Sternfield your only cause for rejecting my own suit?"

Antoinette became deadly pale, and, clasping her hands to her breast as if to keep down her deep agitation, she faltered:

"Colonel Evelyn! Do not speak of my past madness till at least I have acquired sufficient calmness to bear allusion to it. How you must wonder at my folly, condemn and despise me!"

His only reply was to clasp her quickly, closely to his breast, whilst he whispered, "My much-tried, long-suffering Antoinette! Mine own, at last!"

Ah, no farther need of disguise then, and, in broken accents and with panting breath, she faltered forth her gratitude, her joy, her happiness. Much had they to say to each other; and with a childish truthfulness, for which that stern proud man could have knelt and worshipped her, she recounted the history of that long period of dark and bitter trial. True, she hesitated when she came to the part in which he himself had become an actor, when she had to acknowledge how very dear he became to her heart; but still bravely she went on, telling her ceaseless struggles against that new-born love, her temptations and her sufferings; but sparing all the while, as much as was possible, the name of him who had wrought her all that misery.

Her tale concluded, she bowed her head on the arm of the sofa, but he tenderly drew it towards his bosom, whispering, "Here is your resting-place henceforth. O, my beloved, as gold out of the furnace, so have you come purified and perfected out of your fiery trial—all that I had first thought, first hoped you were."

"But, Colonel Evelyn," and she raised her head with a sudden anxious start, whilst the bright rich glow on her cheek faded to a marble pallor, "report must have said so many and such bitter things of me. How can you so fearlessly brave the world's judgment, and make the object of its censure, perhaps scorn, your wife?"

"I have long since ceased to care for the world's opinions or its judgments, and certainly I will never suffer it to influence me where the happiness of my life is at stake. Do not worry your mind with trifles or phantoms, my Antoinette. Thanks to that merciful God whom I so sinfully ignored in the dark days of life's adversity, and to whose love and service your counsels and examples will guide me back, the future lies happy and bright before us. Your father's consent is already obtained." Antoinette joyfully started. "Yes, before renewing my suit to yourself, I thought it but right to speak to him. Without much demur he consented; frankly assuring me at the same time, that, had not circumstances banished Mr. Beauchesne from his native land for ever, he would never have listened affirmatively to my prayer."

"Oh, Colonel Evelyn, I feel almost too blessed," she whispered, tears swelling from her eyes despite every effort. "Leave me now awhile, for I am almost giddy with excess of happiness."

"Not happier, my own, than I am," and he tenderly raised to his lips the hand on the second finger of which Sternfield's wedding-ring still glistened. As his glance involuntarily rested on it, the girl's face deeply, painfully flushed, but he softly whispered:

"Another will soon replace it, beloved. One which will bring you, let us humbly hope, more happiness than it has ever done. But I must leave you for awhile now, for this interview has been an agitating one, and I must be careful of my new-found treasure."

Rapidly to her room sped Antoinette to give vent in tears, in earnest eager prayers of thanksgiving, to the joy which was filling her young heart to overflowing. Ere she had yet half recovered her calmness, a slight tap came to her door, and Mrs. D'Aulnay, half sobbing, half laughing, folded her in her arms.

"Is it not like a romance, a fairy tale, my poor little Antoinette?" she exclaimed. "I have this minute come from Uncle De Mirecourt, who is in the library with that darling Colonel Evelyn, and everything is going on as smoothly as heart could desire."

"And my dear father has really given a cheerful consent?"

"Well he might, child," was the significant reply. "He knew that after the *éclat* accompanying Sternfield's death and the promulgation of the secret which had previously been so carefully kept, he might find it very difficult to get a suitable husband for you. Colonel Evelyn's conduct too was so manly, so honorable throughout. Whilst you were still struggling in the early stage of your terrible attack of fever, he called here almost wild on account of your danger. Your poor father, bowed to the very dust with humiliation and grief, chanced to be in the room into which he was shewn by the half-distracted Justine, who, in common with the rest of the household, seemed to be at her wit's end at the time. The two gentlemen exchanged a few words together, having become acquainted during Uncle De Mirecourt's memorable winter drive to Quebec; and I know not exactly what brought it about, but Colonel Evelyn laid open his heart to your father, exposed his fears, his hopes, his feelings, and received the latter's sanction to his suit if you ever recovered, which at that time was indeed very doubtful. We all agreed we would not agitate you by speaking on the subject till you were sufficiently recovered to let your lover plead his own cause. And now what do you say to my matchmaking talents? Two husbands in the short space of one year! All the young girls in the country will be wild to partake of my hospitality. But here comes that dear old tyrant of a Doctor. He will be puzzled by the rapid rate at which your pulse must be beating now."

Despite the opinions of friends and acquaintances, who had obligingly decided that Antoinette should at once enter a convent, or retire immediately to Valmont, there to live and die in the strictest seclusion, she was publicly united a year after to Colonel Evelyn. It is hard to say whether surprise or indignation predominated; and more than one fair lady expressed unmeasured wonder and contempt at Colonel Evelyn's mad infatuation for a girl who had rendered herself so notorious as the bride had done.

Over Antoinette's future destiny we will not linger. Happiness soon restored to that youthful frame the health which had commenced to give way so rapidly under her early cares and trials. To her devoted, idolizing husband she brought that unclouded domestic felicity he had for so many weary years of his life despaired of ever knowing, and in assuring his happiness, she assured her own.

Louis Beauchesne, who, through the connivance of friends, was fortunate enough to escape from Canada, notwithstanding the strict search instituted for him, never returned to it. He was kindly received in France, which welcomed at that time with open arms the Canadians who chose to leave their native land for her own sunny soil. After a time he formed new ties and friendships which brought him happiness, though they never obliterated from his memory those of his youth and childhood.

The philosophical Mr. D'Aulnay returned with renewed ardor to his books and folios, after the strange period of trouble and bewilderment which had hovered for a time over his household. His fair wife smiled, dressed, and flirted as of old, ever willing to help any of her young lady friends in their love-affairs, but entertaining to the last moment of her career, a prudent horror of secret marriages.

Explanatory Notes

Over half these explanatory notes identify people, places, and events related to Canadian history, particularly during the period of the 1750s and 1760s. Other notes deal with Mrs. Leprohon's fairly frequent references to the Bible and Roman Catholic festivals and saints. Still others explicate allusions to French and English authors and their works. Of the three notes that do not fit easily into any of these categories, one explains a reference to the "Fronde," one the term "Jean Baptiste," and one "the upas-tree." The notes are keyed to the text by page and line numbers.

3.5-7   *the year 176—, some short time after the royal standard of England had replaced the fleur-de-lys of France*] 1763; France officially ceded "Canada, with all its dependencies," to Great Britain by means of the "*definitive Treaty of Peace and Friendship . . . . Concluded at* Paris *the 10th day of* February, *1763*." The year is confirmed by the fact that Madame D'Aulnay's St. Catherine's Eve party was held on a "Thursday" night; in 1763 St. Catherine's Day was Friday, 25 November. See *Documents Relating To The Constitutional History Of Canada 1759-1791*. Selected and Edited with Notes by Adam Shortt and Arthur G. Doughty. 2nd Ed., Pt. 1. Ottawa: King's Printer, 1918, pp. 113 and 115, and CEECT, p. 10.

3.26-28   *Monsieur D'Aulnay, one of the most distinguished among the few families of the old French noblesse*] The name D'Aulnay is not connected with the early history of Quebec but with that of Acadia. Charles de Menou d'Aulnay, sometimes

241

called Charnisay after his birthplace in France, was one of the leading traders in Acadia in the 1630s and 1640s; his ambition to govern the entire colony led him into a protracted fight with another important trader, Charles de Saint-Etienne de La Tour. At various times during their rivalry each man enlisted the help of the Protestant New England colonists; d'Aulnay, however, appears to have always remained a Roman Catholic, while La Tour may have been a Huguenot. François-Xavier Garneau tells the story of the competition between the two Frenchmen in "Guerre Civile En Acadie. 1632-1667," a chapter in *Histoire Du Canada Depuis Sa Découverte Jusqu'à Nos Jours*, but he names d'Aulnay "Charles de Menou, chevalier de Charnisey," and calls him Charnisey for short. He was well known as d'Aulnay, however. In "The Fort Of St. John's, A Tale Of The New World," for example, Harriet Cheney recounts La Tour's battles with "M. d'Aulney, his rival in the government of Acadia" for what is now Saint John, New Brunswick; the story, which ran as a serial in the *Literary Garland* (Montreal) in 1849 in some of the same issues as "Florence; Or, Wit And Wisdom" by "R.E.M.," would certainly have been read by Mrs. Leprohon and may have even helped form her characterization of the D'Aulnays. See H.V.C. "The Fort Of St. John's." *Literary Garland*, NS 7 (1849), 35; *DCB*. Vol. 1, pp. 502-06 and 592-96; and François-Xavier Garneau. *Histoire Du Canada Depuis Sa Découverte Jusqu'à Nos Jours*. 3rd Ed. Québec: Imprimé Par P. Lamoureux, 1859. Vol. 1, p. 149.

4.15   *the capitulation of Montreal*] The "Articles Of Capitulation" of Montreal, "Between their Excellencies Major GENERAL AMHERST, Commander in Chief of his Britannic Majesty's troops and forces in North-America, . . . and the Marquis de Vaudreuil, &c. Governor and Lieutenant-General for the King in Canada," were signed on "the 8th of September, 1760." See *Documents Relating To The Constitutional History Of Canada 1759-1791*. 1918, pp. 25 and 36.

4.24-25   *King George's name*] George III; he had succeeded his grandfather, George II, as King of England on 25 Oct. 1760.

5.4   *Balzac's admired feminine age of thirty*] In *La Femme de trente ans* (1842), Honoré de Balzac provides several descriptions of the beauty and charm of his heroine, Julie d'Aiglemont, at thirty, "ce bel âge . . . , sommité poétique de la vie des femmes." See *Oeuvres Complètes De M. De Balzac*. Vol. 3: *Scènes De La Vie Privée, Tome III*. 1842; rpt. Paris: Les Bibliophiles De L'Originale, 1965, p. 91.

5.30-31   *when the Chevalier de Lévis and his gallant epaulettes left the country*] François de Lévis, Duc de Lévis, who succeeded the Marquis de Montcalm as commander of the French army in Canada after the latter's death at the Battle of the Plains of Abraham in September 1759, left for France on 18 Oct. 1760; his troops had begun to leave in mid-September 1760, shortly after the capitulation of Montreal. See *DCB*. Vol. 4, pp. 477-82.

6.3-4   *a female Carmelite . . . a Trappist's cowl*] Both orders were among the most austere in the Roman Catholic church: the cloistered Carmelite sister led "a contemplative life, a considerable portion of her time being devoted to Divine service, meditation and other pious exercises, the rest occupied with household work and other occupations"; the Trappist (or Reformed Cistercian) took a vow of silence and spent his day in strict observance of a

monastic order that included "seven hours'
sleep . . . ; about seven hours also are devoted to
the Divine Office and Mass, one hour to meals,
four hours to study and private prayers and five
hours to manual labour; in winter there are only
about four hours devoted to manual labour, the
extra hour thus deducted being given to study."
See *The Catholic Encyclopedia*. New York:
Appleton, 1912. Vol. 3, p. 369, and Vol. 15, pp.
25-26.

6.16   *Col. De Bourlamarque*] François-Charles de
Bourlamaque (or Bourlamarque), colonel of
infantry and, after Montcalm's death, the second
in command of the French army, "probably spent
the greater part of the winter" of 1759-60 in
Montreal and returned there in September 1760,
shortly before the capitulation. See *DCB*. Vol. 3,
pp. 84-87. For an example of Mrs. Leprohon's
spelling of the Colonel's name, see "Grace De
Monsieur De Bourlamarque," 1762. In *Collection
De Manuscrits Contenant Lettres, Mémoires, Et Autres
Documents Historiques Relatifs A La Nouvelle-France.*
Québec: A. Coté, 1885. Vol. 4, p. 311.

6.17   *the heroines of the* Fronde] Several noblewomen
played prominent roles in the "*Fronde parlemen-
taire*" (1648-49) and the "*Fronde aristocratique*" or
"*Fronde des princes*," sometimes also called "the
Fronde of the women" (1649-52), civil uprisings
against royal authority that occurred in France
when Anne d'Autriche, widow of Louis XIII, was
Regent and Cardinal Mazarin, her first minister;
included among these aristocrats, known for their
amorous as well as their political intrigues, were
Anne Geneviève de Bourbon-Condé, Duchesse
de Longueville; Marie de Rohan-Montbazon,
Duchesse de Chevreuse; and Anne de Gonzague,
Princesse Palatine. See R. J. Knecht. *The Fronde.*

Rev. Ed. London: The Historical Association, 1986, p. 13, and G.R.R. Treasure. *Seventeenth Century France*. London: Rivingtons, 1966, p. 195.

6.31   fête *of* la Sainte Catherine] Celebrated on 25 November, the feast commemorated St. Catherine of Alexandria, virgin and martyr, patron saint of, among others, "spinsters, young women and girl students." See A. R. Wright. *British Calendar Customs*. Vol. 3: *Fixed Festivals June-December, Inclusive*. Ed. T. E. Lones. London: W. Glaisher, 1940, p. 177.

13.6   *the* seigneurie . . . *of Valmont*] There is no seigneury of Valmont among those known to have existed in New France in the government of Montreal, Trois-Rivières, and Quebec. The parish of Notre-Dame du Mont-Carmel de Valmont, however, a few miles north of Cap-de-la-Madeleine, was created in 1858 by the Roman Catholic bishop of Trois-Rivières and granted civil status in 1859; the "de Valmont" portion of the name was added by the post office so that it could distinguish the new parish from that of "Mont-Carmel, comté de Kamouraska. On lui a sans doute donné ce nom . . . parce que la montagne se trouve comme jetée dans la vallée ou la plaine, à laquelle elle est intimement liée." If, as the novel suggests, Mrs. Leprohon's "Valmont" was a day's drive (approximately thirty to thirty-five miles) west of Montreal, it would have been located within the seigneury of Nouvelle-Longueuil. "The westernmost seigneury conceded on the St Lawrence before the conquest," it was granted in 1734 to Paul-Joseph Le Moyne de Longueuil (1701-78), known as the Chevalier de Longueuil, son of Charles Le Moyne de Longueuil (1656-1729), first Baron of Longueuil.

At the time of the Conquest, Paul-Joseph played an active role in the campaign against the British; governor of Trois-Rivières from 1757 to 1760, he was one of the most important officers and seigneurs who left for France after the capitulation of Montreal. See *DCB*. Vol. 2, pp. 401-03, and Vol. 4, pp. 463-65; *Historical Atlas Of Canada. Volume I From the Beginning to 1800*. Ed. R. Cole Harris. Toronto: University of Toronto Press, 1987, Plate 51; and Pierre-Georges Roy. *Les Noms Géographiques De La Province De Québec*. Lévis, 1906, pp. 477-78.

13.9-16   *Rodolphe De Mirecourt . . . Arthur De Mirecourt*] In assigning Antoinette her ancestry, Mrs. Leprohon seems to be thinking again of the Le Moyne family. Charles Le Moyne de Longueuil et de Châteauguay (1626-85) acquired Île Perrot in 1684; when he died the next year, it was listed among his possessions as "Le fief *Maricourt*, ci-devant appelé l'île Perrot." His fourth son, Paul Le Moyne (1663-1704), added "de Maricourt" to his name; his house in Montreal was called both "*Maison Maricourt*" and "*Hôtel Maricourt*." In April 1760, his great-niece, Agnès-Josephe Le Moyne de Longueuil, daughter of Charles Le Moyne, the second Baron of Longueuil (1687-1755), and her husband were granted by the young widow of Charles Le Moyne, the third Baron of Longueuil (1724-55) " 'un fief en la baronnie de Longueuil' " called " 'de Maricourt'." Later in the same year this fief was sold to a Montrealer named Germain Marcourt. See *DCB*. Vol. 1, pp. 463-65, Vol. 2, pp. 403-05, and Vol. 3, pp. 384-85; Alex Jodoin and J. L. Vincent. *Histoire De Longueuil Et De La Famille De Longueuil*. Montréal: Imprimerie Gebhardt-Berthiaume, 1889, pp. 78 and 148; and E.-Z.

Massicotte. "Histoire Du Fief De Maricourt."
Bulletin Des Recherches Historiques, 38 (1932),
631-33.

13.26-28   *such pitying glances . . . when allusion was made to the*
land of "snow and savages"] In *Candide ou*
l'optimisme, 1759, by François-Marie Arouet *dit*
Voltaire, Martin, explaining to Candide that both
England and France suffer from "une . . . espèce
de folie," comments, "vous savez que ces deux
nations sont en guerre pour quelques arpents de
neige vers le Canada, et qu'elles dépensent pour
cette belle guerre beaucoup plus que tout le
Canada ne vaut." Although in terms of the
chronology of her plot Mrs. Leprohon is using it
anachronistically, she is undoubtedly alluding to
Voltaire's "quelques arpents de neige," the phrase
that became a symbol for French Canadians of
their abandonment and even betrayal by France at
the time of the Seven Years' War (1756-63). See
The Complete Works Of Voltaire. Vol. 48: *Candide ou*
l'optimisme. Ed. René Pomeau. Oxford: The
Voltaire Foundation, 1980, p. 223.

22.2-5   *St. Catherine's Eve . . . which answers so nearly to our*
Hallow-E'en] Both these celebrations preceded
solemn holy days in the Christian calendar; in
North America in particular they became occa-
sions for settlers to gather for eating, drinking,
dancing, and other forms of merry-making
before winter set in. Both festivals were also tradi-
tionally associated with marriage and the divina-
tion of a future marriage partner. In Quebec, for
example, many marriages were solemnized on 24
November, and the "dance of the old maids," in
which the unmarried women paraded before the
unattached men in the community, frequently
took place. See QQLA, Archives de Folklore,

Boite VII, "La Sainte Catherine, 25 Novembre" and "Halloween"; for a discussion of these festivals in England, see *British Calendar Customs*. Vol. 3. 1940, pp. 107-19, and 177-86.

28.6-7   *the capitulation of Montreal to the combined forces of Murray, Amherst, and Haviland*] In 1760 Major-General Jeffery Amherst, commander-in-chief of the British forces in North America, organized a three-pronged assault on Montreal: he himself led an army down the St. Lawrence from Lake Ontario; Colonel James Murray, governor of the British garrison of Quebec, came up the St. Lawrence with his forces; and Brigadier-General William Haviland and his troops made their way to Montreal via Lake Champlain. On 6 September, when Amherst and his army landed at Lachine, all three forces were in place, and the city was surrounded; two days later the "capitulation of Montreal" occurred. See *DCB*. Vol. 4, pp. 20-26, 334-36, and 569-78.

28.28   *the treaty of 1763*] The Treaty of Paris, signed 10 Feb. 1763. For a complete text of this treaty, see *Documents Relating To The Constitutional History Of Canada 1759-1791*. 1918, pp. 113-26.

29.15-30   *General Murray . . . remarks: "When it had been decided . . . it was intended to subject them"*] In this passage, and throughout Chapter 5, Mrs. Leprohon is following Garneau's *Histoire Du Canada*; although her version of Garneau is similar to Andrew Bell's in several respects, it is likely that she was doing her own translation. See *Histoire Du Canada*. 1859. Vol. 2, p. 395, and *History Of Canada, From The Time Of Its Discovery Till The Union Year (1840-1)*. Trans. Andrew Bell. Montreal: John Lovell, 1860. Vol. 2, pp. 318-19.

29.31   *chief-justice Gregory*] William Gregory, an Irishman who studied law in the Middle Temple in London in the early 1740s, served as the first chief justice of the newly-established British Province of Quebec from 1764 to 1766. In describing him, Mrs. Leprohon is following Garneau who says that he was "tiré du fond d'une prison pour être placé à la tête de la justice," and that he "ignorait le droit civil et la langue française." His imprisonment, in England in 1760, was in fact due to debt, not to crime as Garneau implies; otherwise his opinion about Gregory's unsuitability for the Quebec post seems accurate. See Francis-J. Audet. *Les Juges En Chef De La Province De Québec 1764-1924.* Québec: Action Sociale, 1927, pp. [7]-12, and *Histoire Du Canada.* 1859. Vol. 2, pp. 394-95.

29.34   *the attorney-general*] George Suckling; a lawyer and businessman in Nova Scotia before coming to Quebec, Suckling served as the first attorney-general in Quebec from 1764 to 1766. According to Garneau, "Le procureur général n'était guère plus propre à remplir sa charge" than Gregory. Governor Murray, who arranged the dismissal of both Gregory and Suckling, commented, "our chief Judge and Attorney General are both entirely ignorant of the Language of the Natives, are needy in their Circumstances and tho perhaps good Lawyers and Men of integrity, are ignorant of the World, consequently readier to Puzzle and create Difficultys than remove them." See *DCB.* Vol. 4, pp. 724-26; *Histoire Du Canada.* 1859. Vol. 2, p. 395; and NA, Colonial Office 42 Canada, Vol. 25, p. 457, James Murray to Lords of Trade, 3 Mar. 1765 (NA Microfilm B-30).

30.8-17   *The dismemberment of their territory ... and finally New Brunswick was detached, and endowed with a separate government and the name it bears to-day*] The apparent anachronism in this passage translated from Garneau with regard to the date (1784) of the creation of New Brunswick is due to Mrs. Leprohon's rendering of "Bientôt encore" as "and finally" in the clause "Bientôt encore la Nouveau-Brunswick en fut détaché" and the inclusion of this clause as part of Garneau's previous sentence about the territory given to Newfoundland, Nova Scotia, and "aux colonies voisines" by the Treaty of Paris. See *Histoire Du Canada*. 1859. Vol. 2, p. 389.

41¹.4   *an Act of the Provincial legislature*] That is, An Act for removing the old Walls and Fortifications that surround the City of Montreal, and otherwise to provide for the Salubrity, Convenience and Embellishment of the said City, Provincial Statutes of Lower-Canada 1801-1804 (1st Sess.), c. 16. See *The Provincial Statutes Of Lower-Canada . . . Volume The Third*. Quebec: P. E. Desbarats, 1801, p. 116.

58.36-37   *seven years long, as Jacob waited for his bride*] Compare Genesis 29:18; Jacob, son of Isaac, goes to Laban, his mother's brother, to seek permission to marry one of his two daughters, "And Jacob loved Rachel," Laban's younger daughter, and promised to serve him "seven years" for her. See *The Interpreter's Bible*. Vol. 1. New York and Nashville: Abingdon Press, 1952, p. 700.

77.3   *"They whom God hath joined let no man put asunder"*] Compare Matthew 19:6, where Jesus, answering a question asked by the Pharisees on the legality of divorce, replies, "What therefore God hath joined together, let not man put asunder." In "The Form Of Solemnization Of Matrimony" of the Anglican church, the form that Dr. Ormsby would most probably be using, the sentence is quoted by the priest just before he pronounces that the couple being married are "Man and Wife." See, for example, *The Book Of Common Prayer*. Oxford: University Press, 1858, No. 20, "The Form Of Solemnization Of Matrimony," and *The Interpreter's Bible*. Vol. 7. 1951, p. 480.

116.26-28   *our Divine Master Himself told us that he came to seek, not the just, but sinners*] Compare Mark 2:16-17; when "the scribes and Pharisees" ask the disciples why Jesus eats and drinks with "publicans and sinners," Jesus, hearing the question, "saith unto them, They that are whole have no need of the physician, but they that are sick: I came not to call the righteous, but sinners to repentance." See *The Interpreter's Bible*. Vol. 7, pp. 673-75.

124.18   *St. Anthony*] A hermit known for the strict discipline of his ascetic life, St. Anthony of Egypt was the founder of Christian monasticism; his feast, celebrated on 17 January, probably commemorates the day of his death in A.D. 356. See *Butler's Lives Of The Saints*. Edited, Revised And Supplemented By Herbert Thurston And Donald Attwater. Vol. 1. New York: P. J. Kenedy, 1963, pp. 104-09.

131.13-14   *our Divine Teacher said, Judge not lest ye be judged*] Compare Matthew 7:1-2; Jesus, teaching his followers, says, "Judge not, that ye be not judged. For with what judgment ye judge, ye shall be judged: and with what measure ye mete, it shall be measured to you again." See *The Interpreter's Bible*. Vol. 7, p. 324.

153.21-27   *a modern French writer has said that in wedded life, next to love, hatred is best; that anything is better than the terribly monotonous, hum-drum indifference with which so many married couples regard each other, and under the influence of which life becomes like a dull, stagnant pool, without wave or breeze ever breaking the surface*] The exact source of this statement has not been found; the boredom of marriage, however, was frequently mentioned by nineteenth-century French novelists like Balzac, Flaubert, and Stendhal. In *Le Rouge et le Noir* (1830), for example, the narrator comments, à propos of Mme de Rênal's affair with Julien Sorel:

> Étrange effet du mariage, tel que l'a fait le XIXe siècle! L'ennui de la vie matrimoniale fait périr l'amour sûrement, quand l'amour a précédé le mariage. Et cependant, dirait un philosophe, il amène bientôt, chez les gens assez riches pour ne pas travailler, l'ennui profond de toutes les jouissances tranquilles. Et ce n'est que les âmes sèches, parmi les femmes, qu'il ne prédispose pas à l'amour.
>
> La réflexion du philosophe me fait excuser Mme de Rênal.

See Henri Beyle *dit* Stendhal. *Le Rouge et le Noir Chronique du XIXe siècle.* Ed. Pierre-Georges Castex. Paris: Éditions Garnier Frères, 1973, pp. 147-48.

160.25-30 *a city . . . besieged and bombarded twice . . . environs . . . in which three sanguinary battles have been fought . . . all bear melancholy traces of our country's struggles and fall*] Mrs. Leprohon is paraphrasing Garneau's description of Quebec and its environs in the early 1760s:

> A peine se seraient-ils aperçus qu'ils sortaient d'une longue et sanglante guerre, sans les affreuses dévastations qui avaient été commises, surtout dans le gouvernement de

Québec, où il ne restait plus que des ruines et des cendres. Ce district avait été occupé pendant deux ans par des armées ennemies; la capitale avait été assiégée deux fois, bombardée et presque anéantie; les environs, qui avaient servi de théâtres à trois batailles, portaient toutes les traces d'une lutte acharnée.

Quebec was bombarded by the British in the summer before the Battle of the Plains of Abraham on 13 Sept. 1759, and by the French in the spring of 1760, after their victory at the Battle of Sainte-Foy on 28 April; these two, plus the Battle of Montmorency on 31 July 1759, when the British attempted to capture Montmorency heights, are Garneau's "trois batailles." See *Histoire Du Canada.* 1859. Vol. 2, p. [384].

162.13   *Jean-Baptiste*] An ordinary or a representative member of French-Canadian society. See, for examples of the term's use in both English and French, *A Dictionary of Canadianisms on Historical Principles.* Ed. Walter S. Avis. Toronto: Gage, 1967, p. 392, and La Société Du Parler Français Au Canada. *Glossaire Du Parler Français Au Canada.* 1930; rpt. Québec: Les Presses De L'Université Laval, 1968, p. 92.

166.30-167.8   *the remark made by his Majesty George the Third to Madame De Lery . . . 'If . . . fair conquest'*] In the summer of 1763, Gaspard-Joseph Chaussegros de Léry and his wife, the former Louise de Brouague, were the first Canadians presented at the court of George III:

The young and gallant Monarch on receiving Madame de Lery, who was a very beautiful woman observed to her:

> "If all the Ladies of Canada are as handsome as yourself, I have indeed made a conquest."

See *Collection De Manuscrits . . . Relatifs A La Nouvelle-France*. Vol. 4, p. 313.

167.9   *the mission of Mr. De Lery*] Garneau, whom Mrs. Leprohon is following, implies that Chaussegros de Léry was one of the agents sent to London by the Canadians who had remained in Canada "pour présenter leurs hommages à George III et pour défendre leurs intérêts"; whatever they did in London on behalf of their fellow citizens, de Léry and his wife, who had left Canada for France in 1761, also arranged their return to Quebec, where they arrived in September 1764. See *DCB*. Vol. 4, pp. 145-47, and *Histoire Du Canada*. 1859. Vol. 2, p. 388.

167[1].1   *Garneau*] Mrs. Leprohon has translated the story from *Histoire Du Canada*. 1859. Vol. 2, p. 388.

172.25-27   *through weal or woe . . . till death doth part us*] Compare the pledge made by the woman during the Anglican marriage ceremony to her "wedded husband, to have and to hold from this day forward, for better for worse, for richer for poorer, in sickness and in health, to love, cherish, and to obey, till death us do part." See *The Book Of Common Prayer*. 1858, No. 20, "The Form Of Solemnization Of Matrimony."

194.2-3   *Like St. Paul's relapsing sinners, the last state of the man is worse than the first*] In Hebrews 6:4-6, St. Paul writes:

> For *it is* impossible for those who were once enlightened, and have tasted of the heavenly gift, and were made partakers of the Holy Ghost,

And have tasted the good word of God,
and the powers of the world to come,

If they shall fall away, to renew them again
unto repentance; seeing they crucify to
themselves the Son of God afresh, and put
him to an open shame.

Mrs. Leprohon combines St. Paul's notions about
the "relapsing sinner" with Jesus' comments about
the "unclean spirit" in Matthew 12:43-45:

When the unclean spirit is gone out of a
man, he walketh through dry places, seeking
rest, and findeth none.

Then he saith, I will return into my house
from whence I came out; and when he is
come, he findeth *it* empty, swept, and
garnished.

Then goeth he, and taketh with himself
seven other spirits more wicked than him-
self, and they enter in and dwell there: and
the last *state* of that man is worse than the
first.

Another rendition of the "unclean spirit" story
can be found in Luke 11:24-26. See *The Interpre-
ter's Bible.* Vol. 7, pp. 404-05; Vol. 8. 1952, p. 209;
and Vol. 11. 1955, pp. 651-52.

209.1   *his shadow, like that of the upas-tree*] First described
in English in 1783, "the Upas tree," said by the
apparently pseudonymous J. N. (or N. P.) Foersch
to exist near Batavia (Djakarta), Java, was sup-
posed to be so poisonous "that from fifteen to
eighteen miles round . . . not only no human
creature can exist; but that, in that space of
ground, no living animal of any kind has ever
been discovered." See Foersch. "Description Of

The Poison-Tree, In The Island Of Java." Translated From The Original Dutch, By Mr. Heydinger. *London Magazine*, NS 1 (1783), 512-17. Since this is evidently the earliest recorded use of the noun in English, Mrs. Leprohon may be committing an anachronism in employing the term as she does in Dr. Manby's soliloquy of 1764.

217.7-8 *St. Helen's, then belonging to the Barons De Longueuil*] Charles Le Moyne de Longueuil et de Châteauguay acquired Île Sainte-Hélène in 1665; it became part of the Barony of Longueuil in 1700 when his son, Charles Le Moyne de Longueuil (1656-1729), was created Baron de Longueuil by Louis XIV. The first Baron's great-great-grandson, Charles William Grant (1782-1848), sold it to the British government in 1818. See *DCB*. Vol. 1, pp. 463-65, and Vol. 2, pp. 401-03, and *Histoire De Longueuil Et De La Famille De Longueuil*. 1889, pp. 619-20.

225.8   *"ruling habit, strong in death"*] Compare Alexander Pope, "Epistle I. To Sir Richard Temple, Lord Viscount Cobham," 1733, 1. 263, where Pope, complimenting Lord Cobham on the patriotism that is his "ruling passion," writes:

> And you, brave COBHAM, to the latest breath
> Shall feel your ruling passion strong in death:
> Such in those moments as in all the past,
> "Oh, save my Country, Heav'n!" shall be your last.

See *The Twickenham Edition of the Poems of Alexander Pope*. Vol. 3, Pt. 2: *Epistles To Several Persons (Moral Essays)*. Ed. F. W. Bateson. London: Methuen, and New Haven: Yale University Press, 1961, p. 38.

Bibliographical Description of 1864 Lovell Edition

A bibliographical description follows of the first edition of *Antoinette De Mirecourt*, the copy-text for the CEECT edition, published by John Lovell in 1864. In this transcription, the differences between the size of capitals in different lines have not been noted, and the form (thin/thick, swelled, etc.) and length of rules have not been specified.

First Edition

Title-page: ANTOINETTE DE MIRECOURT; | OR, | 𝔖ecret 𝔐arrying and 𝔖ecret 𝔖orrowing. | A CANADIAN TALE. | [rule] | BY MRS. LEPROHON. | [rule] | 𝔐ontreal: | PRINTED BY JOHN LOVELL, ST. NICHOLAS STREET | 1864.

This title-page is reproduced as an illustration in the CEECT edition.

Size of leaf: 175 × 120 mm.

Collation: 8°, *A*⁴ B-T⁸ U-V⁸ W-X⁸ *Y*⁴ χ¹, [$1 signed], 185 leaves, pp. *i-v* vi *vii-viii* 9 10-16 *17* 18-24 *25* 26-38 *39* 40-48 *49* 50-53 *54* 55-59 *60* 61-65 *66* 67-74 *75* 76-86 *87* 88-99 *100* 101-105 *106* 107-117 *118* 119-127 *128* 129-139 *140* 141-150 *151* 152-166 *167* 168-177 *178* 179-190 *191* 192-202 *203*

204-213 *214* 215-219 *220* 221-231 *232* 233-242
243 244-249 *250* 251-257 *258* 259-268 *269*
270-280 *281* 282-294 *295* 296-308 *309* 310-328
329 330-339 *340* 341-360 *361* 362-369 *370*

Contents: p. [i] half-title, p. [ii] blank, p. [iii] title-page, p. [iv] blank, pp. [v]-vi "PREFACE.", p. [vii] blank, p. [viii] blank, pp. [9]-369 text, p. [370] blank

"THE END." appears on p. 369.

Head-title: "ANTOINETTE DE MIRECOURT." appears on p. [9].

Running-titles: From pp. 10-369 "ANTOINETTE DE MIRECOURT." appears on each page, except the first of each chapter.

"ANTOINETTE" is spelled "ANTOINETSE" on p. 38, and "ANTOIFETTE" on p. 206.

Casings: The casing of the copies examined is blue or salmon cloth with a bead-grain or a fine dotted-line-ribbed pattern. Both the upper and lower covers are blind-stamped with two concentric rules and an oriental scrollwork design in each corner. The spine is blind-stamped with double rules at the top and bottom and gilt-stamped "ANTOINETTE I DE I MIRECOURT".

Notes: Four different decorative rules appear at the end of some chapters. The rule on p. vi is repeated on pp. 59, 150, 190, and 360. The rule on p. 48

appears again on pp. 86, 127, 177, 202, 328, and 339. This rule is damaged in all appearances and is very faint on p. 339 in some copies. The rule on p. 53 is repeated on pp. 99 and 166. The rule on p. 219 also appears on p. 308. The first, third, and fourth rules are inverted in one instance each. A wavy rule appears below the head-title on p. [9] and the heading "PREFACE." on p. [v].

The OONL copy is inscribed by Mrs. Leprohon's eldest child, Claude de Bellefeuille Leprohon, on the recto of a blank leaf preceding the half-title. In the same copy, gatherings M, V, W, X, and *Y* are on a lighter weight of paper.

Copies: OKQ LP PS8423 E67A7; OKQ LP PS8423 E67A7 copy 2; OLU PR9298 L6A75; OONL PS8423 E6A65 Reserve; OTU B-11 1847; QMBN S823.89 L55; QQLA PS8424 L599 A711 1864

The two OKQ copies and the OLU, OONL, and OTU copies were microfilmed for CEECT by Icon Microfilm And Image Management Systems, Ottawa, Ontario.

Published Versions of the Text

The following is a list of editions, periodical versions, and one photographic reprint of *Antoinette De Mirecourt*. At least one location is given for each entry. The information on the title-page of each version is recorded and relevant information not appearing on the title-page is inserted in square brackets. Notes explain further distinguishing characteristics of each version. One other possible periodical appearance of *Antoinette De Mirecourt* is discussed in a note at the end.

1864

First Edition

First Impression

Antoinette De Mirecourt; Or, Secret Marrying and Secret Sorrowing. A Canadian Tale. By Mrs. Leprohon. Montreal: Printed By John Lovell, St. Nicholas Street, 1864.
  Copies: OKQ OLU OONL OTU QMBN QQLA
  Note: See CEECT, pp. 257-59 for a bibliographical description of the first edition.

Subsequent Impression

Antoinette De Mirecourt; Or, Secret Marrying and Secret Sorrowing. A Canadian Tale. By Mrs. Leprohon. Montreal: Printed By John Lovell, St. Nicholas Street, 1864; rpt. Toronto: University of

Toronto Press, [1973]. Toronto Reprint Library of Canadian
Prose and Poetry. General Editor: Douglas Lochhead.
Copy: OOCC
Note: This is a photographic reprint of the 1864 John Lovell
       edition.

1973

Second Edition

Antoinette de Mirecourt or Secret Marrying and Secret Sorrowing.
Rosanna Leprohon. Introduction: Carl F. Klinck. General
Editor: Malcolm Ross. New Canadian Library, No. 89.
[Toronto]: McClelland and Stewart Limited, [1973].
Copy: OOCC

French Translation

1865

First Periodical Appearance

"Antoinette de Mirecourt, Ou Mariage Secret Et Chagrins
Cachés." Roman Canadien Par Madame Leprohon, Traduit
De L'Anglais, (Avec la bienveillante permission de l'auteur,)
Par J. A. Genand. *Ordre* (Montreal), 31 Mar.-13 Apr., 19
Apr.-21 Apr., 26 Apr.-7 June, 12 June-23 June, 30 June-12
July, and 17 July-4 Aug. 1865.

Copy: OONL

Note: The installments appeared on page one of this semi-weekly newspaper under the heading "Feuilleton de *L'Ordre*." In some issues the installment is continued on page two. The continuation of Chapter XII in the 10 May issue is misnumbered as XI. The issues of 13 April, 19, 26, 28, 31 July, and 2 August contain two installments each.

First Edition
(printed from the same typesetting as
the first periodical appearance)

Antoinette De Mirecourt Ou Mariage Secret Et Chagrins Cachés. Roman Canadien. Par Madame Leprohon, Auteur de: Ida Beresford, Eva Huntingdon, Clarence Fitzclarence, Florence Fitz Hardinge, Eveleen O'Donnell, Le Manoir De Villerai, etc., etc. Traduit De L'Anglais, Avec la bienveillante permission de l'auteur, par J. A. Genand. Montréal: C. O. Beauchemin & Valois, Libraires-Editeurs, Rue St. Paul, 237 et 239, 1865.

Copy: QQLA

Note: The text for this first edition has been occasionally corrected and revised, and the text that appeared on the second page of several issues reorganized in wider columns of type.

1866-67

Second Periodical Appearance

"Antoinette De Mirecourt." *Pionnier de Sherbrooke* (Sherbrooke,

Quebec), 20 Oct.-22 Dec. 1866; 5 Jan.-6 Apr., 27 Apr.-22 June,
6 July-4 Oct. 1867.
Copies: OONL (microfilm) QQLA
Note: The installments appear on page one of this weekly
    newspaper under the heading "FEUILLETON." In the
    27 Sept. and 4 Oct. 1867 issues, the installment con-
    tinues on the second page. Chapter XX and the con-
    tinuations of Chapters IX, XXV, XXVII, XXIX, XXX,
    and XXXI are misnumbered at least once.

1881

Second Edition

*Antoinette De Mirecourt Ou Mariage Secret Et Chagrins Cachés. Roman
Canadien.* Par Madame Leprohon. Traduit De L'Anglais.
Montréal: J. B. Rolland & Fils, Libraires-Editeurs, 1881.
Copies: OOCC OONL QQLA
Note: An alternate title-page appears in the OOCC and
    QQLA copies. Its capitalization and line-breaks differ,
    but its substance is identical.

1886-87

Third Periodical Appearance

"Antoinette De Mirecourt" Traduit De L'Anglais Par J. A.
Genand. *Nouvelles Soirées Canadiennes* (Montreal), 5 (1886),
324-36, 359-84, 416-32, 465-80, 519-28, and 561-73; 6 (1887),
47-96, 149-[192], 234-40, 270-88, 325-36, 361-84, and 417-32.

Copies: OONL QQLA

Note: Chapter XXVIII and the continuations of Chapters XXX and XXXII are misnumbered. Pages 177-92 in Vol. 6 are misnumbered as 173-88.

NOTE:

An undated clipping apparently from the Montreal *Life* held in the C. C. James Collection at Victoria University Library, Toronto, indicates that Mrs. Leprohon's "story of Montreal after the Conquest" had "just been commenced in *Life*." Unfortunately, few copies of this periodical that began in 1891 are available, and those that are do not contain *Antoinette De Mirecourt*. If the story did appear in *Life*, however, it was probably serialized in the 1890s, for Mrs. Leprohon's son, writing in 1911, encloses in his letter a "short Biography of my dear Mother, which I have found in the Montreal Life printed many years ago." See C. C. James Collection, Box 4, and NA, Mrs. C. M. Whyte-Edgar Collection, MG30, D261, File 10, ALS, R. E. Leprohon to Mrs. Whyte-Edgar, 15 Mar. 1911.

Emendations in Copy-text

This list records all the emendations made in this edition of *Antoinette De Mirecourt* to its 1864 Lovell copy-text, except those silent changes noted in the introduction. Since the 1864 edition is the only version of the novel in English that carries authority, the editor of the CEECT edition is the sole source of these emendations. Each entry in this list is keyed to the page and line number of the CEECT edition. In each entry the reading of the CEECT edition is given before the]; the reading in the copy-text is recorded immediately after the]. In the entries the ~ indicates that the same word (and nothing else) appears both in the copy-text and the CEECT edition; the ∧ indicates that a punctuation mark or other accidental in the CEECT edition is omitted in the copy-text. A solidus, /, indicates where the word was broken at the end of a line in the copy-text.

22.26	De Mirecourt] de ~
23.36	yourself."] ~. ∧
31.2	D'Aulnay] d'Aulnay
42.27	requisite] requsite
43.28	exquisite] exqusite
47.8	'tis] " '~
51.12	child?] ~?"
53.24	they] the
54.21	Mrs.] ~ ∧
58.21	"that] ∧~
59.6	rejoined,] ~.
74.8	it is so] it so
78.22	" 'Tis] ∧'~
79.20	creature?] ~?"
85.23	"Sit] ∧~
86.20	Major's] major's
86.20	contracted] contractcd

91.2	"Antoinette] ∧~
91.16	"Think] ∧~
92.7	ratified."] ~.∧
101.6	than] then
101.32	scene."] ~.'
105.11	De Mirecourt] de ~
106.15	"that] ∧~
109.24	ultimately have] ultimatelyhave
113.19	De Mirecourt] de ~
115.2	good-humoredly] ~-hnmoredly
115.28	"Nay] ∧~
127.3	De Mirecourt] de ~
127.21	Evelyn," interrupted] ~, "~
130.14	"Though] ∧~
131.30	D'Aulnay] d'Aulnay
133.34	De Mirecourt] DeMirecourt
134.1	"In] ∧~
139.2	passed] pased
141.18	"Oh] ∧~
143.13	Antoinette,"] ~,∧
143.14	"One] ∧~
143.37	"and] ∧~
145.14	myself."] ~.∧
150.22	Mademoiselle] Mademoisolle
157.14	Why,] ~∧
163.8	"And] ' nd
163.31	a minute's]~ minutes'
169.1	be] he
169.11	"It] ∧~
169.34	spoke. "Have] ~." ~
176.7	it.] ~."
176.13	"Your] ∧~
176.26	will] wil
178.31	give] ~ give
179.2	imagine."] ~.∧
185.25	moment"] ~ '

197.31   had been] been
199.10   apparent] ap/parent
201.27   allusion] illusion
204.9   "to] ∧~
208.26   gentleman] gentlemen
217.34   Sternfield] Stern/field
227.29   strength."] ~.∧
234.30   agitation] agita-/ ion
236.6   blessed,"] ~,∧
236.27   "I] ∧~
236.30   desire."] ~.∧

Line-end Hyphenated Compounds in Copy-text

The compound or possible compound words that appear in this list were hyphenated at the end of a line in the copy-text used for this edition of *Antoinette De Mirecourt*. They have been resolved in the CEECT edition in the manner indicated below. In order to decide how to resolve these words, examples of their use within the lines of the copy-text itself were sought, and the spelling that appeared there adopted. In cases where the spelling of compound or possible compound words within the lines was inconsistent, the spelling most frequently used within the lines has been adopted. When these compounds or possible compounds appeared only at the end of a line in the copy-text, the *Oxford English Dictionary* was consulted for examples of how they were spelled in the eighteenth and nineteenth centuries, and their resolution based on this information. The words in this list are keyed to the CEECT edition by page and line number; a word appears each time it has been resolved in the copy-text.

1.9	reading-matter	50.14	to-day
10.22	drawing-rooms	54.21	well-pleased
15.33	daughter-in-law	55.12	drawing-room
17.15	drawing-room	56.4	breast-pocket
23.6	bright-eyed	59.12	to-day
32.30	exquisitely-finished	60.3	super-refined
32.32	gayly-tasseled	64.27	never-to-be-recalled
35.28	self-examination	71.34	drawing-rooms
36.9	love-poems	74.23	over-tasked
36.12	day-dreams	75.34	footsteps
36.24	drawing-rooms	76.5	intellectual-looking
39.2	richly-decorated	77.32	commonplace
42.31	half-maddened	82.12	pocket-money
43.32	round-eyed	82.28	to-morrow

271

86.22	quick-eyed	148.20	marriage-vow
92.27	marriage-service	153.18	self-sacrificing
99.9	commonplaces	162.19	lookers-on
100.6	well-loaded	162.24	fellow-traveller
104.23	good-naturedly	164.11	rose-water
105.6	Manor-House	167.32	contra-danse
106.4	headache	169.26	sitting-room
107.1	co-parishioners	184.32	well-known
107.17	half-unintelligible	186.13	straightforward
109.33	half-hour	188.17	re-entered
110.29	anything	194.27	moonlight
112.26	sitting-room	207.29	horsewhip
114.32	to-day	210.24	good-humoredly
115.2	good-humoredly	212.5	wrong-doing
116.12	town-life	214.15	reperused
120.1	ill-natured	218.35	true-hearted
121.29	dinner-dress	226.7	smooth-faced
128.8	new-comer	230.13	red-coats
130.24	woman-hater	230.18	statue-like
131.33	misspent	232.22	kind-hearted
132.34	bride-elect	234.37	long-suffering

Line-end Hyphenated Compounds in CEECT Edition

This list records compound words hyphenated at the end of a line in this edition of *Antoinette De Mirecourt* that should be hyphenated in quotations from it. All other line-end hyphenations should be transcribed as single words. The words in this list are keyed to the CEECT edition by page and line number; a word appears each time it is hyphenated at the end of a line.

4.1	well-lighted	68.32	well-feigned
5.6	heavily-ringed	69.11	drawing-room
8.4	bed-room	71.28	half-hour
17.22	light-hearted	74.8	to-night
19.6	pre-occupied	75.16	new-born
22.31	splendidly-proportioned	76.26	life-long
		79.13	evening-dress
25.10	pink-cheeked	82.19	to-morrow
32.30	exquisitely-finished	83.19	love-affair
32.36	dressing-room	83.31	love-engagement
33.21	new-comer	86.17	ante-room
33.22	out-stretched	91.17	wedding-ring
37.2	half-open	91.28	scandal-mongers
37.28	driving-party	98.17	sitting-room
40.27	well-got-up	100.6	well-loaded
41.7	wide-spread	104.29	to-night
43.15	over-valued	104.32	tear-stained
47.33	self-command	106.1	well-founded
48.3	dash-board	107.5	sitting-room
53.9	drawing-room	107.17	half-unintelligible
54.21	well-pleased	108.19	Manor-House
67.34	hall-door	110.10	drawing-room
68.12	to-morrow	120.1	ill-natured

273

120.2	mess-table	187.17	acacia-boughs
121.29	dinner-dress	188.1	sitting-room
123.7	woman-like	189.18	to-morrow
124.3	soft-breathed	195.18	to-morrow
124.36	thorough-breds	196.20	narrow-paned
126.28	sleighing-party	200.24	novel-reading
129.5	over-crowded	210.35	good-natured
135.17	pre-occupation	211.18	hot-tempered
136.5	over-crowded	215.21	to-morrow
142.2	sun-browned	216.14	out-houses
144.33	over-strained	218.30	to-morrow
147.2	well-known	224.20	new-comer's
148.1	ill-starred	224.27	moon-struck
153.13	every-day	229.19	re-entered
164.4	snow-shovels	230.31	eye-lids
174.11	self-command	234.37	long-suffering
186.23	to-night		